He bent down and next to Laurie's.

He felt her instantly stiffen ... given her any warning. He hadn't given it much thought himself. He'd just been playing along and it had seemed like the natural thing to do.

Her lips were soft and pliable, and oh, so inviting. He'd meant just to brush, the slightest touch, but his lips caught the taste of wine from her and his gentle brush became instantly more intense.

Only the briefest few seconds had passed but he was conscious of the audience around them—and conscious of the fact that if she did object, she might not want to do so in front of others.

He pulled back, but felt her lips still connected with his. It was as if she didn't want the kiss to end. As their noses brushed against each other he opened his eyes. Her dark brown eyes were already open, staring straight at him.

She looked a little stunned. As if she didn't quite believe the kiss had happened. Her hand came up automatically to her lips, which seemed even redder than before.

Her eyes still hadn't left his. All he could see was how chocolate-coloured they looked in this light and the definite dilation of her black pupils. His body reacted instantly—a natural response. Her hips were still pressed against his and her eyes widened, but the smile that appeared on her face was one of pure mischief.

THE HEIR
OF THE CASTLE

BY
SCARLET WILSON

Published in Great Britain 2014
by Mills & Boon, an imprint of Harlequin (UK) Limited,
Eton House, 18-24 Paradise Road, Richmond, Surrey, TW9 1SR

© 2014 Scarlet Wilson

ISBN: 978 0 263 91284 5

23-0514

Harlequin (UK) Limited's policy is to use papers that are natural, renewable and recyclable products and made from wood grown in sustainable forests. The logging and manufacturing processes conform to the legal environmental regulations of the country of origin.

Printed and bound in Spain
by Blackprint CPI, Barcelona

Scarlet Wilson wrote her first story aged eight and has never stopped. Her family have fond memories of *Shirley and the Magic Purse*, with its army of mice, all with names beginning with the letter 'M'. An avid reader, Scarlet started with every Enid Blyton book, moved on to the Chalet School series and many years later found Mills & Boon.

She trained and worked as a nurse and health visitor, and currently works in public health. For her, finding Mills & Boon was a match made in heaven. She is delighted to find herself among the authors she has read for many years.

Scarlet lives on the West Coast of Scotland with her fiancé and their two sons.

This book is dedicated to all those little girls who
ever dreamed of being Liesl and dancing in
the gazebo in a pink floaty dress.

CHAPTER ONE

'THANK YOU FOR coming to the last will and testament reading of Angus McLean.'

The solicitor looked around the room at the various scattering of people, some locals, some not.

Get on with it, thought Callan. He'd only come because the ninety-seven-year-old had been like a father to him. Thoughtful, with a wicked sense of humour, and a real sense of community about him. He'd taught Callan far more than his father had ever taught him.

He wasn't here to inherit anything. He could have bought the castle four times over. He'd offered enough times. But Angus hadn't been interested. He'd had other plans for the estate. And after pretty much living there for part of his life Callan was curious as to what they were.

The solicitor started reading. 'Some of you are here by invitation. Others have still to be contacted. As you may well be aware Angus McLean had a considerable estate.'

He started with some charitable donations, then moved on to the staff that had served Angus over the years—all of them left sizable bequests that would see them into a comfortable age.

Then he cleared his throat and looked nervously

around the room, his eyes deliberately skittering past Callan.

Uh-oh. The castle. What has old crazy done now?

'Most of Angus McLean's friends and relatives knew that Angus was a bachelor. It was always assumed—at least by those of us who knew Angus well—that Angus had no children.' He hesitated. 'But it seems that wasn't the case.'

'What?' Callan couldn't help it. He'd spent most of his life around Angus McLean. Never once in all those years had Angus ever mentioned any children.

Frank, the family solicitor, was clearly not designed for situations like this. His legalese seemed to leave him and he laughed nervously. 'It appears that in his day Angus McLean was a bit of a rogue. He had six children.'

Heads shot around the room, looking back and forth between each other aghast.

But a few heads stayed steady—as if they'd already heard the news.

Callan couldn't believe his ears. 'Six children? Who on earth told you that?' This had to be rubbish. Was a bunch of strangers trying to claim part of the McLean estate?

Frank looked him clearly in the eye. 'Angus told me,' he said quietly.

Callan froze. Every hair on his body standing on end. It couldn't be true. It just couldn't.

Frank cleared his throat nervously. 'As a result of Mr McLean's heirs—and with some further research—we've discovered there are twelve potential inheritors of the estate.'

Callan shook his head. No. Twelve people all wanting a part of Annick Castle. It would be sold without hesitation to the highest bidder. Everyone would want their share of the cash. Angus would have hated that.

'On Mr McLean's instructions, all twelve potential inheritors are to be invited to attend a weekend at Annick Castle.' He bit his lip. 'With true Angus McLean style, they are to be asked to take part in a Murder Mystery Weekend—with the winner becoming the sole heir of Annick Castle. After confirmation of their claim with DNA testing, of course.' His eyes finally met Callan's. 'Mr McLean's last wish was that Annick Castle stayed in the family and was inherited by one person.'

The words chilled Callan to the bone. It was exactly the kind of thing Angus would have said—the only thing they'd ever argued about in this world. But Callan had always assumed there was no real family to inherit, at best, or worst, a few far-flung distant cousins. Nothing like this.

Chaos erupted all around him. Voices shouting and asking questions, people talking amongst themselves, pulling phones from their pockets and dialling numbers frantically.

There was a reporter in amongst the mix who walked out with his phone pressed against his ear. Who inherited Annick Castle was big news—particularly when it was being decided in such an unusual manner. It was one of the few privately owned castles in Scotland.

Callan stood up and walked outside into the rain and biting wind. His eyes landed on the building in front of him. Annick Castle. The place he'd called home for the last twenty-five years.

From the first night Angus had found him cowering in the bushes, hiding from the drunken, abusive bully that was his father, he'd welcomed him into his home. It had become his haven. His safe place. And in later years, when Angus had become frail and needed support, Callan had been the one to provide it.

Annick Castle was the place he'd laughed, cried and learned to be a man.

And it was all, doubtless, about to be destroyed by some stranger.

'Sign here, please.'

Laurie looked up at the electronic screen placed under her nose. She looked around; her secretary had vanished and the courier looked impatient. She lifted the electronic pen and scrawled her signature. 'Thanks.'

She stared at the envelope. It was hardly unusual. A letter from another firm of solicitors. She put it on the pile on her secretary's desk. It would need to be logged in the system.

She rubbed her forehead. Yet another tension headache—and it wasn't even nine a.m. She would be here for at least the next twelve hours. She sighed and picked up the court papers she would need for later and headed back to her office.

Five minutes later Alice appeared at her office door. 'Laurie, did you see who signed for this letter?'

Laurie looked up. It was the heavy cream envelope. 'Yip. It was me.'

Alice looked a little embarrassed. 'Sorry I missed it.' Her hand rested on her slightly protruding stomach. 'I've been at the bathroom three times already this morning.'

Laurie waved her hand. 'No worries.'

Alice smiled. 'I think you should look at this yourself. It's not work-related. It's personal.' She crossed the office and laid the now opened envelope on Laurie's

desk. Receiving letters from other solicitors was an everyday thing. But none of them had ever been personal.

Laurie looked up at Alice's retreating back as she
closed the door behind her.

Why had she closed the door? Alice had already
seen the contents of the letter and unless Laurie was in
a meeting with clients her door was always left open.
It felt kind of ominous. Was someone suing her? But
if they were, surely that would be work-related, not
personal?

She picked up the envelope and turned it over in her
hands. She didn't recognise the logo on the outside.
Ferguson and Dalglish.

She pulled the letter from the inside. Heavyweight
white bond paper. Exactly like the kind they used for
legal documents. Her eyes scanned the page…*'as the
daughter of Peter Jenkins you've been identified as a
possible heir to the estate of Angus McLean…invited to
attend Annick Castle…'* The next page gave contact details and a map of how to get there. The letter dropped
from her hands. Her heart was thudding against her
chest and she couldn't help but automatically shake her
head. This was crazy. This was mad.

As the daughter of Peter Jenkins… Her father had
died more than ten years ago. He'd never known who
his own father was and had always been curious, but
apparently his mother had never told him and refused to
discuss the matter. Who on earth was Angus McLean?
Was he the father he'd never known?

Because that was what this letter implied. What a
way to find out.

She felt her stomach clench a little. Angus McLean
could have been her grandfather. Why hadn't he contacted her when he was alive? Why wait until he was

dead? It almost seemed pointless. And it was certainly pointless for her father.

Her fingers flew over her keyboard, pulling up a search engine and typing frantically. He wasn't hard to find. Angus McLean, died aged ninety-seven, one month ago. Never married. And apparently no children.

She let out a stream of words into the air. Really?

She scanned the letter again. How many children did this guy have? And had any of the others actually been acknowledged?

The phone rang and she ignored it. Whatever it was it would have to wait. She typed again.

A picture appeared before her and she took a sharp breath, her head moving closer to the screen. Annick Castle. On the west coast of Scotland.

Only, it didn't really look like a castle. More like a beautiful stately home perched on a cliff above the sea with gorgeous surrounding gardens and a swan pond. It was stunning, made of sand-coloured stone, with drum towers at either end and complete with cannons on the walls overlooking the sea.

She looked at the photo credit. The picture was taken twenty years before. Did Annick Castle still look like that?

Her curiosity was definitely piqued. What kind of a man stayed in a place like that? And why would he have family that he never made contact with?

She scanned the letter again. In her haste to read she'd missed the last paragraph.

You are invited to attend Annick Castle to take part in a Murder Mystery Weekend along with eleven other identified family members in accordance with Angus McLean's Last Will and Testa-

*ment. The winner of the Murder Mystery Weekend
shall inherit Annick Castle, familial claim shall
be verified by DNA testing.*

It didn't say that. It *couldn't* say that.

Lawyers all over the world would be throwing up
their hands in horror.

She screwed up her eyes and pinched her nose, then
looked from side to side. This was a joke. This was an
elaborate hoax. Somewhere, in this room, there must
be a hidden camera.

She stood up and walked around. First to the bookshelves on the wall, then to filing cabinets next to the
door. She couldn't see anything. But weren't cameras
so small now that they could be virtually invisible?

She opened her door and looked outside. Everyone
was going about their business. No one was paying her
the slightest bit of attention. It was a normal day at Bertram and Bain, one of the busiest solicitors' in London.
Twenty partners with another thirty associates, special-
ising in employment law, partnership law and discrimination law. The phones started ringing around seven
in the morning and continued until after nine at night.

Organised chaos.

The tiny hairs on her arms stood on end as if a chill-
ing breeze had just fluttered over her skin. She closed
the door and leaned against it.

What if this wasn't a joke? Eleven other family members. Who were they?

She was an only child, and as far as she'd been aware
her father had been an only child too. After he'd died,
her mum hadn't coped too well and was now living in
the sun in Portugal with a little help from Laurie.

She walked back to the desk and ran her finger over the thick paper of the letter.

Family.

She'd felt totally lost since her dad had died. She didn't have a million relatives scattered around the world. There was just her, and her mum.

And now this.

What if she did have relatives she'd never met?

She tried to swallow the lump in her throat as she sagged back down into her chair. Dad would have been so intrigued to receive something like this. He'd always been curious about his father. It made her miss him all the more. She was going to find out the things he'd never known. Who was Angus McLean? Why did he live in a castle? And why on earth hadn't he made contact with his potential family members while he'd still been alive?

She was trying not to be angry. She really was.

She read the letter once more. Property law wasn't her forte, but could this even be legal? There were some differences between English and Scots law, but she wasn't sure if this was one of them.

A Murder Mystery Weekend to decide who inherited the castle?

There was no getting away from it: Angus McLean must have been stark raving mad.

She blinked. A bit like how she'd been feeling lately.

Maybe it was a family trait. The thought didn't really fill her with pleasure—only fear.

She watched as people marched past the glass in her office wall, all with a purpose, all with not a minute to spare.

Exactly as she felt.

How many holidays was she overdue now?

She straightened in her chair, the thick paper between her fingers.

Her father had been a grocer, her mother a shop assistant. No one had been more surprised than Laurie when she'd excelled at school. She liked learning. She liked finding out things. And she'd got swept along with the potential and expectations of her exam results. The careers advisor who'd pushed her towards university. The teachers who'd encouraged her to excel. Her father had cried the day she'd been accepted at Cambridge to study law.

And it had only taken her two months to realise that she hated it.

But, by then it was too late. She couldn't disappoint her dad. Not when he'd spent every waking hour working to help her achieve what he thought was her 'goal'. And especially not when she could hear the pride in his voice every time he told someone his daughter was going to be a lawyer. Turning her back on law would be like trampling on his grave.

She'd been miserable here for months. Always smiling, always agreeing to do more, to work late, to help others out. Never mind the hours she put in at the office, there was never really time off at home. Aches and muscle pains, sleepless nights, tension headaches, all signs that her body needed a break.

And maybe this was a sign.

No matter how ridiculous it sounded.

Her fingers tapped out the email quickly—before she had a chance to think straight and change her mind. She picked up the files on her desk and carried them outside.

Alice was worried. Laurie could tell by the frown on her forehead and the way her pencil was banging on the desk.

Laurie took a deep breath and gave her a smile, lifting a pile of Post-its from her desk. She started slapping them on the files. 'I'm taking some time off. Pink for Frances, green for Paul and yellow for Hugo. After I've been at court this afternoon there's nothing they can't handle. Ask them just to pick up where I left off.'

Alice nodded, her mouth gaping open as Laurie handed her the instructions from the letter. 'Can you book me a train ticket and sort out some accommodation for me?'

Alice put her pencil to good use and started scribbling. 'You're going to go? Really? When do you want to leave?'

'Tomorrow.'

'Tomorrow?' Several heads poked up at the surprise in Alice's voice from the pods around them.

Laurie nodded. 'I'm supposed to be there Friday through to Monday evening.'

Laurie Jenkins taking a holiday. It was unheard of.

Maybe it was time for change.

Callan stared at his watch for the twentieth time. This was his last pickup of the day.

Thank goodness. So far, there had been the loud Canadians, the over-excited Americans, the bad-tempered Irishman with the very sweet Irishwoman, and several others from around Scotland. Once the hoity-toity lawyer arrived from London he was all done.

He must have been mad. Why on earth was he agreeing to be part of this ridiculous debacle?

He sighed. What was the bet that Ms Lawyer was extra tired and extra crabbit? By his estimations she'd have travelled four and a half hours from London to Glasgow, another four hours from Glasgow to Fort Wil-

liam, and the last part of the journey on the steam locomotive.

He leaned back against the stone wall of the old station. He could see the steam in the distance. She could
have stayed on the train from Glasgow—it did come
on to Mallaig—but like any good tourist she must have
preferred to take the *Harry Potter* train and cross the
viaduct.

It wasn't really a problem. He couldn't blame her
desire to see the stunning Scottish countryside. It just
meant she was a later arrival than everyone else.

The train pulled into the station and the tourists piled
out. Most of them would be staying overnight in Mallaig—a coach was parked outside the station to trans-
port them to their accommodation.

It took a few moments for the steam and chattering
crowds to completely clear.

Wow! That was Mary Jenkins? So, not what he was
expecting.

Instead of an iron-faced middle-aged woman the
smoke cleared around a long-haired brunette, with slim
pink Capri pants, a white loose tunic and a simple holdall in one hand. Far from looking tired, she was fresh-
faced and brimming with excitement.

Callan was used to beautiful women—he'd dated
enough of them—but this was a shock to the system.
Her clothes highlighted her curves, the swell of her
breasts beneath the thin tunic and her Capri pants showing a hint of lightly tanned skin.

She walked over quickly. 'Callan McGregor? Thank
you so much for meeting me.' She reached over and
grasped his hand firmly between both of hers.

Zing. What was that? A wave of tiny electric shocks
shot up his arm.

'It's a pleasure to meet you.' She waved her hands around. 'What an absolutely gorgeous setting. I've had an absolute ball on that train.' She pointed to the camera around her neck, nestled next to a gold locket. 'I must have taken around a hundred pictures.'

He was trying to remain calm. He was trying not to let the corners of his mouth turn upwards in surprise. It wasn't just that she was pretty—she was gorgeous. Warm brown eyes, clear skin, curls bouncing around her shoulders and full pink lips. 'Mary Jenkins?' he queried. The name just didn't suit her at all.

She let out a laugh. Nothing quiet and polite, but a deep, hearty laugh that came all the way up from her painted pink toes. 'What? No one has ever called me that! It's Laurie. Laurie Jenkins. My father called me after his elderly aunt Mary, but I've always been known by my middle name Laurie.'

He nodded. The Mary Jenkins he'd pictured in his head had looked nothing like the Laurie Jenkins standing on the platform before him. Around twenty years of nothing.

Was she really old enough to be a lawyer?

She shuffled some papers in the front pocket of her holdall. 'Let me take that for you,' he said as he reached down and swung it up onto his shoulder. It was light. It was surprisingly light. Maybe Laurie Jenkins wasn't planning on staying long? Unlike the Canadians, who appeared to have brought the entire contents of their house with them.

He ushered her along the platform towards his car, trying not to watch the swing of her hips and shape of her curved backside. *Focus.* That zing was still bothering him. Callan McGregor didn't do 'zings'.

He waited for the comment—there weren't many

people with a pristine James Bond DB5 in this world. One of the few over-the-top purchases since he'd made his fortune. But she just happily climbed in the front seat and pulled on her seat belt. 'Do you know much about Angus McLean?'

He was thrown. He was totally thrown.

Not only had every other single person made a passing comment on the car, every other single person's first question had been about the castle—leaving him in no doubt why they were there. They could recognise money at a glance.

He should have walked away. After the reading of the will he should have left the solicitor's office and just kept on walking. Walked away from the madness of all this.

But something deep inside wouldn't let him. Whether it was a burning curiosity of what would happen next. Whether it was some bizarre desire to actually meet some of Angus McLean's relatives. Or whether it was some deep-rooted loyalty to the old guy, and some misplaced desire to try and maintain the integrity of the castle.

He waited until she was settled and then he pulled out of the car park.

'Well?' She was obviously determined to find out a little more. Her fingers were clenched tightly in her lap, her index fingers rotating around each other over and over. It was the first sign she wasn't quite as relaxed as she seemed.

'Angus was a good friend.'

She raised her eyebrows. The sixty-five-year age difference was completely apparent and must be sparking questions in her brain.

'So, you're not one of his relatives?' She hesitated. 'I

mean, you're not one of…my relatives?' Her voice tailed off and she shook her head with a little half-smile. 'I can't get used to the thought of any of this. It was only ever me, my mum and my dad. My dad died ten years ago. I never imagined anything like this would happen. It all seems so unreal—like I'm caught in a dream.'

'Oh, it's real all right,' he muttered under his breath. Then he shook his head and gave a woeful smile. This woman really didn't have a clue how he felt about any of this. 'I guess the *Harry Potter* train will do that to you.'

Her face broke into a wide, dreamy grin. 'It was fantastic. My secretary booked it for me. I haven't had a holiday in a while and she obviously knew I would like it.'

He tried not to let his ears prick straight up. She hadn't had a holiday in a while. What did that mean? Did she work for some hotshot company that made their employees work one hundred hours a week? Or did she just not have anyone to go home to? His eyes went automatically to her hand, but she'd moved it, jamming her left hand under her thigh and out of his sight.

'How did you meet?' Her voice cut through his thoughts. Boy, she was persistent. She still hadn't even mentioned the castle.

A shadow passed across his face and his lips tightened. 'I met Angus when I was a small boy. I spent quite a bit of time at Annick Castle.'

Something flickered across her face—doubtless another question—but something obviously told her to change tack and she let it go.

'So, what's going to happen this weekend? Are you organising things?' Did she think he was an employee? Even though he was offended, it was a reasonable assumption. After all, he had picked her up from the station.

He signalled and turned off the main road, passing some stone columns and an extravagant set of entry gates, and heading down a long, sweeping driveway.

He shook his head and his words were spoken through gritted teeth. 'The Murder Mystery Weekend is nothing to do with me. It's being organised by some outside company.'

She shook her head. 'It's the most bizarre thing I've ever heard. Is it even legal? Inheritance law isn't my field of expertise, but I've never heard of anything like this in my life.'

'Neither have I.' The words almost fell out of his mouth. He wasn't embarrassed to say he'd spent the last week locked in a bitter war of words with Frank. But the solicitor had been unrepentant. He'd tried to talk Angus out of it. He'd talked him through all the legal implications, the challenges that might be brought against the decision. They'd even brought a doctor in to give a statement that Angus was of sound mind as he wrote the will.

But Angus McLean had been as determined as he always was in life. This was the way he wanted to do things, and nothing, and no one, could change his mind.

Callan could see Laurie looking around, taking in the impossibly long sweeping road to the castle, and the huge gardens. The car followed the bend in the road and she let out a little gasp, her hand going to her face.

'Oh. Wow.' Annick Castle was now clearly visible. Rebuilt in the seventeen-hundreds, the impressive building had over sixty rooms and a large drum tower at either side. It was clear the first glimpse of the castle took her breath away.

But instead of feeling secretly happy and proud, Callan could barely disguise his displeasure. Was she thinking that the castle might be hers after the weekend? The last guests from Canada had immediately asked what rooms were the best and whipped out a portfolio with extensive notes on the property. He'd almost ejected them from the car on the spot.

But Laurie wasn't quite so brazen. Or maybe she was just better at hiding it?

She shook her head, her eyes open in wonder. 'I just didn't expect it to be so big.' She pointed over at the sea wall. 'I knew it was supposed to be on a cliff top. I guess I just hadn't really realised how impressive it would be.' She fumbled in her bag and produced a tissue, dabbing at her eyes. 'My dad wouldn't have believed this. He would have thought he was in a dream.'

For the tiniest second Callan almost felt sorry for her. He knew that three of Angus's children had died: Laurie's father, another woman from England and a son who'd lived in Canada. Laurie was an only child, but the son in Canada had three sons and two daughters, and the woman in England had had three children. It took the total number of possible inheritors to twelve. All of whom were now here.

They pulled up outside the main entrance and Laurie jumped out automatically. 'I'll show you to your room and introduce you to the staff,' Callan said gruffly.

'My room?' She looked shocked, and then shook her head. 'Oh, no, I'm not staying here.' She started to fumble in her bag for her paperwork. 'My secretary will have booked me in somewhere.'

Callan was starting to run out of patience. 'She has—here.'

Laurie's chin practically bounced off the driveway.

'But I thought you'd just brought me here to show me where the castle was.'

He shook his head and shrugged his shoulders. 'It's part of the stipulation of the weekend.' Nothing he had any control over.

He waited until she'd extricated the crumpled paperwork from her bag and stared at it a few times as if she was still taking all of this in.

'Like I said, come and I'll introduce you to the staff.'

Her eyes widened. 'There's staff?'

He frowned. 'Of course there's staff. A place like this doesn't look after itself.'

That was the trouble with all these people. None of them knew or understood a thing about Annick Castle. None of them appreciated the people who'd spent their life working here. It didn't matter most of the staff had been left bequests, it was the actual castle that mattered to them—just as it mattered to Callan.

Laurie was still standing in amazement outside. The sun was starting to set over the horizon, leaving her bathed in a warm glow of pink, orange and lilac. With the beautiful sea in the background she could have been starring in a movie. With her dark eyes, long chestnut curls about her shoulders and her curves highlighted in her white tunic, Laurie Jenkins could prove quite a distraction.

She was the youngest relative here by far. And for a second he almost forgot that: the fact she was a relative—a potential inheritor. A complete stranger who would probably sell Annick Castle to the highest bidder as soon as she could.

It made the hackles rise at the back of his neck.

All day he'd picked people up and dropped them off. And there was no getting away from it. Some of them he already hated. They'd asked the value of the property, its potential price on the open market and how soon the inheritance would take to sort out.

So it didn't matter how Laurie looked, or how she acted.

The truth was—she was the same as all the rest.

What was wrong with this guy? Ever since he'd picked her up at the train station he'd acted as if she'd jabbed him with a hot poker.

She had no idea what his role was here. It was a shame, because if he could actually wipe the permanent frown off his face, he would be attractive. And not just a little attractive. The kind of guy you spotted at the other side of a room and made your heart beat faster kind of attractive.

When she'd spotted him at the station she'd almost turned around to look for the film camera. Were they shooting a new film, and he'd been brought in as the resident hunk?

She smiled to herself. His hands had been firm. Was the rest of him? It certainly looked that way—his shirt did nothing to hide the wide planes of his chest.

Mr Silent and Brooding was obviously not planning on telling her much. She was trying to push aside the fact he was impossibly tall, dark and handsome. And she was especially trying to push away the fact he'd fixed on her face with the most incredible pair of green eyes she'd ever seen. Ones that sent a little shiver down her spine.

But nothing he'd said had exactly been an answer, and now she'd finally met someone who knew Angus McLean her brain was just bursting with questions. It was her duty to her dad to find out as much as she possibly could. She followed him inside and tried to stifle the gasp in her throat.

It was the biggest entrance hall she'd ever seen, with a huge curved staircase running up either side around the oval-shaped room. These were the kind of stairs a little girl would dream of in her imaginary castle. Dream that she was walking down to meet her Prince Charming. If only.

Callan dropped his car keys into a wooden dish with a clatter.

Fat chance of that happening here.

She shook hands with a grey-haired woman with a forehead knotted in a permanent frown just like Callan's. Maybe they were related?

'This is Marion. She's the housekeeper. If you need anything you'll generally find her around the kitchen area.'

Laurie couldn't imagine a single occasion she'd want to seek out the fearful Marion but she nodded dutifully and followed him up the stairs.

There was an old full-length portrait at the top of the stairs of a young woman in a long red dress. Something about it seemed a little odd and she stopped mid-step. Callan gave her a few seconds, then finally smiled in amusement. It was the first time today he'd looked even remotely friendly.

'You're the first person that's noticed,' he said quietly.

'But that's just it. I know I've noticed something—' she shook her head '—but I don't know what it is.'

He pointed at the portrait's serious face. 'It's an optical illusion. *She's* an optical illusion.'

'But, what…how?' She was even more confused now.

Callum pointed to the stairs. 'It doesn't matter which

side you walk up. It always seems as if she's looking at you.'

'Impossible!' She couldn't even make sense of the words.

He folded his arms across his chest and nodded to the other flight of stairs. His face had softened slightly. He was much more handsome without the permanent frown. 'Go on, then, I'll wait.'

She hesitated for a second but the temptation was just too great. She could only pray he wasn't playing some kind of joke on her. She raced down one side and halfway up the other.

Her arm rested on the ornate banister, her eyes widening. The serene young woman was staring right at her—just as she'd been on the other staircase. She lifted up her hands in exasperation. 'But that's impossible. How old is that painting? Did optical illusions even exist back then?'

A cheeky grin flashed across his face. 'Did rainbows?'

She felt the colour flood into her cheeks and a flare of annoyance. Of course. Nature's greatest optical illusion. Now she felt like a prize idiot. Something tightened in her stomach.

She hated anyone thinking she was dumb. The only real joy in being a lawyer was the recognition that most people assumed you had to be smart to do the job in the first place.

But Callan didn't seem to notice her embarrassment. He was looking at the painting again. 'Angus liked to have fun. Once he discovered the painting he was determined to own it. It's nearly two hundred years old. He put it there as a talking point.' There was obvious affection in his voice and it irritated her even more.

Who was this guy? He'd already told her he'd spent some time living here. But why?

Why would Angus McLean take in a stranger, but ignore the six children that he had? It didn't make sense.

All of a sudden she was tired and hungry. The long hours of work and travelling had caught up with her and all she wanted to do was lie down—preferably in her bed in London, not in some strange castle in Scotland.

'Nice to know he had a sense of humour,' she muttered under her breath as she brushed past him.

'What's that supposed to mean?' snapped Callan.

She took a deep breath and turned to face him. 'It means I'm tired, Callan. I've been travelling for hours.' She lifted her hands in exasperation. 'And it also means I've just found out about a family that's apparently mine.' She cringed as some of the relatives walked past downstairs, talking at the tops of their voices about the value of the antiques.

She looked Callan square in the eye. If she weren't so tired she might have been unnerved. Up close, Callan's eyes were even more mesmerising than she'd first suspected and she could see the tiny lines around the corners. He was tired too.

She took a deep breath. 'I didn't know Angus McLean, but, just so you know, you might have him up on some sort of pedestal—but I don't. I'm not impressed by a man who lived in this—' she spun around '—and spent his life ignoring his six children.' She folded her arms across her chest. 'Nice to see he got his priorities in order.'

CHAPTER TWO

JUST WHEN, FOR the tiniest second, he thought one of Angus's relatives might not be quite as bad as the rest, she came out with something like that.

Callan felt a chill course over his body as he swept past her and along the corridor. 'You're right. You didn't know Angus. And you have absolutely no right to comment.' His blood was boiling as he flung open the door to her room. 'Here's your room.' He stopped as she stepped through the doorway. Her head was facing his chest, only inches away from his. All it would take was one little step to close the distance between them.

It didn't matter to him how attractive she was. It didn't matter that he'd noticed her curves at the railway station, or the way she kept flicking back her long shiny brown curls. All that mattered to him was the fact she'd said something he didn't like about the old man that he loved.

But Laurie Jenkins was having none of it. She folded her arms across her chest again. 'That's just the thing, Callan. I *do* have a right to comment—because, apparently, I'm family.' She let the words hang in the air as she walked past him into the room.

Callan's blood was about to reach the point of eruption.

The very thing that knotted his stomach. Family. And the fact he wasn't.

He still hadn't got over the fact Angus McLean had six children he'd never once mentioned. The reality was he was still hoping it wasn't true—that someone would give him a nudge and he'd wake up from this nightmare.

Nothing about this seemed right. Angus had been the perennial bachelor, even in old age. Why on earth would he have children and never acknowledge them? It seemed bizarre.

Angus had had the biggest heart he'd ever known.

But then, he'd only known Angus for the last twenty-five years. Maybe in his youth he'd been a completely different person?

It bothered him. It bothered him so much he hadn't slept the last few nights.

And now that he'd met some of the relatives it bothered him a whole lot more.

One of these money-grabbers was going to inherit Annick Castle. A place full of history and rich with antiques. A place full of memories that not a single one of them would care about.

Why hadn't Angus let him buy it? He'd known that Callan loved it every bit as much as he did. It just didn't make sense.

The family stuff. It enraged him more than he could ever have imagined.

Laurie was standing looking out of the window across the sea. Some of these bedrooms had the most spectacular views. He knew—his was just above.

And this complete stranger had just put him perfectly in his place.

She was right—she was family. The one thing he wasn't.

He dumped her bag on the bed. 'Dinner is at seven.'

He didn't even wait for a response. The sooner he got away from Ms Jenkins, the better.

Laurie breathed out slowly, releasing the tight feeling that had spread across her chest.

What on earth was wrong with her? And why had she just offloaded to the one person who could actually tell her something about her grandfather?

Common sense told her it wasn't wise to alienate Callan McGregor. He could probably tell her everything she could ever want to know—and a whole lot more besides.

She sagged down onto the bed. The bedroom was big, with panoramic views over the sea. How many people throughout the ages had stood at her window and looked out at this view? The sun had set rapidly leaving the sea looking dark, haunting and cold. Was it possible that the sea looked angry—just like Callan McGregor?

The history of this place intrigued her. It would be fascinating. If only she could take the time to learn it.

Her hand smoothed the coverings on the bed, taking in the carpet, curtains and other soft furnishings. At one time these must have been brand new and the height of fashion. But that time had clearly passed. How did you update a castle? She didn't have a clue.

It wasn't that anything was shabby. It was just— tired. A little dated maybe. And obviously in need of some TLC.

Angus had been ninety-seven when he'd died. How often had he looked around the castle to see what needed replacing and updating? And how much would all that cost?

She shifted uncomfortably on the bed. She'd heard some of the conversation of the other relatives downstairs. They'd virtually had measuring tapes and calculators out, deciding how much everything was worth and where they could sell it.

It made her blood run cold.

This castle was their heritage. How could people immediately think like that?

She walked over to her bag and shook out her clothes. She was only here for a few days and had travelled light. One dress for evenings, some clean underwear, another pair of Capri pants, some light T-shirts and another shirt. What else could she possibly need?

An envelope on the mantelpiece caught her attention. *Ms Mary Laurie Jenkins* was written in calligraphy. She opened it and slid the thick card invitation out from inside.

It was instructions for the Murder Mystery Weekend: where to report, who would be in charge and a list of rules for participation.

Under normal circumstances something like this would have made her stomach fizz with fun.

But how could she even think like that when there was so much more at stake?

The whole heritage of this castle was dependent on the winner. And the weight of the responsibility was pressing on her shoulders. She fingered the curtains next to her. She knew nothing about Annick Castle. She had no connection to this place. She wouldn't even know where to begin with renovations or upkeep. Or the responsibility of having staff to manage.

Working as a solicitor was a world away from all this. Everything and everyone wasn't entirely dependent on her. There was a whole range of other bodies to share the responsibility. Thank goodness. She couldn't stand it otherwise.

All of a sudden she wanted to pick up her bag and make a run for it. She shouldn't have come here. She shouldn't have agreed to be any part of this.

This whole thing made her uncomfortable. She looked at the invitation again. *Costumes supplied.* What did that mean? There was another little envelope with a character profile included, telling her who she was, and what her actions should be.

1920s. Lucy Clark. Twenty-seven. Heiress to a fortune. Keen interest in pharmacy. In a relationship with Bartholomew Grant, but also seeing Philippe Deveraux on the side.

It was a sad day when the pretend character you had to portray had a more exciting love life than you had.

It could be worse. Her card could have told her she was the killer. But maybe that came later?

Then again what did 'keen interest in pharmacy' mean? Was she going to poison someone?

Under normal circumstances this might be fun.

But these weren't normal circumstances, and now she was here, and had actually seen Annick Castle, the whole thing made her very uncomfortable.

She glanced at the clock. There was still time before dinner to freshen up and get organised.

Maybe once she'd eaten that horrible little gnawing sensation at the pit of her stomach would disappear?

Or maybe that would take swallowing her pride and apologising to Callan.

Maybe, just maybe.

* * *

Callan had finally calmed down. He'd had to. Marion, the housekeeper, had flipped when one of the ovens had packed in and she'd thought dinner wouldn't be ready on time. It had taken him five minutes to sort out the fuse and replace it.

Dinner would be served on time.

Served to the twelve strangers who were roaming all over the castle.

Which was why he was currently standing in his favourite haunt—the bottom left-hand corner of the maze in the front garden.

Callan could find his way through this maze with his eyes shut—and he had done since he was a boy. It was one part of the garden that was kept in pristine condition with the hedges neatly trimmed.

Other things had kind of fallen by the wayside recently. Bert, the old gardener, couldn't manage the upkeep of the gardens any more. The truth was he probably needed another four staff to do everything that was required. Twenty years ago there had been a staff of around six to look after the grounds alone, but gradually they'd all retired or left. And the recession had hit. And Bert had become very set in his ways— not wanting others to interfere with 'his' garden. In the meantime the maze, the front garden and the rose garden were almost in pristine condition. As for the rest...

He was thankful for the peace and quiet. All of a sudden his safe haven seemed like a noisy hotel. Everyone seemed to talk at the tops of their voices, constantly asking questions. He'd tried to hide out in the library for a while, but even there he'd been disturbed by some of the relatives wondering if there were any valuable first editions.

If he'd had his way he would have locked some of the rooms to stop their prying eyes, not to mention their prying fingers. He'd caught one relative in his room earlier and had nearly blown a gasket.

A flash of red caught his eye, along with the sound of laughter and heels clipping on the concrete path. He took a few steps forward, crashing straight into Laurie as she rounded the corner of the maze.

'Oh, sorry.' She was out of breath and her eyes wide. 'Isn't this just fabulous?'

As much as he hated to admit it her enthusiasm was clearly genuine.

'How long has the maze been here? I had no idea something like this existed. It's amazing.'

He narrowed his gaze. He could barely focus on the question because his eyes and brain were immediately struck by the sight in front of him. The 1920s-style flapper dress skimmed her figure, hiding it beneath shimmering red glass beads. A feather was slightly askew on her head and he automatically reached up to straighten it. 'What on earth are you wearing?' Damn. There it was again—as soon as his hand touched the soft hair—the mysterious spark from earlier.

'This?' Her eyes widened again and she gave a little spin, sending a cascade of sparkling red lights scattering around them. She wrinkled her nose as she came to a halt. 'Well, I hardly brought it with me, did I? I got it from the costume room. Haven't you got into character yet?' She held out her black-satin-gloved hand to shake his hand. 'I'm Lucy Clark. Apparently an heiress and up to all things naughty with two different men.'

If he'd been anywhere else, at any other time, he would have acted on the current of electricity that was sizzling between them. He thought he might have imagined it, but his palm was tingling. He rubbed it fiercely against his thigh.

The Murder Mystery Weekend. The last thing on his mind right now. He hadn't even opened the envelope that had been sitting above the fireplace in his room. And he had no idea what room in the castle had been deemed the 'costume' room. His fingers burrowed into his jacket pocket and he pulled out the crumpled envelope. 'Oops.' He shrugged.

She shook her head. 'Come on, Callan, get into the spirit of things.' She reached out to grab his envelope, then pulled her hand back. 'I better not.' She leaned forward and whispered, 'I don't want to find out you're secretly a mass murderer.'

He shook his head and pulled the card from the envelope. He must have been out of his crazy mind to have agreed to be part of this.

Then again, he hadn't really agreed. Frank, the solicitor, had informed him that Angus had expected Callan to make his guests feel welcome and help oversee the weekend's activities. He'd had half a mind to walk away.

But his loyalty to Angus ran deep. Too deep.

If he walked away then he'd never find out who inherited the castle, or their plans for it. A tiny seed started to sprout in his brain.

Maybe being here wasn't so crazy after all. Sure, inheriting a castle sounded good on paper, but once Angus's relatives realised the implications, the upkeep, the financial commitments, he was pretty sure they would all run screaming for the hills. Maybe he could make them an offer? He'd always been prepared to pay a fair price, and if Angus wouldn't accept it, maybe one of his children would?

His eyes fixed on Laurie. She was young. She was a

lawyer in London. She wouldn't want to be landed with a castle in the Highlands.

For the first time this weekend he actually paused to think. Maybe he should play nice?

He squinted at the name on his card. He hadn't paid attention to any of the instructions about the Murder Mystery Weekend. 'It appears I'm Bartholomew Grant, thirty-three, a stock-market trader.'

A cheeky smile appeared on her face along with the tiniest flush of red. 'Hmm…Bartholomew Grant. Well, whaddya know? I believe you're one of my two adoring men.' She gave a little wave of her hand. 'Here's hoping you can play the part, Callan.'

The feather was bobbing in the wind. The shimmering red glass beads picking up the soft lights from the open doors of the drawing room. She hadn't donned a short bob wig in keeping with the time; instead she'd left her long brown curls snaking around her shoulders.

She was watching him through her dark lashes with her big brown eyes. His eyes dropped automatically to her left hand. He couldn't see anything through the satin gloves. No telltale lumps with giant diamonds. Surely a successful woman like Laurie must be attached?

She leaned forward again, this time the round neck of her dress gaping and giving a little glimpse of cleavage.

He blinked. What was he doing? Why was his brain even going there? He had far too much to think about this weekend. The last thing he needed was to get distracted by someone he'd never see again.

'Do you think you can play the part, Callan? Or is it all just too much for you?' Her voice was low and husky. She tilted her head to one side. 'Do you even know how to play nice?'

The words made him start. In another world Laurie Jenkins could be quite mesmerising. But he wasn't the kind of guy to fall for a coy smile and the flutter of some eyelashes.

'Maybe I just like to pick my play friends carefully,' he shot back.

She folded her arms across her chest. 'Well, that's a shame. You're the only person around here who looked as if they might be capable of holding a normal conversation. I couldn't get a word in edgeways with the Americans, the Canadians were too busy Googling antiques, and—' she flung her hands up '—the two people that I think are my aunt and uncle from other parts of England have spent the last hour dozing on one of the sofas in the drawing room.'

He couldn't help but smile. He'd already figured out she wanted to meet her family, but it seemed nothing was going to plan. He reached out his hand and grabbed hers, leading her over to a bench near the entrance to the maze and pulling her down next to him.

'What did you think was going to happen this weekend, Laurie?'

He could see her take a deep breath as she glanced around them. The splendour of the castle was behind them and even though the grounds weren't officially lit, the smooth front lawn, maze and rose garden were impressive to say the least. And she had no idea that just beyond that copse of trees lay a swan pond with slightly untrimmed foliage. She really had no idea about this place at all. She shrugged her shoulders, 'I thought this would be a chance to meet some family. There's only me and my mum now, and she lives in Portugal.' She gave a little shake of her head. 'She really couldn't cope when my dad died.' Her eyes had lowered and he resisted the temptation to reach over and squeeze her hand. But her fingers had already moved, automatically going to her throat and catching the gold locket around her neck.

He might not know her, but the pain on her face was real. She'd clearly adored her father.

She lifted her head, turned and stared up at the castle. 'I have no idea what my dad would have made of all this.' Her eyes were shimmering now with unshed tears. 'He so wanted to know about his father. His mum just wouldn't tell him anything.' She lifted her hand and held it out. 'This would have fascinated him, and the thought that he had other brothers and sisters scattered around the world...' She let out a sigh and shook her head. 'That would have blown his mind.'

Callan shifted uncomfortably on the seat. All of a sudden his reaction earlier seemed a bit snappy.

Now he understood a little of what she'd said. It seemed odd to him that Angus had never acknowledged the fact he had children. How must it seem to the newly acquired relatives? To know that Angus had provided for them in his will, but never acknowledged their existence?

He'd been so wound up with how he was feeling he hadn't given much thought to anyone else.

'I had no idea that Angus had children. He never mentioned it. Never mentioned it at all.' He pressed his lips together. 'It just doesn't seem like him at all. The Angus McLean I knew had the biggest heart in the world.'

'How did you know Angus? You seem a bit young to have been friends.' Her brow was furrowed, as if she was trying to sort out in her head where Callan fitted into all this.

He chose his words carefully. Her question wasn't

unexpected. 'Angus helped me out when I was younger. And friends—that's exactly what we were. He was one of the best friends I had.'

'And you stay here—in the castle?' He could almost see the questions spinning around in her head.

'Not exactly. I live in Edinburgh most of the time. I have a house there. But I've always had a room here with Angus. He needed a bit more help in the last few years.'

There was so much more she clearly wanted to ask. He could almost sense her biting her tongue. Instead her eyes fixed on the maze and gardens in front of them.

'Do you know much about the estate?'

The words sent his hackles up. He tried not to let it show, but every question he'd more or less been asked by the relatives in the last twelve hours had revolved around money. He found it impossible not to grit his teeth. 'I know every field, every tree, every fence and every stream. I've been in and around Annick Castle since I was a young boy.'

But Laurie hadn't noticed his tension; she was lost in a world of her own. 'Lucky you.' There was a wistful tone in her voice as she leaned back on the bench and looked up at the elegant façade of the castle. She sighed. 'This would have been my dream when I was a little girl, living in a place like this.' She held out her hand. 'I can only imagine what it must be like to play in a maze like this every day or to run up and down those fairy-princess stairs.' She gave him a mischievous smile. 'Go on, tell me. Did you ever slide down those banisters?'

He could feel his natural protective instincts kick in. Did he really want to tell her that he and Angus had regularly had competitions to see who was the fastest sliding down either side?

All of a sudden this was personal. These were his personal memories of his time here with Angus McLean. And he didn't want to share them.

He didn't want any of these people staying here. He really just wanted them all to leave. The piece of paper in his hand crumpled under his grip.

She was puzzling him. She wasn't talking about money. She was talking about people and family. But maybe she was just cleverer than the rest? And what was more she was persistent. 'Or did Angus forbid you from doing things like that?'

The words jolted him. Jolted him from a whole host of memories that flooded his brain. Diving in the swan pond, trying to build a raft to sail across it, swinging from the rope swings that he'd made amongst the trees. Angus wasn't the kind to forbid him anything. He lifted his heavy eyelids and caught her staring at him with those big brown eyes. 'Only if he caught me,' he said quietly.

The moment passed just as quickly as it appeared. 'Shouldn't we be going?' He stood up. 'You've got a Murder Mystery to solve.'

'Oh, that.' She stood up, her dress catching the light again. 'I'd almost forgotten about that.'

How could she forget about that? It was the key to owning this castle. Surely it should be the first thing on her mind.

He led her towards the open doors to the drawing room. 'Let's get this over with.' She sighed, then turned around. Her hand reached up and rested on his chest. 'Callan, tomorrow, will you show me around the grounds of Annick Castle? I'm only here for the week-end and I'd like to see as much as I can.'

His immediate response caught in his throat, because his immediate response was to say no.

The last thing he wanted was to be the genial host, showing everyone around the castle he considered a home.

But Laurie seemed a little more measured than the rest. A little more interested in the history of the castle as a whole.

Her hand was still resting on his chest, almost burn-ing a hole through the thin cotton of his shirt. She bit her lip. 'I was also wondering if I could see some pictures of Angus. See what he looked like.' Her eyes drifted off... 'I kind of wonder if my dad looked like him at all...' then came back to meet his '...or if I do.'

The hairs were standing up at the back of his neck—and it wasn't the cool evening breeze. It was her. And the effect she was having on him.

Had anyone else asked to see pictures of Angus? He couldn't remember, but they must have—surely? If someone told him he'd a long-lost relative the first thing he'd want to do would be see what they looked like.

He gave a little nod. 'I know where some of the fam-ily pictures are kept. Leave it with me. I'll let you see them tomorrow.'

She gave a nervous kind of smile. 'Thank you, Cal-lan. That will be nice. And the tour?'

Her big brown eyes were fixed right on him. She ob-viously wasn't going to let this go.

He wanted to say no. He really did. But how could he?

He could almost hear Angus's voice in his ear. *Show*

them around, make them fall in love with the place as much as we did.

'Fine. I'll meet you just after breakfast.'

She gave a little nod of her head. 'Thanks.'

He gestured towards the dining room. 'You better go on. I'll be a few minutes getting changed.' He turned and walked off along the corridor.

Dinner with the twelve potential inheritors of Annick Castle.

He really couldn't think of anything he wanted to do less.

CHAPTER THREE

BY THE TIME Laurie reached the dining room most of the other guests were already seated. It seemed there was no opportunity to pick your own seat. The calligraphy from the character envelopes had been carried on to the name cards on the table.

She gave a little sigh as she sat down. Her character was between both men she was apparently seeing, which meant that Callan would be next to her again.

A man around twenty years older than her sat down on her right at the *Philippe Deveraux* card. She tried not to smile. In real life he wasn't exactly her taste, but she held out her hand politely. 'Pleased to meet you.' She nodded at her card. 'I'm Lucy Clark, but I'm really Laurie from London. My father was one of Angus McLean's children.'

Her companion smiled. 'Then that makes you my niece. I'm Craig Fulton. From what I can gather, I think I am the youngest of Angus McLean's children.' He leaned forward conspiratorially. 'And I'm not sure that I'm comfortable with dating my niece.'

Laurie felt a wave of relief rush over her. Thank goodness. This could have been awkward.

'What do you do in London, Laurie?'

'I'm a lawyer.'

His eyebrows rose. 'Well, that will come in handy with all these shenanigans. Is this even legal?'

She shook her head. 'Scottish law and English law can differ. I'm just as in the dark as you are.'

The chair next to her was pulled out and Callan sat down beside her. He'd changed into a hunting-style jacket, obviously in keeping with the style of the evening.

But Craig persisted. 'But you must know something?'

He was making her uncomfortable. 'Actually, I don't. This isn't my area of expertise. I practise employment, partnership and discrimination law.'

Craig threw up his hands. 'What use is that to anyone?'

Now he'd really annoyed her. And it was clear that Callan was about to intervene, but she lifted her hand and laid it on his jacket sleeve to stop him. She smiled sweetly at Craig and spoke quietly. 'Why don't you ask my last client? I won him an award of half a million pounds.'

Craig choked on the wine he was currently necking down at a rate of knots. Leaving his neighbour on the other side sharply hitting his back for him.

Callan shot her a smile. 'Touché,' he whispered.

She smiled. 'I'm nobody's shrinking violet…' she leaned forward to whisper in his ear '…and I hate anyone implying otherwise.'

Callan lifted his glass. 'I'll remember that.'

The food appeared moments later, all served by a harassed-looking Marion and a young girl who looked too terrified to speak.

Everything was beautiful. From the chicken liver

pâté, to the chicken breast stuffed with haggis. All accompanied by copious amounts of free-flowing wine.

After such a long journey Laurie could feel the wine go straight to her head and stopped after the second glass.

The doors to the garden had been left wide open, and, instead of feeling cold, Laurie found herself appreciating the clean sea air that circulated around them. It was the first time in for ever she could remember having a clear head. Sure, if she'd drunk much more wine it could have made her wobbly, but for the first time in months she didn't feel at her muggiest, with a persistent headache thumping in the background.

She tried to remember when the headache had actually left her. It had been there so frequently she couldn't recall. She really should get out of the city more. Was it on the steam railway that she'd finally felt her head clear? Maybe there was a lot to be said about highland views and sea breezes.

It didn't matter that the air in the room was fraught with tension. It didn't matter that she was lost amongst a sea of relatives, some of whom she wasn't sure she even liked. It didn't even matter to her that Callan was constantly prickly around her.

This was the first time, in a long time, she finally felt relaxed. Her body almost didn't recognise the signs. What she really wanted to do right now was climb the curved staircase, open her bedroom window to the sea air and slip under the covers of that comfortable-looking double bed.

She almost didn't care about the inheritance aspect of the journey.

Almost.

Because from the moment she'd set foot in this place she'd loved it.

It made her toes tingle. It made her breath catch in her throat. It made the tiny little hairs on her arms stand on end.

She couldn't even begin to imagine the fabulous history of a place like this. And all she wanted to do was drink it in.

And if that meant having to play nice with Mr Callan McGregor, then she would. Because he seemed to be the only person who could tell her what she wanted to know.

The dinner passed by in a flash, then Frank the solicitor appeared again and ushered them all into the drawing room.

Laurie almost let out a sigh. It was after nine o'clock at night and after a long day's travel she really just wanted to go to sleep.

She'd tried to speak to Frank earlier but it had been very apparent he didn't want to be seen in discussion with her. Maybe he was worried he would get accused of showing her favour because she was a fellow professional? All she'd wanted to ask him was a little about Angus McLean. But it wasn't to be.

Frank read out a list of rules about the Murder Mystery Weekend, about them staying in character and when they would be expected to meet. He also introduced some people from the company running the weekend's activities: Ashley, a blonde woman in a pale pink 1920s dress, Robin, a dark-haired man dressed in hunting regalia and John, who was dressed as a butler.

Tea and coffee were provided on a table at the side and Laurie made her way over to grab a cup. The rest of the guests were told to mingle and familiarise themselves with each other. As she poured the coffee into one of the pale blue china cups another one was slid alongside.

'Pour me one too, would you? I'm going to fall asleep in here. Playing nice doesn't agree with me.'

Laurie smiled at Callan's voice. 'You and me both. I had no idea I'd be so tired after the journey. All I want to do right now is go to bed.'

Should she have said that out loud? There was kind of an amused glint in Callan's eyes. For a second she felt a flare of panic. What did he think she meant? For a horrible moment she thought he might have taken it as an invitation. The colour started to flood into her cheeks, and she did what she always did when she was embarrassed—she babbled.

'It's such a long journey up by train. The steam locomotive was fabulous, I wouldn't have missed the gorgeous scenery for anything, but when it gets to this time at night, and especially after that beautiful dinner, I just want to go and lie down. Alone—I mean,' she added hastily.

But Callan was laughing and shaking his head. It was obvious he'd picked up on her anxiety.

She said the first thing that came into her head. 'What about you, Callan? Is there a Mrs McGregor to go home to?'

Had she actually just said that out loud? Please let the ground open up and swallow her whole. Wine and tiredness obviously weren't a good mix for her.

Callan shook his head, and was it her imagination or did he just glance at her left hand?

'No. There's no Mrs McGregor. I've been a bit of a workaholic these last few years.'

'And any mini McGregors?' In for a penny, in for

a pound. It seemed prudent to ask, particularly after what had been learned about Angus McLean in the last few weeks.

There was no hesitation. He shook his head. 'I can assure you, if I had any kids they would be permanently attached to my hip.'

There was no mistaking that answer. Callan McGregor would never do what Angus McLean had—whatever his reasons might have been.

'What about you, Laurie? Are you like your character—do you have more than one attachment?' There was a cheeky glint in his eyes as he asked the question.

Laurie rolled her eyes. 'I should be so lucky. I don't have enough hours in the day for myself let alone anyone else. Do you know, I think this is the first time I haven't had a headache in months.'

He leaned forward. 'It's all this good Scots air. It does wonders for your health.' For a second, her breath was caught in her throat as the aroma of his woody aftershave invaded her senses. It was delicious.

She gathered herself and smiled. 'Yeah, but it's making me exceedingly tired.'

'You mean you don't want to go and play nice with the relatives?'

Laurie took a deep breath. She knew the correct answer to this question, but it just couldn't form on her lips. She gave a little shrug. 'Yes, yes, I do. But right now I'm just too tired to care.' She looked over to the middle of the room where they were all currently holding court, talking—no, shouting—at the tops of their voices.

She gestured over to the other side of the room. 'The person I'd really like to sit down with at some point is Mary from Ireland. She'll have been my father's half-sister. And she looks really like him. I'd like to get a chance to talk properly to her.'

The lights flickered out and the room was plunged into darkness, followed by a theatrical scream. And even though she should have half expected it, it really did make her jump.

Callan's arm slid around her waist. Even though she couldn't see a thing, she could sense him leaning closer to her. And it was her natural instinct to move a little closer to him. 'You okay, Laurie?' His warm breath tickled her cheek. More of the aftershave. It was scrambling her senses and rapidly turning into her new favourite smell.

She clutched the cup in her hands. Her hands had started to tremble. The last thing she wanted to do was shatter some priceless china on the parquet flooring. 'Yes, thanks,' she whispered.

'I'm sure this will all be over in a second...' his voice was low, the curls around her ear vibrating with his tone '...and hopefully then we can all get off to bed.'

The words sent a shiver down her spine. Something she hadn't felt in a long time. Something she hadn't had *time* to feel in a long time.

The realisation was startling.

She'd only been here one evening and everything about this place was surprising her.

She'd yet to feel a connection to any of her relatives—the one thing she would actually have liked.

But she couldn't get over the connection and tingle she'd felt to this place from the moment she'd stepped inside. She was under no illusion that Annick Castle would actually ever be hers. But she hadn't expected the place to take her breath away. She hadn't expected to get the tiniest sensation of belonging from just look-ing out of a window across an ocean.

None of that made any sense.

But what made even less sense was the man standing next to her, and the fact her skin was on fire beneath his fingertips. She didn't even know him. She wasn't sure if she even *liked* him. He was grumpy. He was prickly.

But something made her feel as if Callan McGregor was the one true person about here she could trust.

Then there was the fact she knew he was single. It seemed to have made her stomach do dangerous som-ersaults.

And he seemed fiercely loyal to a man she knew nothing about.

The lights flickered back on around them. It only took her eyes a few seconds to adjust. The blonde woman Ashley from earlier was now lying on the floor, with a blood stain on her dress. Thank goodness she could still see the woman's slight chest rising and fall-ing, otherwise she might have been totally convinced.

Robin—the man in hunting clothes—immediately launched into his act. 'Call the police, there's been a murder! Everyone stay where you are—you'll all be questioned.'

Callan took a deep breath. 'Oh, joy. Let the mayhem begin.' He was shaking his head again and he moved his arm from her waist. She was surprised by how much she could feel the imprint of his hand on her side. She was even more surprised by how much she still wanted it to be there.

He took a few steps over to the door, looking back across the room. There was something in his eyes, and she couldn't tell what. Was it a memory? Happiness or sadness? No, it was something else, a wistfulness.

'Angus would have loved this,' he said under his breath as he headed out of the door.

CHAPTER FOUR

LAURIE PUSHED OPEN the door to the kitchen. It was ridiculously early but there seemed to be a whole army of pigeons nestling outside her castle window. And the truth was she'd had the best night's sleep in a long time. Whether it was the good Scottish clean air, or the immensely comfortably mattress, something had made her feel as if she were sleeping in a luxury hotel.

Marion the housekeeper was *not* in a sunny mood. She glanced at her watch. 'It's only six. Do you want breakfast already?' Her face was red, her brow wrinkled and her shoulders hunched as if an elephant were sitting on top of them. And there was a tiny little red vein throbbing at the side of her eye. The woman looked as if she were about to spontaneously combust.

Laurie crossed the huge kitchen and laid her hand on Marion's arm. 'No, of course not, Marion. I'm more than capable of fixing my own breakfast.'

Totally the wrong thing to say.

'That's what I'm here for, that's what I get paid for! You shouldn't be in here at all.' Her feet were crossing the kitchen in shuffling steps like a tiny little wind-up toy. 'I've got sixteen people to fix breakfast for and four staff. Then there's the morning coffee and cakes and all the veg to prepare for lunch. The butcher meat hasn't arrived yet and someone pushed *this* under the kitchen door.' She brandished a crumpled piece of paper in her hands. 'I mean, how many allergies can one person have? What on earth am I supposed to do? And did they have these allergies last night? Because no one said a word then—and all the plates came back clean. How am I supposed to deal with that?'

Laurie nodded her head and took the piece of paper from Marion's hand. She blinked at the list. It was the kind of thing that got printed in national newspapers when movie stars handed them to their chefs. She glanced at the name and stifled her smile.

She put the piece of paper on the table and tried to smooth it with her hand. 'Why don't you let me deal with this, Marion?' She met the woman's angry eyes. 'Let's face it, if they were this allergic to food they probably died in their bed last night after the amount they put away at dinner.'

There it was. The tiniest glimmer of a smile. The slightest sag of her shoulders showing a bit of relief. 'Do you think?'

Laurie nodded. 'Leave it with me. If there's anything that is a true allergy and not just a preference or a request, I'll let you know.'

She looked around the kitchen, trying to choose her words carefully. 'Is there anyone else to give you a hand? You're not expecting to do all this yourself?'

Marion bristled and Laurie winced, bracing herself for another onslaught. But it didn't come. It was almost as if it hovered in the air for a few seconds before Marion took a deep breath and calmed herself down.

'One of the girls from the village nearby is coming to help out. She should be here at seven. She's good with breakfasts—just not so good with baking.'

Laurie ran her hand along one of the dark wood worktops leading to the Belfast sinks. There was a huge Aga stove taking up one end of the kitchen and a gas hob with sixteen burners in the island in the middle. There was a huge range of copper-bottomed pans hanging along one wall and shining silver utensils hanging along another. At some point this kitchen had been renovated, keeping the best of the old with the most practical of the new. It was the kind of kitchen used in TV shows, or period dramas.

She loved it. She absolutely loved it.

There was a navy and white striped apron hanging on a hook at the side and she picked it up and put it over her head. 'Okay, if you have help with the breakfasts that should be fine. I'm happy to help with the baking. What kind of thing would you like?' She bent down and started opening cupboards looking for cake tins and mixing bowls. 'I can do carrot cake, fruit loafs, lemon drizzle, cupcakes, tray bakes or sponges.'

She straightened up. Marion was looking at her in horror. 'You can't possibly help with the baking. You're a guest.' She looked as if she was about to keel over and faint.

Laurie smiled and shook her head. 'And you're a member of staff that has had their workload increase tenfold overnight.' She sighed. 'Let me help you, Marion. Baking is about the only skill I have to offer.' She shrugged. 'To be honest I'm not that enamoured by some of my potential relatives and I'd prefer to stay out of the way in the meantime.' She glanced out of the kitchen window and across to the beautiful rose gardens. 'I'd much prefer to be in here.'

Marion frowned. The wrinkles in her forehead like deeply dug troughs. It seemed to be the natural position her face returned to after every interaction. 'You really want to help?'

Laurie nodded. 'I really want to help.' Just being in the kitchen helped. She could already feel some of the tension starting to leave her body, particularly around her neck and shoulders. The thought of staying in the kitchen and not having to participate in small talk with the crazy relatives was like a weight off her back.

The thought of not being under the watchful glare of Callan McGregor was also playing around the back of her mind. Why did he bother her? Why was he floating around in her thoughts? And more importantly, why had he hovered around the edges of her dreams last night?

Marion thudded a stained and battered recipe book onto the worktop. 'Can you follow a recipe?'

Laurie smiled. 'Of course I can.'

And that was it.

Acceptance. Acceptance into the murky depths of the castle kitchens.

Marion bustled around her. 'You'll find all your ingredients in here…' she opened the door to a huge walk-in pantry '…all your fresh goods in here…' another door to a chilled walk-in larder '…and all the equipment you'll need here.' She flung open a door to every baker's dream—a full array of scales, mixing bowls and every baking implement known to man.

Marion folded her arms. 'We've just had a delivery of strawberries. How do you feel about making a fresh cream and strawberry sponge?'

'Sounds good.' Her mouth was watering already.

'And an iced gingerbread and some flapjacks too?' The frown was on its way back.

Laurie nodded. 'No problem, Marion. Leave it with me.'

Marion gave her a little nod and bustled off to the other side of the kitchen where the girl from the village had arrived and was hanging up her coat.

Laurie started to gather all the things she would need. Peace perfect peace. Just what she wanted.

Callan pushed open the door to the kitchen and immediately started to choke, the thick white smoke clawing and catching at the back of his throat.

But it wasn't smoke, and the immediate burst of pure adrenaline started to fade. In amongst the white cloud around him, all he could hear was raucous laughter.

And what was more he recognised that laughter. He just hadn't heard it in a while.

Marion's laugh seemed to come from the very bottom of her feet and reach all the way up her tiny frame to the top of her head. It was a deep, hearty laugh that should come from someone double her size. And he loved it.

Callan waved his hands in front of his face, trying to clear the white, smoky haze.

'Marion? Are you all right in there?'

There was another sound, another laugh. This one verging on hysteria. And he recognised it too. He'd heard it at the train station yesterday.

The white haze gradually cleared, settling around his shoulders and every surface in the kitchen in a fine white powder.

Marion was holding onto the side of one of the worktops to keep herself from falling over. Laurie was sitting in the middle of the floor, a huge sack of white flour burst all around her, covering her hair, face, shoulders and legs and making her look like a snowman in the middle of summer.

He shook his head, taking in the scene around him. 'What on earth happened?'

Laurie opened her mouth to speak, then burst into a fit of laughter again.

Marion shook her head. 'Miss High-and-Mighty on the floor didn't realise quite how heavy the flour sacks were. She thought she could just pick it up and throw it over her shoulder.' Her shoulders started to shake again. Even though she was dusted in white powder her cheeks were flushed with colour. She rolled her eyes. 'Seems like the sack taught her a lesson.' She started laughing again.

Callan held out his hand. 'Laurie? Are you okay?'

Her slim hand fitted easily inside his and he gave her a firm tug to pull her up from the floor.

'Whoop!'

Maybe the tug was a little more than he realised, as she catapulted straight towards him, her flour-coated hands landing squarely in the middle of his navy jumper. 'Oops, sorry, Callan.'

She even had flour smudged on her nose. And he resisted the temptation to wipe it clean.

'What are you doing in the kitchen, Laurie?'

She tried to shake off some of the flour. 'I'm help-ing. I got up early and offered to help Marion with the baking for later.'

'You did?' He was astounded. It was the last thing he was expecting.

Laurie was a potential inheritor of the castle and estate. Why on earth would she want to be helping in the kitchen? She was a lawyer, for goodness' sake. His suspicions were immediately aroused.

She reached over and started trying to brush the flour from the front of his jumper. Long sweeps with the palm of her hand across the breadth of his chest, sweeping lower and lower... His body gave a jolt at his immediate reaction. He stepped back. Seemed as if it wasn't only his suspicions that could be aroused around Laurie Jenkins.

He lifted his hands and brushed the cloud of flour off for himself. 'Leave it,' he said a little more brusquely than he meant to.

Laurie stepped back and rested her hand on Marion's shoulder. 'I'm so sorry, Marion.' She looked around the powdered kitchen. 'I'll clean up, honest, I will.'

But Marion shook her head firmly. 'Forget it. You've done enough this morning.' She gave her an unexpected wink. 'Anyway, you'll not clean to my standards. June and I will manage.'

Callan shook his head. 'Marion, if you needed help in the kitchen, why didn't you let me know? I could have tried to get you some extra help for the weekend.'

He was cursing himself inside. He should have planned ahead. But the truth was, he'd been so angry about the whole scenario—the whole some-stranger-will-inherit-Annick-Castle—that he hadn't properly considered the staff there.

He knew they'd been catered for in Angus's will. But that wasn't the same. That wasn't the same as considering the pressure they would be under this weekend, or the way they would feel about having to deal with a whole host of strangers—one of whom could become their new potential boss. It wasn't just the twelve potential inheritors—some of them had brought husbands or wives with them, then there was the Murder Mystery Weekend staff too.

It wasn't like him to be so blinkered. He hated that he hadn't considered the people he'd been amongst for years.

But Marion didn't seem so bothered. It was odd. For as long as he'd known her she'd been prickly and difficult. As if a little invisible force field stopped those around her from getting too close.

The laughing he'd heard a few moments ago had been the first he'd heard her laugh like that in years. She had a twinkle in her eye. Laurie Jenkins was currently digging her way under that force field. And he'd no idea how she'd managed it.

Marion tilted her chin, a stern look in her eye. The kitchen was her domain. 'Let me manage things in here, Callan.' Her hand swept towards the table at the far end of the kitchen. 'Laurie seems to be managing fine. She's done a good job.'

He tried not to flinch. Praise indeed from Marion and he followed her gaze to three cakes covered with glass domes and protected from the flour attack, sitting on the far-away table.

He walked over. 'You made these?' It didn't matter that he tried to hide his surprise, the rise in inclination of his voice was a dead giveaway.

He felt Laurie appear at his side, their arms almost touching. She was smiling. She looked happy—no, she looked relaxed. The first time she'd appeared that way since she'd got here. 'Strawberry sponge, orange-iced gingerbread and flapjacks for Mr Allergy.'

He raised his eyebrows. 'Mr Allergy?'

She waved her hand. 'Don't ask. I think a pop music diva has a shorter list of demands than he has.'

He wrinkled his nose. 'So, if you've made all these, what's with the flour?'

She smiled. 'I was going to make a chocolate cake for dessert tonight.'

'Aren't you supposed to be taking part in the Murder Mystery Weekend?'

His head was spinning. Surely, the whole point of coming here was to see if she could be the potential inheritor of Annick Castle. Everything had been clearly spelled out in the letter. Why on earth was she wasting her time in the kitchen?

'Yeah, well, I suppose so.' Her eyes fixed on the gardens outside, drifting away to her own little world. What was the story about Laurie Jenkins?

There it was. That little flicker on her face. Did she even know that happened? That little glimmer that looked a lot like hope. Right now it was fixated on the rainbow explosion that was the rose flower beds outside. Usually the castle gardens had regimented colours, red in one, pink in another, yellow and white in others. But this year he suspected Bert the gardener had fallen foul of his own poor eyesight.

Nothing had been mentioned. Nothing had been said. And the effect was actually startling. An explosion of colour right outside the kitchen windows.

Laurie turned to face him. 'To be honest I was hoping to take a walk around the gardens today.' She hesitated. 'You've already shown me the maze—how about the rest of the gardens? Isn't there a swan pond?'

Callan nodded automatically. 'Aren't you supposed to take part in all the designated activities?'

She shrugged. 'I'll make an excuse. As long as I hand in my card at the end saying who I think the murderer is, I don't suppose it will matter. Anyway, I'll be there for dinner tonight.'

She really didn't care. She really didn't want to take part.

He was astonished. Did she know what she was giving up?

But Laurie was peering out of the window again, across the gardens to the wall next to the sea that was lined with cannons. 'Can we get down on the beach from here?'

He nodded. 'It's not the easiest path.'

'I think I'll manage.' She'd lifted one eyebrow at him, as if daring him to imply anything otherwise.

He wasn't sure whether to be angry or intrigued.

The whole purpose of the weekend was to find out who would inherit the castle. Laurie was a lawyer. Maybe she'd found a loophole in all this and knew she could mount a legal challenge. The thought sent a prickle across his skin.

He'd been assured that no matter how crazy this whole scheme appeared, legally it was watertight—whether he liked it or not.

But that would be an explanation as to why she didn't really want to engage with the Murder Mystery Weekend. Why she wanted to spend her time exploring the estate. Maybe she was already drawing up plans in her head about what she wanted to do with the place, or how to sell it off for the highest profit.

'Callan?' Her voice was quiet and her hand rested gently on his.

His mind was running away with him again. Every time he thought about this place or the people in it, his mind naturally went for the worst-case scenario.

He looked down, trying to ignore the warmth spreading up his arm. She was looking up at him with her smudged nose and hair and her big brown eyes. Questioning the fact that for a few minutes he'd been lost in a world of his own.

There was still a light dusting of flour across the pink shoulders of her shirt. Her dark brown hair was swept up in a clasp, with stray strands escaping. The flour was like the first fall of snow at the start of winter.

She blinked, her cheeks flushing a little as he continued to stare. Her head tilted to the side. 'What time can we meet?' she prompted.

He started. Meet. Yes. That was what he was supposed to be doing.

'Half an hour.' His words came out automatically. 'I'll meet you in the entrance hall.'

She gave a little nod of her head and disappeared through the kitchen door.

Callan stared at his hand. The skin that she'd touched felt on fire. He couldn't understand. It just didn't figure.

Laurie just didn't figure.

A movement caught his eye. Marion was staring at him with her arms folded across her chest.

'What?' The words snapped out, louder than intended.

She gave him a little knowing smile, then turned her back and started busying herself around the kitchen.

For the first time, in a long time, Callan felt unnerved. And he couldn't quite work out why.

CHAPTER FIVE

LAURIE WASN'T QUITE sure why her stomach was churning, but it was. She frowned at her reflection in the floor-length mirror. Red Capri pants probably weren't the most appropriate for a cliff-side clamber but that was the trouble with travelling light. Thank goodness Marion had found her a pair of wellington boots, and they even matched her trousers.

She took a deep breath, grabbed her jacket and headed along the corridor towards the stairs. The phone in her pocket beeped and she pulled it out. Work.

Her stomach sank like a stone. Funny how a simple text could have that effect on her. A missing file. On a Saturday. She glanced at her watch. If she'd been in London right now she'd probably have been in work too. How sad was that? She couldn't help but glance at the mysterious woman in the portrait at the top of the stairs. Was it possible that her glare was even more disapproving than normal, and even more focused on Laurie?

She wondered if this castle had any ghosts. She'd need to ask Callan about that later. She tapped out a quick reply with a number of locations for the missing file.

As she reached the bottom of the curved staircase Robin, the Murder Mystery Weekend co-ordinator, rushed over, clipboard in hand. 'Ms Jenkins, I didn't see you at breakfast this morning. Was something wrong?'

Yet another person with a disapproving glare. She shrugged. 'Sorry, I was busy.'

He frowned. 'You do realise that in order to get a good idea of who the murderer is, you have to take part in all the activities.'

She bit her tongue to stop the words rolling off that she really wanted to say. It wasn't his fault Angus McLean had made this a stipulation of his will. This was just a guy doing a job.

She gave him her sweetest smile. 'Some of the activities just aren't for me.'

He looked horrified. 'But you have to take part. You have to speak to as many of the other characters in order to build up an idea of who the murderer is.' He eyed her haughtily. 'And they need the opportunity to speak to you too.'

She sighed. 'Listen, you and I know that I'm not the murderer, so it doesn't really matter whether the other "characters"—' she lifted her fingers in the air '—speak to me or not. As long as I tell you at the end who I think is the guilty party, everything will work out fine.'

'Ms Jenkins, you're really not entering into the spirit of things. It spoils things for all the other participants too.'

She was starting to get annoyed now, and feel a little guilty, which made her even madder. She straightened herself up to her full five feet five inches. 'Well, I guess since the other participants are my new-found family, it's up to me whether I want to spend time with them or not.'

She turned and strode away as best she could in the ill-fitting red wellies. Callan was leaning against the wall next to the door with his arms folded across his chest and an amused look on his face. He pulled the main door open and picked up a jacket. 'Ready?'

There was a little spark of something in his eyes and if he said something smart right now she would take one of these wellies off and hit him over the head with it.

'Ready.' She barely turned her head as she walked straight out of the door and onto the gravel courtyard.

This place was driving her crazy.

She spun around, hands on her hips, and Callan nearly walked straight into her.

'What kind of person was Angus McLean?'

He started. 'What?'

'What kind of person was Angus McLean? Was he some kind of sick sadist that would try and pitch his unknown relatives against each other for some kind of pleasure? Did he actually think anyone would agree to this?' Now the words were coming out she couldn't stop them. 'Was he sane? Did a doctor check him over after he wrote that mad will?'

Callan hesitated for the tiniest second, then obviously thought better of getting into an unwinnable fight with an angry woman. He put his arm around her shoulders and steered her in the direction of the stairs, leading down to the impeccable gardens, fountain and maze. Her feet moved without her even really realising it, the weight of his arm behind her just making her flow along with his body. Before she knew it she was guided along to the bench in front of the trickling fountain.

Callan nudged her to sit down and she did. With a thump.

It was as if all her frustration was coming out at once.

Callan waited for a few minutes, letting them sit in silence and listen to the peaceful trickle of the fountain.

It was a beautiful setting. The bronze fairy was spouting the water from her mouth, through her hands. The water flowed down into the round pond with a mosaic bottom of blue and green tiles. The sun was high in the cloudless sky and the temperature was warm in the shelter of the lowered set of gardens.

Eventually Callan spoke, his voice deep and calm. He was leaning forward, his arms resting on his knees. 'Angus McLean was completely sane. Frank Dalglish, the solicitor, was worried there might be a legal challenge to the will and made sure that Angus was examined by a doctor.'

'Oh.' Laurie's brain was spinning, questions firing everywhere, but Callan's voice had a real weight to it. He was completely sincere. And she realised he probably wasn't amused at her outburst. She could smell his aftershave again, the one that seemed to play with her self-control and turn her brain to mush. Or maybe that was just the sight of his muscled arms?

'He was no sadist. And he certainly wasn't sick. Angus McLean was one of the best guys I've ever met.' He leaned back against the bench and ran his fingers through his hair, mussing it up. She liked it better that way. He shook his head. 'Truth is, Laurie, I don't understand any of this any more than you do. I spent twenty-five years around Angus McLean. I never suspected for a second that he had children. I could never understand why he wouldn't sell me the place. He kept telling me he wanted to keep it in the family—but as far as I knew, there wasn't any.'

He was upset. He was hurting. No matter what her thoughts were on Angus McLean she had to try and remember that this was someone who had been dear to Callan. His experience was totally different from hers.

Something registered in her brain. She looked up at the castle.

It was hard to believe but as a potential inheritor of Annick Castle she hadn't even given a moment's thought to how much it could actually be worth.

She gulped. The figures dancing around her brain made her mind boggle. She turned to face him. 'How on earth could you afford to buy a place like this?' She held up her hands. 'I have no idea how much Annick Castle would cost, but what kind of job do you have?'

She couldn't even begin to understand how someone could make enough money to buy Annick Castle. Her question probably seemed cheeky, but she was the kind of girl who usually said what came to mind. And she wasn't going to stop just because she was here.

'If I tell you will you be able to reply in one hundred and fifty characters or less?'

It took a few seconds for the penny to drop. She couldn't help it; her mouth fell open.

'You? You own Blether?' She couldn't believe it. The Scottish equivalent of Twitter, with a slightly longer letter count, had started as a rival company six or seven years before. It had taken the advertising market by storm. Those ten little letters made all the difference, but still allowed short, sharp messages.

He gave a rueful smile and nodded. 'Guilty as charged. I owned an Internet search engine before that. Blether came about almost by accident.'

She was stunned. Everyone knew exactly how successful the company was, but she'd never really heard anything about the owner. 'How so?'

'I was annoyed one night and came home and spouted off to Angus about it. He told me to stop bellyaching and do something about it. He challenged me to make something bigger and better.'

She shook her head. 'And the name?'

He shrugged. 'How could it have been anything else? Blether—the Scots word for people who talk incessantly.' He raised his eyebrows at her. 'You should be able to relate.'

Her reaction was automatic; she elbowed him in the ribs. 'Cheeky.'

They sat quietly for a few more seconds as she tried to take in everything he'd just told her. He must be worth millions—no, probably billions—and here he was, sitting at Annick Castle for a crazy Murder Mystery Weekend. It just didn't make sense.

'So, your background is in computers, then?'

He shook his head. 'It should be, but it isn't. I did pure mathematics at university.'

'You did?'

He smiled and looked up at the castle. She could see the fondness in his eyes, see the memories flit across his face. 'I wasn't doing too well at school before I met Angus. My father didn't believe in homework. And as a child I had other skills that were my priority.'

Something about the way he said the words sent a chill down her spine. He hadn't emphasised them, or been too explicit, but it was almost as if the skills he was hinting at were survival skills.

'Once I started spending time with Angus he used to sit me down at the kitchen table at night and go over my homework with me. He was methodical—and strict. He discovered I had a natural aptitude for maths and he bought me textbooks and journals that challenged me.'

'So you did your homework here?' It seemed the safest question to ask, without prying too much.

'Pretty much. Angus helped me with my exams. He even helped me fill in my application for university.'

'Where did you go?'

'I got into Cambridge—and Oxford, but in the end I went to Edinburgh. I didn't want to leave Scotland.'

'You didn't?' She didn't mean to sound so surprised; it just came out that way. It hadn't even occurred to her for a second to turn down her university place at Cambridge. Did people actually do that? And how distracted would she have been if she'd met Callan at university?

He stood up and arched his back, obviously trying to relieve some tension. 'Look around you, Laurie. What's not to love?'

It was the way he said the words. So simple. Without a second thought.

And she did look around her.

At the magnificent sand-coloured castle looking out over the Scottish coastline.

At the immaculate maze.

At the colourful, impeccably kept gardens.

At the forest and vegetation around them, set against the start of a mountain range.

It was almost as if something sucked the air out of her lungs.

She lived her life in London. She spent her day jumping on and off the tube, breathing in other people's air. She was surrounded by high-rise buildings and streets that often never saw any sunlight. Continual fights over parking spaces, and eternally rising rents.

She didn't have a single friend in London that had a garden. Her own flat had a window box that she rarely filled with flowering shrubs—on the few occasions that she had she often forgot to water them.

She couldn't remember the last time she'd walked

on grass. How long had it been since she'd gone to Hyde Park?

'You want me to tell you a little of the history of the place?'

She nodded. She knew absolutely nothing about Annick Castle.

Callan sat back on the bench, resting his arm along the back as she settled next to him. His arm was brushing the top of her shoulders. It was as if a whole host of butterflies were flapping their wings against her skin. 'The castle was built originally in the fifteen-hundreds.' There was a gleam in his eyes. 'There's even a rumour that Mary Queen of Scots once stayed here. It was enlarged, rebuilt and the gardens planted in the seventeen-hundreds. The Earl of Annick's family owned the estate for years. They were connected to the Kennedy family in Scotland who can trace their ancestry back to Robert the Bruce. In later years they had connections with some of the most powerful families in America.'

'I had no idea. So how did the castle end up in the hands of Angus McLean?'

'There were a number of properties like this all over Scotland. Some of them were poorly maintained because of the costs involved, others just weren't lived in all year round. In 1945 a lot of them were handed over to the National Trust in Scotland. But this one had caught the eye of Angus's father—he owned a pharmaceutical company and was about the only person who hadn't gone bankrupt after the Second World War. He bought the place for a song.'

Laurie let a hiss of air out through her lips. Maybe not this castle, but something had been here for five hundred years. It was amazing. All that history in one place.

She could be sitting in the same place that Mary Queen of Scots had once stood.

Callan had reached out his hand towards her and she took it without question, letting him pull her up from the bench. Warmth encapsulated her hand. There was a chilly breeze coming off the sea and part of her wished he would wrap her in his arms.

'Come on,' he said. 'You wanted to see the grounds. Let's go down to the swan pond.'

She followed him along the gravel path, winding past the fountain and flower beds. Small things started to prick her mind. Some of the plants here were a little wilder, a little less trimmed. The bushes weren't quite as shaped as the ones underneath the castle windows.

'Who looks after the grounds, Callan?'

He turned, his hand gesturing towards another set of steps. 'Bert mostly. He has a few of the local boys who come and help him, but he generally scares them all off within a few months.' He pointed back at the perfect green lawn. 'Last year Angus persuaded him to let another company come in and cut the lawns and do the edging.' He rolled his eyes. 'You've no idea the fight that caused.' There was a real affection in his voice.

She walked down the steps that were sheltered by some thick foliage. When she reached the bottom she let out a little gasp. She turned to face Callan. 'When you said swan pond I was thinking of something much smaller.'

He gave a nod and a smile. 'Some people don't even know it exists. The castle grounds are sheltered and on an incline. It means that you have to walk down steps at each level.' They walked closer to the edge of the pond. It was the size of around four football pitches and Laurie could see a few white swans bobbing in the middle.

'What's that over there?' There was an elegant glass and white metal gazebo on the other side of the pond. 'It looks as if you lifted it straight out of *The Sound of Music* and put it there.'

Callan nodded. 'What if I told you it had a bench that ran all the way around the inside?'

'Really?' Her stomach gave a little flutter. Her mind instantly had her inside the gazebo with Callan twirling her around in his arms. The chemistry between them seemed to increase the more time she spent with him; it was getting hard not to acknowledge it. Did Callan think so too?

She wasn't sure. He nodded and gave her a half-smile. 'Really. It's just coincidence. It's more than a hundred years old. Angus's parents had it built. The swan pond was his mother's favourite spot, but she didn't like sitting in the sun.'

'It's gorgeous. Can we go around?'

He glanced at his watch. 'Maybe later. We've still got a lot of ground to cover.'

Laurie glanced down at her footwear. If she was going to visit the castle's own *Sound of Music* gazebo she didn't really want to do it in red wellies. It kind of spoiled the mood. 'Okay, then, where to next?'

Callan led her up another set of steps that took them around the other side of the castle. They passed outbuildings that looked a little worse for wear. A set of unused stables and a round stone building that was almost falling down.

The stonework on this side of the castle wasn't as clean as the front and there were a number of slates on the ground. Were they from the roof?

The round building was fascinating and she couldn't

help but go and peer through the doorway. 'What was this?'

'It was one of the old icehouses on the estate. They used to cut ice from the swan pond and store it here for use in the house. The old icehouses were the forerunners of refrigeration. And watch out—you probably need a hard hat to go in there.'

'Wow. What other buildings are there?'

'As well as the gazebo at the swan pond, there is an orangery. It was built in 1818. It was used later as a ca-mellia house and had one-inch-thick glass, a dome top and a furnace at the back of the building to supply un-der-floor heating. They used to think that delicate flow-ers needed to be grown in hothouses. There also used to be a pagoda overlooking the swan pond, but it fell into ruins—only the foundations are left now.'

This place was truly amazing—she didn't even know the half of it. No wonder Callan loved it so much. 'What was that for?'

'The lower level was the swan house and aviary with the gazebo or teahouse above. During its time the avi-ary housed specimens of gold and silver pheasants, pi-geons of fancy varieties, kites and hunting hawk. It's also thought that one time a monkey was housed here, giving the pagoda its local nickname of the "monkey house".'

She shook her head. 'I had no idea the estate was so big.' She was also astounded at Callan's knowledge and the way everything just tripped off his tongue. 'Did you ever see it?'

He wrinkled his brow. 'It was partially standing when I was a boy. There was still some glass and stone remaining. And there's more. There are old gatehouses, a water house and a gas house all around the grounds of the estate. There's an old dairy, a stonemason's and another set of stables.'

Laurie had no idea about any of this. When she'd done the Internet search for Annick Castle, she'd only really looked at the pictures of the actual castle. She hadn't read up on how big the estate was or what it contained.

They'd reached the wall again that looked out over the sea. She placed her hands on her hips and looked around her. 'This place is just amazing.' She sighed.

'Yeah. It is.' Callan had that look again, the one where he just drifted off and she couldn't help but wonder what was going on in his head.

She cleared her throat. 'I hope you don't mind me saying, but parts of it look a little…run-down.'

He didn't hesitate. 'I know. You're right. I tried to speak to Angus about it for the last few years. But I've got no control over what happens on the estate, and I had no right to order repairs—even though I was willing to pay for some of them myself.'

'He didn't want to maintain the castle?' It sounded odd. And she couldn't imagine why.

Callan leaned back against the wall. 'He just grew old—and stubborn. And he wouldn't let me help him with his finances.' He shrugged his shoulders. 'I was worried he didn't actually have any money left. He still had his faculties but his decision-making processes, well—they just seemed to disintegrate.'

'And yet he still managed to make the strangest will in the world?'

'There's no cure for old age, Laurie.' He gave a nod towards the next set of steps. 'Come on. Let's put those wellies to good use.'

He removed a thin piece of rope closing off the

steps and started down them. Laurie made to follow and stopped dead. It wasn't a traditional set of steps. They were precarious, cut into the cliff side with only a thread rope as a handhold. At places they looked almost vertical.

Callan moved down them easily, sure-footed without a second's hesitation. He made it look easy.

Except it was far from easy.

'Come on,' he shouted over his shoulder. 'If you fall you'll only land on me.'

Part of his confidence annoyed her—which was silly. He'd lived here for a good part of his life. He could probably go down these steps with his eyes shut.

Venturing down them in a pair of somebody else's ill-fitting wellies was an entirely different story. In some ways she might have taken great pleasure in landing squarely between his shoulders. In another, despite his bravado, it was likely they would both tumble down the cliff face and land in the rocks below. Quite frankly, she wasn't that brave.

She took her time as she edged down the steps, shouting down to Callan in an attempt to appear casual, 'You never told me, how did you end up going from pure mathematics to computers?'

He was so far beneath her now. The noise from the crashing waves below almost drowned out his reply. 'Boredom, or luck, I guess.'

She took the next few steps a little quicker. She was becoming more sure-footed, the thin rope slipping easily through her fingers. She knew her brow was wrinkled as she took the last few steps towards him. 'I don't get it. Boredom? Whoops—'

The last few steps were slicked with moss and lichens, the thick soles of the wellies having hardly any grip at all. His hands planted firmly on her hip bones, stopping her from losing her balance completely.

She was one step above him, meaning they were almost face-to-face.

If the breath hadn't exited her lungs so quickly she might have smiled. The view was good here.

Any woman would tell you that from first glance Callan McGregor was a fine figure of a man. But this close she could see everything—his slightly tanned, slightly weathered skin. The smattering of tiny freckles across his nose. Her hands had lifted to stop her falling and were now naturally placed on the breadth of his chest. After a few seconds she could feel the heat from his skin seeping through his cotton shirt onto the palms of her hands.

She should move them. She really should. But right now they felt superglued to his chest.

She caught her breath. 'Boredom?' she asked softly.

They were so close now the crashing waves were merely background noise. He hadn't moved his hands; they were still firmly on her hips, steering her closer to him.

He blinked. If he'd been any closer those long eyelashes of his might have brushed her cheek. She shouldn't feel so comfortable. Under normal circumstances she would have jumped back, hating her personal space being invaded without her say-so.

But nothing about this weekend had been normal. Why change anything now?

From this position she had a real clear view of his green eyes. Bright green eyes. Unlike any she'd seen before. There was nothing pale or wishy-washy about them. She'd seen an emerald this green once before on the jewellery shopping channel. Was it from Colombia?

It had been three carats, with a single carat diamond on either side. Probably the most gorgeous ring she'd ever seen and well out of her price range. Funny how the billionaire's eyes reminded her of that.

He tilted his head to one side. 'Just because I had a natural talent for maths didn't mean I had to spend my life doing it.'

He said it as if it made perfect sense.

A gust of wind swept past her, pushing her even closer to him. Every hair on her arms stood on end. But it wasn't the wind. It was him. His touch. And his words. Doing a whole host of strange things to her.

It was more than unsettling. She tried to pull her tongue down from its current position of sticking to the roof of her mouth. It wasn't often in this life that Laurie found it difficult to talk.

'But what did Angus say? Didn't he tell you to find a career related to your degree?' She'd already realised there was no point asking what his father thought. He hadn't even mentioned his mother at all. And she couldn't ask the question that was throbbing in her head right now: *What would my father have thought if I'd walked away from law?* Because neither Callan nor she would know the answer.

Callan smiled. A smile that reached right up into those green eyes. Little wrinkles appeared around them. Good wrinkles. He looked so much better when he smiled rather than the permanent frown that had been on his face since she'd met him.

'Angus would never have told me to do something that made me unhappy. I'd completed my degree. It was up to me to find my place in life.'

He said the words so easily. As if it was the way it

should be for everyone and she felt her stomach twist in tight knots.

Why couldn't she have said something like that to her father? Only hers hadn't been an ordinary kind of degree. What else could you do with a law degree if you didn't practise law? Sure, there were some students in her class who hadn't gone on to complete their professional qualifications after sitting their exams. They'd moved into other professions.

But she wasn't exactly sure what. Truth was, she'd been too scared to pay too much attention to any other options. It had almost been easier to work on the assumption that there was none. She would never have disappointed her father. She just couldn't have.

Horrible things were jumping around in her mind. What would have happened if she'd told her father that she didn't like her degree? What would have happened if he'd still been alive and she'd told him she hated her job? She could feel tears prickling in the backs of her eyes. All of a sudden she felt cold. Really cold. Did this make her a coward?

'Laurie?' Callan's voice was quiet; she could feel his warm breath on her cheek, see his eyes full of concern.

'But what if you can't find your place in life?' she whispered. *Or, you're too scared to.*

She was going to cry, any second now she was going to burst into tears, on the edge of the Scottish coastline with a virtual stranger.

Callan didn't say a word. He slipped his arm around her shoulders, holding her close to his side, and guided her down the last few steps onto the thin line of shingle beach. Judging from the moss and lichen on the shingles, this part of the coastline must regularly be underwater.

The warmth from his body was comforting. The feel of the arm around her shoulder was reassuring—protective almost. He hadn't asked her any questions. It was almost as if he knew she was upset and he sensed not to push her.

They walked a few hundred yards along the coastline and he stopped at the rock face. 'Look,' he said, his mouth brushing against her ear.

She lifted her head. Carved into the rocks in front of her were three arches—as if someone had tried to create a house out of one of the natural caves. The arches were on three levels, almost as if it had been someone's home.

'What on earth is this?' It was a perfect distraction. So unusual, and so mysterious that she couldn't help but ask the question and push the other heavy thoughts from her mind.

'Welcome to the history of Annick Castle. This part of the coast was a notorious centre for smuggling and the fortified caves beneath the castle were ideal for hiding contraband from the Revenue Officers. For centuries the Annick Kennedys and others on the estate were either directly involved in smuggling, or turned a blind eye to it, in exchange for a share of the profits.'

'No.' Laurie felt her eyes grow wide. 'Really?' This was fascinating to her. A whole part of her family history she knew nothing about. 'So, you're telling me my relatives were involved in smuggling?'

Callan smiled as they entered the cave. 'It seems that way. This was all long before Angus's time, but it is amazing, isn't it? And it's part of the heritage of Annick Castle.'

He sounded a little wistful as he said those words. They stood for a moment in the cave. It wasn't quite as dark as she'd thought, the carved windows letting in lots of light. It was damp and slimy, with the water lapping around her wellies. There was a ledge high above her at the second window.

Laurie pointed. 'I take it the contraband had to be moved up there at high tide?'

Callan shrugged. 'I would assume so.' He walked over and touched one of the walls. 'Just imagine if these walls could talk. What do you think they would tell us?'

She walked over and laid her hand on the damp, cold wall next to his. 'How many of those smugglers died on the rocks out there? This doesn't look like the easiest bit of coast to navigate—not that I know anything about sailing.'

Callan nodded. 'That's a good point. This is a pretty treacherous part of the coast. Even today, sailing around here isn't really encouraged. I can remember a few wrecks over the years.' He gave a little smile. 'When I was a young boy I spent most of my time down here fighting imaginary pirates.'

She could almost imagine him dressed up with a pretend sword, swooping in and out of the atmospheric cave. 'Was it safe to play down here?'

He laughed. 'I take it these days it would need a whole health and safety check before anyone set foot on those steps. But when I was young Angus could always tell me the tide tables. As long as it wasn't high tide, I was allowed to come and play.' He gave her a measured look. 'Do you think you would have come and joined me?'

The question took her by surprise. A million thoughts and possibilities had floated around her head. What if Angus McLean had made contact with her dad years ago? What if she'd had a chance to spend summers here—to spend summers playing in *The Sound of Music* gazebo, pretending to be Liesl? What if she'd had a chance to grow up around Callan McGregor?

She pushed the thought from her mind and met his smile. 'I was a girl's girl. Pirates and damp caves would have horrified me. I guess, as every little girl would, I would have dreamed of being a fairy princess in the castle. To be honest, I would probably have spent most of my time sweeping up and down that fabulous staircase. Hours of fun presenting myself at the ball.' She gave an imaginary curtsey. He went to speak but she raised her finger. 'But as a teenager, I would have put a no-fly zone around the gazebo and spent every evening re-enacting the dancing scene, singing "Sixteen Going on Seventeen" with the gentleman of my choice.'

Callan raised his eyebrows. 'And who might that have been?'

He moved a little closer. Or did she just imagine it?

Nope. His fingers had definitely edged nearer hers on the wall. 'That all depends.'

'Depends on what?'

His voice had grown quieter, huskier. It was sending shivers down her spine and her body was reacting in the most natural manner—moving even closer to hear his words.

'Depends on who the hero of the moment was.' It was the perfect time to tease him. And she had to tease him. Because otherwise she might end up wishing for something else entirely. 'When I was sixteen I went through a real retro phase—I loved Marty McFly from *Back to the Future*. I wanted him to magically appear in his DeLorean and take me off. By seventeen I'd moved on completely and thought I would marry a member of Take That.'

Callan cringed. 'Save me from boy bands!'

She shook her head. 'It was downhill all the way from there. I still had a tiny bit of retro films going on. Indiana Jones was definitely my overall favourite.'

He raised his eyes. 'So, no pirates?' His eyes were darker in here. He was standing with his back to the incoming light, making his pupils even bigger.

It was easy to imagine what film he was talking about now. She smiled. 'No, funnily enough, pirates never did it for me.'

He blinked. Thick, dark lashes over bright green eyes nearly obliterated by the huge pupils. 'Pity.'

He said the word so quietly it was almost a whisper. But it was the hidden implication. The expression on his face. Laurie was frozen. She couldn't move. No, she didn't want to move.

She knew exactly what he was thinking. Because her mind was in the same place.

She was in the same position as earlier. Inches away from Callan McGregor. Except this time she wasn't standing on a set of exposed steps; this time she was standing in a darkened cave.

Any second now he might move closer. She couldn't help it. Her lips felt instantly dry and she ran her tongue along them.

He lifted his hand and her breath caught in her throat. Was he going to kiss her? But no. He reached up and touched a long brown curl, pushing it back over her shoulder. 'You're a strange one, Laurie Jenkins.'

She tilted her head to the side. 'What do you mean?'

He sighed. 'I mean, I haven't found you stealing the family silver. You don't seem that interested in the Murder Mystery Weekend, but you *do* seem really interested in the castle.'

'That's because I am.' It was the simplest answer because it was true. It was cold in here. If she just inched forward a little…

'But why? Because of how much it will be worth if you inherit it?'

His words sounded harsh. And they offended her. She pulled back.

'Is that what you think?'

Callan hadn't moved his eyes from hers. 'That's just it, Laurie—I'm not sure what I think.'

She moved a little backwards. His gaze was starting to unnerve her. But she was determined to speak her mind.

'I want the opportunity to meet other members of my so-called family. I'm still not sure how I feel about all this. Most of the time it makes me angry. You talk about Angus McLean with great affection, Callan, but for me—he's just some unknown guy that ignored his children. I can't get my head round that at all.' She lifted her hands up. 'And this, a castle, spectacular grounds, caves and a history just waiting to be learned. It's more than I could ever have imagined. I'm trying to decide how much I want to be part of all this—if at all.'

His expression changed quickly. He looked almost scornful. 'You mean you don't want to inherit the castle?'

She shook her head. He really didn't understand her at all. And she wasn't even sure she could put it into words. She could barely understand it herself. 'I mean, I don't know what I would do with it, Callan. Look at me.' She put her hand on her chest. 'I'm a London girl from a small family. I'm a lawyer. What do I know about castles? I've never seen anything like this before. How on earth would I fit in? You've had the benefit of being here since you were young. You grew up here. You know everything there is to know—'

'Or not.' His words were quick. She'd forgotten Angus hadn't told him about his children either. This must be even harder for him than it was for her.

He'd cut off her frustration mid-sentence. And she just couldn't find the words to continue. She needed some time. She needed some time to get her head around all this.

She took a deep breath in the vain hope it would fill her lungs and straighten out her head.

Work. Getting away from work had been the first step for her.

The letter and invite to Annick Castle had been the starting point in the process, but now she was away and out of her usual environment she was scared of how she was feeling. She was scared by how much she was embracing things, relishing the change and enjoying little things she would never usually experience.

She was scared of the horrible feeling in the pit of her stomach when she realised she would have to board a train in a few days to head back down to London.

Back to the long hours, aching muscles and tension headaches. Back to a life that revolved completely around work. She'd long since abandoned her gym membership after she'd only found the time to go twice. Was that what she really wanted?

The waves started to lap in around her feet. Callan looked down. 'Time to go. The tide comes in quite slowly at this time of day. We've got around twenty minutes to get up the steps.'

He strode out of the cave into the bright sunlight while Laurie stood for a few seconds longer.

She took a deep breath. What was she doing? She

had no idea who Callan McGregor was. Every time she was around him she was unsettled.

She couldn't help but feel a tiny bit envious of the fact he'd grown up here.

She couldn't help but feel even more envious that Angus never had any expectation of him beyond going to university.

She squeezed her eyes tightly shut. This was disloyal. She wasn't even going to allow herself to think like that.

It was time to get a hold of herself. Time to stop with the crazy thoughts and focus on the reason she was here—to try and get to know her family members.

She lifted her head and walked back outside into the sunlight.

CHAPTER SIX

'Knock, knock.'

Callan cringed. He'd recognise that high-pitched voice anywhere. It was Robin, the Murder Mystery Weekend organiser. It didn't matter where in the castle he tried to hide, the guy seemed to have an inbuilt antenna and could find him anyway.

Robin stuck his head around the door. 'Dinner will be served in ten minutes. We were hoping you would have made it to the pre-dinner drinks. You did agree to participate.' There it was. That tiny disapproving edge to his voice that he seemed to have in every conversation with Callan. It was almost as if he were an eighty-year-old grumpy headmaster trapped inside a gangly twenty-five-year-old's body.

Callan tried not to say what he was really thinking. He stared at the crumpled piece of card he'd been given earlier with his instructions. They included *Flirt with Lucy Clark, get into an argument with Philippe Deveraux*. No problem. If the man was drunk again and put his hands on Laurie he'd do more than argue with him.

Where had that come from? The thought surprised him. He'd only known the woman two days and already she was getting under his skin.

Who was he kidding?

She'd probably got under his skin from the second the smoke had cleared at the railway station and he'd caught sight of the curvy brunette. But when they'd been standing on the steps earlier and he could see her brown eyes filled with tears he couldn't help but feel protective towards her. Something was going on with Laurie Jenkins—and it was nothing to do with inheriting a castle. The question was, did he really want to find out?

Did he want to get to know any of Angus's relatives who were milling around the place he thought of as his home? Once one of them inherited it, he would have to clear out his things and start staying in his Edinburgh town house. And even though he owned a beautiful home he couldn't bear the thought of that.

The place he called home was here.

'Callan, can I count on you?'

Robin. He'd forgotten he was even there. He gave the organiser a quick nod and watched him scuttle off.

Callan closed his computer. He was doing exactly what he'd been dreading. Examining the castle accounts. In the interim period between Angus dying and the castle being handed over he'd been appointed as caretaker. The upkeep of the castle was huge. Heating, lighting and maintenance costs were astronomical. The roof needed some repairs. They needed to employ more staff to help Bert with the grounds. Whoever inherited Annick Castle was going to get a nasty shock.

A horrible little coil of guilt was snaking around him. He should have stepped in earlier. He should have spoken to Angus about how run-down parts of the estate were becoming.

But the truth was he had too much respect for Angus to ever have done that.

But maybe there was a little hope. Maybe if he made more of an effort to talk to the relatives he could plant the seeds about how costly the castle would be. With any luck he could put in a generous offer and buy the castle, just as he'd always wanted to.

It seemed mercenary. It seemed calculating. But none of these people felt the way he did about the castle. The only one who'd shown any real interest in anything other than its retail value was Laurie, and even she'd admitted that she'd be out of her depth.

He picked up the jacket that was sitting on the Louis XV armchair. It was the same one he'd worn the night before. He'd no idea whose idea it had been that all the guests should dress in 1920s clothes but this was as far as he'd go.

He could hear the noise in the main drawing room as he descended the stairs, some laughter louder than others.

He saw Laurie as soon as he entered the room. She was sitting next to another woman on one of the red velvet chaises longues. It was Mary, from Ireland, the one aunt that she'd really wanted to talk to.

She was wearing an emerald-green dress with beading around the scooped neckline. It skirted the top of her knees and she had a matching pair of shoes. Her hair was swept back on one side with an elaborate clasp made of jewels and blue and green feathers. Was that a peacock? He couldn't help but smile.

The dress could have been made specifically for her. It skimmed her curves, hinting at them without giving too much away. The dress colour accentuated the light tan of her skin and the glossy chestnut of her hair that hung in curls around one shoulder. She'd applied some heavier make-up, her eyes outlined in kohl and her lips red and glossy. It was all he could do to stop himself staring at them.

But what he noticed most about her was how animated she seemed. She was clutching a photograph in one hand that she'd obviously been showing to her aunt and the two of them were talking at once. Her eyes were sparkling, her other hand gesturing frequently, and her aunt Mary seemed equally engaged.

Laurie was the only person in the room he was interested in talking to, but he couldn't disturb them. He walked over to the sideboard where a vast array of drinks was laid out. He didn't for a second imagine that any of the bottles had been half empty when they'd been put out, but most of them were well on their way to being finished.

He poured himself some soda water and gritted his teeth. He did drink alcohol himself—in moderation. But he hated being around people that were drunk. Having an alcoholic as a father did that to you. When his father had succumbed to alcoholic liver disease a few years ago Callan had actually felt a sigh of relief. It was as if he could finally shake off that part of his life.

He looked around the room again. He was still finding it hard to get his head around the fact that he was surrounded by Angus's relatives—Angus's *family*. Twelve people who'd never had a single conversation with Angus McLean in their lives, one of whom could inherit the thing he'd held most dear. No matter which way he looked at it, it still didn't make sense.

But as much as he didn't want to admit it, he was noticing a few similarities in some of the guests. Two of the sons definitely looked like Angus—one so much so that Marion had commented it was like being around a younger version of him.

One of his daughters had identical blue twinkling eyes and a dimple in her right cheek. He couldn't see any physical similarities in any of the other relatives.

Family. Why hadn't Angus surrounded himself with these people?

He'd never really understood the whole 'Annick Castle should be kept in the family' ethos and had questioned Angus about it on more than one occasion.

But Angus had made comments about family on other continents. Callan's problem was he'd imagined that was some distant far-flung second cousin who'd eventually inherit the castle. He'd always had the thought at the back of his mind the said cousin wouldn't want to move continent and change their life, so would be happy with a financial offer instead.

But he hadn't imagined this. He hadn't imagined children.

It made it all so much more personal.

He watched as Laurie threw back her head and laughed, revealing the paler skin of her throat. It was the same hearty laugh he'd heard in the kitchen earlier. He liked it, but from the way Laurie had acted earlier today he guessed she didn't get to do it often enough.

It was as if the rest of the room just faded into oblivion whenever she was around. At least that was what happened in his head. This woman was invading every part of his senses. Even when he wasn't with her he was thinking about her, and when he *was* with her it was all he could do to keep his hands to himself.

What had she meant—*What if you can't find your place in life*? She was a lawyer living in London. She'd gone to Cambridge to do her degree. Surely she'd already found her place in life?

He knew she was successful—he'd Googled her.

There didn't seem to be any bad reports about her work and the case she'd quoted the other night—about winning a client half a million pounds—had been entirely true.

And why was Laurie Jenkins intriguing him so much? Why, when she'd looked as if she was about to burst into tears on the coastal steps, had he just wanted to put his arms around her?

Everything about her drew him in like a magnet. Her sparkiness, her ability to cut through the crap, but still have a hint of vulnerability about her. She spoke with love about her father, disappointment that he hadn't got to meet Angus McLean and she didn't try to hide her disdain that Angus hadn't met his children.

He couldn't blame her. And as much as that hurt him, part of him was pleased that she didn't tiptoe around him.

So what was it that was making Laurie Jenkins unhappy? Because he could see it. See it in her eyes when she had those fleeting moments off in a little world of her own. He could sense it in the little gaps in conversation as she tried to take in the beauty of Annick Castle and its surroundings.

All he knew was he liked it better when Laurie had a smile on her face and that twinkle in her brown eyes. He liked it better when he could hear the laughter that seemed to come from the very bottom of her soul. Just as she was now.

Her eyes met his across the room and she paused for a second, then lifted the glass of rosé she had in her hand towards him and gave him a little smile of acknowledgement.

'Dinner is served, everyone.' Robin's voice jolted him.

Callan caught Robin's steely glare clearly directed at

him. Darn it. He'd forgotten about flirting with Laurie and causing an argument. To be frank it was the last thing on his mind. Flirting with Laurie he could do in a heartbeat, but the argument? He really couldn't be bothered. He'd just need to remedy that at dinner.

Laurie walked straight over to him as they entered the dining room and reached the table, her green dress swishing around her with the sway of her hips as she moved. 'I met my aunt Mary,' she said. 'And she's fabulous. It's so strange how some of her mannerisms are the same as my dad's. Even though they never met. I can't believe it.'

She glanced at the table with the name settings and promptly reached over and swapped hers with someone else's so she could sit next to Callan. He raised his eyebrows at her but she shook her head and said quietly, 'Don't want to be stuck between those two—they've spent the whole evening arguing.'

He smiled and whispered in her ear. 'Don't you think you might be spoiling the activities of the night by doing that?'

She gave him a wink. 'I'm quite capable of sorting out my own activities for the night.'

He liked it. Her cheeky side that he'd only glimpsed on a few occasions. Most of the time Laurie Jenkins was obviously on her guard around him. And who could blame her? She'd walked into a weekend full of strangers. Some of whom were friendlier than others.

'I'll bet you are,' he replied. If he thought about that too long his imagination would run riot.

'Did you speak to any of your other relatives?'

She rolled her eyes. 'Yes, and no. Mary was great. Joe from Canada was great too.' She wiggled her hand

and pointed at the name cards she'd moved. 'I'm not so sure about Arnold and Audrey.'

Callan raised his eyebrows. 'Were they taking pictures while they spoke to you?'

Laurie nodded and moved to the side as her dinner plate was put in front of her, the feathers in her hairclip brushing against his face. 'Yes! And what's that little black book they continually scribble notes in? What on earth are they up to?'

She straightened up, leaving her perfume wafting around him. Something spicy, more sensual than the floral scent she'd been wearing today. It wound its way around him, prickling his senses.

He waited until all the other guests had been served, then picked up his knife and fork, trying to clear his head. Marion had got some help this evening and things certainly appeared to be going more smoothly. Like all the food that came out of her kitchen the chicken Caesar salad looked delicious. If only he could concentrate on it.

He gave her a smile. 'I hate to think what they're up to. You know I caught one of them in my rooms yesterday?'

'You're joking? Really?' Her mouth was hanging open. 'What on earth were they doing?'

He shrugged. 'I didn't wait to find out. I just shouted at them, told them my rooms were private and showed them out.'

Laurie shook her head. 'That's just ridiculous.'

'I think we should change seats.' The interruption was brisk. Callan heard the male voice in his ear and felt the hand pressing heavily on his shoulder. He resisted his first reaction. Although Craig had obviously had a bit too much to drink again this evening, Callan's instruction card for this evening had told him to flirt with Laurie's character and get into an argument with Craig, or his alter ego Philippe Deveraux. He'd paid little enough attention to the Murder Mystery Weekend without trying to wreck the one small part he'd been asked to be involved in. He would give him the benefit of the doubt. For five minutes only.

He stood up. 'I think you'll find Ms Clark has decided she wants my attention this evening.' He looked down at the dinner table. 'I think you'll also find that the entrées have already been served. Take a seat, Mr Deveraux.'

From the corner of the room he could almost see the Murder Mystery Weekend organiser clapping his hands with glee.

Craig looked momentarily confused, then obviously realised he was supposed to be in character. 'You've monopolised Laurie—I mean, Ms Clark's attention all day. It's time to let her mix with some other company.'

Callan wondered exactly how far he was supposed to go with this. As Laurie lifted a glass of wine to her rose-red lips he had an instant spark of inspiration. Or maybe it was her scent that was still permeating his skin? Whatever it was, he reached down and pulled her to her feet.

After all, he had agreed to play along.

'I think you'll find Ms Clark is already spoken for, Mr Deveraux. I suggest you take your seat.' And at that, he bent down and brushed his lips next to Laurie's.

He felt her instantly stiffen in shock. He hadn't given her any warning. He hadn't given it much thought himself. He was just playing along and it seemed like the natural thing to do.

Bartholomew Grant would surely want to stake his claim on his girlfriend?

His hand was around her waist, supporting her as she leaned back a little. Across the table Auntie Mary burst into a round of applause.

Her lips were soft and pliable, but, oh, so inviting. He meant just to brush the slightest touch, but his lips caught the taste of wine from her and his gentle brush became instantly more intense. He felt her hands place on his chest. For an instant he wondered if she was going to push him away, but she didn't. Instead her hands rested lightly—just as they had done earlier that day on the steps.

Her scent wound its way around him, rich, sultry and exotic. It was truly intoxicating. If he didn't stop now, he never would.

Only the briefest few seconds had passed but he was conscious of the audience around them, and conscious of the fact if she did object, she might not want to do so in front of others.

He pulled back but felt her lips still connected with his. It was as if she didn't want the kiss to end. Had she felt the same connection he had? As their noses brushed against each other he opened his eyes. Her dark brown eyes were already open, staring straight at him.

She looked a little stunned. As if she didn't quite believe the kiss had happened. Her hand came up automatically to her lips, which seemed even redder, even fuller than before.

Her eyes still hadn't left his. All he could see was how chocolate-coloured they looked in this light and a definite dilation of her black pupils. His body reacted instantly—a natural response. Her hips were still pressed against his and her eyes widened, but the smile that appeared on her face was one of pure mischief.

As if on cue, one of the other guests stood up and started shouting—obviously all part of the activities. Callan stepped back, releasing his hand from around her back, and reluctantly sank back down into his seat. 'Sorry, if I took you by surprise,' he murmured.

She lifted her glass and took another sip of wine. There was a cheeky glint in her eyes. Laurie Jenkins wasn't upset or offended. Quite the opposite, in fact. It made the blood race through his body. 'Seems like it was surprises all round,' she said softly.

Up close the green dress was perfect for her skin tone and chestnut-coloured hair. Her cheeks glowed and the red gloss on her lips shined. The beads around the neckline caught the candlelight in the room and dazzled. She looked as if she belonged on a magazine cover, or an old-fashioned portrait. But here she was sitting at his side.

He wanted to sweep the rest of the guests away. He wanted to erase the Murder Mystery Weekend completely. He wanted the chance to get to know Angus McLean's granddaughter on his own, with no distractions.

But the long evening stretched ahead of them. He spoke solicitously to the other guests around him. He ate the steak placed in front of him. But all the while his eyes were watching her every move. Every sip of her wine. Every mouthful of delicious food.

Laurie knew it. And she was enjoying it. Seemed like teasing Callan was the order of the night.

The play-acting continued around them. Callan hadn't paid attention to a single part of it. He leaned over and whispered in her ear. 'Do you have any idea who the murderer is?'

She looked up through her darkened lashes. 'Of course I do, Callan. I've known from day one. But it wouldn't be fair if I told you. You have to guess for yourself.'

'But I don't need to guess. I don't have anything to inherit.' As soon as he said the words he could feel them wash over his body like an icy wave.

It kept coming back to this. One of the people at the table would inherit the place he called home.

Part of him wanted to behave like a child. Part of him wanted to scream and shout that even though DNA might say they were related to Angus, none of them had been his family.

He was Angus's family.

He'd been the one to make adjustments to Angus's rooms so it was easier for him to get about. He'd been the one who'd eventually had to help him in and out of the bath and shower. He'd been the one who'd tried to persuade him to eat and drink as he'd started to fade away. He was the one that had sat by his bedside while his chest rattled night after night.

He was the one that held his hand while he died.

He was the one that shed a mountain of tears.

Not one person in this room knew a single thing about Angus. They weren't family. No matter what the DNA said.

And it made him angry.

It made him angry to see relatives examining the antiques and trying to find their value on the Internet. It made him angry to hear them discussing market values. Had they no respect?

'Callan? Are you okay?'

Laurie was looking at him with those big brown eyes again.

It was so easy to get distracted by her. It was so easy to forget that she might actually be the person to inherit Annick Castle.

Why couldn't he have met her in a bar? Why couldn't he have just met her in the street?

Anywhere but here. And any set of circumstances but these.

Callan was usually good with people. He could usually tell the charlatans at fifty paces.

And there was definitely more to Laurie than met the eye.

But could it all just be a game?

He had to remember she could inherit this place. He had to push aside the way his pulse quickened when she entered a room, and raced when she shot him one of her winning smiles.

She was a lawyer. She was on the ball. And despite how uninterested she acted, she'd probably checked out all the legal implications before she got here. Was there a chance she was playing him?

A horrible sensation crept over his skin. Who better to tell her everything she'd need to know about Annick Castle than him? There was no one. No one else.

He'd noticed her talking to Frank Dalglish yesterday when she'd arrived, but Frank wasn't giving anything away. He was much too cautious for that.

And she'd just told him she already knew who the murderer was. At the end of the day that was all that was needed to inherit Annick Castle. He had no idea what would happen if more than one person got it right. Doubtless, Frank would have instructions for that scenario too.

He'd thought Laurie was genuinely interested in the place and the people. But maybe she was just killing time? Come Monday and the announcement of who would inherit, a totally new Laurie Jenkins might appear.

'Callan?' Laurie was tugging his arm now, concern written all over her face. 'What's wrong?' she hissed.

Robin was finishing a long diatribe at the end of the table. It seemed everyone had been listening but him. Some people were even taking notes. Had he given away a clue as to who the murderer was—or wasn't?

Truth was he didn't have a clue. About anything.

'Tomorrow night, more will be revealed as Annick Castle hosts its very own ball.' Robin's normally high-pitched voice was practically squeaking with excitement. 'Formal dress will be required—all available from our costume room, of course. I look forward to seeing you all there.'

Laurie gasped and put her hand up to her mouth. He could almost see all her childhood fantasies dancing about in her head.

Callan pushed his chair out and stood up. 'Sorry, Laurie, something's come up. We'll talk later.' He couldn't stand it. He couldn't stand the thought of all this merriment in Annick Castle.

Not when Angus McLean wasn't here to see it.

None of this seemed right. None of it at all.

CHAPTER SEVEN

THIS WAS, WITHOUT doubt, Laurie's favourite room in the whole castle.

She leaned back in the well-worn leather chair and turned the pages of the book in front of her. It was one of the classics—*Anne of Green Gables*—and she'd never had the chance to read it before.

Her feet were tucked under her and the sun was streaming through the multi-paned windows. She took a deep breath. She loved that. The inhalation of the smell of books and wood.

The library was one of the grandest rooms in the castle. Set in the base of one of the large drum towers, the circular bookshelves ran along the inside of the room on three different levels. There was even a sliding set of stairs that allowed you to reach the books on the top level. But the real pièce de résistance was the views all around the tower. Sitting in the middle of the room Laurie could see the sea on one side and the beautiful gardens on the other. The room was every book lover's dream.

The knock at the door startled her. She'd closed the door and turned the key in the lock in order to try and have a little privacy. Just her, the views, the books and a steaming-hot cup of lemon tea.

She shrank down into the chair. It was silly. No one could see through the door. No one could really know she was in here. Maybe if she just kept quiet they would go away?

But no. The knock was more insistent this time, sharper and louder. She cringed.

'Laurie? Laurie, I know you're in there. Can you open the door, please?'

She straightened in her chair. Callan.

After his abrupt departure last night she hadn't seen him again.

She had no idea what she'd said or done to upset him. One minute they'd been almost flirting, the next second he'd disappeared. She'd made excuses as soon as she could and tiptoed up the stairs to bed. She hadn't really been in the mood for socialising after that, her excitement about the ball all but crushed.

The knock came again. 'Laurie? Will you let me in, please?'

She sighed. Callan. This was his home. She couldn't really keep him locked out. He probably had a master key somewhere anyway.

She walked over and opened the door, not even waiting to speak to him but crossing back to her chair, sitting down and picking her book back up.

He was carrying a tray in his hands that he set down on one of the tables before turning and locking the door again.

The fresh smell of his aftershave drifted across the room. She was trying to make a point by ignoring him.

But ignoring a six-foot-four man who'd just locked them both in a room was kind of hard.

That and the smell of bacon rolls that was floating across the room towards her.

Her stomach betrayed her and rumbled loudly. A plate landed on her lap. 'Can I interest you in some breakfast?'

She looked up. 'Is this an apology?'

He hesitated. 'It's a peace offering.'

'Did you bring ketchup?'

He lifted the bottle and shook it.

She held out her hand. 'Let me think about it while I'm eating.'

He sat down in the chair next to her with his own bacon roll and a cup of tea.

He smiled. 'I see you went for the old lock-the-door-and-keep-them-out trick.'

She was mid-chew. 'Sometimes it feels as if there are just too many people about. I mean, I know it's a big place—it's a castle, for goodness' sake. And I can always lock myself away in my room. But it's weird—sometimes I feel I just need a little space. A little time out.'

He nodded. 'I get it. I do. And I get agitated every time I see a measuring tape.'

She burst out laughing. 'I know. They were doing it again last night as I was going to bed. What is the obsession with that and taking pictures with their phone?'

He shook his head. 'I'm trying hard not to think about it. I'm sure if I go online I'll probably see half the furniture and antiques in this castle listed for sale.'

She was horrified. 'Callan? Do you really think that?'

He shrugged his shoulders. 'What other reason is there? I take it they're sending the pictures to someone to get things valued first.'

She shook her head. 'That's horrible.'

'That's life.'

He said the words so simply. As if he was finally trying to accept the fact that in the next few days Annick
Castle would have a new owner. She couldn't imagine
how he must be feeling. If people came into her home
and started doing things like that—well, she couldn't
be held responsible for her actions.

Their eyes met and there it was again. That connection she felt every time she was around him. Her breath
hitched in her throat. She didn't want to drag her eyes
away from his. What she really wanted was to get to
the bottom of what was happening here.

They hadn't discussed it. They hadn't acknowledged
it. Surely this wasn't just in her head?

Callan looked away and she took a steadying breath,
bringing herself back to reality. She had to think about
normal things. Things that weren't Callan McGregor.

Focus. She took a sip of her tea and looked around
the room. That bacon roll had really hit the mark. 'I still
don't get it. How did Angus McLean manage to have
so many children that no one knew about?' She stood
up and started walking around the room.

There were a few pictures of Angus in here. One
with him in his army uniform in World War II. Another
with him looking a little older and standing in front of
the sign for Ellis Island in New York.

Callan walked over next to her. 'I've been trying to
figure it out—believe me.' He pointed to the picture of
Angus in his uniform. 'I've worked out that Angus was
stationed in a few places throughout World War II. He
was down in England for a time, then over in Canada
just after the war. I think that accounts for two—or
maybe even three of his children.'

'What about this one—the New York picture?'

He nodded. 'He was apparently sent there after the

war to negotiate deals for the pharmaceutical company.' He raised his eyebrows. 'That would be another child.'

'Wow. The guy certainly got about.' She wrinkled her nose. 'What about my Irish relatives, then? Did he go to Ireland?'

Callan shook his head. 'I don't think so. But Mary said her mother was originally from Scotland and moved over to Ireland as a young woman.'

'A young woman with a baby on board?'

Callan shrugged. 'It's just as much a mystery to me as it is to you, Laurie.'

She couldn't help it. Talking about Angus McLean just made her frustrated. 'But how? How could he have six children and not bother with them?'

Callan slumped down into the chaise longue and put his head in his hands. She was staring out at the gardens thinking what a beautiful environment this would have been to be raised as a child. 'I've got some boxes of paperwork—old things, to go through. Maybe I'll find something there that will shed some light on all of this.'

'Should you be doing that?' Her lawyer head was instantly slotting into place. Callan wasn't related to Angus.

He looked up at her. His brow was wrinkled again and the green of his eyes seemed to make her want to step closer. He ran his fingers through his dark hair. 'That's just it, Laurie. I might not be family, but I was named as Angus's next of kin. So, until all this is sorted, I'm pretty sure I'm allowed to sort things out. At least that's what Frank tells me.'

'Wow.' She sat down next to him and automatically put her hand on his leg. It was meant to be friendly. It was meant to be reassuring—or supportive. But it was none of those things.

It was her fine fingers feeling his thick, muscular thighs. How did a guy with a desk job get thighs like that? And what did they look like when he wasn't fully dressed?

The wayward thoughts made her blush and her instant reaction was to pull her hand away. But Callan stopped that. He put his hand over hers and gave it a squeeze.

She could swear that right now a thousand butterflies were fluttering over the skin on her hand. She couldn't stop staring at him. Even though she wanted to.

She must look like some star-struck teenager, hardly appealing.

'Didn't you know he'd named you as his next of kin?' Great. Her voice had turned into an unintelligible squeak.

He shook his head. 'Maybe I should have guessed. As far as I knew, Angus didn't really have anyone else to name as next of kin. But we'd never talked about it. I found out as he became really unwell. Frank told me.'

'But he didn't tell you the rest?'

Callan raised his eyebrows. 'That he had six mystery children? Oh, no. Frank didn't mention that.'

'Have you asked him about it?'

'That's just it. I'm not entirely sure how much Frank knows. He said he's checked back and Angus's family have dealt with Ferguson and Dalglish solicitors for years. As far as he can see, Angus was contacted at various points in his life and made payments.'

'What kind of payments?'

'I guess it must have been some sort of child support. All of this happened before I was even born.'

Laurie shook her head. 'Isn't there anyone else you can ask?'

He lifted one hand and held it up. 'Like who? Angus was ninety-seven. All his friends and acquaintances are long since gone.'

It made sense. Whether she liked it or not.

But here was the thing. She wasn't really concentrating on why Angus McLean had only acknowledged his children financially. She was far too interested in the fact that their fingers were still intertwined on his thigh. Her ability to concentrate on anything else was fading fast.

Laurie pointed at one of the photos. Anything to try and keep herself distracted. 'I have to say, I can't really see any family resemblance between Angus and my dad. I can definitely see a resemblance with some of the other relatives. I notice lots of subtle similarities between Mary from Ireland and my dad. They're half-siblings. It's only natural. But it just feels really strange. It's almost like having a little part of him back.'

Her eyes instantly filled with tears. She hadn't meant to say that out loud. She didn't want to get emotional in front of Callan.

But Callan didn't hesitate. He stood up in front of her and pulled her up, enveloping her in his arms.

She'd never been the kind of girl to act like a shrinking violet. She'd never been the kind of girl that needed rescuing by some dashing guy.

But just that act of kindness—that feeling of someone putting their arms around her—made her breath hitch in her throat. How long had it been since this had happened?

It was so nice to feel the warmth of someone's body next to hers. It was so nice to be comforted—to not feel alone any more—that for a few seconds she went with her natural responses and just buried her head against his chest. She could hear his heart thudding in her ear through the thin cotton of his shirt. She could feel the rise and fall of his chest next to her skin.

It was warm. It was comforting. It was something else entirely.

What would it be like if this could be the sound she woke up to every morning?

Her brain was doing crazy things to her today. If he'd hovered around the edges of her dream the night before, then there was no denying that he'd had the starring role last night. It was funny the things an unexpected kiss could cause to pop up in a dream.

He pulled back a little. 'Are you okay?' Before she had a chance to speak, his hand came down and tilted her chin up towards him. 'I'm sorry, Laurie. I don't mean to be a bear. I've been so caught up in the fact that Annick Castle will soon be gone that I've not really thought about how all this might be affecting others—affecting you.'

There was real sincerity in his words, real concern in his eyes. She should feel comforted. She should feel reassured. But all she could feel was the blood currently buzzing around her body.

'Angus's funeral was only a month ago. And all this has come as a bolt out of the blue. I still wake up in the morning and it takes me a few seconds to remember that he's not here any more. It takes me a few seconds to realise I'm in the middle of all this. I feel as if I haven't really had a chance to say goodbye to him yet.'

His words stopped her blood buzzing. Stopped it dead.

She could relate. She could totally relate. Grieving was a completely individual process, but Callan's sounded similar to how she'd felt.

This time she reached out to him. And it was the most natural thing in the world for her. Her hand reached up and cradled the side of his cheek.

'I hated that. That few perfect seconds where everything was all right—just as you woke up. Then, that horrible sicky feeling you got as soon as you remembered. It was like that when my dad died. It took months for it to go away, Callan—and even now, ten years later, tiny little things—a headline in a paper, a picture of something, or someone saying something totally random to me—can bring it all flooding back. It doesn't go away. It never goes away.'

He hadn't moved. He was just watching her with his steady green eyes. He probably didn't realise it, but she could see the myriad emotions flitting behind his eyes.

She was starting to see a clearer picture now. She'd been making assumptions. But it was clear to her now that, in Callan's head, Angus had been his father figure. The person he'd relied on, the person he'd looked up to. How would she feel if she were in his shoes?

His arms were still around her waist. Her hand was still on his cheek. She almost felt frozen in time. She could stay like this for ever.

For the first time, in a long time, she felt as if she was home. Home in Callan McGregor's arms. The realisation was startling. It didn't matter how she felt about Angus McLean. She had to respect the fact that, for Callan, he'd been family.

'What happened to your own mum and dad, Callan?'

It was an intrusive question and she felt him bristle under her touch. But it was just the two of them, with no interruptions. If she wanted to understand Callan McGregor better, she had to ask.

His eyes fixed on hers and she could almost see his

mind jumble around trying to decide what to say. 'My mother was never really around. I'm not entirely sure what happened in their marriage. It was only me and my dad since I was a young boy. My dad would never talk about her.'

'Do you remember anything about her?'

'I remember the police coming to the door of our house when I was fifteen to tell my dad she was dead. I was more or less staying with Angus all the time by then, but I went home on occasion.'

'What happened to her?'

He shook his head. 'I didn't actually find out until years later. She had a mental health condition—schizophrenia. She'd taken an accidental overdose.'

'That's awful. Do you think she left because of her mental health problem?'

'No. I think she left because of my dad.'

His answer was instant. The next question was poised on her lips, but something told her not to ask it. Not to pry. Callan took several deep breaths. Even sharing that little part of himself had been hard for him.

He pulled back and she was surprised by how hurt she felt as he walked across the room, picking up the plates and cups and putting them on the tray.

She didn't want him to leave. She wanted him to stay here, with her. And that made her insides curl up in confusion.

'I'll take these back to the kitchen. Are you baking today?'

The conversation was clearly over. At least that part of it was.

She took a deep breath and smiled. 'I think Marion has me lined up to make a raspberry cheesecake and some more gingerbread.'

'You could leave the staff to it, you know.'

'No. I couldn't. I like being in the kitchen. Next to this room—' she held out her arms '—it's the place I feel most at home.'

She hadn't meant to say it like that. She hadn't meant to imply that she was thinking of this place as home. Because she wasn't. Really she wasn't. Her mind was getting jumbled with the huge range of emotions Annick Castle was conjuring up for her. And something flickered across his face. A look of discomfort, that was quickly replaced by a quick nod of the head.

'I'm going to go for another walk later—back around the grounds. Or, do you want me to help you with Angus's boxes?' It was a measured question. It was her trying to offer a hand of friendship.

Was she really comfortable making that offer? Who was she to go through Angus's things? Grandfather or not, she hadn't known him and never would. Not the way Callan had.

But she'd seen the look in Callan's eyes earlier. She'd seen how hurt he was, how he was struggling with his bereavement. And while she didn't have any loyalty to Angus, she did have a burning desire to support Callan.

She'd been there. She knew how hard this was. Her mother had fallen to pieces and if it hadn't been for her university friends, she would have too. Having people around to support you made all the difference.

Callan shook his head. 'I'll be fine. I probably won't get much done today. I have to make some calls and answer some emails for the day job.'

She smiled. 'You mean you need to Blether?'

He laughed. 'Absolutely. I need to Blether.'

She took a deep breath. This was difficult. She was struggling with this. She didn't really know who Callan

McGregor was. But he'd shared a little of himself with
her today. He'd held her at the bottom of the cliff steps.
He'd kissed her last night. He'd hugged her today. This
was the closest she'd got to a man in months. And he
set every nerve in her body on fire. There was something between them. For her, there were blurred lines
all over the place. She just wasn't sure what this was.

'Well, you know where I'll be if you're looking for
me.' Her eyes fixed on his.

And he held her gaze. For longer than ever before.
She could practically hear the air in the room sizzle
between them. Was something else going to happen?

He tore his gaze away and fixed a smile on his face.
'Yes, I do. Thanks, Laurie.' Then he picked up the tray
and disappeared down the corridor.

She didn't know whether to laugh or cry.

At first glance the kitchen seemed empty and Laurie
walked across the room and started washing her hands
at one of the Belfast sinks. It only took her a few minutes to collect all the ingredients from the larder, including the fresh raspberries that had been picked from
the castle gardens this morning. She breathed in deeply;
they smelled gorgeous.

She lifted the large glass mixing bowl and whisk
out from the cupboard at her feet and started adding
her ingredients for the cheesecake. Marion appeared at
her elbow. 'Hi, Laurie, are you sure you're still happy
to help?'

She jumped about a foot in the air. 'Where on earth
did you come from, Marion? I was sure there was no
one else in here.'

Marion laughed and tapped the side of her nose. 'I'm

like the genie in the lamp. I know all the hiding places around this kitchen.'

Laurie stared at her for a few seconds, trying to work out if she was joking or not.

Marion smiled. 'I was in the pantry. You were so deep in concentration that you didn't notice me when I came out. What are you fretting about? Is it about the castle?'

Laurie set down the wooden spoon she held in her hand. 'No. It's not about the castle. Not at all.' She looked around her. 'But that's probably what I should be worrying about, isn't it?'

'Aha.'

'Aha? What does that mean?' Marion was giving her a strange kind of smile as she started to collect her own set of ingredients.

'It means I always know what's going on in this place.'

'Well, I don't. Why don't you share it with me?'

Marion was practically chuckling. 'I bet it was Callan that was on your mind.'

Her cheeks flushed instantly. The woman was a mind reader. 'Why do you think that?' Had people noticed they'd been spending time together?

'Because I've been here a long time. I notice things. I particularly notice things when it comes to Callan.' Her voice had a little protective edge to it. 'I heard about the kiss,' she added.

'How long have you been here, Marion?' Curiosity was piquing her interest, particularly now Callan had revealed a little part of himself to her.

'More than forty years.' She said the figure with pride.

'And you haven't thought about retiring?' She knew

instantly it had been the wrong thing to say as Marion bristled.

'I have no intention of retiring,' she said stiffly. 'As long as I can still do my job I'll be here.'

'Of course. I didn't mean anything by it, Marion. Forty years is a long time.' She started mixing the ingredients in her bowl. 'You must have been here when Callan first appeared,' she added carefully.

Marion's keen eyes locked with hers. 'What did he tell you?'

'He told me Angus found him as a young boy. He told me about his mother. And about the fact Angus named him as next of kin.'

Marion raised her eyebrows. 'He told you quite a lot, didn't he?' Her eyes swept up and down the length of Laurie. 'He doesn't usually share much about himself.' She stopped, then added, 'But then he doesn't usually kiss girls in front of a room full of strangers.'

Laurie gave a little smile. 'I get that.'

She mixed slowly. Had she been misleading about how much Callan had told her? She was itching to know more, but she didn't want to come right out and ask.

After a few guarded seconds Marion started to speak, her eyes fixed on the wall. She'd obviously drifted off into some past memory. 'I'll never forget that night for as long as I live. When Angus came in here with Callan bundled up in his arms, freezing and soaking wet after hiding from his brute of a father.' She shook her head. 'We made a pact.'

Laurie felt her heart start to race. Did she really want to know this? Should she be upfront and tell her Callan hadn't told her this part? But the truth was she did want to know this. She wanted to understand why Callan was so fiercely loyal to Angus. She wanted to try and understand the connection between the two men.

'All of us. Me, Angus and Bert. We were the only three here that late at night. But we promised there would always be a place here for Callan. There would always be somewhere safe he could come where people would be concerned about him.' Her voice drifted off a little, and Laurie could see the tears forming in her eyes. 'Where people could show him that they cared what happened to him.'

She looked out of the window. 'Social services weren't the same as they are nowadays. Children were left in conditions they shouldn't be. Everyone knew that.' She turned to face Laurie. 'Do you know after his drunken rage his father didn't even know that Callan had gone? It was two days before he turned up here looking for him.' Laurie could hear the disgust in her voice. 'We all knew that his mother was gone. But no one really knew why. We didn't know about the schizophrenia then.' She waved her hand. 'That all came much later.' She shook her head. 'We guess that his father got worse after his mother left. But we don't know that for sure. Maybe his father's drinking contributed towards his mother's mental health condition? All I know is, that must have been a terrible environment for a wee boy to be in.'

Laurie was shocked. No wonder Callan only shared little pieces of himself. What had he been subjected to at home?

Marion hadn't said the words but the implication about his father being a drunk was clear. She couldn't help the automatic shiver that ran down her spine. No child should be subjected to a life like that.

Her eyes fixed on the contents of the bowl as she

stirred. She could feel the tears prickling in her eyes. Her natural thoughts were to compare Callan's upbringing with her own.

She'd had a mum and dad who had loved her dearly and doted on her. Callan's life had been nothing like that. And no matter what her thoughts about Angus McLean, thank goodness he'd recognised a child in need and had reached out to him.

She felt a hand resting on her back. Marion's. 'I know,' came the quiet words of understanding. Marion could obviously see the whole host of emotions flitting across her face.

She waited a few minutes, lost in her thoughts. 'Marion, if you've been here that long, tell me about my grandfather. Tell me why he didn't acknowledge his children.'

She couldn't stop this. It played on her mind constantly. She already knew Callan's thoughts on all of this. Maybe Marion could offer better insight?

Marion shrugged her shoulders. 'I'm not sure, Laurie. It seems odd. But Angus McLean's life wasn't entirely easy. He was much more involved in the pharmaceutical business than his colleagues thought. He would spend hours in the laboratories. He was involved in all the developmental work. Lots of people just thought Angus dealt only with contracts and sales—but that wasn't true at all.'

There was something strange about her words. Something Laurie couldn't quite put her finger on.

'But lots of people have difficult jobs, Marion. That doesn't stop them keeping in contact with their kids.'

Marion's lips pressed firmly together. 'Things aren't always what they seem, Laurie. And remember, times have changed rapidly over the last few years. Angus did what he thought was right for his children.'

Money. Marion was talking about money. So, she wasn't wrong about this vibe. There was definitely something that Marion wasn't telling her.

'All the money in the world doesn't make up for not having your dad when you need him, Marion. I can't imagine not having my dad there. I'm a grown adult now, and I still struggle with the fact I can't pick up the phone and speak to him every day.'

'I understand that, Laurie, really I do. But everyone's life circumstances are different. That's all I'm saying.' She picked up the mixture she'd been preparing and started dividing it into tins. It was clear that from her perspective the conversation was over.

Laurie followed suit. It only took a few minutes to finish whisking the cheesecake and put it in the fridge to set. The gingerbreads were ready for the oven and now all she had to do was wait.

'Have you finished up?'

She nodded. 'Is there something else you need a hand with?'

Marion shook her head. 'We're all ready for the ball tonight. The turkey and the beef joints are in the oven. The veg are all prepared. And I've got a few girls coming in from the village to help serve again.'

'What else is happening tonight?'

Marion rolled her eyes. 'I have no idea. I do know that there's a string quartet coming. They are expected to arrive in the next few hours. As for the rest of Robin's plans? Your guess is as good as mine.' She brushed her hands together and glanced over at the ovens. 'If you're finished up I'll be happy to take everything out of the oven for you.'

Laurie smiled. 'Has Callan been nagging you about me being in the kitchen?'

Marion laughed. 'Don't you worry about Callan nagging me. I've been dealing with that for years.'

Laurie took off her apron and hung it back up. 'I'd quite like to go for a walk around the grounds before tonight—you know, to clear my head.'

Marion nodded and looked at her carefully. 'We all need to do that sometimes. Even Callan.'

Her feet had already carried her to the door but she turned as Marion spoke again. 'Laurie—just so you know. That's the first time I've ever known Callan to be so...' she was obviously searching for the right word '...affectionate in public.'

Laurie's heart gave a little leap. She gave Marion a little smile and fled out of the door. Annick Castle was going to land her in a whole heap of trouble.

CHAPTER EIGHT

CALLAN CHECKED THE records one more time. Annick Castle was in trouble. Lots of trouble. It was losing money like a leaky sieve. In a few weeks' time he and Frank would have to hand over all this information to the new owner. What would they think? Because right now, all paths seemed to lead to the fact that Angus McLean hadn't been managing at all.

He could see what the problems were. The biggest, and most obvious, was that Annick Castle had no income. The gas and electricity bills had quadrupled in the last ten years, but, then again, so had every family's in the country.

Annick Castle wasn't environmentally friendly. It was a draughty old girl, in rapid need of some maintenance. But even then his hands were tied. There were no modern windows to keep the freezing winter temperatures out, no proper insulation, no modern heating or modern appliances. The whole place really needed to be rewired. But rewiring was more than a little expensive, and the damage that would be incurred rewiring a building like this would be astronomical. The heritage people would have a fit. As for the roof…

He hadn't even had a chance to glance at Angus's boxes yet. All his time had been taken up with trying to sort out the accounts. It wasn't just the castle. The family fortune had been damaged by the stock-market crash, some unlucky investments and poor interest rates. He was going to have to try and find some solutions—fast.

He closed the computer program and grabbed his jacket. The walls were starting to close in around him. He needed some fresh air and that was one thing Annick Castle had in abundance. It was time to find Laurie. She was the only person around here he wanted to spend any time with.

Part of him felt a little guilty that he didn't want to spend more time around Angus's children or grandchildren. Truth was, some of them he didn't even like.

And a tiny part of him said why should he spend time with people that Angus hadn't? And until he got to the bottom of that he wouldn't be able to understand it.

But Laurie was different. She wasn't constantly assessing the value of the castle. She wasn't aligning herself with estate agents as he'd heard one of Angus's sons doing yesterday.

Laurie was the only one of Angus's relatives he felt a connection to. He couldn't understand it. He couldn't understand it at all, but after several hours surrounded by computers, paperwork and figures he found himself craving her company again.

It would be so much easier if he could put Laurie Jenkins in a box where she wasn't a possible inheritor of the castle, and she wasn't Angus McLean's granddaughter. Then maybe he would be free to try and figure out what it was about her that drew him like a moth to a flame.

The scent of gingerbread had drawn him to the kitchen. But the evidence of her baking was sitting on two wire cooling trays with no sign of Laurie at all.

He walked out into the grounds. His first guess had been the gazebo next to the swan pond. He'd noticed the gleam in her eyes when she'd first seen it and the whole host of other thoughts that was obviously flitting around her mind. But even from the top of the steps leading to the lowered gardens it was clear she was nowhere in sight.

His steps carried him onwards, quickening as his brain went into overdrive. *Please don't let her have headed to the caves.* It was odd. He hadn't given a second thought to any of the other relatives injuring themselves on the cliff-side stairs—even though they would probably sue Annick Castle—his only thought was for Laurie. The thought of her on those stairs sent a shudder down his spine. He really needed to see about something more substantial than a piece of rope to block them off.

He rounded the drum tower and stopped dead.

There she was. A yellow hard hat perched precariously on her head as she skirted around the edges of the round icehouse. She hesitated at the entrance, glancing at the roof, then in the blink of an eye she disappeared inside.

He resisted the temptation to shout at her, striding over and grabbing one of the other hard hats outside and jamming it on his head. He'd warned her about this place. It wasn't safe. Part of the roof had already fallen in, and other parts looked distinctly dangerous.

He stuck his head inside. It was much darker in here. The only window was boarded up and there was no lighting, no electricity. The place hadn't been used in over one hundred years.

'Laurie? What are you doing?'

She was standing in the middle of the icehouse, looking up at the part of the ceiling that had fallen in. Could she be any more dangerous?

'I just wanted to get a feel for the place, Callan. You talked about the history of the caves, but what about the history of this place?'

He folded his arms across his chest. 'It was an ice-house. It stored ice that was brought up from the lake. It took the ice to the kitchen. End of.'

She walked over towards him. Even in this dim light he could see the sparkle in her eyes. Her voice changed timbre. 'Callan McGregor, are you using your stern voice on me?'

'Do I need to?' His response was instant because Laurie Jenkins had gone from the middle of the room to directly under his nose. Didn't she realise what those big brown eyes did to the men around her? Had this woman no idea of the electricity she could spark with those few words? She was flirting with him. She was definitely flirting.

'Hmm…' She was looking up at him through half-closed lids. In another life he'd have called them come-to-bed eyes. But Laurie didn't seem the type.

But type or not, her very presence was having instant effects on his body.

She gave a shiver and he frowned. 'Are you cold, Laurie?'

Why hadn't he even considered that? He'd picked her up from the railway station; he knew she'd travelled light. He was wearing a big thick parka, the one he always used for tramping around the grounds of Annick Castle. But Laurie only had on a light summer jacket. It might be nearing the end of summer, but she obviously hadn't banked on the Scottish coastal winds.

'Isn't it weird? How even though this place hasn't

been used in years, it's just still so…cold.' She gave a shudder and wrapped her arms around herself.

Callan moved closer, opening his jacket and putting one arm around her shoulders. He couldn't quite fit her inside, but she slid her arm behind his waist and pressed her body up next to his.

He tried to focus. 'What are you doing in here anyway?'

She smiled. 'It's this place. I like it. I love the shape—the circular building is gorgeous. And it's bigger than you'd expect. Why didn't Angus do something with this? Turn it into something else?'

Callan shook his head. 'Like what? He's already got two unused sets of stables, a gazebo, an orangery, an old water house, an old gas house, and—' he gestured out beyond the doors '—a whole set of mystery caves.'

But Laurie was deep in thought, her mind obviously taking her off into her own world. 'This could be a gorgeous coffee shop,' she murmured, 'right next to the castle, with views over the sea and over the gardens if this place had windows in it. It could make a fortune.'

The words sent prickles over his skin. Did Laurie know more about Annick Castle than she was letting on?

But she was obviously wrapped up in her own ideas. 'Can't you see it, Callan?' She held her arms out. 'Just think, wooden tables and chairs with red and white checked tablecloths. A whole variety of teas.' She pointed to the other side of the round house. 'There could be a whole circular serving area over here and one of those gorgeous coffee machines.' Her eyes were lit up. 'I can practically smell the different kinds of scones, gingerbread, sponges and chocolate buns. You could serve local produce from the neighbouring farms, maybe even from the castle gardens?' She was walking around, obviously seeing the whole thing in her head. 'It could be great. Two kinds of homemade soup every day and a different variety of scone.' She came back over and slid her arm around his waist again.

He could feel himself bristle. 'What's the point? The castle isn't open to the public. Who would come to a coffee shop?'

'But maybe it should be.' Her eyes looked up and met his.

He drew in a sharp breath. Her words put him instantly on the defensive.

And Laurie seemed to sense that, but she waved her hand. 'Oh, don't get all crabbit with me, Callan. I'll be the first person to admit I know nothing about Annick Castle. But I'm not blind. I can see buildings lying in ruins. I can see the tiles and slates off the roof. That can't be safe. That can't be good for the castle. Don't you want to see things restored? Wouldn't you like it if that gorgeous pagoda that used to house birds down at the swan pond could be rebuilt? You already told me the upper floor used to be a teahouse. It seems like somebody, somewhere, at one time thought it was a good idea.'

He tried not to be defensive. He tried not to take it as a criticism. But the thought of a whole bunch of strangers tramping around Annick Castle didn't fill him with joy.

He had to be rational about this. He had to put his business head on and think with his head and not his heart. 'Do you think people would want to come and see around Annick Castle?' There were a hundred little thoughts currently sparking around his brain. He'd only ever thought of Annick Castle as a home. He'd

never even considered anything else. And deep down
he knew Angus wouldn't approve of having strangers
on his property. But the sad fact was that times had
changed, the comfortable nest egg the family used to
have was gone, and so was Angus. It was certainly
something that the new owner could look into.

'Why ever not? There's another castle about a hundred miles down the coast that's open to the public.
They have a kids' playground, a teahouse, an old book-
shop and stables too. Why couldn't Annick Castle be
like that?'

He could feel the hackles go up on the back of his
neck, instantly suspicious of her wider knowledge.
'How do you know that?' His voice was low. It was
practically a growl. But Callan McGregor couldn't hide
how he felt about things. Had she been planning this all
along? He hated feeling as if he'd been duped.

Her arm slid out from around his waist. She folded
her arms and stood in front of him. All of a sudden the
dim light in the icehouse didn't seem tranquil or romantic, it felt oppressive.

'I know because I looked it up on the Internet, Callan. What did you think? That I'd planned all this
before I got here?'

The words stuck in his throat. He was being ridiculous. He *knew* he was being ridiculous. He just couldn't
help it. As soon as anyone started making suggestions
about Annick Castle he could virtually feel his own
portcullis slide down in front of him.

The protection of Annick Castle lay at the very es-
sence of his heart and soul. He couldn't see past it. He
couldn't see around it.

And being around Laurie just seemed to heighten
every emotion that he felt. Magnify it ten times over.

He seemed to seesaw between high as a kite and lower than the belly of a snake all in the blink of an eye.

Laurie was annoyed. It was practically emanating from her pores. And boy was she beautiful when she was angry. Her dark eyes flashed, 'Get over yourself, Callan. I *get* that you love this place. I *get* that it means everything to you. But if you find yourself unable to have a rational, reasonable conversation about the place then I've got to ask the question if you're the right person to be custodian of this place in the first place. I'm making one tiny suggestion.' She held up her finger and thumb with the minimum of space between them. 'That's all. The very least you can do is listen.'

'It's not one tiny suggestion, Laurie.' He held up his finger and thumb too, but then he held his arms open wide. 'This is the kind of suggestion you're making. Annick Castle hasn't been open to the public since its first building was put up in the fifteen-hundreds. That's more than five hundred years of history.'

She stepped closer, gritting her teeth. 'Exactly. Five hundred years of history that should be shared with others.'

Their faces were inches apart. Even in this dim light he could see the normally hidden tiny freckles that were scattered across her nose. He didn't even want to start thinking about those brown eyes again. In years gone by Laurie Jenkins would probably have been labelled an enchantress with eyes like those.

And she was obviously determined to get her point across. 'Don't you think visitors would love to know about the links with Mary Queen of Scots? Don't you think there must be dozens of little boys who'd want to explore the smuggler's caves and think about pirates? Don't you think there must be a hundred crazy women like me who'd love a chance to sit in the gazebo that matches the one in *The Sound of Music* and dream their afternoon away?'

He could see the passion in her eyes. Passion in them for Annick Castle and what it represented and he couldn't help but smile.

'You've really got it bad for that gazebo, haven't you?'

His words broke the tension in the air between them in an instant.

Her face broke into a smile too and she rolled her eyes. 'You have *no* idea how much I love that gazebo.'

'Every little girl's dream?'

'Oh, *way* more than that.'

'Better than the castle double staircase?'

She grinned. 'Yip. Even better than the castle staircase.' She moved back towards him. 'Why is it that we always head towards a fight? What is it I do that upsets you so much?'

'I keep asking myself the same question.' His voice had deepened; it was quieter—a virtual whisper. The words seemed to echo around the circular building.

She edged a little closer and he found himself doing the same thing. Any second now he could reach out and touch her. Touch the soft skin of her face, run his fingers through her loose curls. Or just grab her with both hands and pull her body next to his.

Her sultry perfume was winding its way around him again—like the Pied Piper's music had lured the children of Hamelin. He couldn't control it.

He couldn't help the grin spreading across his face.

She blinked, her long dark eyelashes brushing against his lowered head. It was torture. 'And have you found the answer yet, Callan?'

Even the way she said his name sent shivers down his spine. His hands reached up and cradled her hips. 'It's as much a mystery to me as it is to you. Maybe we're just two people with a lot at stake.'

She squeezed her eyes shut. 'Not the answer I was looking for.'

It wasn't the answer he'd wanted to say either. But he couldn't articulate what he really wanted to say. He couldn't sort it out in his head. And until he did that, how could he say anything?

He couldn't tell her that she was driving him crazy. He couldn't tell her that he hadn't been able to sleep since he'd kissed her. He *definitely* couldn't tell her what she'd been doing in the five minutes' worth of dreams he'd had last night.

And no matter how much his body was reacting around Laurie, no matter how much he felt drawn to her. No matter how much he was attracted to her both physically and emotionally, he still had the tiniest doubts in his head. Doubts placed there by his love of Annick Castle. And until that was resolved he couldn't feel free to make any kind of other decision.

'It's the best I can do right now.'

She stepped backwards and gave him a gentle smile. 'I know, Callan, I'm finding this just as hard as you are. You aren't the only person with something at stake.'

She gave him a wink, but it wasn't the playful kind of wink he'd experienced from Laurie before. This was different. It was more resigned. Almost sad.

She looked out of the doors, her eyes drifting over towards the crashing waves. 'There's something about this place, Callan. I can't tell you what it is. I can't put my finger on it. But Annick Castle, it just draws you in and holds you here.'

He understood. He understood completely. He always had, right from the first time he'd stayed here. Was it the dream of living in a castle, or was it just the austerity of the building, the magic of the surroundings?

And this was it. This was the tiny thing that kept creeping up on him. It was the long tendrils of jealousy that flickered around him when someone else said those words. When Annick Castle had that effect on *them*.

Her words tailed off. 'But is it the castle…' then her dark eyes fixed on his again and a jolt shot through him '…or is it you?'

She disappeared out of the door before he could reply.

His skin prickled. It didn't matter what his selfish thoughts were. Laurie Jenkins had just laid it on the line.

Big time.

She'd only lain down on the bed for a few minutes. But it seemed as if the comfortable mattress and high thread-count sheets had lulled her off into a deep sleep. As her eyes flickered open the sun was lowering in the sky outside her window. It wouldn't be sunset for a few hours yet but she'd slept much later than she'd expected.

A wave of panic swept over her as she glanced at her watch. She jumped from the bed and ran to the door. The ball was tonight and she had nothing to wear. She hadn't even given it a thought; she'd been too busy baking in the kitchen and spending time with Callan. The costume room was on the floor underneath and her feet thudded heavily down the stairs. She'd always managed to find something suitable before; she would just have to grab the first thing that fitted.

Robin was flapping around the room. Flapping. It was the most accurate expression for him. 'There you are! Where have you been? You're the only person who hasn't chosen a costume.'

'Sorry, Robin, I fell asleep. I'll just take whatever you think is appropriate.'

He pointed to the wall. 'I'd already picked out a few possibilities for you.'

There were four dresses hanging from part of the coving on the wall. Should he really be doing that? Wouldn't that damage the paintwork? She shuddered to think.

The costume room was packed full of colourful clothes, all hanging in rails by gender and size. Some women would absolutely adore this, but Laurie had never been the kind to spend hours mooning over clothes. She appreciated beautiful things, but didn't want to spend the time having to find them. The last two dresses she'd had from this room Robin had recommended to her.

She walked over to the four dresses. All beautiful. All full-length. She wasn't quite as elegant as others might think. There was a high possibility of her catching her feet in these dresses and tumbling down the curved staircase. That would make for an interesting ball.

She reached out and touched one. There was a variety of colours. Gem colours. Ruby red, emerald green, sapphire blue and silver. All sparkling. All gorgeous.

She wrapped her arms around herself and turned to face Robin.

'What's wrong?' he demanded. 'Don't you like them?'

She screwed up her face; she really didn't want to hurt his feelings. She hesitated before speaking. 'I think they're all beautiful. But I'm worried about wearing something full-length. It just isn't me. There's a strong likelihood I'll fall over and ruin them.'

He scowled and touched the red one. 'It's a ball, Laurie. You're supposed to wear something full-length—you know, a *ball* gown. I thought you might go for this one. It's almost identical to the dress the girl is wearing in the picture at the top of the stairs.'

He was getting tetchy. She looked again. It was. It was perfect. A little more old-fashioned than the others but almost a perfect replica. Why couldn't she imagine herself wearing it? It was so thoughtful that Robin had tried to take in the surroundings. But she just couldn't picture herself walking down the stairs in that dress. If there were ghosts in this castle they'd probably push her down in disgust at her attempts to look regal.

She shook her head. 'I'm sorry, Robin. I just don't think they're right for me.'

He let out a loud sigh and threw up his hands. 'Okay then, Laurie. What is it? What is the dress you see in your dreams?'

She laughed. 'It depends entirely what I'm dreaming about.'

'Pfft.' He waved his hand in disgust and touched his finger to the side of her forehead. 'What is it, Laurie? What's the one that you keep in here?' Then his finger came down and pressed on her chest bone. 'Or more importantly, what's the one you keep in here?'

She flinched. 'It's the dress Liesl wore in *The Sound of Music*.' The words came straight out without a second thought.

'No!' He was excited, and obviously a little surprised. He didn't even have to ask what dress she was referring to as he clearly already knew. He flung his arms around her. 'Oh, Laurie, you are going to love me!'

He disappeared in a flurry, snaking amongst the rails of clothing.

She caught her breath; he couldn't have what she was looking for—could he? She stood on her tiptoes. Robin had disappeared from sight. She'd no idea where he'd disappeared to, then she heard an exclamation of pure pleasure. 'I've got it!'

He snaked his way back through to her, a pale pink dress held in a plastic cover in his hands. Her heart started to beat a little faster and she was sure her eyes must have been as wide as saucers. 'No. You can't have.'

'I can.' He swept the dress past her in pleasure, holding it up under the light. 'A genuine, replica Liesl dress.' She'd never seen him look so pleased with himself.

Laurie could hardly contain her excitement. She reached out her hands to touch the dress, then snatched them back again.

Robin lifted his eyebrows; it was almost as if he understood. He slipped the dress out of its protective cover and held the hanger in one hand and let the dress rest on his forearm.

It was the palest pink chiffon, as light as a whisper. Elbow-length chiffon sleeves, a tiny bow in the middle of the gathered bodice, and a knee-length swishy skirt. It was exactly the same as the dress in the film.

There were no sequins. No floor-length glamour. No jewels. But beauty was in the eye of the beholder and it was the most perfect dress she'd ever seen.

The colour was so pale. On so many other women the colour would completely wash them out. But Laurie had slightly sallow skin, and with her dark eyes and long brunette curls there was no doubt it would suit her to perfection.

'Will it fit me?' She was almost too scared to ask.

She had curves. She certainly wasn't the tiny frame of the actress who'd played Liesl in the film.

Robin nodded with pride. 'I promise, it will be a perfect fit.'

She held out her hands. She had to touch it and she couldn't wait to try it on.

Her feet flew up the stairs even quicker than she'd come down. She slammed the door behind her and stripped off her clothes in an instant, sliding her arms through the delicate material.

It fell over her head as light as a feather. Her eyes were closed and she spun around to where the full-length mirror was, praying inside her head that it would look okay.

She opened her eyes. It looked more than okay. It was more perfect than she could have imagined. It was almost as if it had been made especially for her.

She glanced at her watch. She'd only half an hour to get ready. She pulled the dress over her head again and switched on the shower. It only took her a few minutes to put her long hair in sticky rollers. There was a knock at the door.

She panicked and grabbed a towel to hold in front of herself in her undressed state. She opened the door just a crack. It was Robin, holding two pairs of shoes in his hands.

He rolled his eyes at her. 'You dashed off so quickly I didn't have time to give you some shoes. Take your pick.' He held up the first pair. 'Nude shoes—' then held up the other '—or gold sparkly sandals. Not strictly Liesl,' he whispered, 'but aren't they gorgeous?'

He set them on the floor just outside her door. 'I'll leave them here.' He sashayed back down the corridor as she clutched at her towel and grabbed the shoes.

She could hear the strains of music downstairs. The string quartet had obviously arrived and was setting up. Robin had also left her a card with her instructions for her character this evening. She hadn't even glanced at it and it made her feel guilty. He'd obviously just pushed the boat out to give her what she wanted. The least she could do was try and fulfil her duties for this evening.

But the shower was calling and time was ticking onwards. She didn't want to be late.

She got ready in double-quick time, pulling out her rollers at the last possible second and letting her curls tumble around her shoulders. At the last minute she fastened her gold locket around her neck, giving it a little kiss. 'You've no idea what's going on, Dad,' she whispered. 'I just hope you'd approve.'

She slipped one foot into one of the nude shoes and pulled the straps of one of the gold sandals over the other. A quick glimpse in the full-length mirror told her everything she wanted to know.

The nude shoes were abandoned and the straps on the sandals quickly fastened into place. A little brush of eye shadow and mascara and some rose-coloured lipstick and she was ready.

She read over the instructions on the card once more. She really didn't have much to do this evening. A simple conversation with one of the other guests, which would obviously lead them to think her a suspect. Robin was planting red herrings all over the place.

She didn't really care. It wasn't important. Not to her.

She wanted to enjoy herself. She wanted to enjoy spending the evening in Annick Castle when it would look at its finest. Where she could imagine bygone eras and what the nights had been like for the people who used to be residents here.

Where she could spend some more time with Callan McGregor.

Where she could try and figure out what was going on in her head whenever she was around him.

Tiny pieces were fitting into place. Callan had opened up a little, but after Marion's telling comments she finally felt as if she could start to appreciate the loyalty he felt towards Angus McLean.

It was exactly the same as the loyalty she felt towards her father. She had one final glance out of the window towards the sea and then walked across the room, pulling the door closed behind her.

She walked along the corridor. How would she feel about going back to her flat in London? Being surrounded by the compressed air of the city again instead of the fresh coastal winds of the Scottish Highlands?

Her feet carried her along the corridor. One foot in front of the other.

One foot in front of the other. Much as her life had been for the last eight years. But was that enough? Didn't she want more out of life?

Her eyes had been opened in the last few days to a whole host of possibilities—both personal and professional.

How would it feel to get up every morning feeling excited about going to work? How would it feel to be doing something else entirely?

She reached the top of the curved stairways and looked down to the magnificent hallway. Which set of stairs, one or the other? And how did you choose?

She glanced at the red-dressed woman in the portrait at the top of the stairs. Her haughty expression hadn't changed. But there was more. Something else when you looked a little closer. Something in her eyes. Something pleading. Was it desperation?

There was a shift in her peripheral vision.

Callan. He was waiting at the bottom of the stairs for her. It didn't matter which set of stairs she walked down. The outcome would be the same.

It was almost as if someone had turned on a glistening chandelier in her head.

The last few days had been the oddest of her life.

Relief. That was what she'd felt as soon as she'd set foot in Annick Castle.

No tension headaches. No aching joints or sleepless nights. Her stomach coiled at the realisation that was coming over her.

She couldn't go back. She couldn't go back to Bertram and Bain. No matter what happened here.

Just the recognition in her brain felt like a huge weight off her shoulders. The logistics of how she might do that were too complicated for her to figure out herself. She had ongoing cases—responsibilities to clients. It was only fair that she work a period of notice.

The fear of stepping outside her ordered life was terrifying. She really needed to speak to someone about it. But who? Most of her friends were in the profession, and they would be horrified and try to talk her out of it.

Callan. He was the only person she could talk to about it.

He was the only person she wanted to talk to about this.

And there he was—waiting for her. Everything about this just seemed right.

She took the first step.

CHAPTER NINE

CALLAN WAS AGITATED. He'd spent the last five minutes walking about the drawing room, dining room and kitchen. Searching everywhere for Laurie, but she wasn't here yet.

Everyone else seemed to be accounted for. Most were sipping drinks and listening to the string quartet—who were surprisingly good. Marion was a blur in the kitchen; service would begin shortly. So where was Laurie?

For a horrible fleeting second he wondered if she'd decided to leave. To get away from Annick Castle and to get away from him.

She'd left that question hanging in the air between them. She'd been disappointed he couldn't acknowledge what was happening between them. And he'd been disappointed too.

If he got her on her own again he wouldn't make the same mistake.

The momentary thought of her leaving vanished as quickly as it had come. He'd seen the look in her eyes. He'd seen the way she felt about her surroundings. Laurie wasn't ready to leave yet. No matter how many difficult conversations they had.

Then he froze. There she was. Standing at the top of the curved staircase.

Looking as if she belonged. Looking as if she was meant to be here.

She was a vision. No ball gown. Nothing ostentatious.

It took him a few seconds for the vaguely familiar-looking dress to click into place in his head. Of course. He should have known.

He watched her carefully. She was deep in thought, her hand resting on the carved banister. She was taking long slow breaths, then her eyes met his and she gave him a smile as her feet started to descend the stairway.

She was breathtakingly beautiful. Her shiny dark curls danced around her shoulders. The simple pink chiffon dress floated around her, emphasising the curves of her breasts and hips.

But it wasn't just her beauty that was captivating. It was something else. It was the feeling that she looked totally at home—that walking down this staircase was what she was supposed to be doing.

He met her at the bottom of the stairs. 'Should I break into song?' he said quietly.

He couldn't wipe the smile from her face. Her eyes sparkled and her cheeks were flushed. 'I need to talk to you. I need to tell you something.'

He frowned. 'Is something wrong?'

She shook her head, making her curls bounce around. 'No. I think for the first time in a long time, something is right.'

He had no idea what she was talking about. All he could see was how happy she looked, how relaxed. It was almost as if the weight of the world had been lifted off her shoulders. What on earth had happened?

He crooked his elbow towards her. 'Shall we go into dinner?'

She nodded and slipped her arm through his. 'I can't wait for this to be over,' she whispered in his ear.

'Me either. Do you have anything to do this evening?'

She shrugged. 'I've to have a conversation with someone and say a few things that will make them suspicious of me.'

'I've to do something similar.' They'd reached the dining room by this point and he pulled out her chair for her, ignoring the seating plan at the table. As she sat down he moved the cards around.

She arched her eyebrow at him. 'I've taught you well.'

He sat beside her. 'You have. I feel kind of guilty—I haven't really paid much attention to what's been happening this weekend.' He didn't mean for the words quite to come out like that. He'd been paying far too much attention to what was happening between them, just not the events of the Murder Mystery Weekend.

He could see her pause momentarily before she took a sip of her rosé wine. 'I haven't either,' she said, her eyes fixing on his.

For a moment he felt relief. She hadn't misunderstood. She was staring at him with those big brown eyes. He couldn't blink. He didn't want to do anything to break this moment. She knew he was invested heavily in Annick Castle. She knew how important it was to him. She knew he loved it with every breath that he took.

So, to allow himself to be distracted away from the events of the weekend spoke volumes. He was only just beginning to realise how much.

Laurie Jenkins was occupying every waking minute

of his thoughts. She was burrowing under his skin with her questions, her logic and her passion for everything around her. Maybe he should be worried. Maybe, given the set of circumstances he was in, he should be acting with more caution. But Laurie was the first woman he'd ever really felt a true connection with.

Of course, he'd had girlfriends. He'd even lived with one woman for a couple of years. But he'd never felt this. He'd never felt drawn to someone so much.

And it wasn't for any of the reasons most people would suspect. It wasn't her connection to Angus—if anything, that was more of a hindrance than a help. And it wasn't the possibility she could inherit Annick Castle.

No. This was simple. This was all about her, Laurie Jenkins, and him, Callan McGregor.

He would have felt this way no matter where he'd met her. Whether it had been some noisy bar in London or Edinburgh, or some workplace environment. The fact that he'd met her here—in one of the most beautiful settings in the world—was just an added bonus.

One he fully intended to take advantage of.

He gave her a smile. There was a whole host of other thoughts going on in his head that he almost hoped she could see. 'I guess it's only good manners for us to stay as long as it takes to fulfil our duties.'

She nodded solemnly, with a wicked smile dancing across her lips. 'I guess you're right.' She leaned forward and whispered in his ear, 'How long *exactly* do you think that will take?'

Their eyes met again and stayed that way until Robin clapped his hands together to draw their attention. 'Good evening, people. This is the last night of our Murder Mystery Weekend. There have been more than enough clues left for you all to have some idea of who the murderer could be. I'd ask you *all*—' he emphasised the word and looked pointedly in the direction of Laurie and Callan '—to pay special attention to the actions you've been asked to take this evening that will help all parties have an equal chance of winning the castle.'

Callan felt a cold wave wash over his skin. Robin made it sound as if they were winning the lottery—not an ancient piece of history. He tried to push his thoughts aside. He had to come to terms with this. He had to move past this and accept Angus's decision. The boxes upstairs flickered into his mind again. He had to spend some time looking through them. Not that it would make any difference to the eventual outcome.

A slim hand slipped under the table and gave his hand a squeeze. Even now Laurie was taking his thoughts into consideration. The touch of her silky skin sent a shot of electricity up his arm, setting his senses on fire. And in a world of uncertainty there was one thing that he knew for sure. Nothing would douse these flames.

He kept his voice low. 'How quickly can you eat dinner, Laurie?'

She smiled as a bowl of soup was placed in front of her. 'Quicker than you can imagine.' She looked around her. 'This is my last night in Annick Castle. Let's blow this place as quickly as we can.'

She was laughing. She wanted to escape the confines of the dining room and their other companions and he felt exactly the same.

Dinner had never seemed such a protracted affair. The food was as delicious as always. But every single mouthful seemed to take for ever. People were too busy talking to eat their food. In between courses Callan walked around to the other side of the table and had the conversation that his card had instructed him to. It was over in the blink of an eye. He made sure of it.

And Laurie had done the same. But she didn't seem to walk—she floated. Something was different with her tonight. And he couldn't wait to find out what.

The clock ticked slowly. By the time dessert arrived Callan wanted to refuse it and leave. But it was Marion's speciality, rhubarb compote with crème anglaise and he could never offend her by not eating her food.

Laurie was more relaxed. She happily sipped her wine and ate her food, chatting to all those around her. By the time Robin announced time for coffee in the drawing room Callan was almost ready to explode.

He didn't hesitate. He grabbed her hand and pulled her towards the open glass doors leading out to the gardens. 'Ready to leave?'

She flashed him a smile. 'Around two hours ago.'

'Really? You seemed so comfortable.'

'I'm just a better actor than you.' She squeezed his hand. 'Where are we going?'

They'd walked out to the stone patio that overlooked the maze. There was smoke around them, a haze. A natural mist that was lifting from the sea as the warm summer air met the cool sea breezes. If he didn't know any better he'd suspect some film director was pumping it around them to set the scene.

But Callan didn't need anyone else to set the scene for him. He'd arranged that for himself.

He looked down at her. 'In that dress? There's only one place we can go.'

They didn't even wait to walk along the paths but just cut across the lawn towards the stairs that led to the lowered gardens. His hand was grasping hers tightly and she could scarcely keep up with his long strides, the damp grass wetting her feet through the open gold sandals. As the grass was wet the ground underneath it was soft, her spindly heels sinking rapidly into the pliable earth. She stumbled as her heel caught and her foot slipped out of the shoe.

Callan's strong arms closed around her, catching her before she collided with the damp grass. 'Careful!'

He reached back and extracted her shoe from the ground, kneeling down to slip it back over her foot. His gentle touch around her foot was sending a whole host of delicious tingles down her spine as he refastened the straps. 'Isn't this what Cinderella did? Lose her shoe as she ran away from the ball?'

She smiled at him. Her one leg that was on the ground was feeling distinctly wobbly. 'I guess that makes you my Prince Charming, then?'

His hand slid along her lower leg. The tingles were getting *so* much worse. 'I guess it does.' He stood up, stopping in front of her for a few seconds. She caught her breath.

This was so real now.

Tonight was their last night together. And expectations were causing the air between them to sizzle.

He reached out and took her hand again, this time walking with a little more care, a little more measure.

As they reached the top of the stairway she let out a little gasp. Something she totally hadn't expected. Lights around the gazebo.

'I didn't realise,' she began. 'Is there an electricity supply down there?'

The rest of the swan pond was in complete darkness. Even the steps they were standing on now had no lighting.

'No. Just be thankful for modern technology.'

She took a few tentative steps down the first few stairs and screwed up her nose. 'What is it then?'

'Solar lights. Small white ones lighting around the base of the gazebo, and some coloured butterfly lights strung along the outside.'

'They're beautiful, Callan. Just beautiful.' She tilted her head as she looked at him. 'Have they always been there? I didn't notice them the other day.'

He shook his head. 'I put them there today.'

There was a little soar of pleasure in her chest. It was almost as if, with every step, a notch on the dial between them turned up. She felt curious. 'Did you know? Did you know about the dress?'

'No. But I knew about your daydream. You told me. You told me what you wanted to do.'

Her heart squeezed in her chest. She hadn't told him everything she wanted to do. Some thoughts were entirely private. But here, and now, someone had valued her enough to make her little girl dreams come true. Someone she'd only known for a few days, but felt a whole-hearted connection to.

'Thank you,' she whispered.

He kept her hand in his as she walked gingerly down the steps and they walked along the white stone path around the edge of the swan pond. She could hear the swans rustling in the bushes at the side of the pond. Some of them were floating near to the edges, obviously asleep. It was such a peaceful setting at night.

The gazebo with its soft lights was glowing like a beacon in the middle of the pitch-black night. Twinkling like a Christmas tree in the middle of summer. The air around them was still with hardly a breath of air. Apart from the occasional animal noise all she could hear was their steps on the path, the stones crunching beneath their feet. It was magical.

They reached the entrance to the gazebo and Callan pushed the door open. It creaked loudly. Almost in protest at being disturbed. She liked the idea that none of the other guests had been here. She liked the thought that this was her and Callan's private space.

It probably wasn't too surprising. Most of the other guests were older than her and Callan. The steps to the lower garden were steep, not the most conducive to those who weren't as steady on their feet.

She held her breath as she stepped inside. Wow. The glass panels inside reflected the string of tiny butterfly lights outside. And as they bobbed around outside, the multicoloured lights reflected across the floor inside like a rainbow.

It was better than a movie effect. This was real.

She felt his hands on her waist and spun around to face him, her hands reaching up and resting on the planes of his chest.

He smiled down at her. 'So, Laurie. What is it you wanted to talk to me about?' He was standing over her. Only inches away.

She was trying to concentrate. She was trying not to focus on the rise and fall of his chest beneath the palms of her hands. She was trying not to dare recognise the fact she could feel the gentle echo of his beating heart beneath her fingertips.

It was time. It was time to tell someone else her plans. Her hopes for the future. It didn't matter that she didn't know where those plans would take her. She only knew they wouldn't keep her in London any more.

Callan's green eyes were focused on her. And they

soothed her. And they ignited a fire within her belly. A surge she hadn't felt in a long time.

'You know I work as a lawyer in London.'

He nodded.

'When you told me that you worked in computers instead of mathematics I was surprised.'

'Why?' His voice was quiet. 'Lots of people do degrees in one field and take jobs in another.'

She hesitated. This was hard. She was trying so hard not to say anything she would regret. 'It's a bit more difficult when you've studied law. It's not such a generic field. Once you've done a law degree there's really only one way you can go.'

'I get it. Like why would you study medicine if you don't want to be a doctor? But why would you do a law degree if you didn't want to be a lawyer?'

It made so much more sense when he said it out loud. It also made her feel foolish. Foolish for taking so long to put this into words.

She lowered her head, blinking back the tears that had automatically formed in her eyes. There was a lump in her throat. She felt his warm hand sweep back the hair that had covered her face, pulling it back to the nape of her neck where his gentle figures rested. 'Laurie?'

The tears started to flow. 'I knew right from the minute I got there that I didn't want to do a law degree. I'd done well at school. My guidance teacher persuaded me to apply for the best possible degrees for my results. It seemed natural. It seemed the sensible thing to do.'

'You were thinking with your head instead of your heart?'

He whispered the words as if he understood.

She nodded desperately. 'My dad—he was just so

happy, so proud when he knew I'd been accepted to Cambridge. He'd never imagined his daughter would do so well. And neither did I. It all seemed like a dream at first.' She shook her head, fixating on the flickering lights outside. 'Then my dad just worked so hard, such long hours to make the dream a reality and all of a sudden I felt as if I couldn't get out. I couldn't say anything. How could I disappoint him when he was working so hard? What kind of a daughter would that make me? It was like being on a train ride I couldn't get off.'

His hand cradled the side of her cheek and his fingers brushed away one of her tears. 'You felt like you couldn't tell him?'

She nodded again as the tears just seemed to flow from her eyes like a tumbling river's stream. 'I didn't want to do anything to disappoint him. I didn't want to do anything to make him sad.' She could hear the desperation in her own voice. 'But when you said that Angus had no expectation of you beyond finishing your own degree…' Her voice tailed off. 'It just seemed unfair. You make it sound so easy.'

Her hands were resting on his shoulders now and one of his hands drifted along the length of her arm, settling back to her waist where he pulled her closer.

The temperature had dropped around them. Or maybe it was just the atmosphere that was making her breath send little clouds in the air around them. The hairs on her arms were standing on end. Or maybe it was being here with Callan, the man who had no expectations of her and only a steady admiration in his eyes.

'I know you lost your dad a few years ago, Laurie. So what now? You're an adult. There's no one to disappoint. You can decide what happens next. You can decide what steps you take. Where do you want to go, Laurie? Where do you want to end up?'

The words were measured. His other hand had reached her waist and both were pulling her even closer to him. She could almost hear music in the air between them. And it was as if they weren't talking about her career choice any more. It was so much more than that.

Where do you want to end up? The million-dollar question. It was everything that sparked in the air between them. Every impulse that fired in her skin whenever he touched her. Every dream that featured him in high-definition detail.

A smile came across his face. The air in the room was closing in on them. Pressing around every inch. His grip on her waist tightened and he lifted her in the air, as if it were something he did every day, making her breath catch in her throat as he took a few steps and stood her on the thin bench that ran around the inside of the gazebo.

'Maybe it's time to forget, Laurie. Let's pretend you don't need to think about any of these things.' He waited, then reached and wiped another tear from her cheek before adding, 'And neither do I. You told me earlier what you wanted to do. Why don't you just let me give you your dreams tonight?' She heard his voice break and it squeezed at her heart.

Tomorrow everything changed for both of them.

Tomorrow the person who would inherit Annick Castle would be announced. She doubted it would be her. And in a way, she didn't want it to be. She had no idea what to do with a place like Annick Castle, even though it had wound its way into her heart.

Right now, she was more concerned about what it might do to Callan. What it might do to the small boy who had found a haven—a safe place in Annick Castle. It didn't matter what she thought of Angus. It didn't matter to her at all.

All that mattered to her was what Callan thought of him. How Callan McGregor would feel. Because Callan McGregor was a keeper. She knew that in her heart.

She would never do anything to hurt him. Never do anything to keep him from his dream.

The realisation was startling. Two, in one night.

And even though she couldn't think about it right now they were probably interconnected. The decision about walking away from her job felt freeing. Like spreading her wings and flying high in the air.

She didn't feel guilty about it. She didn't feel irresponsible. It was time to start living her life for herself. Not for anyone else.

Her legs were trembling. She looked around her. It was beautiful. It was the perfect setting. And Callan was the perfect man to share it with.

'Are you going to be my prince tonight, Callan?' She held out her shaking hand towards him.

He gave a little smile. 'Aren't I supposed to be your Rolfe?'

She wrinkled her nose. 'He turned out to be a traitor. I'd rather go with the prince theme.'

He took her hand in his. 'Does this mean I have to dance and sing? Because, I warn you. This might not work out the way you imagined it.'

Her voice was low and husky. 'You've no idea what I've imagined, Callan.' His eyes widened as his smile spread across his face. He gave a mock bow.

'Ms Jenkins, can I have this dance?'

She gave a little curtsey as he took her hand and her steps quickened around the circular bench. Callan laughed, keeping pace with her as she started to run, letting the rainbow-coloured reflections of light dance across the pale chiffon of her dress. Her gold shoes sparkled in the dim lights but the one thing that stood out for her was the green of Callan's eyes. They didn't leave her. Not for a second.

'You're planning on making me dizzy, aren't you?' he quipped as she started around the circle for the fourth time.

'I might never get to do this again,' came her instant response.

He stopped dead. As if the realisation had just hit him.

Her breath caught in her throat, her heart beating rapidly against her chest. Did she really want this to be the last time for her and Callan?

She could see his quick breaths, see the glimmer of uncertainty across his eyes followed by a look of firm decision.

His hands swept around her waist, lifting her up and spinning her around as if she were as light as a feather. Her arms caught around his neck and she laughed as he continued to spin her round, her dress billowing out around them. He stopped slowly, holding her in place for a few seconds before gradually beginning to lower her down. Her face was just inches above his. She didn't want him to stop touching her; she didn't want him to stop holding her.

'Are you going to kiss me again, Callan?' she whispered. 'Do I get a little warning this time?'

'How much warning do you need?'

'About this much.'

She started to kiss him before he'd completely lowered her to the floor. This time she was ready. This time she initiated it. This time there were no spectators.

There was just her and Callan. A perfect combination.

It wasn't a light kiss. She wasn't gentle. She knew exactly what she was doing. This was happening because she wanted it to happen. This wasn't about her job. This wasn't about Angus McLean. This wasn't about Annick Castle.

This was just about her and Callan.

And it felt so right.

Their kiss was intensifying; the stubble on his chin scraped her skin. His hands ran through her curls, locking into place at the back of her head as he tried to pull her even closer.

The chiffon material on her dress was so thin, all she could feel was the compressed heat from his body against hers.

Her hands ran across the expanse of his back; she could feel his muscles rippling under his shirt. One of these days she'd ask him how he got those.

Or maybe he could show her…

He pulled his head back from hers, still holding her head in place. With slow sensuous movement he slid his hands down her back, around her hips, and stroked upwards with his palms towards her breasts.

She wasn't in a fairy tale any more. She was in a positively adult dream. One where she only dared imagine the outcome.

'Laurie,' he murmured as he rested his forehead against hers.

'Yes.' She could hardly breathe. She would scream if he stopped touching her. This was meant to happen. They were meant to be together.

She'd never felt a connection like this. Her one-track mind knew exactly where this would go. And she couldn't think of a single reason to stop it happening.

She didn't want to have regrets in life. She had too many of those already. And Callan could never be regret. Not when he made her feel like this.

She stood on her tiptoes and kissed his nose. She ran her fingers through his dark hair as she looked into his eyes. He didn't need to ask the question out loud.

She already knew her answer. Her hands cupped either side of his face. 'Yes, Callan,' she breathed.

And he took her hand in his and led her back to the castle.

CHAPTER TEN

HE DIDN'T WANT to wake up. He didn't want this day to begin.

This was the day where two things he loved could slip through his fingertips.

All of a sudden he was instantly awake, his eyes fixating on the rain battering on the windowpane. Love. Where had that come from?

With the exception of Angus, Callan couldn't remember the last time he'd ever had a thought like this. Callan 'cared' about people. He didn't love them.

He'd 'cared' about some women in the past. He'd worried about them. He hadn't wanted to hurt their feelings. He'd wanted to take care of them.

None of these things applied to Laurie. He'd have to multiply everything by a thousand to get even close.

From the first second he'd glanced her through the steam on the train platform she'd started to burrow her way under his skin and into his heart.

Her reactions had been totally different from everyone else who could inherit the castle. She'd walked the estate, she'd asked questions, she'd shown an interest that was above and beyond the monetary value. She'd seemed invested in the place.

Her connection with Marion had taken him by surprise. He suspected it had taken Marion by surprise too. She wasn't known for sharing her domain. But apparently Laurie had sneaked under her radar too. She'd done nothing but sing Laurie's praises to him—all with a twinkle in her eyes.

What sat heaviest on his chest was his loyalty to Angus. He knew instantly that if Angus had met Laurie he would have loved her. He would have loved her spark, her inquisitiveness, her cheek and her ability to run rings around Callan.

He just couldn't understand why Angus hadn't met his children. Hadn't loved his children the way he'd loved him. Nothing about it seemed right. And until he could sort that out in his head he would never be able to move forward.

And today was a day for moving forward.

He turned on his side. Laurie currently had her back to him, the cotton sheet had slipped from her shoulders and his eyes carried along the curves of her skin. She was sleeping peacefully and his hands were itching to touch her again.

He wanted to ask her to stay. He wanted to ask her to stay here with him. To stay anywhere with him.

But what could he offer her?

Her words had almost broken his heart last night when she'd told him how she hated her job. It would be so easy for him to tell her just to pack it all in, forget about everything and move up to Edinburgh with him. Money wasn't an object for Callan.

But he knew in his heart that Laurie wasn't that kind of girl.

And the outcome of Annick Castle was still hanging over his head like a black thunder cloud. Until that was resolved his stomach would constantly churn.

He slid his feet to the floor as something flickered into his brain. Laurie had told him she knew who the murderer was. How on earth could she know? He was embarrassed to say that he hadn't been paying enough attention to even hazard a guess.

Was there even a tiny chance that Laurie could inherit the castle?

A shiver crept down his spine. How would that make him feel? He didn't even want to consider that for a second. What was developing between him and Laurie could be destroyed by something like that.

He took a deep breath as he watched her sleeping form. She had a one in twelve chance of inheriting the castle. He watched her gentle breathing, in and out, in and out, her hair framing her face and her tongue running along her rose-pink lips.

He didn't want anything to mess this up. Nothing at all.

He stood up. The boxes. He still hadn't had a chance to go through Angus's boxes. He had to do it now. Time was running out. He might have access to these things now, but in a matter of days he would have to walk away from Annick Castle and leave everything behind. He had to use the opportunity to find out what he could now.

He pulled a shirt over his head and some trousers on. He would do it now while Laurie slept. There was no point disturbing his sleeping Cinderella.

Her eyes flickered open and for a second she was startled. For the last few days she'd woken in a room with a peaceful yellow colour scheme. The pale themes of blue unsettled her. Her reactions were instantaneous.

She pulled the sheet over her naked body and flipped over onto her back.

Nothing. No one.

Callan wasn't there.

She was instantly caught by the pain in her chest. The expanse of the bed seemed huge. The dip where he should be lying seemed like a giant chasm. Where was he? Was he embarrassed? Was he ashamed of what had happened last night? Why wasn't he still lying here next to her?

Her beautiful pale pink chiffon dress was lying in a crumpled heap on the floor. Robin would have a fit. Her gold glitter sandals were strewn across the floor, obviously left exactly where they'd fallen. She cringed as she looked around the rest of the room. Even though this was obviously Callan's room, there was no visible sign of him.

It made her stomach churn. She pulled the sheet around her like a toga as she stood up and her eyes swept the room. There was nothing else for her to wear except the clothes she'd discarded last night. And who knew where her underwear was?

She rummaged around the floor eventually finding her bra and pants and pulling them on. Her Liesl dress was a crumpled wreck. It seemed to echo exactly how she felt. Talk about doing the next-day walk of shame.

Thankfully the corridor was empty. She fled down the staircase as quickly as possible and slammed her door closed behind her.

Her half-empty rucksack lay on the floor. Going home. After the announcement today she would be going home.

Her eyes filled with tears. Everything last night with

Callan had been perfect. But deep down both of them had known they were saying goodbye.

How could there be a happy ever after for them? What on earth did she expect to happen?

She pulled out some clothes. A pair of Capri pants and a slightly wrinkled shirt that she'd already worn. If she'd thought about it a bit more she could have asked Marion where she could launder her clothes. But there was no point now. No point because she wasn't staying.

There was something pushed under the doorway. She'd completely missed it. She tore the envelope open. Was it from Callan?

Of course it wasn't. He'd left her sleeping alone in his room; why would he push a note under her door? It was from Robin. Asking her to write the name of the person she suspected as the murderer and return it to him before eleven that morning.

That was easy. She grabbed a pen and scribbled the name. She didn't even have to think about it.

Part of her wanted to hide away in her room. *Her* room. It wasn't her room. It was part of the castle. After today she would probably never see this place again and it was about time she accepted that.

She'd probably never see Callan again. But that thought made her legs buckle and left her sitting on the window seat looking out at the crashing sea.

The rain was battering down outside. It was the first day of bad weather she'd experienced here and all of a sudden she felt very sorry for the bygone smugglers. It must be terrifying down at the caves in weather like this. She could feel the wind whistle through the panes of glass. The temperature was distinctly lower. Or maybe it was just her mood.

It was time to step away from Annick Castle and Callan McGregor. It was time to go back to London and sort her life out.

One thing hadn't changed. She didn't want to be a lawyer any more and she needed to take steps to make a change. She could do that. She could do that now.

Annick Castle had changed her. It had given her some perspective on life. Meeting some of her unknown relatives had been enlightening.

She would have preferred it if some of them had remained unknown. But there was a few she had felt some kind of affinity towards. She would love to go and visit her auntie Mary in Ireland some time. She would love to show her some more pictures of her father so she could see the family resemblance between the two of them.

As for Angus McLean? She'd grown tired of wondering why he'd abandoned his children. She'd grown tired of wondering why he'd been able to show love to some unknown child, then split his heart in two with the contents of his will.

She'd grown tired of it all.

There was a thin layer of dust over the boxes. No one had touched them in years.

He'd found them in the back of a cupboard in Angus's room, hidden amongst shoes and old smoking jackets. He'd been curious at first, wondering if they would reveal something about Angus's unacknowledged children.

But they were something else entirely.

Medical files. And lots of them.

It took Callan a few minutes to work out what he was looking at. At first they seemed totally random. Patients allocated numbers instead of names. They were ancient—some more than seventy years old. And the initial sense of unease he'd felt at looking at someone's medical files rapidly diminished.

The files all seemed to have one thing in common. A big red stamp with deceased across the front.

But there was more than that. All of these people seemed to have died within a very short period of time. A window of six months back in the 1940s just after the Second World War had ended.

It took him a little longer to work out entirely what they were telling him.

Angus's father had owned a pharmaceutical company. These were all records of drug trials. Nowadays clinical drug trials were scrutinised, monitored and regulated beyond all recognition. Seventy-five years ago—not so much.

And whatever drug these people had been trialling seemed to have had an extreme adverse effect. All the patients taking it had died within six months.

All except one. Patient X115. Otherwise known as Angus McLean.

It was a horrible moment of realisation. Scribbled notes were all over the file that was obviously Angus's.

Scribbled notes that revealed that as one drug trial patient after another died, Angus McLean had fully expected to die himself within a few months.

He'd had no idea what was wrong with the medication, but all the other patients—twenty of them—had died within a short space of time.

Callan leaned back against the desk. He'd been sitting on the floor, the files scattered all around him. People had been paid a fee all those years ago to take part in drug trials. Things weren't so carefully monitored.

And although the medical files were full of things he didn't understand, there were a few things that he did understand.

According to the post-mortem results most of the patients had died of some kind of accelerated blood disorder. Angus McLean had thought he was living on borrowed time. He'd fully expected to die along with the rest of the group.

Except he hadn't. He'd outlived them all by almost seventy years.

Was this the reason? The reason why he hadn't had contact with his children, but had instead made some kind of financial recompense?

From the dates he could see, at least three of his children had been born during wartime. Communications were limited. It wasn't like today where a ping of an email signified the arrival of a message from half-way round the globe. He'd moved around a lot during, and directly after, the war. It was entirely possible that Angus hadn't found out about some of his children until after the war—right around the time he'd just taken part in the disastrous drug trial.

Callan's head was spinning. He couldn't really draw any conclusions from this. He was guessing.

But Angus had been a gentle-natured man. Callan didn't really want to believe he'd deliberately left his children without a father. But how would Angus have coped, forming a relationship with these children, whilst he was living in fear he would die at any moment? Leave them to suffer the bereavement of losing their dad? Maybe, if Angus had died quickly, it would have been better not to meet them. And although he didn't agree with it, he could maybe understand it a little better.

* * *

But Angus would never have left his children unsupported. That did seem like something he would do. Provide for them. And if this was the only explanation Callan could find, then he'd take it.

Maybe he'd thought leaving them Annick Castle would make up for the fact they hadn't had a father figure in their lives. How had he felt as one year after another had passed? Had he realised he'd managed to run the gauntlet that the others in the drug trial had failed?

Callan leaned forward. There was a collection of black-and-white photos at the bottom of the box. Some of women. Some of children. One, a picture of Angus with his arm around a woman.

This was it. This was the only sign that Angus McLean actually had family. No letters. No gushy cards. No sentimental keepsakes.

Callan felt a rush of unease at the similarities between himself and Angus.

If someone searched his personal belongings what would they find? No pictures or memorabilia about his father. No trace of the man at all. One slightly crumpled picture of his mother, along with an album of family snaps of him as a baby or a young boy accompanied by an unknown arm holding him, or a set of unidentified legs.

He opened the lid of the other box, fully expecting to find similar contents. But this was different. This held a leather-bound photo album.

He opened the first page. It was some old pictures of Angus as a young boy with his mother and father. Family snaps had obviously been few and far between then.

He flipped the pages. Angus as he was growing up.

In school uniform. In hunting gear. In his army uniform. In a dinner suit.

And then there was Callan. As a small child sitting at the kitchen table that still existed, laughing heartily with Angus laughing next to him. Callan had no recollection of the picture ever being taken, but that tiny snapshot in time struck him like a bullet through his heart.

He flicked again. Him and Angus on every page. Fishing. Horse-riding. Sitting in the grounds. Digging the gardens with Bert. Standing on the cannons in the castle grounds. Sailing across the swan pond in the most rickety paddle boat that ever existed. It had subsequently sunk to the bottom of the pond never to be seen again.

Callan standing at the castle doors holding some kind of certificate in his hands. He had a vague recollection of it being his exam results that gained him his place at university. All little moments in time.

He'd been feeling annoyed. He'd been feeling spurned by the fact Angus wouldn't sell him Annick Castle. Deep down he'd been hurt that Angus hadn't considered him in his will.

But here it was. Captured for posterity. Exactly what Angus had left him.

A life.

A safe haven.

Love.

The things he'd needed to shape him and become his own man.

A tear dripped down his face.

Now he understood.

He'd always known how much he'd owed Angus. But here was something to cherish and keep. To help him remember that memories were more precious than material things. None of Angus's children had shared any of these moments with him.

The gift that Angus had left him was the most precious of all.

CHAPTER ELEVEN

THE GONG SOUNDED dead on eleven. Laurie had never heard the gong used before. She'd noticed it standing in the entrance hall and wondered what it had ever been used for. It was almost like the start of one of those movies, except Robin wasn't dressed in a loincloth.

Everyone was gathering in the drawing room. It seemed to be the room where Angus's relatives had spent most of their time.

The rain was battering the windows with a ferocity she'd never seen. It seemed fitting on a day like this. It was almost as if the weather could read how she was feeling.

She filed in and took a seat. Frank, the family lawyer, was standing in the corner of the room. He looked as if he wanted to be sick. Robin stood next to him along with the guy John who had been playing the butler, and the girl who'd been murdered on Friday night.

There was the sound of hurried footsteps outside. Callan appeared with Marion and Bert by his side. It was only fitting. They should all hear who would own Annick Castle together.

Her eyes fixed on the floor. After Callan had abandoned her in the bedroom she didn't even want to look him in the eye. She certainly didn't want to have a conversation with him in front of anyone else. Whatever she had to say to Callan she could say in private before she left.

But Callan seemed to have entirely different thoughts.

He crossed the room in a matter of seconds, sitting on the chaise longue next to her. 'Laurie, I'm sorry. I had to go and look through Angus's papers this morning. You won't believe what I've found.'

What? Her head whipped up. She couldn't help but frown. 'But you left this morning.' She shook her head. 'I woke up and you were gone.' She couldn't hide the confusion in her voice. And she didn't care what he'd found.

He smiled, obviously unaware of the turmoil she'd felt. 'You looked so peaceful. I didn't want to wake you. I meant to come back and bring you breakfast in bed, but once I started going through Angus's boxes I just lost all track of time.'

There was no time to reply. No time to try and think clearly. Frank cleared his throat loudly. 'Thank you for gathering here this morning. In accordance with Angus McLean's will, today we will reveal who has inherited Annick Castle. Once the announcement is made, we will make suitable arrangements for a DNA test to be carried out to confirm the family connection. Once this has been confirmed, the process of passing on Annick Castle will take a few weeks.'

Frank looked around the room. He was clutching cards in his hands—the cards where everyone had written who they thought had carried out the murder.

He was obviously feeling the strain. The colour in his face was rising, probably in line with his blood pressure. He gave a nervous smile. 'It turns out that only one person correctly identified the murderer. There was provision in the will if more than one person had guessed correctly, but that won't be necessary now.'

Heads were glancing around the room. Everyone wondering who had been right. 'So, who was the murderer?' Craig snapped, the tension obviously getting too much for him.

Frank nodded. 'The murderer was John. The butler did it,' he said simply.

There were gasps around the room, along with several expletives.

'That's not fair!'

'I hardly spoke to him.'

'He was only ever in the background.'

'I never even had a conversation with him!'

Robin was instantly on the defensive. 'We conducted everything with absolute precision. The clues were all there if you looked for them.'

Laurie was frozen. Her throat dried in an instant. She couldn't hear anything. She couldn't hear because the thudding in her ears was getting louder and louder. Sweat. She'd never experienced sweat like it. Appearing instantly all over her body, running down the length of her back and collecting between the cups of her bra. She was freezing. She felt as if someone had just plucked up her body and dropped her in the raging sea outside.

People were still ranting. Callan was just frozen in the chair beside her, holding his breath while he waited for the announcement.

The announcement that would mean any chance they had of having any kind of relationship would disappear in an instant.

Frank's grey eyes locked on hers. 'Congratulations, Laurie. Pending a DNA test, Annick Castle is yours.'

The room erupted.

'It's a fix!'

'She's obviously in league with Frank—you lawyers stick together.'

'She's hardly even been here!'

'She's in cahoots with that man—Callan. The rest of us never really stood a chance!'

She felt numb. There was good reason she didn't like some of her relatives. Her vibes about most of them hadn't been wrong. Any tiny flicker of doubts she'd had about the personality traits of some her relatives were now being revealed in 3D multicolour. She felt as if she couldn't breathe. The air was coming in, but she couldn't get it back out.

From the corner of her eye she saw her auntie Mary give her a little smile and blow her a kiss. She was sitting on the other side of the room and her elderly bones couldn't possibly navigate the melee between them.

It was the first sign of hope. The first glimmer of a good-luck wish.

She was scared to look sideways. She was scared to look at Callan. Part of her wished he'd jumped up to defend her once the rabble had started. But he hadn't—he'd been silent.

Frank was trying to push his way through the crowd. At this point it looked as if he might be trampled by the objectors.

She stood up and turned to face Callan.

He hadn't moved. He looked shell-shocked. The smile on his face earlier had vanished. His green eyes lifted and met hers.

She could read everything on his face and in his eyes. He'd been taking steps forward. He'd been trying to move past the fact that Annick Castle would be inherited by someone else. And he'd been getting there. In tiny baby steps.

But this was entirely different. This changed everything. The pain and confusion was etched in his eyes. Both of them knew this wasn't her fault. This was something that neither of them had control over. Or did they?

Could she have done something to prevent this happening? Could she have done something to allow them to cling onto the hope of developing a relationship together?

She was so confused right now.

Panic started to grip her. She'd written that name on the card without a second thought. Her reactions had been automatic. She should have guessed wrongly. But it hadn't even occurred to her at the time.

Pain started to spread across her chest. She was starting to feel woozy. The room was closing in around her. She couldn't bear the look on Callan's face. The look that said everything had just changed. His pain was too much for her to bear. And the ramifications made her feel as if everything was out of her control.

Her feet started to move. She started to push her way through the bodies. She had to get outside. She had to get some air.

Marion reached out to her on the way past but she didn't even slow her steps. She couldn't.

She pulled the main door open. The wind and rain howled around her but she didn't even care. She just walked. And kept on walking.

Her shirt was soaked in seconds, her hair whipping around her face. But all she could think about was the air. It was what she needed.

Her legs carried her around to the front of the castle—

the most exposed edge facing the sea. She leaned
against the wall and tried to take some deep breaths.

The wind was working against her—almost suck-
ing the air from her lungs as she tried to pull it in. She
bent over, arms around her waist and counted to ten.
One, two, three…

She lifted her head again. This time she felt the cold
coursing through her. This time she looked at the castle
she could inherit.

Tears started to pour down her cheeks. This was
hers. This *could* be hers.

It was almost unbelievable. To go from a girl with
only one known living relative, to a girl with a huge
array of aunts, uncles and cousins, and the inheritor of
a castle all in the space of a few weeks.

The castle loomed in front of her. Dominant. Intimi-
dating. A whole world of problems.

But she didn't feel like that about it. She looked at
the sandy-coloured storm-battered building with its in-
tricate-paned glass windows and drum towers.

She loved it.

She loved it with her whole heart.

But she loved something or someone else a whole
lot more.

Genetically she might have a right to Annick Castle. But there were some things so much more important than genes.

'Laurie!' The shout came from her side.

Callan was running towards her, followed by Frank
bundled up in a rainproof mac. Frank's umbrella caught
in the high winds, turning instantly inside out and making him spin around blindly.

Callan reached her, soaked and windswept by the
battering rain. He put his hands on either side of her

shoulders. 'Laurie, are you okay? What happened? You ran out before we had a chance to talk.'

She shook her head. Would he notice her tears in amongst the torrent of rain?

Callan was shaking his head in wonder. An amazed smile appeared on his face. 'How did you know? How did you know it was the butler? We've hardly been there this weekend.' He was shouting now. She could hardly hear him above the roar of the waves below.

She lifted her hands. 'Who else could it be? There were twelve of us. It couldn't be any of us, Callan. That would have been unfair. It had to be you, Robin or John. And when the murder took place, you had your arm around me the whole time.'

The recognition dawned on his face. He'd obviously never given the whole weekend much thought. He'd been too wrapped up in the outcome. Too wrapped up in the fate of Annick Castle.

He grabbed her hand. Frank had reached him now and was starting to babble. She couldn't hear a single word he was saying in the braying winds. 'Come on,' shouted Callan. 'Let's get inside.'

He pulled her towards a back door. It must have been a servants' entrance and it took them along a back corridor until they reached somewhere she was much more familiar with. Much more comfortable with—the library.

Callan waited until Frank had joined them and locked the door behind them. Rain was dripping from every part of her. Callan lifted a throw from the back of one of the chairs and stood in front of her, gently rubbing her sodden hair and face.

Callan was so wrapped up in what he wanted to tell her he couldn't contain himself. 'I found medical files,

Laurie. Files that were part of a drug trial seventy years ago. Angus was a participant. Everyone else died within six months. He must have thought he was going to die too, Laurie. That's why he didn't meet his kids—just provided for them financially.'

She hadn't spoken. She hadn't responded. And his voice tailed off to be replaced with a concerned expression on his face. There was a second of recognition. Recognition that she was long past the point of caring about Angus McLean.

'Laurie? Isn't this what you wanted? You're the only relative here who has shown any real interest in Annick Castle.' He hesitated. 'I'll need to go over the castle accounts with you, but some of the things you suggested might be part of the way forward for Annick Castle.'

Frank stepped forward. 'I have to warn you I think there might be some legal challenges from some of the unhappy parties. There's nothing we can do to prevent that. But no matter what their challenges, Angus's will is rock solid. He made sure of that. It might just tie us up in court proceedings for some time.' He rustled some papers. 'Now, can we make some arrangements for your DNA test? It's just a simple cheek swab, and I'd expect the results back relatively quickly.'

'Stop.' She lifted her hand. 'Stop it. Both of you.'

Callan froze. He'd been mid-rub of her hair, which was still stubbornly dripping on the floor below. She shivered. The impact of the rain and wind was starting to affect her body's reactions. Frank's mouth was still open—poised mid-sentence.

'I can't do this.'

'What?' Both voices, in perfect unison.

Callan's brow instantly wrinkled. 'What do you

mean you can't do this? You are the perfect person to do this, Laurie.'

'No. No, I'm not.' She shook her head fiercely. 'If I'd thought about this more carefully I would have put the wrong name on the card.' Frank looked horrified, but she continued before he could say anything else. 'I'm not the right person to look after Annick Castle. It doesn't matter that I'm a relative of Angus McLean. It doesn't matter at all.'

She walked over and picked up one of the photographs of Angus in his army uniform. 'I didn't know this man. I didn't know this man at all.' She pointed to herself. 'And he didn't know me. I didn't matter to him. My father didn't matter to him. I don't care what his reasons were.'

Her brain felt as if it were scrambled. She didn't feel rational. She didn't feel in control.

'Laurie, hold on. Let me show you what I found—'

'No. Don't, Callan. I don't want to hear it. The fact is, I'm a lawyer. And I'm not even going to be that for much longer. But it doesn't matter. What do I know about a place like this? I wouldn't even know where to begin. It's already starting to fall apart.' She held out her hands. 'This is a piece of history. This is something that should be protected and preserved. This is something that other people should enjoy.'

'But you can do that, Laurie. You've already considered what could happen with Annick Castle. Let me tell you what I found.'

She felt herself start to sway. Her legs were turning to jelly underneath her and she slumped down into one of the nearby chairs.

She took a few seconds, then lifted her head. 'Frank,

if you need to do a DNA test on me, then that's fine. Do it. But I need you to do something else for me.'

'What?' Frank looked bewildered, as if the whole event were taking place in a parallel universe.

She loved Callan. She absolutely loved him. If she kept Annick Castle they would never have a chance. This would always be Callan's home. And she would always be the person that had taken that away from him. And she loved him too much for that.

She'd seen the flash in his eyes back in the drawing room. She didn't need him to spell it all out to her.

She wanted to believe that he really hadn't meant to leave her this morning. But deep down she couldn't entirely be *sure*.

And she needed to be sure. She needed to know that Callan McGregor was with her because he wanted to be, not because she was a route to something else that he loved.

She needed him to love her, just as much as she loved him. The only way to find out if that was true was to take Annick Castle out of the equation.

To put right something that was wrong.

She looked over at Callan's face. She loved him. She loved him with her whole heart. There was only one action she could take right now and it was something she was proud to say that her dad had taught her. *Do the right thing.*

'I want to give Annick Castle to Callan. I want the castle to be looked after by the person who deserves it most.'

CHAPTER TWELVE

'WHAT?'

Callan couldn't believe his ears. This day was getting madder by the second.

'You can't do that.'

'Yes, I think you'll find I can. Can't I, Frank?'

Frank nodded numbly.

Callan knelt down in front of Laurie. She looked exhausted and she was still soaking wet. They were all soaking wet. 'Laurie, you've had a shock. You're not thinking clearly.'

Her words were crisp. 'I'm thinking perfectly clearly, Callan. If Annick Castle is mine, then I can do what I want with it.'

He shook his head. 'But Angus wanted it to go to family. *You're* his family, Laurie, not me.'

She leaned forward, her face inches away from his. 'And I can see exactly how much that hurts you, Callan. What is a family anyway? Is it the person that created you genetically? Or is it the person that's loved you, protected you and sheltered you from the world? Isn't family the people who've taken care of you, helped you do your homework, played with you and looked out for you when you were a kid? Shaped you into the adult you've become? What does the word family mean to you, Callan?' She reached out her finger and touched his chest. 'What does it mean to you in here?'

He couldn't speak. He felt totally blindsided by her. It was as if she could see inside his head. See every bad thought that had entered his brain. Every time he'd bitten his tongue this weekend to stop him saying something he shouldn't.

He knew exactly what she meant. He'd heard her talk about her father. She'd loved him unconditionally— much like the way he'd loved Angus. Whenever she was thinking deeply about something she fingered the gold locket around her neck, the one her father had given her. The love she felt for her father had lasted long after her father's death. And he felt the same; he'd never forget Angus.

'Angus was my family,' he whispered. His throat felt dry and scratchy. Saying the words still hurt. Facing up to the fact that Angus hadn't thought of him as family still hurt. But now he'd discovered so much more.

He reached over and took her hand. 'Let me show you something—something I just found.'

He didn't wait for her response; he just pulled her along behind him. Down the corridor and up the carved staircase towards the room that held Angus's things.

Laurie hadn't stopped crying yet. Slow tears were still trickling down her cheeks. She reached over and put her hand on his cheek. 'What is it, Callan? Because I can't deal with this right now. I can't deal with you.' She pressed her hand to her chest.

He dropped down onto the carpet and pulled the photo album from the top of the box. 'I don't want you to give me the castle, Laurie. It's not right. It's not the way it's supposed to be.'

She lifted her head up. He could see the determined

look across her face. The kind of look that dared anyone to argue with her. 'I don't agree with what Angus
has done. And I don't need to. But I can put right what
I think is wrong.'

Callan shook his head. Every other relative had
looked as if they wanted to sell the castle. Laurie was
the only person who hadn't considered that. Did she
have any idea what the castle was really worth?

'Laurie, I have to tell you. I'd planned to speak to
whoever inherited the castle to see if they would accept my offer. I'd always planned to try and buy Annick
Castle. I certainly don't want you to give it to me.' He
placed the album in her hands. 'But this is what Angus
McLean left me. Something so much more important
than a castle.'

He was starting to panic. This didn't feel right. Callan McGregor was always entirely above board. He
didn't want Laurie to give him the castle. No way.

How would that look?

Particularly now—when he wanted her to stay.

This confused everything. He'd wanted to ask her to
stay this morning. Before any of this happened. And he
should have asked her. He should have asked her then.

He wanted her to understand everything. He wanted
her to look through the album and realise he believed
she was right. The gift that Angus had given him was
security. A place where a little boy could thrive and be
loved by a family. The people who stayed here were
his family. Blood didn't matter. Genetics didn't matter.

But Laurie's face was blank. Was she listening to
him at all? She still hadn't opened the album. The album
that told the story of his life. He had to try something
else.

'I'll buy it from you. We'll get an independent survey, an independent evaluation.' He was starting to babble, but he just couldn't help it. He felt as if everything was slipping through his fingers. Which was strange, because up until a few days ago his priority had been Annick Castle. A few days ago, this would have been exactly what he wanted.

And part of him still wanted it. Just not without her.

He shook his head. 'I've looked at the accounts. Things aren't good. Annick Castle is in trouble. The nest egg that Angus used to have just isn't there any more. You've seen for yourself that there are areas that need attention. And with a place like this there are no simple fixes. Even things that seem simple need a master craftsman. Traditional materials, specialist trades, everything has to meet the standards for listed building consent. Things need to change around here.'

Laurie stood up. 'What are you talking about, Callan? I've told you. I want to give you Annick Castle. I don't want your money. I don't want you to buy it from me. It doesn't even feel as if it should really be mine.' She flung her hands in the air, letting the album fall to the floor. 'It's ridiculous. I inherit this place on the basis of the name I wrote on a card?' She turned to face Frank too. 'Tell me this isn't fundamentally wrong—because we all know it is. This place, never mind its monetary value, what about its heritage value, its history? These are the things that are important. These are the things that make Annick Castle special.' She turned back to Callan. 'Angus was wrong. Annick Castle should always have been yours. You're the one with the connection with this place. You're the one who loves it. It should be yours.' There was real passion in her voice. As if she knew, as if she understood.

And he could recognise it. Because he understood completely.

He placed his hand on her arm. 'But that's just it, Laurie. I'm not the only one with a connection to this place, am I?'

He watched her eyes widen. She started to stutter, 'B-but...'

'Tell me.' He stepped forward and placed his hand on her chest. 'Tell me how Annick Castle makes you feel in here, Laurie.'

She didn't answer. She couldn't answer.

'I could see it, Laurie. I could see it in your eyes, in everything you did this weekend. From the moment you saw this place, from the moment you set foot in this place, Annick Castle started to get under your skin. You asked questions, you took an interest in everything that happens around here. You looked at this place with a fresh set of eyes.' His voice lowered. 'You introduced me to ideas that I would never have considered myself.' He shook his head as he grew more determined—as he started to see in his head exactly what he wanted to happen.

It was like standing at the railway station again, watching the smoke clear around Laurie's curves. He just knew.

'I can't do this without you, Laurie. I don't want to do this without you. This morning, when I woke up I watched you sleeping. I wanted to ask you then. I should have asked you then.'

'Asked me what?'

'To stay. To stay with me.' The words that had been skirting around the edges of his brain for the last few hours. It was so much easier to say them out loud than he could possibly have imagined.

He sat her down on the chaise longue next to the window and put the album in her lap, flicking past the first few pages of Angus's photographs and onto the pages that showed him as a young boy.

He could see her sharp intake of breath. 'Laurie, I don't care what you do with Annick Castle. If I ever want to move on, I have to let it go. I have to get past this. But I can't get past you.'

Her eyes widened as he turned the pages, letting her see every year of his life recorded by Angus. Letting her see the love between them, letting her see the warmth and security that he'd been provided with. Letting her see his family.

'What is this?' she murmured.

'This is me. This is the legacy that Angus left me.' He put his hand over hers and squeezed tightly. 'It means so much more than bricks and mortar. Angus, and the people here, helped me grow into the man I am today.' He traced a finger down her cheek. 'One that knows if you love someone, you should always put them first.'

Her voice trembled. 'What do you mean you can't get past me, Callan? What are you saying?'

'I'm saying whatever your decision—about Annick Castle, or about your job—I want to be in your life. I want to be part of your life.' He put both of his hands on her cheeks. 'I want to be your family.'

Tears glistened in her eyes.

'You have to know that I've never connected with anyone the way I've connected with you. I don't want to let you go. I don't want this weekend to end.' He held up his arms. 'I wanted to ask you to stay with me this morning, Laurie, but I didn't know where I'd be. I didn't know what I'd have to offer you.'

Her voice cracked. 'Why would you need to offer me anything, Callan? I don't expect anything from you.'

'But that's just it, Laurie. I want you to. I want to be part of your life. I want to be here for you. Wherever you want to be, just tell me. I can find a way to make this work.'

He could see her breath catching in her throat.

Her head was spinning. He was asking her to stay. He was telling her he wanted to be with her. But he hadn't said the words. The three little words she needed to hear.

She took his hands from her cheeks and intertwined her fingers with his. It had finally stopped raining and the sun was peeking out from behind some clouds. Beneath them the gardens lay out in all their coloured glory. Who wouldn't want to look out at that every single day?

She took a deep breath. 'I've been so confused, Callan. You're right. From the moment I set foot in Annick Castle I feel as if it's got a hold on me. I love this place. I love every single part of it.'

She hesitated. Should she say the next part?

'You've made some of my dreams come true, Callan. I never expected it. I never imagined it.'

His hand clasped over hers. 'Every girl should have their own *Sound of Music* gazebo. Every girl should have their own princess staircase.'

'But I don't want every girl to have you.' Did she just say that out loud? In another life she might have cringed, but not here, and not now. This was the moment she found out if her life was going to change for ever.

His voice was low and sincere. 'Every girl can't have me. There's only one girl I want. There's only one girl I want in my life, now and always.' His hand reached up and stroked her cheek. 'Know that I will go anywhere with you, any time.' He shrugged his shoulders. 'I can Blether all over the world, but there's no one else I want to blether with. It's you or nobody. I love you, Laurie Jenkins. Please say you'll stay with me. Please say we have a future together.'

She reached up and caught his finger in her hand. 'I love you too. I can't imagine spending a single day without you.'

She was going to cry again. The tears were building in her eyes.

'Can I interest you in an Edinburgh town house, Laurie Jenkins?'

'Can I interest you in a slightly dishevelled castle, Callan McGregor?'

He smiled, his eyes crinkling as pulled her towards him in a kiss. 'Let's begin negotiations. I think I'm going to need a good lawyer.'

She laughed. 'I know just the person.'

EPILOGUE

As soon as he walked through the doors all he could smell was the wonderful array of baking. Gingerbread, chocolate cake, freshly baked scones and the bubbling smell of lentil soup. His stomach growled in instant response but there was a bus tour due in an hour. He had to keep his mind on the job. 'Laurie, where are you?'

The former icehouse was exactly as she'd planned. Windows all the way around showing views of the gardens and views of the sea. Red and white checked tablecloths, comfortable chairs at the tables, a separate play area for kids and a *very* expensive coffee machine that Callan had already burned himself on. Still, it was red and matched perfectly. *And* it had put a huge smile on Laurie's face.

She appeared from behind the counter, looking a little flushed, wiping her hands on a towel. 'It can't be that time already?'

He raised his eyebrows. 'It is.'

'But I haven't got changed, or fixed my hair, and my make-up must be halfway down my face.'

He shook his head and put his hands on her waist. 'You look perfect.'

'But I've still to—'

He bent down and kissed her to stop her talking. It

was amazing how often he had to do that. But it worked like a charm every time. She wound her hands around his neck. 'You're distracting me,' she murmured.

'It's my job.'

He pulled back and smiled. 'I have two special customers that we can't keep waiting.'

Fourteen months of blood, sweat, tears and lots and lots of special memories. Annick Castle was theirs. Together. And it was now open to the public. The repairs had been put in order. They'd been exhausting and daunting. There had been hours of planning and negotiations with local authorities. They'd even had to redo the steps down the cliff side and install a proper handrail.

But the important thing was that they'd done them together.

And the truth was he'd never seen her look happier. She gave a nervous laugh. 'Customers. Now I'm really scared.'

'Oh, don't worry. I think they'll like this place,' he said with confidence as she flicked the sign on the door from Closed to Open.

Marion and Bert didn't waste any time. Bert went straight to the strawberry and cream sponge sitting under a glass dome. 'I'll have a bit of that and a mug of tea.' He wagged his finger at Laurie. 'Don't be giving me any of those fancy china cups.'

Marion was the extreme opposite. 'I'll have a toasted scone with butter and jam, and a pot of tea.' She nodded at Laurie. 'And I do want a china cup.'

Laurie scurried off, obviously overjoyed by her first customers. Callan sat down at one of the round tables, staring out at the crashing ocean. It was August. The doors to Annick Castle opened today. His stomach was churning a little at the thought of it.

Part of it was genuine nerves about what people might think of the place he loved. Part of it was fear that things wouldn't work out. Laurie would be devastated. He was beginning to suspect she loved this place even more than he did. Could that even be possible?

He heard the clink of china being set on a table, appreciative voices, then he felt a hand on his back and Laurie slid into the chair next to him, putting a large piece of his favourite chocolate cake on the table in front of him.

'How does it feel?'

She smiled and glanced out of the window, looking the other way towards the gardens. 'It feels right,' she said quietly as she reached over and squeezed his hands.

'No regrets about leaving London?'

She shook her head fiercely. 'Not a single one. I haven't had a tension headache since I moved here.'

'Even with all the hassles with the castle?'

'They weren't hassles. They were teething problems.' She leaned over and kissed him. 'Besides I had someone I could moan to every night in bed with me.'

He gave her a wink as he put a piece of chocolate cake in his mouth. 'I hope that wasn't the only reason you were moaning.' He didn't wait for her reaction before he let out a yelp. 'Ouch! What's that?'

Laurie jumped up. 'What's wrong? Is there something wrong with the cake?'

'There's something very wrong. I just got a lump of something in it.' He couldn't stop the gleam in his eyes as he pretended to fish something out of his mouth.

She still hadn't clicked. 'What is it?' she demanded as she made a grab for his palm. 'Oh!'

The emerald and diamond ring lay in the palm of his hand. He'd wanted to propose to her from the moment she'd moved here. But there was never a more perfect time than now—the first day of their new life together.

'Is that all you can say—oh?'

She smiled. 'Oh, no, you don't, Callan McGregor. I want the whole shebang.'

He slid down onto the floor, kneeling in front of her. 'I should have taken you to the gazebo, shouldn't I?'

She leaned forward and whispered in his ear. 'Don't worry, our last trip to the gazebo seems to have left us with more than memories.'

'Really?' He jumped straight back up and pulled her into his arms, swinging her around. 'Really?' He couldn't believe it. Nothing could be more perfect.

'Really.' She smiled as he lowered her to the floor.

For the first time in years Callan felt flustered. He grabbed the ring and knelt down again in front of her. 'Then I better make this quick, before people start getting out calendars and looking at the date.' He took both her hands in his. 'Laurie Jenkins, I love you more than life itself. Will you do me the honour of walking down our gorgeous staircase in a wedding dress and becoming my wife?' He slid the ring onto her finger.

'I think you're supposed to wait for my answer.' She smiled.

He leaned forward and kissed her, laying his hand gently on her stomach. 'It seems to me that you've already realised I've got no patience. How about we get ready for a castle full of them?'

'I can't wait,' she replied as she kissed him again and again.

* * * * *

Her heart kind of melted about then.

How could she help but melt? He not only made her want to rip off her clothes and climb him like a tree, but he was a very good man. He was constantly finding new ways to show her that he really did care about her and the things that mattered to her. It wasn't his fault that she had trouble trusting her own emotions.

Her throat burned with all the difficult stuff she didn't know how to tell him. "Max, I…" She had no idea where to go from there.

And then it didn't matter what she might have said. He wiped her mind free of all thought by the simple act of lifting her chin lightly with his free hand and lowering his lips to hers.

* * *

The Bravo Royales:
When it comes to love, Bravos rule!

THE PRINCE'S
CINDERELLA BRIDE

BY
CHRISTINE RIMMER

Published in Great Britain 2014
by Mills & Boon, an imprint of Harlequin (UK) Limited,
Eton House, 18-24 Paradise Road, Richmond, Surrey, TW9 1SR

© 2014 Christine Rimmer

ISBN: 978 0 263 91284 5

23-0514

Harlequin (UK) Limited's policy is to use papers that are natural, renewable and recyclable products and made from wood grown in sustainable forests. The logging and manufacturing processes conform to the legal environmental regulations of the country of origin.

Printed and bound in Spain
by Blackprint CPI, Barcelona

Christine Rimmer came to her profession the long way around. Before settling down to write about the magic of romance, she'd been everything from an actress to a salesclerk to a waitress. Now that she's finally found work that suits her perfectly, she insists she never had a problem keeping a job—she was merely gaining "life experience" for her future as a novelist. Christine is grateful not only for the joy she finds in writing, but for what waits when the day's work is through: a man she loves who loves her right back, and the privilege of watching their children grow and change day to day. She lives with her family in Oregon. Visit Christine at www. christinerimmer.com.

For MSR, always

Chapter One

Maximilian Bravo-Calabretti, heir to the Montedoran throne, stepped out from behind a low cluster of fan palms and directly into the path of the woman who'd hardly spoken to him since New Year's.

Lani Vasquez let out a small squeak of surprise and jumped back. She almost dropped the book she was carrying. "Your Highness." She shot him a glare. "You scared me."

The high garden path that wove along the cliffside was deserted. It was just the two of them at the moment. But anyone might come wandering toward them—one of the gardeners looking for a hedge to trim, or a palace guest out for a brisk early-morning stroll. Max wanted privacy for this. He grabbed her hand, which caused her to let out another sharp cry.

"Come with me," he commanded and pulled her forward on the path. "This way."

She dug in her heels. "No, Max. Really."

He turned to face her. She flashed him a look of defiance. Still, he refused to let go of her soft little hand. Her sweet face was flushed, her thick midnight hair loose on her shoulders, tangled by the wind off the sea far below.

He wanted to haul her close and kiss her. But he needed to get her to talk to him first. "You've been avoiding me."

Her mouth quivered in the most tempting way. "Yes, I have. Let go of my hand."

"We have to talk."

"No, we don't."

"We do."

"It was a mistake," she insisted in a ragged little whisper.

"Don't say that."

"But it's the truth. It was a mistake and there's no point in going into it. I don't want to talk about it."

And he didn't want to hear that. "Just come with me, that's all I'm asking."

"I'm expected at the villa." She worked as a nanny for his brother Rule and his wife. They owned a villa in the nearby ward of Fontebleu. "I have to go now."

"This won't take long." He turned and started forward again.

She let out a low, unhappy sound, and for a moment, he was certain she would simply refuse to budge.

But then she gave in and followed. He kept hold of her hand and pulled her along. Not glancing back, he cut off the overlook path and onto the rocky hillside, finding a second path that twisted up and around, through a copse of olive trees and on to where the land flattened out to a more cultivated formal garden.

High, green hedges surrounded them, and they walked on thick grass. The grass gave way to a rose garden. Now, in February, the buds were only just forming on the thorny stems. Beyond the budding roses, he took a curving stone path beneath a series of trellises. Still she followed, saying nothing, occasionally dragging her feet a little to let him know she was far from willing.

They came to a gate in a stone wall. He pushed through

the gate and held it for her, with his free hand, going through after her and then closing it behind them.

Across another swath of lawn, between a pair of silk floss trees, the stone cottage waited. He led her on, across the grass, along the stepping-stones that stopped at the rough wood trellis twined with bare, twisted grapevines. The trellis shaded the rough wood door.

He pushed the door open, let go of her hand and ushered her in first. With a quick, suspicious glance at him, she went.

Two windows let in enough light to see by. Sheets covered the plain furniture. It took him only a moment to whip off the coverings and drop them to the rough wooden floor, revealing a scarred table with four chairs, a sofa, a couple of side tables and two floral-patterned wing chairs. The rudimentary kitchen took up one wall. Stairs climbed another wall to the sleeping area above.

"Have a seat," he offered.

She pressed her lips together, shook her head and remained standing by the door, clutching her book tightly between her two hands. "What is this place?"

"It's just a gardener's cottage. No one's using it now. Sit down."

She still refused to budge. "What *are* you doing, Your High—?"

"Certainly we're past that."

For a moment, she said nothing, only stared at him, her dark eyes huge in the soft oval of her face. He wanted to reach out and gather her close and soothe all her troubles away. But everything about her warned, *Don't touch me.*

She let out a breath and her slim shoulders drooped. "Max. Really. Can't you just admit it? We both know it was a mistake."

"Wrong." He moved a step closer. She stiffened a little,

but she didn't back away. He whispered, "It was beautiful. Perfect. At the time, you thought so, too—or so you said."

"Oh, Max. Why can't I get through to you?" She turned from him and went to one of the windows.

He stared at her back, at her hair curling, black as a crow's wing, on her shoulders. And he remembered…

It was New Year's Eve. At the Sovereign's New Year's Ball.

He asked her to dance and as soon as he had her in his arms, he only wanted to keep her there. So he did. When the first dance ended, he held her lightly until the music started up again. He kept her with him through five dances. Each dance went by in the blink of an eye. He would have gone on dancing with her, every dance, until the band stopped playing. But people noticed and she didn't like it.

By the fifth dance she was gazing up at him much too solemnly. And when that dance ended, she said, "I think it's time for me to say good-night."

He'd watched her leave the ballroom and couldn't bear to see her go. So he followed her. They'd shared their first kiss in the shadows of the long gallery outside the ballroom, beneath the frescoes depicting martyred saints and muscular angels. She'd pulled away sharply, dark fire in her eyes.

So he kissed her again.

And a third time, as well. By some heady miracle, with those kisses, he'd secured her surrender. Lani led him up to her small room in the deserted apartment of his brother Rule's family. When he left her hours later, she was smiling and tender and she'd kissed him good-night.

But ever since then, for five endless weeks, she'd barely spoken to him.

"Lani. Look at me…."

She whirled and faced him again. Her mouth had softened and so had her eyes. Had she been remembering that night, too? For a moment, he almost dared to hope she would melt into his arms.

But then she drew herself up again. "It was a mistake," she insisted for the fourth time. "And this is impossible. I have to go." She headed for the door.

He accused, "Coward."

The single word seemed to hit her between the shoulder blades. She let go of the doorknob, dropped her book to the rough entry table and turned once more to meet his waiting eyes. "Please. It was just one of those things that happen even though it shouldn't have. We got carried away...."

Carried away? Maybe. "I have no regrets. Not a one." He was *glad* it had happened, and on New Year's Eve, too. To him it had seemed the ideal way to ring in a whole new year—and right then, a dangerous thought occurred to him. God. Was there a baby? If so, he needed to know. "We should have been more careful, though. You're right. Is that why you keep running away from me? Are you—?"

"No," she cut in before he could even get the question out. "We were lucky. You can stop worrying."

"I miss you," he said, before she could start in again about how she had to go. "I miss our discussions, our talks in the library. Lani, we have so much in common. We've been good friends."

"Oh, please," she scoffed. But there was real pain in her eyes, in the tightness of her mouth. "You and I were never friends." All at once, her eyes were too bright. She blinked away tears.

He wanted only to comfort her. "Lani..." He took a step toward her.

But she put up a hand and he stopped in midstride. "We've been *friendly*," she corrected. "But to be more is beyond inappropriate. I work for your brother and sister-in-law. I'm the *nanny*. I'm supposed to set an example and show good judgment." She swallowed. Hard. "I never should have let it happen."

"*Will* you stop saying that it shouldn't have happened?"

"But it *shouldn't* have."

"Excuse me. We are two single adults and we have every right to—"

"Stop." She backed a step toward the door. "I want you to listen, Max. It can't happen again. I won't let it." Her eyes were dry now. And way too determined.

He opened his mouth to insist that *it* most certainly *would* happen again. But where would such insistence get him? Except to send her whirling, flinging the door wide, racing off down the walk and out the gate.

He didn't want that. And arguing with her over whether that unforgettable night should or should not have happened was getting him nowhere, anyway. They didn't need arguing. They needed to reestablish their earlier ease with each other.

So in the end he answered mildly, "Of course you're right. It won't happen again."

She blinked in surprise. "I don't… What are you saying?"

"I'll make an agreement with you."

She narrowed her eyes and peered at him sideways. "I don't want to bargain about this."

"How can you know that? You haven't heard my offer yet."

"Offer?" She sneered the word. He held his silence as she nibbled her lower lip in indecision. Finally, she threw up both hands. "Oh, all right. *What,* then? What is your offer?"

"I'll promise not to try to seduce you," he suggested with what he hoped was just the right touch of wry humor, "and you'll stop avoiding me. We can be…" He hesitated, remembering how she'd scoffed when he'd called them friends. "...what we used to be."

She aimed a put-upon look at the single beam in the rough-textured ceiling. "Oh, come on. Seriously? That never works."

"I disagree." Light. Reasonable. Yes, just the right tone. "And it's unfair to generalize. I think it can work. We can *make* it work." Until she admitted that being what they used to be wasn't nearly enough. Then they could make it work in much more satisfying ways.

She hovered there in front of the door, staring at him, unblinking. He stared right back, trying to look calm and reasonable and completely relaxed when in reality his gut was clenched tight and he'd begun to lose hope he would ever get through to her.

But then, at last, she dropped her gaze. She went to the rustic dinner table, where she ran her finger along the back of one of the plain straight chairs. He watched her, remembering the cool, thrilling wonder of her fingers on his naked skin.

Finally, she slanted him a look. "I love Montedoro. I came here with Sydney thinking I would stay for six months or a year, just for the life experience." Sydney was his brother Rule's wife and Lani's closest friend. "Two years later, I'm still here. I have this feeling, and it's such a pow-erful feeling, that Montedoro is my real home and I was only waiting to come here, to find the place I was meant to be. I want to write a hundred novels, all of them set right here. I never want to leave."

"I know. And no one wants you to leave."

"Oh, Max. What I'm trying to say is, as much as I love it here, as much as I want to stay forever, if you or any of your family wanted me gone, my visa would be revoked in a heartbeat."

"How many times do I have to tell you? No one wants you to go."

"Don't pretend you don't get it. Love affairs end. And when they end, things can get awkward. You're a good man, a kind man. But you're also the heir to the throne. I'm the help. It's...well, it's hardly a relationship of equals."

Why did she insist on seeing trouble where there was none? "You're wrong. We *are* equals in all the ways that really matter."

She made a humphing sound. "Thanks for that, Your Highness."

He wanted to grab her and shake her. But somehow he managed to remain still, to speak with calm reproach. "You know me better than that."

She shook her head. "Don't you get it? We went too far. We need to back off and let it go."

Let it go—let *her* go? Never. "Listen. I'm going to say it again. This time I'm hopeful you'll actually hear me. I would never expect you to leave Montedoro, no matter what happened. You have my sworn word on that. The last thing I would ever want is to make things difficult for you."

Heat flared in her eyes again. "But that's exactly what you've done—what you *are* doing right now."

"Forgive me." He said it evenly, holding her dark gaze.

Another silence ensued. An endless one.

And then, at last, she spoke again, her head drooping, her shining, softly curling hair swinging out to hide her flushed cheeks. "I hate this."

"So do I."

She lifted her head and stared at him, emotions chasing themselves across her sweet face: misery, exasperation, frustration, sorrow. After a moment she confessed, "All right. It's true that I miss...having you to talk to."

Progress. His heart slammed against his rib cage.

She added, "And I adore Nick and Constance." His son, Nicholas, was eight. Connie was six. Lani was good friends with Gerta, Nick and Connie's nanny. Rule's children and his often played together. "I…" She peered at him so closely, her expression disbelieving. "Do you honestly think we could do that, be…friendly again?"

"I know we could."

"Just that and only that." Doubt shadowed her eyes. "Friendly. Nothing more."

"Only that," he vowed, silently adding, *Until you realize you want more as much as I do.*

She sighed. "I… Well, I *would* like to be on good terms with you."

Light, he reminded himself as his pulse ratcheted higher. *Keep it light.* "All right, then. We are…as we were." He dared to hold out his hand to her.

She frowned. He waited, arm outstretched, arching a brow, trying to appear hopeful and harmless. Her gaze darted from his face to his offered hand, and back to his face again. Just when he was certain he would have to drop his hand, she left the table and came and took it. His fingers closed over hers. He reveled in the thrill that shivered up his arm at her touch.

Too soon, she eased her hand free and snatched up her book. "Now, will you let me go?"

No. He cast about for a way to keep her there. If she wouldn't let him kiss her or hold her or smooth her shining hair, all right. He accepted that. But couldn't they at least talk for a while the way they used to do?

"Max?" A slight frown creased her brow.

He was fresh out of new tactics and had no clue how to get her to let down her guard. Plus he had a very strong feeling that he'd pushed her as far as she would go for now. This was looking to be an extended campaign. He didn't like that, but if it was the only way to finally reach her, so be it. "I'll be seeing you in the library—where you will no longer scuttle away every time I get near you."

A hint of the old humor flashed in her eyes. "I never scuttle."

"Scamper? Dart? Dash?"

"Stop it." Her mouth twitched. A good sign, he told himself.

"Promise me you won't run off the next time we meet."

The spark of humor winked out. "I just don't like this."

"You've already said that. I'm going to show you there's nothing to be afraid of. Do we have an understanding?"

"Oh, Max…"

"Say yes."

And finally, she gave in and said the words he needed to hear. "Yes. I'll, um, look forward to seeing you."

He didn't believe her. How could he believe her when she sounded so grim, when that mouth he wanted beneath his own was twisted with resignation? He didn't believe her, and he almost wished he could give her what she said she wanted, let her go, say goodbye. He almost wished he could *not* care.

But he'd had years of not caring—long, empty years when he'd told himself that not caring was for the best.

And then the small, dark-haired woman in front of him changed everything.

She turned for the door.

He was out of ways to keep her there, and he needed to accept that. "Lani, wait…"

She stopped, shoulders tensing, head slightly bowed. "What now?" But she didn't turn back to him.

"Let me." He eased around her and pulled the door wide. She nodded, barely glancing at him, and went through, passing beneath the rough-hewn trellis into the cool winter sunlight. He lingered in the open doorway, watching her as she walked away from him.

Chapter Two

"What is going on in that head of yours?" Sydney O'Shea Bravo-Calabretti, formerly kick-ass corporate lawyer and currently Princess of Montedoro, demanded. "Something's bugging you." The women sat in kid-size chairs at the round table in the playroom of the villa Sydney and Rule had bought and remodeled shortly after their marriage two years before.

Lani, holding Sydney's one-year-old, Ellie, kissed the little one's silky strawberry curls and lied without shame. "Nothing's bugging me. Not a thing."

"Yes, there is. You've got this weird, worried, faraway look in your eye."

Okay, yeah. Yesterday's confrontation with Max in the little stone house had seriously unnerved her. She'd thought about little else since then. She'd told no one what had happened on New Year's, not even Sydney. And she never would. But she had to give Syd *something,* some reason she might be distracted—anything but the truth that, while Sydney and Rule and the kids were here at the family's villa, Lani had led His Highness up to her room at the palace and done any number of un-nannylike things to his magnificent body.

Limply, she offered, "Well, the current book is giving me

fits." That should fly. She was in the middle of writing the final book in a trilogy of historical novels set in Montedoro. Syd had been her best friend for seven years and knew that she could get pretty stressed out while struggling with the middle of a book where the story had a tendency to drag.

Syd was so not buying. "The current book is *always* giving you fits. There's something else."

Crap. Lani frowned and pretended to think it over for a minute. "No, really. It's the book. That's all. There's nothing else."

"Yolanda Vasquez, you are lying through your teeth."

So much for the sagging-middle excuse. What to try next?

No way was Lani busting herself. Syd had her back, always. But it was just too tacky to get into, the nanny-slash-wannabe-writer getting naked at New Year's with the widowed heir to the throne—whom the whole world knew was still hopelessly in love with his lost wife. *"Lying through your teeth,"* she echoed brightly. "What does that mean, really? Some expressions are not only overused, they make no real sense. I mean, everything we say, we say through our teeth, right? I mean, unless we *have* no teeth."

Syd didn't even crack a smile. "You think you're distracting me from asking what's up with you. You're not."

"Nani, Nani…" Ellie squirmed around until she was facing Lani. Then she reached up her plump right hand and tried to stick her fingers into Lani's mouth.

Lani gummed them. "Mmm. Yummy, tasty little fingers…" Ellie giggled and bounced up and down. Lani kissed her again, that time on her button of a nose, after which she started squirming again and Lani hoisted her high. Ellie laughed in delight as Lani swung her to the floor.

The little sweetheart was only thirteen months and already walking. For a moment, she wobbled, steadying herself on her fat little feet. And then she toddled to her brother's open toy box and started rooting around in it.

Syd's phone chirped. A text. She took it out and read the message. "Rule. He won't be home till after seven." She started composing a reply. Lani breathed a cautious sigh of relief that the subject of what could be bothering her was closed.

Over at the toy box, Ellie pulled out a soft green rubber turtle, which she carried across the playroom to four-year-old Trevor, who sat quietly building a slightly tilted Lego tower.

"Turt," she said, beaming proudly, and held it out to him as Syd chuckled and texted.

Trev gave Ellie his usual so-patient big-brother look, took the toy from her and set it down on his other side. Ellie frowned and toddled carefully around to reach the turtle again. She bent with great concentration and picked it up. "Tev," she said.

Trevor went on building his tower.

Sydney put her phone down. "So you're *not* going to tell me?"

Resigned to continued denials, Lani dished out yet another lame evasion. "Syd, I promise you, there's nothing to tell." Were her pants on fire? They ought to be.

And right then, before Sydney could say anything else, Ellie cheerfully bopped Trev on the head with the rubber turtle—not hard enough to hurt, but hard enough to get his full attention.

Trev scowled. "No hitting," he said, and gave her a light shove.

She let out a cry as her baby legs collapsed and she landed, plop, on her butt. The impact caused Trevor's shaky tower to collapse to the playroom floor.

Trev protested, "Lani! Mom! Ellie is being *rude!*"

Ellie promptly burst into tears.

Both women got up and went over to sort out the conflict. There were hugs and kisses for Ellie and a reminder to Trev that his sister was only one year old and he should be gentle with her.

Trev apologized. "I'm sorry, Ellie."

And Ellie sniffed. "Tev. Sor-sor." She sighed and laid her bright head on Sydney's shoulder.

Then Sydney's phone rang. She passed Ellie to Lani and took the call, after which she had to go and attend a meeting of one of her international legal aid groups. Lani was left to put the kids down for their nap.

She felt guilty and grateful simultaneously. Once again, she'd escaped having to tell Sydney that she'd had sex with Max on New Year's Eve.

At the muffled creak of one of the tall, carved library doors, Lani glanced up from her laptop.

Max.

He wore a soft white crewneck sweater and gray slacks, and his wonderfully unruly hair shone chestnut brown in the glow from the milk-glass chandeliers above. His iron-blue eyes were on her, and her heart was galloping so fast she could hardly catch her breath.

He'd said he wanted them to be as they used to be.

Impossible. Who did he think he was kidding? There was no going back to the way it had been before. And the more she thought about it—which was all the time since their conversation in the gardener's cottage—the more she was certain he knew that they couldn't go back.

And she would bet that was fine with him. Because he didn't *want* to go back. He wanted to be her lover, wanted more of the heat and wonder of New Year's Eve.

And okay, she wanted that, too. And she knew it would

be fabulous, perfect, beautiful. For as long as it lasted. Until things went wrong.

Because, as she'd tried so very hard to get him to see, love affairs ended. And there were too many ways it all could go bad, too large of a likelihood she'd be put on a plane back to Texas. Yes, all right. It might end amicably. But it also might not. And she wasn't willing to risk finding out which of the two it would be.

She stared in those beautiful eyes of his and thought that she ought to confront him for being a big, fat liar, for saying how he missed her friendship when he really only wanted to get back in bed with her.

But then, who was she to get all up in anyone's face about lying? She'd yet to tell Syd the truth. And she wanted to be Max's lover as much as he wanted to be hers.

However, she wanted the life she had planned for herself more. Risking all of her dreams on a love affair? She'd tried that once. It hadn't ended well.

He gave her a slow nod. "Lani." A shiver went through her—just from the sound of her name in his mouth.

"Hi, Max," she chirped way too brightly.

"Go on, do your work. I'm not here to distract you."

Liar. "Great." She flashed him a smile as bright and fake as her tone and turned her gaze back to her laptop.

He walked by her table on his way to the stairs that led to the upper level. She stared a hole in her laptop screen and saw him pass as a blur of movement, his footfalls hushed on the inlaid floor. He mounted the stairs, his back to her. The temptation was too great. She watched him go up.

At the top, he disappeared from sight and she heard another door open, no doubt to one of the locked rooms, the vaults where the rarest books and documents were kept. She wasn't allowed into any of those special rooms without the watchful company of the ancient scholar who acted as palace librarian or one of his two dedicated assistants.

In fact, she wouldn't be allowed into the library at all at eight o'clock at night if it wasn't for Max.

A year ago, he'd presented her with her own key to the ornate, book-lined, two-story main room. To her, it was a gift beyond price. Now, whenever she wanted to go there, anytime of day or night, she could let herself in and be surrounded by beautiful old books, by a stunning array of original materials for her research.

Library hours were limited and pretty much coincided with the hours when she needed to be with Trev and Ellie. However, most days from about 5:00 p.m. on, Rule and Sydney enjoyed time alone with each other and their children—usually at their villa. They welcomed Lani as part of the family if she wanted to stay on in the evening, but they had no problem if she took most nights off to work on her latest book.

With the key, she could spend as many evening hours as she pleased at the library. And later, at bedtime, her room in the family's palace apartment was right there waiting. Then, early in the morning, it was only a brisk walk along landscaped garden paths down Cap Royale, the rocky hill on which the palace stood, to Fontebleu and the villa.

Pure heaven: the laws, culture and history of Montedoro at her fingertips in the lovely, silent library with its enormous mahogany reading tables and carved, velvet-upholstered chairs. Yes, there were some language issues for her. Much of the original material was in French or Spanish. The French, she managed all right with the aid of her rusty college French and a couple of French/English dictionaries. She knew a little Spanish, but not as much as she probably should, given her Latino heritage. Max, however, spoke and read Spanish fluently and was always happy to translate for her, so the Spanish texts were completely accessible to her, too. Until New Year's, anyway.

It had worked out so perfectly. Lani stayed at the palace several nights a week. She took her laptop and worked for hours. No one disturbed her in the library, not in the evening.

No one but Max—though he didn't really disturb her. He came to the library at night to work, too. An internationally respected scholar and expert on all things Montedoran, he'd written a book about the special, centuries-long relationship between Montedoro and her "big sister," France. He'd also penned any number of articles on various points of Montedoran law and history. And he traveled several times a year to speak at colleges, events and consortia around the world.

Before New Year's, when he would join her in the library, they would sit in companionable silence as she wrote and he checked his sources or typed notes for an upcoming paper or speech. He'd always shown respect for her writing time, and she appreciated his thoughtfulness.

Sometimes, alone together in the quiet, they would put their work aside and talk. And not only in the library. Often when they met in the gardens or at some event or other, they might talk for hours. They had the same interests—writing and history and anything to do with Montedoro.

They'd shared a special kind of friendship.

Until New Year's. Until she finally had to admit that she'd done it again: gotten in too deep with the wrong guy when she needed to be concentrating on the goals she'd set for herself, the goals that she never quite seemed to reach, no matter how hard she worked.

Right now, she should get up and leave—and she would, if only she hadn't foolishly agreed that they could go back to the way they were before.

Right. As if that was even possible.

But still. She'd said she would try. And the hopeless romantic idiot within her wanted at the very least to remain friendly with him, to *be* his friend, which she had been before New Year's, in spite of her denials the other day.

So she stayed in her seat, laptop open in front of her.

A full ten minutes passed before he reappeared on the stairs—ten minutes during which she did nothing but stare at the cursor on her screen and listen for the sound of his footsteps above and call herself five thousand kinds of stupid. When he finally did come down, he was carrying a stack of folders and books.

She waited for him to engage her in some way, her teeth hurting she was clenching them so hard. But he only took a chair across and down from her, gave her another perfectly easy, friendly nod and bent his gorgeous head over the old books and papers.

Well, okay. Apparently, he *was* just there to work.

Which was great. Fabulous. She put her hands on her keyboard and her focus on the screen.

Nothing happened. Her mind was a sloppy soup, a hot mess of annoyance, frustration and forbidden longing. She yearned to jump up and get out of there.

But something—her pride or her promise to him yesterday, maybe—kept her sitting there, staring blankly at her own words, which right then might have been hieroglyphics for all the sense they made to her.

Eventually, she managed to type a sentence. And then another. The writing felt stiff and unnatural. But sometimes you had to write through a distraction. Even a really big distraction, like a certain six-foot-plus hunk of regal manliness sitting across and down from you.

For two full hours, she sat there. So did he, tapping away on a tablet computer, poring over the materials he'd brought down from upstairs. She sat there and she wrote.

It was all just garbage she'd end up deleting, but so what? They were being as they used to be, sitting in silence, working in the library.

Except that it was nothing like it used to be. Not to her, anyway. To her, the air felt electrically charged. Her tummy was one big knot, and the words she was writing made no sense at all.

At ten after ten, she decided she'd sat there writing meaningless drivel and pretending there was nothing wrong for long enough. She closed her laptop, gathered up her stuff and rose.

He glanced up then. "Leaving?"

She hit him with another big, fake smile. "Yeah." She hooked her purse on her shoulder and picked up her laptop. "Good night."

"Good night, Lani." He bent his head to his notes again.

And somehow, she couldn't move. She stood there like a complete fool, staring at his shining, thick hair, at his impossibly broad shoulders to which his soft white sweater clung so lovingly. She wanted to drop back into her chair and ask him about his day, to tell him the real truth—that she missed him in the deepest, most elemental part of herself. That she wished things were different, but she was not a good choice for him as a friend or a lover or anything else, and he ought to know that....

He glanced up a second time. "What is it?" he asked. Gently. Coaxingly.

"Nothing," she lied yet again.

He began closing books and stacking papers. "I need to take everything back upstairs. Only a minute, and I'll walk you out."

"No, really. It's fine, I—"

He stopped and pinned her with a look. "Wait. Please."

The problem was, in spite of everything—all she could

lose, all the ways it wasn't going to work—she *wanted* to wait for him. She *wanted* to be his friend again.

And more. So much more…

"Fine," she said tightly.

He tipped his head sideways. "You won't run out on me?"

She pressed her lips together and shook her head while a frantic voice in her mind screamed, *You idiot, what's wrong with you? Get out and get out now.* "I'll be right here."

He gathered the materials into his big arms and turned for the stairs. She stood rooted to the spot as he went up, knowing she ought to just duck out while he wasn't looking—but somehow unable to budge.

He came back down again and picked up his tablet. "All right. Let's go."

A few minutes later, along a wide, marble-floored corridor on the way to Rule and Sydney's apartment, he stopped at a gilt-trimmed blue door.

She frowned at him. "What's this?"

He clasped the ornate gold latch and pushed the door inward. On the other side, dimly, she saw a sitting room. "An empty suite," he said. "Come inside with me."

She moved back a step. "Bad idea."

He held her gaze, levelly. "A few private minutes together in a neutral setting. We'll talk, that's all."

"Talk." She said the word with complete disbelief.

"And *only* talk," he insisted. He sounded sincere.

And she was tired of resisting, fighting not only him, but also herself. She *wanted* to go in that room with him. It was hopeless. Every minute she was near him only made her want to steal one minute more.

She let him usher her in.

He turned on a lamp. She sat on a velvet sofa and he took a floral-patterned armchair.

"All right," she said. "Talk about what?"

"Why making love with me on New Year's Eve has upset you so much. To me, it was exactly right, a natural step. The *next* step for us. I don't understand why you can't see that."

She stared at him and said nothing. The truth was too dangerous.

He watched her face as though memorizing it. "I miss those black-rimmed glasses you used to wear. They made you look so serious and studious."

She'd had laser surgery six months before. "Life is easier without them in a whole lot of ways."

"Still, they were charming."

She almost messed up and gave him a real smile. But not quite. "You dragged me in here to talk about how you miss my glasses?"

He set his tablet on the low table between them. "Put down your laptop."

She had it clutched to her chest with both hands. It was comforting, actually. Like a shield against doing what she really wanted and getting too close to him. But fine. She set it down—and felt suddenly naked. "This is ridiculous."

"I've been thinking it over," he said as though she hadn't spoken, a thoughtful frown carving twin lines between his straight, thick brows.

"Max. Why are we doing this? There's just no point."

He shrugged. "Of course there's a point. You. Me. That something special between us."

"You still love your wife," she accused. And yeah, it was a cheap shot, the kind of thing a jealous girlfriend looking for promises of forever might be worried about. Lani was not looking for promises of any kind, no way.

He answered without heat. "My wife is gone. It's almost four years now. This is about you and me."

"See?" she taunted, childishly. Jealously. "You're not denying that you're still in love with her. She's still the one who's in your heart."

Something happened in his wonderful face then. Some kind of withdrawal. But then, in an instant, he was fully engaged again. "This is not about Sophia. And we both know that. You're just blowing smoke."

Busted. "Can't you just…? I mean, there have to be any number of women you could have sex with, be *friends* with, any number of women who would jump at the chance to get something going with you."

His mouth twitched. What? He thought this was funny? "Any number of women simply won't do. I want only one, Lani. I want only you."

Okay. Crap. That sounded good. Really, really good. She made herself glare at him. "You're working me. I know what you're doing."

He sat there so calmly, looking every inch the prince he was, all square-jawed and achingly handsome and good-hearted and pulled-together. And sincere and fair. And way, way too hot. "If working you is telling you the truth, then yes. I am shamelessly working you. I waited five endless weeks for you to come to me again, to tell me whatever it is that's keeping you away from me. It was too long. So I took action. I'm not giving up. I'm not. And if you could only be honest, I think you would admit that you don't *want* me to give up."

Why did he have to know that? It wasn't fair. And she needed, desperately, to get out of there. She grabbed her laptop and popped to her feet. "I need to go."

He shifted, but he didn't rise. He stared up the length of

her and straight into her eyes. "No, Lani. You need to stay. You need to *talk* to me."

Talk to him. Oh, no. Talking to him seemed only to get her in deeper, which was not what she wanted.

Except for when it was *exactly* what she wanted.

He arched a brow and asked so calmly, "Won't you please sit back down?"

She shut her eyes tight, drew in a slow, painful breath— and sat. "I'm not…ready for any of this with you, Max."

He reached out and took her laptop from her and carefully set it back on the low table. "Not ready, how?"

Her arms felt too empty. She wrapped them around herself. "It's all too much, too…consuming, you know? Too overwhelming. And what about the children?" she demanded.

He only asked, "What about them?"

"They have a right to a nanny who isn't doing their daddy."

"And they have just such a nanny. Her name is Gerta— and in any case, you're *not* doing me, not anymore."

She let out a hard, frustrated breath. "I'm just saying it's impossible. It's too much."

He kept right on pushing her. "What you feel for me, you mean?"

She nodded, frantically. "Yes. That. Exactly that."

"So…I'm too much?" His voice poured through her, deep and sweet and way too tempting. It wasn't *fair,* that he should be able to do this to her. It made keeping her distance from him way too hard.

She bobbed her head some more and babbled, "Yes. That's right. Too much."

"*I'm* too much and Michael Cort wasn't enough?"

Michael. Oh, *why* had she told him about Michael? She'd dated the software designer until she saw Sydney with Rule and realized that what she had with Michael was…exactly what Max had just said it was: not enough. "You and Michael are two different things," she insisted, and hated how wimpy and weak she sounded.

"But we're the same in the sense that Michael Cort and I are both men you decided not to see anymore."

"Uh-uh. No. I was with Michael for over a year—and yes, I then decided to break it off. But you and me? We're friends who slept together. Once."

His eyes gleamed. "So then, we *are* friends?"

She threw up both hands. "All right. Have it your way. We're friends."

"Thank you, I will—and about Michael Cort…"

"There is nothing more to say about Michael."

"Except that I'm not in the same league with him vis-à-vis you, correct?" He waited for her to answer. When she didn't, he mildly remarked, "Ouch."

God. Did he have to be so calm and reasonable on top of all the hotness and being so easy to talk to and having the same interests as she did? He was a quadruple threat. At least. "Can we just not talk about Michael?"

"All right. Tell me why you find this thing between us… how did you put it? 'Overwhelming' and 'consuming' and 'too much.'"

"Isn't that self-evident?"

"Tell me anyway."

Against her better judgment, she went ahead and tried. "Well, I just…I don't have time to be consumed with, er, passion, now. There are only so many hours in a day and I…" Dear Lord. Not enough time to be consumed with passion? Had she really said that?

"Tell me the rest," he prompted evenly.

She groaned. "It's only that, well, my dad's a wonderful teacher, the head of the English department at Beaufort State College in Beaufort, Texas, which is west of Fort Worth…" He was frowning, no doubt wondering what any of that had to do with the subject at hand—and why wouldn't he wonder? For a person who hoped someday to write for a living, she was doing a terrible job of keeping to the point and making herself understood.

"You told me months ago that your father's a teacher," he reminded her patiently.

"My father is successful. He's head of his department. My mother's a pediatrician. And my big brother, Carlos, owns five restaurants. Carlos got married last year to a gorgeous, brilliant woman who runs her own dancing school. In my family, we figure out what we want to do and we get out there and do it. Okay, we don't rule principalities or anything. But we contribute to our community. We find work we love and we excel at it."

"You have no problem then. You have work you love and you're very good at it."

"Yes, I'm good with children, and I love taking care of Trev and Ellie."

"You're an excellent nanny, I know. But that isn't the work you love, really, is it?"

She folded her hands in her lap and stared down at them—and wandered off topic some more. "My dad wanted me to follow in his footsteps and be a teacher. From the first, I knew I wanted to write. He said I could do both. Of course, he was right. But I didn't want to do it his way, didn't want to teach. We argued a lot. And the truth is I wasn't dedicated to my writing, not at first. I had some… difficulties. And I took my sweet time getting through college."

"Difficulties?"

Why had she even hinted at any of that? "Just difficulties, that's all."

"You're not going to tell me, are you?"

She shook her head tightly and went on with her story. "My parents would have paid for my education, even though they weren't happy with my choices. But I was proud. I wanted to make it on my own."

"You *were* proud?" he teased.

She felt her cheeks grow warm. "Okay, yeah. I *am* proud. I met Syd and we were like sisters from the first. I went to work for her, became her live-in housekeeper before she had Trev, to help put myself through school. And then once I got my degree, I stayed on with her, working for her, but with plenty of time to write. I worked hard at the writing, but it never took off for me. I lacked focus. Until I came here, until I knew the stories I wanted to write. And now I do know, Max. Now I've got the focus and the drive that I need, plus the stories I want to tell."

Max was sitting forward in the chair, his gray-blue gaze intense. "Have I somehow given you the idea that I think you should stop writing and spend every spare moment in bed with me?"

"Uh, no. No, of course you haven't. It's just that I have goals and I need to meet them. I need, you know, to *make* something of myself. I really do, Max."

He went on leaning forward in the chair, watching her. And she had that feeling she sometimes got around him, the feeling that used to make her all warm and fuzzy inside, because he *knew* her, he understood her. Too bad that lately, since New Year's, that feeling made her worry that he knew too *much* about her, and that he would use what he knew to push her to do things his way. He said, "You want your parents to be proud of you—and you don't feel that they are right now."

Her mouth went dry. She licked her lips. "I didn't say that."

He went further. "You're embarrassed that it bothers you, what your parents think. Because you're twenty-nine years old and you believe you should be beyond trying to live up to their ideals. But you're not beyond it, Lani. You're afraid that it will somehow get out that we've been lovers and that your mother and father will read about it in the tabloids, tacky stories of the nanny shagging the prince. You're afraid they'll judge you in all the ways you're judging yourself. You're afraid they'll think less of you, and you already feel they look down on you as it is."

"No. Really, they're good people. They *don't* look down on me, and I love them very much."

"Plus, you're clinging to a completely unfounded idea that I'll grow tired of you and have you banished from Montedoro in shame."

She groaned. "Okay, it really sounds silly when you put it that way."

"Good. Because it *is* silly. I've given you my word that it's never going to happen. And I never break my word." He was frowning again, holding her gaze as though he could look right through her eyes into her mind. "There's more, isn't there? Something deeper, something you haven't told me yet. Something to do with those 'difficulties' you had that you wouldn't explain to me."

Uh-uh. No. Not going there. *Never* going there. "It doesn't matter."

"Yes, it does."

It was long in the past. She'd survived and moved on, and she didn't want to get into it with him now—or ever. She lifted her chin to a defiant angle and kept her mouth firmly shut.

Without warning, he stood. She gasped and stared up at him, a breathless weakness stealing through her at the sheer masculine beauty of him. And then he held down his hand to her. "Take it," he said with such command and composure that it never occurred to her to do anything else.

She put her fingers in his. A dart of hungry fire flew up her arm, across her chest and downward, straight into the secret core of her. She should tell him to let go. But she didn't. She only rose on shaky feet to stand with him and then stared up at him dazedly as hot, sweet memories of New Year's Eve flashed through her brain.

He said gruffly, "There's nothing wrong with wanting your mother and father to be proud of you. It gets dangerous only when you let your need for their approval run your life."

She managed to muster a little attitude. "Do you have any idea how patronizing you sound?"

He only smiled. "Hit a nerve, did I? Also, you should know that very few authors can write a decent book before the age of thirty. Good writing requires life experience."

"Do you think you're reassuring me? Because you're not."

"I'm praising you. You've written five books and you're not thirty yet. One is okay, two are quite good and the most recent two are amazing."

"Five and a *half* books." She was currently stuck in the middle of number six. "And how do you know how good they all are? You've only read the last two." He'd actually offered to read them. And she'd been grateful for his helpful ideas on how to make them better. That was before New Year's, of course.

He added, "*And* you're published."

Yes, she was. In ebook. Just that past December, as a Christmas present to herself, she'd self-published the three women's fiction novels she'd written before she moved to Montedoro. So far, unfortunately, her e-book sales gave a whole new meaning to the word *unimpressive*. She was holding off on self-pubbing the new trilogy, hoping to sell them as a package to a traditional publisher.

And suddenly she got what he was hinting at. "You downloaded the three books I e-pubbed, didn't you?"

One big shoulder lifted in a half shrug. "Isn't that what you put them on sale for—so that people will buy them?"

Her heart kind of melted about then. How could she help but melt? He not only made her want to rip off her clothes and climb him like a tree, but he was a very good man. He was constantly finding new ways to show her that he really did care about her and the things that mattered to her. It wasn't his fault that she had trouble trusting her own emotions.

Her throat burned with all the difficult stuff she didn't know how to tell him. "Max, I…" She had no idea where to go from there.

And then it didn't matter what she might have said. He wiped her mind free of all thought by the simple act of lifting her chin lightly with his free hand and lowering his lips to hers.

Chapter Three

Max knew he was out of line to kiss her.

He'd made a bargain with her to keep his hands to himself, and yet here he was with one hand tipping up her soft chin and the other wrapped firmly around her trembling fingers. It was not playing fair.

Too bad. He wanted to kiss her, and at the moment she was going to let him do it.

So he did. Lightly, gently, so as not to startle her or have her jerking away, he settled his mouth on hers.

Pleasure stole through him. Warm velvet, those lips of hers. They trembled like her hand. He made no attempt to deepen the kiss, only drew in the haunting scent of her perfume: gardenias, vanilla and a hint of oranges all tangled up with that special, indefinable something that belonged only to her skin.

Lani. Yolanda Ynez. Her name in his mind like a promise. Her warmth and softness so close, calling to him, making him burn as he hadn't burned in years.

Making him *feel* as he'd never thought to feel again.

She made things difficult when they didn't have to be.

And yet, there was, simply, something about her. Some combination of mind and spirit, heart and scent and skin and bone that worked for him, that spoke to him. There was something in the core of her that called to him. Something within her that recognized him in a way he'd despaired long ago of ever being known.

He'd been asleep for almost four years, walking through his life like a ghost of himself, a dutiful creature, half-alive.

No more. Now his eyes were open, his mind and body one, whole, fully engaged.

Whatever it took, whatever he had to do to keep feeling this way, he would do it. He refused to go back to being half-alive again.

"Max." She breathed his name against his mouth.

He wanted to continue kissing her for the next century or two. But she wasn't ready for a century of kisses. Not yet. He lifted his head. "Not giving up on you," he vowed.

For once, she didn't argue, only stepped away and snatched up her laptop. He got his tablet and ushered her ahead of him out the door.

"Nicholas!" Gerta Bauer called sharply as the eight-year-old aimed his N-Strike Elite Retaliator Blaster Nerf gun at the back of his unsuspecting sister's head.

Nick sent his nanny a rebellious glance. Gerta narrowed her eyes at him and stared him down. Nick glared some more, but he did turn the toy gun away from Connie's head. He shot the trunk of a rubber tree instead, letting out a "Hoo-rah!" of triumph as the soft dart hit the target, wiggled in place for a moment and then dropped to the ground.

Connie, totally unaware she'd almost been Nerfed, continued carefully combing the long, straight black-and-white hair of her Frankie Stein doll. Meanwhile, Nick grabbed the fallen dart and forged off into a clump of bushes in search of new prey.

Trev, armed with his Supergalactic Laser Light Blaster, charged after him. "Nicky! Wait for me!" He pulled the trigger. The gun lit up and a volley of blasting sounds filled the air.

Gerta chuckled and tipped her head up to the afternoon sun. "Did I tell you that Nicholas is all grown up? He's too old for his nanny. He told me so this morning before school. 'Only babies have nannies,' he said."

Lani, on the garden bench beside her with Ellie in her lap, caught the butterfly rattle the toddler had dropped before it hit the ground. "He's exercising his independence."

"Me!" Ellie demanded, exercising a little independence of her own.

Lani kissed the top of her head and gave her back the rattle, which she gleefully began shaking again. "Is he still throwing fits when it's time to do his homework?"

Gerta's broad, ruddy face wore a self-satisfied expression. "For the past week, he's been getting right to it and getting it done. I took your advice and had his father talk to him about it."

Lani's pulse accelerated at the mere mention of Max. Honestly, she was hopeless, telling him no over and over—and then kissing him last night.

She needed a large dose of therapy. Or a backbone. Or both.

Gerta was watching her. "What's the matter?"

"Not a thing," Lani answered too quickly. Gerta frowned but didn't press her. And Lani asked, "So the homework is getting done?"

Gerta turned her head up to the sky again. "Yes, the homework is getting done."

Ellie giggled and said, "Uh-oh. Poopy."

She definitely had.

Gerta laughed, waved her freckled hand in front of her face at the smell and offered, "You could change her right here on the bench…."

But Lani was already shouldering the baby bag and lifting Ellie into her arms as she stood. "No. It's a little chilly out here." Ellie dropped the rattle again. Lani caught it as it fell and tucked it in the bag. "Plus I doubt a few baby wipes are going to cut it."

Ellie giggled some more and pecked a baby kiss on Lani's chin. "Nani, Nani…" The weak winter sunlight made her hair shine like polished copper. Even with a loaded diaper, she was the sweetest thing. Lani felt the old familiar ache inside as she gently freed her hair from the perfect, plump little fist. It was an ache of love for this particular child, Syd's baby girl, all mixed up with a bone-deep sorrow for what might have been, if only she'd been a little wiser and not nearly so selfish way back when.

Gerta held up a key. "Use our apartment. It's much closer." She meant the palace apartment she lived in with Nick and Connie. And Max.

Lani's thoroughly shameless heart thumped faster. Would Max be there?

Not that it mattered. It didn't, not at all. No big deal. She knew the apartment's layout. She and Gerta sometimes filled in for each other, so Lani had been there to help out with Nick and Connie more than once. Once she'd let herself in the door, she would go straight to the children's bathroom, clean Ellie up and get out. Fast.

She took the key. "Keep an eye on Trev?"

"Will do."

The apartment was quiet when she let herself in. The maids had been and gone for the day, leaving a faint scent of lemon polish detectable when she pushed the door open, but quickly overpowered by what Ellie had in her diaper.

No sign of Max. Lani breathed a quick sigh of relief.

In the children's bathroom, she hoisted the diaper bag

onto one of the long white quartz counters, shifting Ellie onto her hip as she grabbed a few washcloths from the linen shelves by the big tub. Returning to the counter, she pulled the changing pad from its side pocket and opened it up. Ellie giggled and waved her arms, trying to grab Lani's hair as Lani laid her down.

"You need a toy." Lani gave her the butterfly rattle, which she promptly threw on the floor. Lani played stern. "If I give you another toy, you have to promise not to throw it."

Ellie imitated her serious face. "K," she replied with a quick nod of her tiny chin.

There was an apple-shaped teething ring in the bag. Lani gave her that. She promptly started chewing on it, making happy little cooing sounds.

Lani flipped the water on and set to work. She had the diaper off and rolled up nice and tight and was busy using up the stack of cloths, wiping and rinsing and wiping some more, when her phone in the diaper bag started playing "Radioactive." It was the ringtone she'd assigned to her agent, Marie.

Her heart rate instantly rocketed into high gear.

Okay, it could be nothing.

But what if it *wasn't* nothing?

What if this was her moment, the moment every wannabe author dreamed of, the moment she got the *call,* the one that meant there was an actual publisher out there who wanted to buy her book?

She let out a moan of frustration and wiped faster. Not a big deal, she promised herself. She could call Marie back in just a few minutes. If there was an offer, it wouldn't evaporate while she finished mopping Ellie's bottom.

"Let me help," said the wonderful deep voice that haunted her dreams.

Slowly, her heart galloping faster than ever, she turned her head enough to see him lounging in the doorway wearing gray slacks and a light blue shirt.

The phone stopped ringing and she scowled at him. "How long have you been standing there?"

"Only a minute or two." He straightened and came toward her, all confidence and easy male grace. "I was in my study and I heard your voice and Ellie's laughter...." He stopped beside her at the counter. His niece giggled up at him as she drooled on her teething ring. "Give me the washcloth."

"I... What?"

"The washcloth." He reached out and took the smelly wet cloth in his long-fingered, elegant hand. "Return your call."

"No, really. I'll do this. It's fine." She tried to grab it back.

He held it away. "I have two children. I know how to diaper a baby." Ellie uttered a string of nonsense syllables, followed by a goofy little giggle. "See? Ellie knows I can handle it." On cue, Ellie babbled some more. "Make your call," he commanded a second time as he stuck the washcloth under the water. He wrung it out and got to work.

Lani washed her hands, grabbed her phone and called Marie back. She watched Max diaper Ellie while Marie Garabondi, the agent she'd been working with for just over a month now, talked fast in her ear.

Somewhere in the third or fourth sentence, Marie said the longed-for word: "offer." And everything spun away. Lani listened from a distance, watching Max, so manly and tender, bending over Ellie, doing a stinky job gently and efficiently.

And Marie kept on talking. Lani held the phone to her ear, hardly believing, understanding everything Marie was telling her, only somehow feeling detached, not fully present.

She held up her end, answered, "Yes. All right. Okay, then. Great." But it all seemed unreal to her, not really happening, some odd little dream she was having in the middle of the day. "Yes. Good. Let's do it, yes…" Marie talked some more. And then she said goodbye.

Lani was left standing there in the bathroom holding the phone.

Max had finished changing Ellie and lifted her onto his shoulder. She promptly pulled on his ear and babbled out more happy sounds that didn't quite amount to real words.

"Well?" he asked. Lani blinked and tried to bring herself back to reality. "Lani, what's happened?" he demanded. He was starting to look a little worried.

She sucked in a long breath and shared the news. "That was my agent. We have a deal. A very good deal. I just sold three books."

Max smiled. It was the biggest, happiest smile she'd ever seen on his wonderful face. And it was for her. "Congratulations," he said.

Ellie seemed to pick up on the spirit of the moment. She stopped pulling Max's ear and clapped her hands.

Very carefully, Lani set her phone down on the bathroom counter. "I'll be right back."

Max didn't say anything. He just stood there grinning, holding the baby.

And Lani took off like a shot. She ran out into the hallway of Max's apartment, shouting, "Yes! Yes! Yes! Yes!" When she got to the kitchen, she turned around and ran back again, shouting "Yes!" all the way.

Max was waiting, leaning in the bathroom doorway with Ellie in his arms, when she returned to him. "Feel good?"

"Oh, yeah." She wanted to grab him and plant one right

on him, to take his hand and lead him back to the kitchen where they could sit and talk and…

She stopped the dangerous thought before it could really get rolling.

"Nani, Nani…" Ellie swayed toward her.

She took the little sweetheart in her arms. "I'd, um, better get back. Gerta will wonder."

He was still smiling, but there was something somber in his eyes. "All right, then."

Neither of them moved.

"Nani…" Ellie patted her cheek—and then started squirming. "Dow, Nani, dow…"

Lani broke the tempting hold of his gaze. "I need to get back." He was blocking the doorway. "The diaper bag?"

He went and got it for her. "Here you are."

She took it from his outstretched hand and carried the wiggling toddler out of there, away from him.

"It's time and you know it," Sydney said the next day.

They were at the villa, just Syd and Lani, sitting at the table in the kitchen, sharing a late lunch while Trev and Ellie napped.

Everything had changed with that single call from Marie. And the time had come for Lani and Syd to deal with that.

Lani couldn't seem to stop herself from arguing against taking the next step. "But I love Trev and Ellie. And I have plenty of time to write and to take care of them."

Syd wasn't buying. "Why do I have to tell you what you already know? You'll be needing to network, to put together a PR plan. And what about that website you still don't have? And you keep saying you're going to establish more of an online presence, see if you can do more to boost the sales of those three e-books you have out."

"You're making me dizzy. You know that, right?"

"What I'm saying isn't news. It's what we always agreed. As soon as you were making enough with your writing to live on for a year, you would put all your work time into building a career. This sale does that for you."

"I know, but..."

"But what, Lani?"

Lani let out a low cry. "But it's all happening so fast. And what about Ellie and Trev? They're used to my being with them all the time. How will they take it, having some stranger for a nanny?"

"They will do fine." Syd reached across the distance between them and ran a fond hand down her hair. "They grow up, anyway. To a degree, in the end, we lose them to their own lives."

Lani wrinkled up her nose at her friend. "Okay, I get that you're trying to make me feel better. But come on. Ellie's still in diapers and Trev's four. It's a long time until they're on their own. And I know you and Rule are planning to have more children. You need me, you know you do."

"And you need to get out there." Syd set down her fork. "Listen, don't tempt me, okay? You're amazing with the kids. They love you so much—almost as much as I do. You're part of the family and I hate to let you go."

"Then why don't we just keep it like it is for a while?"

Syd refused to waver. "Uh-uh. No. You *need* to do this. And it's not like you're moving back to Texas or anything. You'll see them often, every day if you want to."

"Of course I want to see them every day. I *love* them. I love *you*."

"And *I* love you," Syd said. "So much. I'm so crazy happy for you."

Lani's throat clutched and her eyes burned.

"Oh, honey…" Syd grabbed the box of tissues off the windowsill and passed them to her.

Lani dabbed at her eyes. "Somehow, I didn't expect it to be like this. To get what I've always wanted—and just feel all weepy and lost about it."

"It's all going to work out. Change is a good thing."

Lani shot Syd a sideways look. "Keep saying that."

"You'd better believe I will—until you stop trying to go backward and move on."

Lani pushed her plate away, braced her elbows on the table and rested her chin between her hands. "Unbelievable. Seriously. And yeah. Okay."

Syd chuckled then. "Okay, what?"

"Okay, you can find a new nanny."

"Excellent. You're fired, as of today. And I'm perfectly capable of watching my own children until I find someone else." In the old days, before she'd married Rule, Sydney had worked killing hours at her law firm in Dallas. A full-time nanny had been a necessity then. Now, Sydney had projects she took on, but her schedule was flexible and she enjoyed being a hands-on mom. "And Gerta's terrific. I know she'll be willing to accept a nice bonus and keep an eye on all four kids if I get desperate."

"*I* can help if you get desperate."

"The main thing is you're a full-time writer and you're getting out on your own."

"Yes. Fine. I'll start looking for a place. Something in Monagalla, maybe…" The southwestern ward was close to the palace. It was known as the tourist ward because room rates were relatively low there. But housing in Montedoro didn't come cheap no matter where you lived.

Syd seemed to be reading her mind. "If you need help with the money…"

"Don't even go there. I have enough to tide me over until

the advance check comes. I'm just…a little freaked out at making the move."

"No kidding."

Lani pulled her plate close again. "God. I'm a basket case. Thrilled. Terrified. Sure that Marie will be calling any minute to tell me never mind, it was all a big mistake."

Syd sipped her coffee and set the cup back down with care. "Is it a guy?"

Lani almost choked on the chip she'd just poked in her mouth. She swallowed it whole and it went down hard. "Whoa. That came out of nowhere."

"Did it? I don't think so. Something's been bothering you since the beginning of the year. I keep asking you what. And you keep not telling me. Who is he?"

Lani was so tired of lying. And Syd didn't believe her lies anyway. Still, she tried to hold out. "Syd, come on…"

"No, Lani. *You* come on. Whatever this is, it's got you really on edge. And it's got me more than a little bit worried for you."

"Don't be. I'm all right."

"No, you're not. You're kind of a mess lately."

"Gee, thanks."

"Just *talk* to me."

Lani waffled. "It's only, well, I'm afraid you won't approve."

Syd made a sound that was midway between a laugh and a groan. "Don't give me that. We've been friends for too long. There is nothing…*nothing* you could do that would make me love you any less."

Lani stared at her friend and wanted to cry again. "You are the best. You know that, right?"

"So tell me."

The words were right there. And so she just said them. "I slept with Max on New Year's Eve."

Syd's green eyes bugged out and her mouth fell open. "Max. As in Maximilian, aka my brother-in-law?"

Lani drew herself straight in her chair. "Yes. Maximilian as in the heir to the throne. That Max. You know the one."

"Oh, Lani…" Syd shook her head slowly.

Lani made a low, pained little sound. "See? I shouldn't have told you. Now you've gotta be certain I have a screw loose."

Syd's hand came down on top of hers. She squeezed her fingers tight. "Stop."

Lani turned her hand around and grabbed on to Syd's. "I know you're shocked."

"No—well, surprised, maybe. A little."

"More like a lot."

Syd gave her a patient look. "I knew the two of you were friendly…."

"Right. Just not *that* friendly. I mean, the prince and the nanny ending up in bed together. Ick. It just sounds so tacky."

"I don't want to have to tell you again," Syd scolded. "Stop beating yourself up. You like him. He likes you. You're both single. It happens. Men and women find each other. I mean, where would we all be if it *didn't* happen?" Protectively, she laid her other hand over their joined ones. "I did notice how he was always finding a reason to talk to you, always hanging around with you and Gerta and the children."

"Well, his kids were there, too."

"Lani. Let me make myself clearer. I should have guessed."

"Why should you guess? I mean, everyone talks about how much he loved his wife, about how he'll never get married again, how nobody has a chance with him."

"Nobody until you, apparently."

She pulled her hand free of Syd's comforting grip and ate another chip without really even tasting it. "It was one night, that's all."

Syd leaned a little closer. "Do you want it to be more?"

Lani hardly knew how to answer, so she didn't.

Syd kept after her. "Is he treating you like it never happened or something? Do I need to kick his ass for you?"

Lani pushed her plate away again, then pulled it back, ate a slice of pickle and teased, "You think you could take him? He's pretty fit."

"Answer the question. Has he been disrespecting you?"

"No, he hasn't. He's been wonderful. Last night, he kissed me and said he won't give up on me, even though I've done everything I possibly can to chase him away."

"Wait. Stop. I'm getting whiplash, this conversation is so confusing. He wants to keep seeing you—and you're just not interested?"

Lani pushed her plate aside for the third time so that she could bang her head on the table. Then she sat up, sucked in a hard breath and said, "No, actually, I'm crazy about him."

Syd stared at her for a long time. Then she said gently, "So give him a chance." Lani only looked at her. Syd spoke again. "This is not eleven years ago."

Lani almost wished she'd never confided in Syd about what had happened when she was eighteen, the terrible choices she'd made and the life-altering domino effect of the ugly consequences that followed. But they *were* best friends and best friends shared the deepest, hardest secrets. "I just don't want to get my heart broken, okay? Been there, done that. It almost destroyed me. I don't want to go there again."

"The way I remember it, you broke up with Michael Cort because you wanted more than just safety in a man…."

"Yeah, I know that, but—"

"Save the *buts*. I don't get this. A big part of the reason I went to lunch with Rule that first day I met him was because *you* told me to get out there and give another guy a chance. You knew how many times I'd been messed over, and that I was scared it was only going to happen again. But you pushed me to see that you don't get what really matters without putting yourself out there, without risking big."

"Well, I'm having a little trouble right now following my own advice."

"Just think about it."

"Are you kidding? I do. Constantly. I just made the big sale. I'm living my dream. But all I can think about is this thing with Max."

The apartment, in an old villa on a narrow street in Monagalla, had one bedroom, a tiny kitchen nook and a six-by-ten-foot balcony off the living room that the landlady called a terrace. From the terrace you could see the hillside behind the building, and a forest of olive and rubber trees and odd, spiky cactus plants. Lani took the place because the old Spanish-style building charmed her. Also, it was available immediately at a good price and it was only a short walk from the front door up Cap Royale to the palace.

One week after she got the call from Marie, she moved in. She had all the furniture she needed, courtesy of Rule and Sydney, who had led her down into the warren of storage rooms in the basement of the palace and let her choose the few pieces she needed from the mountains of stuff stored there.

It took her two days to make it livable. She designated half of the living room as her office, positioning her desk so she could look out the glass slider at the little square of terrace and the olive trees on the hillside. And she found a housewares shop nearby where she bought pots and pans, dishes, glassware and cooking utensils. The shop had all the linens she needed, too.

At the end of the second day of fixing the place up, when she had it just the way she wanted it, she cooked herself a simple dinner in her little kitchen and she ate on the plain white plates she'd bought from the nearby shop. After she ate, she sat down at her computer and wrote ten pages and felt pretty good about them. It was well after midnight when she closed her laptop and saw the pink sticky note she'd slapped on the top: *Call parents.*

Actually, she'd been meaning to call them for days now—ever since she made the big sale. They would be thrilled for her, of course. But she'd been putting off making that call.

They loved her and they worried about her. And every time she talked to them they wanted to know when she was coming home. They didn't seem to understand that she *was* home. She'd tried to explain to them that she was never moving back to Texas. So far, they weren't getting it. Sometimes she doubted they ever would.

Midnight in Montedoro meant five in the afternoon yesterday in Texas. Her mom was probably still at her clinic. But her dad might be home. She made the call.

Her dad answered. "Yolanda." He sounded tired but pleased to hear from her. "How are things on the Riviera?"

She told him about the sale first. He congratulated her warmly and said he'd always known it would happen. And then she couldn't resist bragging a little, sharing the dollar amount of the advance.

He got excited then. "But this is wonderful. You won't have to spend your time babysitting anymore. In fact, you could come home. You know your mama and I would love to have you right here in the house with us. But I know you probably don't want to live with the old folks. You would want your own place, and we understand that."

"Well, I already have a place. I moved out of the palace and got myself an apartment."

"But you could—"

"Papi. Come on. I've told you. I don't want to leave here. I love Montedoro and I plan to stay."

"But not forever. Your home is here, near your family. And you're almost thirty. It's time you found the right man and made me a doting grandfather."

She didn't say anything. It seemed pointless to argue.

He kind of took the hint and tried to put a positive spin on what he considered self-destructive stubbornness on her part. "If you have your own apartment there in Montedoro, does that mean you're not babysitting Sydney's kids anymore?"

"Yes. That's what it means."

"Well, I'm glad for that. You have great talent. I always told you that. If you're going to take care of babies, they should be your own."

She couldn't let that stand. "I'm an excellent nanny, Papi. And I enjoyed every moment with Trevor and Ellie."

He got the message. More or less. "Well, of course, you will excel at whatever you do." He said it much too carefully.

That was the problem now, with her and her parents. In the awfulness of what had happened more than ten years ago, something essential had been lost. They continued to go through the motions with each other, but there were barriers, things they didn't dare talk about with each other— or maybe didn't know how to talk about.

She asked how he was feeling, and how Mama was doing. "Fine," he answered. "Very well." And then he told her that her brother, Carlos, and his bride, Martina, had bought a house in San Antonio. Martina's family was in San Antonio, and Carlos would be opening a new restaurant there. "Of course, your mama and I are happy for them, and you know how proud we are of Carlito's success."

"Yes, I know." She made her voice bright. "He's done so well."

"*And* they are already trying for a baby. A first grandchild is a precious thing."

A first grandchild. The words stung, though Lani knew she shouldn't let them.

After that, the conversation really began to lag. She told him she loved him and to give her love to her mother. They said goodbye.

She went to bed feeling empty and lonely and like a failure as a daughter. Sleep didn't come. She just stared up at the ceiling fan, trying to turn her mind off.

But instead, she thought about Max.

She'd had zero contact with him since that afternoon in his apartment when he'd diapered Ellie for her while she took the call from Marie. Nine days. And nothing. She hadn't seen him during the week she was still at the palace. And for the past two days, she'd put all her effort into setting up her place.

He'd made no attempt to get in touch with her. So much for how he wasn't giving up on her. No doubt he'd had enough of her pushing him away. She didn't blame him for that. He'd tried and tried and she'd given him nothing back.

She sighed. So all right. It was over between them.

Over without ever really getting started.

And, well, that was fine with her. It was better this way. Except that it wasn't.

And she was a complete coward who'd driven away a perfectly wonderful guy. Even if he was too much for her, too overwhelming, way more than she'd bargained for. Even if he was probably still carrying a torch for his lost wife. Even if it scared her a lot, how gone she was on him.

She turned over onto her side and punched at her pillow. But sleep wouldn't come. Her mind thrummed with energy. With longing. She started thinking about calling him—and yeah, she knew that was a very bad idea.

So she tried *not* to think about calling him.

And that only made her want to call him more.

She had his cell number. He'd given it to her months ago, long before New Year's, just taken her phone from her one day when they were out in the gardens with the children and added himself to her contacts.

She'd laughed and said she didn't need his number. They saw each other all the time. If something came up and she had to reach him, Rule and Sydney had his landline on autodial.

But he'd said he wanted her to have it. Just in case…

Lani reached out a hand through the darkness and felt around on the nightstand until she found her phone. She punched up his number and hit Call without letting herself stop to think about how it was too late and she'd already blown it and calling him at one-thirty in the morning was hardly a good way to reestablish contact.

Not surprisingly, he didn't answer. The call went to voice mail. She knew she should just hang up. But she didn't.

"Hi, Max. Um, it's me. Lani? Yeah, I know it's almost two in the morning, not to mention you've probably decided you're better off giving me what I said I wanted and leaving me alone. And I, well, I get that. I mean, why wouldn't you finally just give up on me? I haven't been anything but a headache lately. Why wouldn't you just…?" She stopped, closed her eyes and let out a whimper of utter embarrassment. "Okay, this ridiculousness is stopping now. Sorry to bother you. Sorry for everything. 'Night." She disconnected the call, dropped the phone on the nightstand and then grabbed her pillow and plunked it down hard on top of her face.

For several seconds she lay there in the dark, pressing the pillow down on her nose and mouth as hard as she could. But it was all just more ridiculousness and eventually she gave up, tossed the pillow aside and pushed back the covers.

If she couldn't sleep, maybe she could work. Not pages, no. Not tonight. But she did need to get going on a marketing program. She could look around online, see what resources were generally available. She needed to find a website designer. And maybe enroll in a few online classes. Things such as how to make the most of social media and how to create an effective PR plan. When the first book in her trilogy came out, she needed to be ready to promote herself and the books, and do it effectively. Gone were the days when an author could sit around and wait for her publisher to set up a few book signings.

Her phone rang as she was reaching for her robe.

Her heart lurched and then began thudding hard and deep in her chest. Sweat bloomed between her breasts, under her arms and on her upper lip. She craned her head toward the nightstand to see the display.

Max.

She dropped the robe and grabbed for the phone. "Uh, hello?"

"Gerta says you're no longer working for Rule and Sydney." His voice was careful, measured. Withdrawn. Still, that voice had the power to make her breath come uneven, to make her thudding heart pound even harder. "And I understand you've moved out of the palace."

"Yes. That's right. I'm not at the palace anymore. And Max, really, I'm sorry about—"

"I don't want your apologies."

"Um. Well, all right. I'm okay with that."

"You're okay." His tone was too calm. Calm and yet somehow edged in darkness.

"That's what I said, yes."

"You're okay and you're no longer a nanny working for my family. No longer at the palace."

Anger rose up in her. Defensive anger. She reined it in and tried to speak reasonably. "Look, I don't know what's the matter with me. I shouldn't have called you tonight. It was wrong of me to do that and I—"

"Not so."

"Excuse me?"

"You were very right to call me tonight."

"I—"

"But you were *wrong* to run off without a single word to me."

"Max, I did not 'run off.' I moved. I certainly have a right to move without checking with you first."

He was silent.

"Max?" She was sure he'd hung up on her.

"Where are you?" Low. Soft. But not in any way tender.

"I don't—"

"An address. Give me your address."

"Max, I—"

"I must tell you, I could have your address so easily without asking you. Gerta would give it to me. I could get it from Rule. And there are other ways. There are men my family hires to find out whatever we need to know about anyone with whom we associate."

"Max, what are you doing? I really don't like this. Is that a threat?"

"No threat. Only an explanation. I can find out whatever I want to know about you. But I would never do that. I care for you. I respect your rights and your privacy. So please. Give me your address or hang up the phone and never call me again."

"Max, this isn't like you. Ultimatums have never been your style."

"My *style,* as you put it, is not serving me well with you. Make a choice. Do it now." There was nothing gentle in that voice. He didn't grant her so much as a hint of the compassionate, patient Max she'd always known.

Obviously, her sweet and tender prince was being a complete jerk and she needed to hang up and forget about him. Let it be and let him go. Move on. It was only what she'd repeatedly told him she wanted.

He spoke again. "Lani. Choose."

She gave him the address.

Chapter Four

Max was furious.

He'd been furious for a couple of days now. Ever since Gerta had told him that Lani was no longer Trev and Ellie's nanny, that she'd found an apartment and moved into it.

He left the palace by a side door and walked down Cap Royale under the pale sliver of a new moon. It took him eight minutes to reach her street and a minute more to get to her door.

The old villa was locked up at that hour of the night. But she was waiting in the vestibule, as he'd told her to be.

Their gazes locked through the etched glass at the top of the door. She opened it. He went in. She wore yoga pants and a big sweatshirt that made her look small and vulnerable, her hair curling on her shoulders, a little wild, as though she hadn't been able to stop herself from raking her fingers through it.

"This way," she said in a hushed voice, and turned for the stairs.

He caught her arm before she could escape him.

She gasped and faced him, tried to pull away. "Max, I—"

"Nine days," he whispered, pulling her closer, bending

his head to get right in her face. "Nine days. Not a word from you."

"I thought it would be better. You know, to let it go."

"Maybe it would have been. I didn't want to give up on you. I thought it mattered, what we might have had. But a man can be told no only so many times before he begins to wonder how big a fool he really is. When Gerta told me you had moved, I decided that was it. You'd been sending a message and I'd finally received it. I was done with you. I set my mind on forgetting you. Then you called me tonight. Why?"

She drew in a careful breath and let it out slowly. "Let's just go upstairs. Please."

He jerked her closer. The sweet scent of her hair drifted up to him, piercing him like knives.

"Max..." She said it pleadingly.

He wanted to be cruel to her. He wanted to make her pay somehow for being able to just go like that, just walk out of his life so easily. He wanted to get even with her for giving him a taste of heaven.

And then taking it back.

But she was right. They should go to her apartment, where they could close the door and say what needed saying without the possibility of nosy neighbors listening in. He was the Prince of Montedoro, after all. The heir to the throne should know better than to let himself be heard carrying on an intimate discussion in a dimly lit apartment foyer in the middle of the night.

He released her.

She turned again and led him up two flights. Her apartment door was open, soft light spilling out onto the landing. She ushered him in first and closed and locked the door behind them.

They were in the living room. It was small and plain—a sofa and two chairs, her desk facing a sliding door.

She gestured at the sofa against the inside wall. "Sit down."

He did no such thing. They remained near the door, facing off against each other like enemies. "Why did you call me tonight?"

She wore a look of desperate confusion. "I couldn't help it."

"Not good enough." He waited.

Still she only gazed at him, all big, dewy eyes and no answers.

He knew then that he really was a fool. Duped by the best of them. Tricked yet again. "There's nothing here for me. I understand." He did his best to gentle his tone. "It's all right, Lani. We'll do what you wanted. We'll move on. Step out of my way."

She gulped. Hard. "I… Oh, God, Max. Please don't go."

He tried not to waver. But it wasn't easy to cut her free. She'd changed his world, turned the never-ending grayness to warm, soft, beautiful light. When he looked at her, he never wanted to look away. "Give me a reason to stay."

"I…" She shut those enormous black eyes. Gulped again. "I need to…Max, I need to tell you a few things about me, a few not-so-good things." She made a sound then. Ragged, shrill. Not quite a laugh and not exactly a sob. "Scratch that. Worse than not-so-good. Straight-up bad things. I've done some really rotten, crappy, bad things. I thought I had forgiven myself. But now, since New Year's, since I had to admit how much you mean to me, I'm not so sure."

How much you mean to me. Could he count the admission as progress? He searched her face. "I knew there was something."

"I haven't wanted to tell you. I didn't think I could bear to see the disappointment in your eyes."

He dared to reach out and take her hand. Her soft fingers felt good in his, as always. They felt achingly right. Gently, he suggested, "I think that now we should sit down."

She blinked, looking slightly dazed. "Yes. All right."

He turned for the sofa and she followed obediently. Once there, he took her slim shoulders, gently pushed her down and then sat beside her, facing her, laying an arm along the sofa back behind her, hitching a knee up onto the cushions.

She did not turn to him, but sat facing front, hands folded in her lap, staring straight ahead. "When I was eighteen, I fell in love with my dad's best friend. He was forty-five and he was married—well, separated. But still. There had been no divorce. He was a writer, a novelist. His name was Thomas McKneely."

McKneely. Max knew that name. He was pretty sure he'd read at least one of the man's novels and that he'd found what he read funny and smart.

She went on. "Thomas was everything I thought I wanted someday to be. He and my dad had gone to college together. Thomas wrote humorous novels set in Texas."

"I've heard of him." Max kept his voice carefully neutral. "Go on."

"I'd known Thomas since I was a child. I'd always idolized him. He was…bigger than life, you know? Tall and broad-shouldered and handsome, always laughing and saying the cleverest things. He and his wife, Allison, often came to dinner, to the parties my parents would give. And then, in the summer after my senior year, he left Allison. He came to dinner alone one night and he was…different. Kind of sad and withdrawn. But then he looked at me and I knew he really saw me, finally. He saw me as a woman."

He couldn't resist pointing out the obvious. "His best friend's daughter? What a bastard."

"Yeah, well. I *wanted* to get something going with him or nothing would have happened, believe me."

"You were only eighteen. Barely an adult."

She shook her head slowly. "True. I didn't know my ass from up. Some people have seen enough and learned enough to be grown-ups at eighteen. Not me. In hindsight it's way clear I was asking for all kinds of trouble. But I was the baby of my family, totally spoiled, and I thought that if I wanted something bad enough, it had to be okay. So I snuck out to meet him several nights in a row. We were secret lovers. I thought it was so romantic and beautiful and he would divorce his wife and we would be together forever." She put up her hands and covered her face—and then dropped them again. "Young. I was so young. And I really was sure I knew everything, all the secrets of life and love and happiness that my parents just couldn't understand."

"And then?"

"My father found out. He caught me sneaking out and he confronted Thomas. They fought, the two of them, punching at each other, rolling around on the front lawn. My father won. He stood over Thomas and called him a lowlife child-molesting… Well, there were bad names and there were a lot of them. And I…I blamed my dad. I yelled at him that I was eighteen and a grown woman and I had a right to love the man of my choice." She fell silent, staring into the middle distance.

Max wanted to say something, to offer some kind of comfort. But he had no words right then. And when he reached out a hand to her, she leaned away from his touch.

"No," she whispered. "Don't. Let me finish this." He drew back and she went on. "I left with Thomas that night. I moved in with him. I thought we would live on love and he would write more brilliant novels and dedicate them all to me. But what do you know? The summer went by and he wasn't writing and I didn't go away to the University of Iowa as planned. We started fighting. He drank too much. I cried all the time. And then, in October, he told me that I was a spoiled, selfish child and I didn't really have anything to offer him. He went back to his wife." She looked at him then, and her eyes were defiant. "He was a bastard, yes. But he was also right about me." She smiled the saddest smile. "I went home. I didn't know where else to go. My parents forgave me. That's how they are."

He wanted to kill Thomas McKneely. But it seemed to him he'd read the man's obituary already. "I think I read somewhere that Thomas McKneely died."

She made a small sound in the affirmative. "Four years ago. A ruptured aortic aneurysm. Allison was with him right to the end." Lani eased her folded hands between her knees, hunched her shoulders and looked down at the floor. "She was a good wife to him. Truer than he ever deserved. A year after he died, I went to see her, to apologize for all I'd put her through. She was really something, so kind. She said it was all years ago, that I should put it behind me and move on."

"A good woman."

"Yeah. I heard later that she remarried and moved to Florida. I like to picture her there, holding hands on the beach with some handsome older guy."

Max waited, in case there might be more.

And there was. Eventually, she let out a long, slow sigh. "A month after Thomas went back to Allison, I realized that I was pregnant." He swore, with feeling. She gave a sad little shrug. "I didn't know what to do. I just…did nothing. I told no one. I stayed in my room most of the time. My brother, Carlos, came and tried to lecture me. He yelled and told me off, trying to make me snap out of it. I just shut the door in his face. And my poor parents didn't know how to reach me, how to help me. I never actually told them I was pregnant. They found out when I miscarried at the first of the year."

He cast about for something helpful and comforting to say, but all he could think of was, "I'm sorry, Lani. So damn sorry..."

She raked a hand back through her hair. "My parents called an ambulance. They stayed at my side. I lost the baby, but I pulled through all right, physically at least. Mama and Papi were hurt that I hadn't told them about the baby, that they found out only when I was losing it. Children and family mean everything to them. But still, they didn't accuse me or blame me. They tried to see the positive. They said that miscarriages do happen, that someday there would be other babies, that I was young and strong and things would get better in time." She lifted her tear-wet gaze to him. "I meant it when I said that they're good people. They stuck with me and came through for me and they tried to convince me to get help, tried to talk me into seeing a counselor. But I refused. I felt I was dead inside. I *wanted* to die."

He knew then what she would tell him next. "Lani, my God."

She covered her face again. "I had the pain medication they'd given me at the hospital when I lost the baby. I took it. All of it. I was unconscious when my mother found me. She called me another ambulance. It was touch and go for a while, they told me. But, well, here I am. I pulled through."

He touched her arm. "Look at me."

Once more, she lowered her hands and turned her eyes to his. "I was in a psych hospital for several weeks and I got the intensive therapy I needed right then, and for a year more after I got out, I saw a really good doctor who helped me to get well."

He didn't know what to say. So he didn't say anything. Instead, he touched her again, lightly clasping her shoulder, guiding her closer. She didn't resist that time, but melted against him. He pressed his lips to her hair.

She said in a voice barely more than a whisper, "I swear to you, Max. I thought I was over all that, over the past, over my own stupid, blind arrogance, to risk it all on a completely self-absorbed married man more than twice my age. I thought I was, well, if not over losing my baby, at least at peace with it. I thought I had forgiven myself for going against everything I've ever held true and trying to end my life."

"But you're not over it." It wasn't a question.

She put her hand against his chest and tucked her head more snugly under his chin. "I've made a good life, a safe life, with Syd and her family. Kind of, you know, living on the edge of other people's happiness. Loving Syd's children. Writing my stories, but not taking too many chances. Dating safe, kind men like Michael Cort, breaking it off with them eventually because what I had with them was never enough. But then..." She pushed away from him and looked at him. "There was you..."

He pulled her down again and guided her head back to his shoulder.

She said, "I know I tried to deny it that day in the gardener's cottage, but you *were* my friend for more than a year. And it was okay, being friends with you. It was safe, the kind of safe I've always needed, after all that happened eleven years ago."

"You mean it was okay until New Year's. Until we were suddenly more than friends."

"That's right. Then I got scared. Terrified. I've felt this

strongly for a man only once before. And now you know that didn't go well."

"I would never do what he did." He said it quietly, but a little of his earlier fury crept in. He had made his own mistakes, been the worst kind of fool. But at least he'd always kept his promises.

She had tipped her head back, was watching his face. "Of course you're nothing like Thomas. Nothing at all. Oh, Max. If you despise me now, I do understand...."

He traced the line of her hair where it fell along her cheek, his anger fading away. "You're harder on yourself than I could ever be."

She gazed up at him pleadingly. "Just tell me. Do you despise me?"

"No. How could I? You made some bad choices. Everybody does. You learned from those choices and you came through to be who you are right now. I have no problem with that. I'm only grateful you're finally able to tell me about it."

"But, well..." She put her hand against her throat.

"What?" he demanded. "Tell me."

"Oh, Max, I hate to have to say it, but you see now, don't you, why I said it would be better if we both just moved on?"

Move on now? When he was finally breaking down the walls with her? No. "I don't see that. I don't see it at all."

"But you should. You really should."

"Shh." He cradled her closer. "I don't want to move on, Lani. I want to stay right here with you."

She hitched in a sharp breath. "You really mean that?"

"I do."

She laughed then, a low laugh. There was something deeper than humor in the sound. "I think you must be out of your mind. I'm a mess. It's not pretty."

"You are something of a mess, I'll give you that—but you are very, very pretty."

She sat up and made a show of tossing her head. "What are you telling me? That at least I'll have my looks to fall back on if all else fails?"

He grinned at that, and then he said in all seriousness, "It matters to me, that you trusted me, finally. That you took that kind of chance on me. But you have to stop running away from me."

"I get so scared that I'll ruin everything—and then I ruin everything…"

He finished for her. "By running away."

"Yes. That's exactly right."

"Stop doing that," he instructed sternly.

"I will. I promise you, Max." She made a low, nervous sound. "So…we're good, then?"

He reached out, eased his fingers up under the thick fall of her hair and wrapped them around the soft, warm nape of her neck. "We are excellent." He gave a tug.

And she came to him, leaning close, smelling of gardenias and oranges. Her soft breasts brushed his chest. He felt the promise of that softness, even through the layers of their clothing. And her mouth was right there, an inch from his. "Oh, Max…"

He claimed her lips. She opened, sighing. He tasted her. He wrapped his arms around her and kissed her for a long time, sitting there on the old sofa in her plain living room.

"Lie down," she whispered against his mouth.

He admitted reluctantly, "I can't stay…"

"I know."

"New Year's was beautiful," he told her, his voice rough with the memory of it, with the reality of her right now, in his arms. "But next time, I want to go slow, to have the whole evening together."

"All right. Yes."

"That is a word I love to hear you say."

"I'll say it some more then. Yes, yes, yes, yes—and now, tonight, won't you stay just a little longer?"

She was way too tempting. So he let her guide him down to stretch out on the cushions—after which she promptly wriggled away and got rid of her shoes and then his, too. He put his feet up on the sofa and reached for her, pulling her against him so she was lying on top of him.

And she gazed down at him, eyes bright as stars now. "You were so angry when you got here. I was sure it was over, that I had pushed you too far and there was no hope."

"I'm not angry now."

"And I'm so glad. It all seems a little unreal, though. I can't believe I finally put it all out there, told you everything. And you didn't walk out. You're still here, in my apartment, holding me tight…"

"I'm here," he promised. "I'm right here." He stroked her back and smoothed her hair. "Sunday," he whispered.

She let out a low, husky laugh. "Comes after Saturday, last I heard."

"*This* Sunday, day after tomorrow…"

"What about it?"

"You, me, breakfast with the family in the Sovereign's apartments." It was a tradition. He had eight brothers and sisters. They all tried to show up for the family Sunday breakfast whenever they could manage it. In recent years, there were wives and husbands and children, too. Some Sundays it was a big group.

She pulled away enough to make a pained face at him. "Sunday with your family. I don't know. What will they all think?"

"They will be happy for me, that I've found someone special again at last."

She laid her head against his chest. "Your mother is so amazing. I'm kind of intimidated by her."

"There's no reason to be."

"Oh, come on. Some say she's the best ruler Montedoro's seen in five hundred years."

"Yes, she is."

"And she's as beautiful as she is brilliant. Why wouldn't I be intimidated?"

"She will see us together and she'll be glad. She's like all good mothers. She wants her children to be happy."

"You have to see that it could be awkward. Everyone will know for sure that you've got something going with the nanny."

"But you're not the nanny. Not anymore. So that's a non-issue—not that it ever mattered to me, anyway."

She lifted her head and gazed at him steadily. "You really do mean that."

"Yes, I do."

"I am so crazy for you, Max." Her voice was soft, full of wonder.

He guided a lock of hair behind her ear. "Hold that thought—and you are coming with me and Nick and Connie to breakfast on Sunday. Stop trying to get out of it."

"Oh, all right. Fine. I'll be there."

"Yes, you will. And tonight, dinner. I'm taking you out."

She made a breathless little sound. "A real date."

"Exactly. Be ready at seven."

For once, she didn't argue. She brushed a kiss across his cheek and whispered, "Yes, Your Highness."

He held her tighter. "You and me," he said, to make certain she understood. "For all the world to see."

"I'll be ready."

"That's the spirit. Kiss me again." She did, wrapping him in her softness, in the scent of her hair. When she lifted her head, he groaned. "On second thought, maybe I should stay a little longer...."

She brushed another light kiss against his mouth. "I wish. But I know you like to be there, in the morning, for breakfast with Connie and Nick." And with that, she slid off him, bringing another groan from him as she shifted away. Kneeling, she handed him his shoes. He sat up and put them on.

Then she followed him to the door.

"It's so strange," she whispered, her hands on his shoulders, her forehead pressed to his. "I'm almost afraid to let you go. I'm afraid that in the morning, I'll wake up and this will all be a dream."

He tipped up her chin, kissed her one more time. "It's already morning, my darling. And this is no dream."

When he was gone, Lani wandered to the sliding door and stared out at the night, at the shadowed olive trees on the hill beyond the terrace. She was smiling to herself. Eventually, she turned and went to bed, feeling light as a moonbeam, her feet barely touching the floor.

She peeled off her yoga pants and sweatshirt, took off her bra and her panties. Naked, still smiling, she climbed between the sheets and closed her eyes. She was asleep in seconds, a deep, contented dreamless sleep.

Chapter Five

"Dinner out tonight with Max?" Syd laughed in delight.

"Shh." Lani pointed at Ellie, who was asleep on her lap.

Syd lowered her voice. "Good for you." They were sitting in the kitchen at the villa. Trev had made short work of his lunch and gone off to the playroom. "Good for both of you."

Lani stroked Ellie's silky curls. The little one muttered a nonsense word in her sleep. Lani whispered, "That's not all. He asked me to come with him and Connie and Nick to Sunday breakfast with the family. I said I would."

"Wow. The man is not fooling around."

"He's…something special."

"You really told him everything, the whole story?"

"I did. And he was wonderful."

"*You* are wonderful," Syd declared. "Remember that."

Lani grinned. "Well, you are my best friend. You have to say that."

Syd seemed to study her. "You know, it feels kind of right, the more I think about it. You and Max not only both love sitting in the library talking Montedoran history for half the night, but you've also both seen some rough times. You fell for an egotistical, alcoholic SOB who broke your heart and practically cost you everything. He lost Sophia

so suddenly, so tragically." His wife had died in a waterski-
ing accident. "You both deserve a big dose of happiness."

Sophia. Lani had seen pictures of her—in Max's apartment and in the long hallway to the throne room, which was
lined with portraits of generations of Calabrettis. She'd been
tall, slim and elegant. With auburn hair and hazel eyes. "It's
strange about Sophia," she said. "Somehow, Max seems…
protective of her, of her memory. Or maybe it's just that he
never says much about her, about his life with her."

"You're worried about that?"

"I guess so. A little. It's like…there's a mystery there."

"Think how you'd feel if he never *stopped* talking about
her."

Lani considered that option. "Good point. I suppose I
should just admit I'm jealous of her. She was so beautiful.
The daughter of a Spanish grandee. And I've heard the stories. That they had loved each other since they were children, that they always knew they would marry."

"Yeah. And they married early. I think Rule told me they
were both twenty. Pretty young."

"Maybe it's just that he will never get over her, really,
and that bothers me. I mean, who wants to compete with
a memory?"

For that remark, Syd gave her an eye-roll. "Well, you
could start by not borrowing trouble. The man is showing
clear intent when it comes to you. He's heard your darkest,
deepest secrets and he's still hanging in. He's bringing you
to breakfast with the family."

"Okay, I hear you. I've got nothing to complain about."

"The big question is do you want to be the Princess Consort one of these days?"

"Oh, come on."

"What do you mean, come on? It could happen. It seriously could. You know how the Bravo-Calabrettis are.

They marry for love. If you two have that, well, wedding bells will be ringing."

"No, they won't."

"They could. They absolutely could."

"Syd, everyone knows that Max is never getting married again."

"Everyone *assumes* that Max is never getting married again. That doesn't mean he won't."

"Yes, it does. He told me so himself, months and months ago."

"Wait a minute. You two discussed getting married months and months ago?"

"Not like that, not in terms of him and me. It just came up naturally out of another conversation."

"Another conversation about…?"

"Syd, honestly. You are so pushy sometimes."

"It's part of my charm. Another conversation about…?"

Lani gave in and told her. "The Prince's Marriage Law." The controversial law decreed that each of Montedoro's princes and princesses had to marry by age thirty-three or be stripped of all titles and disinherited. The law was put in place to help ensure early marriages, like Max's to Sophia, because early marriages are more likely to be fertile and provide potential heirs to the throne. "We were in the library at night, just Max and me, and we were discussing the Marriage Law. We went on from there to talking about marriage in general. I told him how I didn't think I was even cut out for marriage, or that I would ever have children. And he said he understood, that he didn't plan to marry again, either."

Syd made a humphing sound. "That is all just so wrong in so many ways."

"It's how I feel—and how he feels, too. Not everybody wants to get married. Not everyone is cut out to be a mother."

"If anyone is cut out to be a mom, it's you. You're letting what happened in the past steal your future from you."

"Syd. I'll say it again. It's how I feel." Ellie stirred in her arms. Syd opened her mouth to argue, but Lani put a finger to her lips and pointed at the baby. They were quiet for a moment, waiting, as Ellie sighed and settled back into sleep.

Syd whispered, gently now, "People change. You might find, as time goes by, that you want a life with the right man, you want children of your own to raise. And as for Max, well, whatever he said in the library months and months ago, that was then."

"Then?"

"Yeah, *then,* when you were calling yourselves 'friends.' Everything is different now."

"Not *that* different."

"Oh, yeah. *That* different. Wait and see. And remember this conversation, because one of these days in the not-too-distant future, I'm really looking forward to saying I told you so."

After she left Syd, Lani went to the library and worked for a while. The ancient librarian, Oliver Laurent, greeted her with more enthusiasm than he'd ever shown her before. He brought her some reference books she needed on Montedoran law in the sixteenth century to help her work out a plot point. And then he congratulated her on her big sale.

"His Highness Maximilian told me about it a week ago," the librarian said. "He's quite pleased, as are we all—and really, you've been coming here to work and study for almost two years now. I think it's time you called me Oliver."

"I would like that. But you will have to call me Lani."

He said he would be delighted. And then he slid her a

sly sideways glance. "You will be sure and tell us when the books will be available?"

Lani took the hint. She thanked him for his good wishes and promised to provide signed copies to the library, to him personally and to his assistants as soon as she received her author's copies—which, she warned, would be more than a year away for the first of the three books.

At four, she went out into the gardens looking for Gerta, who often brought Constance and Nick outside after school. Gerta greeted her with a hug. Connie had a friend over. They were playing with their dolls a few feet from the bench where Gerta sat.

Lani sat next to Gerta and asked, "Where's Nick?"

"Still at school." Both Nick and Connie attended Montedoro's highly rated International School. "They have an after-school swim program now."

"That's perfect for Nicky. He can swim off some of that energy."

"He's a handful, all right. How's the new place?"

"Cozy."

"Ah. You like it, I think."

"I do. And Gerta, I…" Somehow, she didn't know how to go on.

A small smile tipped the corner of the older nanny's mouth. "You and His Highness, eh?"

Lani stole a quick glance at the two little girls. They were busy with their dolls, lost in their own world. "How did you know?"

"I have eyes. And ears. Also, you should have seen his face when I told him you were no longer Trev and Ellie's nanny and that you had left the palace."

Lani felt more than a little ashamed. "He was really angry that I didn't tell him."

"Oh, yes. He was tense and preoccupied for days. Then

last night late, I thought I heard him go out. And this morning at breakfast he was all smiles."

"We worked it out, I guess you could say. And tonight, we're going to dinner."

Gerta nodded. "He's a good man, the prince. He was the sweetest little boy, so helpful and kind. I keep hoping Nicky will grow to be more like him."

"It's the age. Most eight-year-olds are ready to run the world—or at least to knock themselves out trying to get things their way." Lani still wasn't sure of how Gerta felt about her seeing Max. "You're…okay then, with the idea of Max and me spending time together?"

"You make His Highness happy. And I did help to raise him. He may be a grown man, but to me, he's still the good little boy who always wanted to do the right thing and would tell me he loved me when I tucked him in his bed at night. So if you make him happy, I'm happy." Gerta patted her hand. "The question is, are *you?*"

"Yes, of course, I…" She blew out a slow breath. "I have to admit. It's all kind of new and scary."

"Only if you make it that way," said Gerta. "Life is short. Savor every minute."

"I'll try."

Gerta tipped her face up to the thin winter sun. "I admit it might get a little difficult when the press gets hold of it."

"Don't remind me."

"You'll be fine. Do what they all do, all the Bravo-Calabrettis. Hold your head high, show them no weakness and never let them see you cry."

Max came to get her that night in a black limousine. His driver held the door for her and she ducked into the waiting embrace of the smooth leather seat.

But she wasn't careful enough of her short black dress.

It rode way up. The driver shut the door and she tried to be subtle about tugging the skirt back down where it belonged.

Max watched her plucking at her hem, a smile flirting with those fine lips of his, looking every inch the prince in one of those suits that probably cost more than she made in a year—well, last year anyway. This year would be better due to that nice, fat advance check she was getting.

"Nervous?" He leaned a little closer. He smelled wonderful, as always, a heady combination of subtle, expensive aftershave and pure manliness.

"I feel…I don't know. Naked, somehow."

He leaned closer. "You're not. You look beautiful and all the naughty bits are covered."

She poked him with her elbow as the driver pulled away from the curb. "It's not what I meant."

He grew more serious. "You're still afraid to be seen in public with me."

She put on her seat belt. "Well, yeah. I mean, being as how you're such a complete loser and all."

He hadn't hooked his seat belt. So it was easy for him to slide the rest of the way across the plush leather. He put his arm around her. "You're mean when you're nervous. I don't care. I like you next to me, whatever mood you're in."

She liked having his arm around her, liked the feel of him, of all that hot and muscled good-smelling manliness pressed against her side. "If we get in a wreck, you could go through the windshield."

He nuzzled her neck. "I'll take my chances."

"Spoken like a man born to privilege."

He caught her ear and worried it a little between his teeth. She felt a rush of heat across her skin. "I love to touch you. I love that you're finally *letting* me touch you…."

She couldn't stop herself. She turned to him. They shared a kiss. It was slow and very sweet. The feel of his mouth on hers was a miracle to her. She could just climb in there and swim around in all that heat and wetness. Finally, she whispered against his lips, "I'm not walking into a restaurant on your arm looking like I just had sex in the car. So slide back to your side of the seat, please."

He chuckled. But he did as she asked. "It's going to be fine. No one will bother us. You'll see."

"I know that. I've seen how careful the reporters are here." In Montedoro, the tabloid journos kept their distance from the princely family. Security was unobtrusive, but everywhere. Reporters and photographers who got out of line were quickly escorted to the French border and invited firmly never to return. "It's only…"

"Say it." He did that thing, holding her eyes, making her feel she could trust him with anything. Her life. Her future. Everything she'd almost thrown away in the past.

She tried to explain. "Everything's changed overnight. Since New Year's, I've been running away from you. Now I need to stay right here beside you. I'm not sure of how to do that yet."

He offered his hand. She took it and twined her fingers with his. His touch soothed her frazzled nerves. "I'm here." He made the two words into a promise. "Hold on to me."

She dredged up a smile for him, one that hardly trembled at all.

The restaurant was beautiful, in the Triangle d'Or, the area of exclusive shops and hotels in the harbor area near the casino. And Max was right about how they wouldn't be bothered.

Yes, people stared when she walked in on Max's arm, but then they went back to their own meals, their private conversations. The staff was right there when needed, invisible when not. And if paparazzi lurked nearby, she never spotted one.

As the meal progressed, she relaxed a little. They talked of things they always used to talk about, before New Year's. He brought her up to date on his progress with his second nonfiction book, a chronicle of Montedoro's two hundred years as a Spanish protectorate. They discussed her new contract and her plans to go to New York in a couple of months, as soon as she finished the book she was working on. She would meet with Marie and with her new editor.

Max said he would be speaking at Columbia University in April. He sipped the really excellent Cabernet he'd ordered for them. "Let's go together, combine business with pleasure."

The unreality of all of it—the two of them, out for an evening like any two ordinary people might do, casually discussing a trip together—hit her all over again. "Can we get through breakfast Sunday with your family before we start planning for two months out?"

He ate a bite of artichoke heart. "Fair enough," he replied in a neutral tone.

After that, he seemed a little subdued. Not withdrawn, exactly, but careful. She knew it was her fault, for being snippy and difficult. She knew she should apologize.

But she was feeling just edgy enough that she'd probably only hurt his feelings again. Better for him to be on his guard against her.

The lamb came. It was fabulous. They had soft cheeses with wonderful little bits of crusty bread. And the dessert cart pretty much took her breath away.

She couldn't decide.

He told the waiter, "We'll have the chocolate cake and the crème brûlée."

She saw no reason to argue. "Good choices."

He shrugged. "Someone had to make a decision."

She felt defensiveness rise, and reminded herself that she'd already been crabby enough for one evening. So she beamed a big smile at the waiter. "Put the chocolate cake right here in front of me."

They shared both desserts. She tried to have only a taste or two. But she ended up unable to resist devouring every last bite of the cake. He ate most of the crème brûlée, so she told herself they were even.

There were more stares when they left the restaurant. But really, the curious glances weren't that hard to ignore. Lani started thinking that being stared at all the time was like anything else. If it happened enough, you got used to it. Maybe eventually, she would be like Max, confident and graceful in just about any situation.

When they stood outside across from the casino and the world-famous Fountain of the Three Sirens, he asked, "Would you like to play the tables for a while?"

She answered truthfully. "I would rather be alone with you."

He put his hand at the small of her back then, the light touch possessive and also somehow tender. She sucked in a sharp breath and glanced up into his waiting eyes.

"There you are," he whispered, for her ears alone. "Good to see you again."

"All right," she confessed. "I *have* been nervous."

"Not so much anymore?"

"It's getting better all the time."

The long black car drifted up and stopped at the curb in front of them. They got in. When he pulled her into the circle of his arm, she didn't even complain about the safety issues of driving around without her seat belt.

She put her head on his shoulder. "Where are we going?"

He touched his lips to her hair. "Around the block. I have a villa on Avenue d'Vancour."

"Your villa." Just the two of them. Alone. "Perfect."

Five minutes later, he still had his arm around her. Her head was comfortably tucked into his shoulder. And they were driving in circles.

She observed, "It's a very long way around the block."

He ran his hand down her bare arm, stirring a row of happy goose bumps. "Evasion maneuvers, just throwing off any nosy reporters—here we are."

"It's beautiful." In the classic Mediterranean style, the two-story villa was yellow stucco with white trim. The driver turned the car into the side driveway that curved around to the back.

They got out onto a walkway paved in white stone. In-ground lights showed them the way, across a pretty patio to a pair of French doors. Light glowed from within. Max ushered her into a living area that adjoined a large open kitchen.

A middle-aged woman in a plain black dress came toward them. Lani recognized her. She was Max's personal housekeeper and cook. "Sir," she said.

"Hello, Marceline."

Marceline gestured at the ice bucket on the low coffee table. "I've opened the champagne and left you a few treats there on the counter, and in the refrigerator."

Max thanked her. With a quick nod, she went out the way they had come in. He shrugged out of his jacket and tossed it across the sofa. Then he turned to Lani and smiled, and she realized there was nowhere else she'd rather be than right there, with him. "Let's go upstairs."

"Yes."

He handed her the two flutes waiting on the coffee table and he took the bucket of ice and champagne. They went through a central hallway to the front foyer and up the curving white stairs.

Halfway down the upper hall, he led her into a large bedroom suite. He set the bucket down on the coffee table, took the flutes from her and poured them each a glass.

There was a terrace that looked out over the sea. "Let's go out there," she said.

"It will be chilly."

"Just for a minute."

So they went out on the terrace and admired the Mediterranean gleaming under the new moon. When she shivered, he stood behind her and wrapped her in his strong arms.

He brushed a kiss above her ear. "This was my parents' villa. They bought it when they were newlyweds, a quick and easy getaway from the palace. I was almost born here."

"Almost?"

"It's tradition that the heir to the throne should be born at the palace. My mother went into labor here. The story goes that she felt the first twinge at noon and I popped out at a quarter of one. She barely made it to the palace on time." There was laughter in his deep voice. "All of us were like that, eager to get into the world. My mother had easy pregnancies and quick births."

"Which would explain why she was willing to go through all that nine times."

"Eight," he corrected. "Remember, Alex and Dami are twins."

"Oh, well. *Only* eight—and that's just another way your mother is amazing."

"Some have remarked that a ruling princess should be more delicate."

"Jealous much?"

He gathered her closer. "Yes, I believe that they are."

She sipped her champagne and shivered in the wind off the water, even with his warm arms holding her close.

"Ready to go in?" He rubbed his cheek against her hair.

Another shiver went through her, as much from anticipation as the chill in the air. "Yes."

Inside he took her hand and they went to the bed. The covers were drawn invitingly back. He set down his flute on the inlaid night table, took hers and set it beside his.

Then he cradled her face between his two strong hands. "Am I rushing you?" He rubbed his nose against hers, breathing in, scenting her.

Her heart thrummed a deep, hungry rhythm under her breastbone. "No." Breathless. Yearning. "Absolutely not."

He pressed his cheek to hers. Already, she could feel the slight roughness, the beginnings of his dark beard. He said, "The first time I saw you was outside my parents' palace apartment. It was in mid-May, not long after you came here with Sydney. You had Trevor in your arms. You were bringing him to Sydney and Rule, I believe."

She seemed to recall that. "You smiled at me, didn't you?"

He kissed her lips, a brushing caress. "You barely remember."

"Everything was so new, so completely outside of my experience."

"I was just another Bravo-Calabretti prince among so many, eh?"

"Never."

He chuckled against her mouth. "Liar. I knew you hardly saw me. But *I* saw you. I wanted to touch your cheek, to learn the texture of your skin. I wanted to get close enough to know the scent of you."

She hardly knew how to answer. "Oh, Max…"

He took her shoulders and turned her around. "You have

no idea how rare that moment was for me. I find most people interesting. You could say I'm socially adept. It's part of my position as heir, to be good with people. But to be… swept away at the sight of a woman. No. Usually, there's a distance I feel, a need to be careful, to proceed slowly. The sense that I will never really know them, be open to them. Not with you. Right away, I knew I wanted you, wanted to be with you."

His words excited her. They also surprised her. "I had no clue you felt that way."

He went on. "The second time I saw you was in the garden by the topiary hedges, with Trevor again. I ducked away so you wouldn't see me. By then, I'd decided that I was *too* attracted to you and I would be wiser to avoid you."

"Too attracted? Seriously? How could I not have picked up on that?"

"Yes, well. I didn't want you to know."

She leaned back against him. "Ah. Right."

He linked his arms around her waist. "And then I saw you in the library and I was intrigued. I wanted to know what you were doing there, with your laptop, so serious and intent, those charming black-rimmed glasses you wore then sliding down your nose. I asked Oliver Laurent about you. He said he believed you were writing a novel."

She could feel him growing hard against the small of her back and she settled in closer, savoring the power in his arms as they tightened around her. "Yes," she said on a whisper.

"Yes, what?" His voice teased in her ear.

"Yes, I saw you there several times before you ever spoke to me. I knew who you were by then. I remember us sharing nods and polite smiles."

"I kept waiting for my interest in you to fade. I was absolutely certain it would." His palms glided up her rib cage. He cradled her breasts. She gasped, a tiny sound. He pressed his lips against her hair and whispered, "It only got stronger. Finally, I gave in to it and spoke to you."

Even through the fabric of her dress and bra, the feel of his hands on her was so lovely. "I remember that day." She held back a moan of pleasure and felt all the more aroused as he found her nipples with his thumbs. "We argued about Anastagio the Great." An early Calabretti lord, the deposed Anastagio had turned to piracy to reclaim what he'd lost. Later, he'd recaptured Montedoro from the Genoese. "I said he was a genius. You said he was a murdering thief willing to do anything to regain the power he'd lost."

"I'd never met a woman so fascinated by Montedoran history." He nuzzled her ear and continued to do naughty things to her breasts. "Through the whole of our first conversation, your eyes didn't glaze over once."

"It was a fascinating conversation."

"To you and to me, which is exactly my point."

She rubbed back against him, shamelessly. "After that first time we talked, you were always kind to me. Friendly. Easy to talk to—about books and history, about your work and mine, about the children. I knew you liked me. But that you wanted me? I swear, I didn't know, not for months and months. Even when you asked me to dance that first time, I assumed you were only being kind."

"Denial." He breathed the word against her temple.

She confessed it. "Yes. I never let myself admit what was happening between us until I had no choice."

"Until New Year's Eve."

"Yes. New Year's Eve..."

His hands left her breasts. She wanted to grab them back. But then he touched her hair, smoothing it to the side. She understood his intention and reached back to guide the dark strands out of his way. He took the zipper down. "I read you correctly. I knew I would never get near you unless you trusted me first. It took a very long time to gain your trust." He guided the dress forward, off her shoulders. It dropped to her waist.

"I had no idea what you were up to…." She looked down at the twin swells of her breasts cradled in the black lace of her bra. Her skin felt thin and acutely sensitized.

He made her burn by the simple act of running both palms so lightly up and down her bare arms. "You didn't *want* to know what I was up to."

"Max, I…" She tried to turn around to him.

He caught her shoulders and held her in place facing away. "You're not an easy woman to get close to. Still, I want you. Why is that?"

"Um, because you're a glutton for punishment?"

He chuckled then, a rough, low, exciting sound. "There could be some truth in that." And then he buried his face against her neck. He scraped his teeth across her skin and she moaned. "Take off the dress." The words seemed to burn themselves into her yearning flesh.

She eagerly obeyed him, pushing the dress down. It fell to the rug. He took her by the waist and lifted her out of it effortlessly, as though she weighed no more than a glass of champagne, setting her down again closer to the head of the bed, but still facing away from him.

He hooked a finger under the strap of her bra next and guided it down so it fell along her arm. The other received the same treatment. And then he undid the clasp. Instinctively, she lifted her hands and caught the cups against her chest.

"Let it go." A command.

By then, she wanted nothing so much as to obey him. She did. The bra dropped to the side of the bed and slid off to land near the toes of her black high-heeled shoes. She waited, her breath uneven, yearning for him to touch her breasts again.

Instead, he trailed both index fingers slowly along her sides, from just under her arms down into the cove of her waist and outward, following the swells of her hips, pausing at her panties. And then inward, tracing the elastic from each side across her lower belly. Until those clever, knowing fingers met in the middle right below her navel.

Her belly muscles twitched in anticipation.

And he didn't disappoint her. He dipped both fingers lower. She moaned at that, and moaned again when he cupped her through her panties.

He whispered, "Take these off, too." And he let go of her.

Trembling, eager, she did what he commanded. Stumbling a little as she lifted one foot and then the other to get them off and away.

He touched her, his hands on her hips again, steadying her. "Lani…" It sounded so good to her, so right, her name from his mouth. She had no idea at that moment why she had ever run from him. Here, with him, was exactly where she wanted to be.

She stood up straight again.

And he guided her hips, turning her at last, until she was facing him.

A kiss. Sweet, wet. Endless. Her breasts brushed the fabric of his beautiful dress shirt, the slight friction increasing her already considerable arousal. And her hands strayed up, her fingers sifting into his hair, clasping his neck.

Images of their one time before, at the first of the year, floated in her mind. He had seemed shier then, somehow. More careful of her, almost reverent.

Not so reverent now.

More forceful. More sure. She found she was wild for both sides of him. Forceful or tender, his caresses excited her. His kisses carried her away, made her forget all her fears and doubts and hesitations, all her past sins, until there was nothing but the sound of his voice in her ear, the wonder of his hands on her flesh.

He clasped her waist. She gave a soft cry of surprise as he lifted her, setting her down on the side of the bed.

"Don't move," he instructed.

So she sat there on the silky sheet, naked in her high-heeled shoes. He undressed swiftly, in a ruthless economy of movement, shucking everything off from his tie to his socks and silk boxers in no time at all.

His body was so beautiful, broad and strong, the muscles sharply defined beneath bronze skin. He worked out several times a week in the training yards of the Sovereign's Guard, he'd told her. *I'm a geek and proud of it. A very fit geek.*

She grinned at the memory, and kicked off her shoes.

He bent close so suddenly that she gasped. "What's funny?"

"You." She kissed him, quick and hard. "Total geek, really buff."

He caught her mouth again and kissed her endlessly, wrapping his arms around her as he did it, coming down to the bed with her, rolling until she was on top. She braced on her hands and gazed down at him.

And then he smiled. Slowly. "I have you where I want you now."

She'd ended up with her knees to each side of his lean waist and he was pressed against her in exactly the right spot. "Or maybe *I* have you...."

He slid a hand down between them. She hitched in a hungry breath as he touched her. "Wet," he said softly, appreciatively.

With a low, pleasured sound, she bent close and kissed him again.

And then they were rolling. And he was on top. She looked up into his eyes as he caressed her, making her wetter, hotter, ready for him. He groaned and he bent his head and captured her breast as below he went on caressing her.

She threaded her fingers in his hair, holding him to her as he drew her nipple into the wetness beyond his lips, as he touched her, fingers delving in. It was good. It was so sweet. Without shadows, without fear.

Right now, she was lost in him, joyfully, all her worry and hesitation about where they might go from here banished. Gone.

He rolled her on top again, pulling her down to him, kissing her, deep and slow and endlessly. And then they were on their sides, facing each other. He said her name. She gave his back to him.

Within that sweet heat pulsing between them like a beating heart, the past didn't matter and the future was of no concern. He wrapped her close, scooted back—and pulled open the little drawer in the bedside table. He took out a condom.

They laughed together, breathless and eager, as he fumbled to get the wrapper off.

"Here. I'll do it." She took it from him and managed it easily.

He said, "Well done."

And then she rolled it down over him smoothly, fitting it snugly at the base. "I do good work."

"Come here." He flipped her onto her back once more and rose up above her.

She opened to him, reaching up to bring him down to her, taking his weight gratefully, wrapping her legs around him, crying out as he entered her in one smooth, hard thrust.

"Wait." He held still, hips flexed, fully within her.

"Oh, my…"

He braced his forearms on the pillow, to each side of her head. "Still. Be still. Don't move."

"Oh, my, oh, my…"

He lowered his mouth and he kissed her, his tongue sliding inside, tasting her as deeply as he was buried in her below.

She ached with the pleasure of it. She moaned into his mouth. And still, he held steady as he went on kissing her.

Finally, when she thought she would go mad with the sheer unbearable goodness of it, with the burning need to move, he lifted his head and he stared down at her, eyes gone from iron-gray to the sweetest, cleanest blue.

She panted, dazed, gazing up at him. "Now? Please?"

His mouth twitched. "Say that again?"

She punched him on his big arm. "You are torturing me."

He was merciless. "Again."

"Please?"

"Please what?"

"Please, Max, I need to move."

"Ah. Move? Really?" And then he did it. A smooth, hard flex of his powerful hips. "Like this?"

She had no words left. Which wasn't really a bad thing. Because finally, he was willing.

He did it again. "Answer me. Like this?"

"Yes," she somehow managed to croak out.

"Say it again."

And she did. "Yes. Yes, yes, yes…"

And at last, they were moving. Moving together. Rising and falling, faster and harder. Until there was only the two of them on a high wave of pleasure, rising and rising higher, opening outward to light up the night.

Chapter Six

"I'm not sure about Sunday," she told him a little bit later, as they stood in the kitchen wearing matching silk robes he'd pulled from a closet, drinking champagne and eating red-hearted slices of a Montedoran orange.

He reached out, wrapped a hand around the back of her neck and brought her right up close to him. "Forget it. You're not backing out." He kissed her.

She tasted the oranges, tart and sweet, as she sighed into his mouth. "It seems a little too soon, that's all."

He looked at her patiently. "All right. I'll play along. Too soon? How do you figure that?"

She stammered out the best explanation she could think of on such short notice. "Well, I mean, we really only barely got something going between us last night. You know, in a real, sincere, both-on-the-same-page and we-want-to-be-together kind of way."

His eyes were iron-gray. But at least he wasn't scowling. Then, unfortunately, he started talking. "I'm not going to argue with you about it. I'm not going to point out that we should have been together months ago, but you needed forever to admit that this is important, this thing between us."

"But you *are* arguing."

"No, *you* are. You're going. No excuses." He offered her

a slice of orange. She pushed it away. That didn't stop him from reminding her, "You agreed to go. Keep your word. Do not disappoint me."

"You used to be so patient."

"And look where being patient got me."

"If you would only—"

"No. I mean it. There is no 'if only' here. Last night, you made a choice to tell me your secrets, to go forward with me. You said you would go to Sunday breakfast. There's nothing to argue about here. You're going."

She thought of his children then. "What have you told Nick and Constance about me?"

He looked at her sideways. "What do you mean?"

"Do they know I'm invited for Sunday morning?"

He gazed off toward the French doors. "Well, I…"

She drew in a breath and let it out slowly. "You haven't talked to them."

"I only thought—"

"Max. Come on. You *didn't* think."

He got that look, his I'm-the-prince-and-you're-not look. "We have to start somewhere."

"And we have. We went out. We're here, in your villa, sharing champagne and oranges after mind-altering sex."

His lips twitched. "Mind-altering, was it?"

"I'm only asking why you need to rush things."

"I'm not rushing. You are dragging your feet. I will tell Nick and Connie that you'll be with us for Sunday breakfast."

Another awful thought occurred to her. "You *have* told your parents I'll be there, right?" The silence was deafening. "Oh, God, Max. You haven't told them. You're bringing me to a private family breakfast—and I'm a surprise."

"It's not a formal event. It's easy and comfortable, open-ended. There's plenty of food for whoever can make it.

Husbands, wives, children, dear friends, girlfriends, boy-friends and all variety of significant others are welcome."

"Meaning you *haven't* told them."

"I just explained. It's not necessary that I tell them."

"Oh, really? How many significant others have you brought to your family's Sunday breakfast since you lost your wife?"

He set down his empty champagne flute. Slowly. "All right. You're the first."

"So it's very likely I will be a surprise. Possibly a big surprise. I don't want to be a big surprise. If you're going to hold me to this—"

"I am. Absolutely."

"Then you will tell your parents and your children that I will be there."

He picked up the bottle and poured them each another glass. "All right. I'll tell them."

She didn't know whether to be relieved—or more anxious than ever. "I still think it's too soon."

"You're going. That's that."

All her clothes were wrong.

Lani knew this because the contents of her closet were strewn across the bed and she still hadn't decided what to wear to Sunday breakfast with the princely family. Yeah, okay. She should have given it some thought before now. But she'd been busy all day Saturday writing and researching—not to mention creating her Facebook profile and fan page, setting up a Twitter account, reserving her domain name and signing up for a couple of online classes.

Who had time to think about what to wear? She stood in front of the mirror mounted on the closet door and scowled at her reflection. There was nothing wrong with her slim gray skirt and blue silk blouse—but nothing particularly right about them, either.

She'd pinned her hair up. Should she take it down?

The intercom down the hall buzzed. That would be the driver of the car Max had insisted on sending for her.

"Oh, help!" she moaned aloud. And then she grabbed her gray suede pumps and her blue faux crocodile purse and raced to the door.

The driver let her off at the palace entrance closest to Max's apartments.

The guard there checked her ID against his handheld device and admitted her with a quick nod. She hurried down one gorgeous hallway and then another, the heels of her pumps echoing on the inlaid floors. When she got to Max's door, she paused to smooth her hair and straighten her blouse. A buzzer sounded inside when she pushed the little button by the door.

The housekeeper, Marceline, answered with a polite smile and a pleasant, "Come in. They're almost ready, I believe."

"Lani. You're right on time." Max entered the foyer from the apartment's central hall, wearing tan slacks and yet another beautiful soft sweater, looking casual and confident and way, way hot—and making her certain all over again that her clothes were all wrong. He herded Nick and Connie in front of him.

Nick, in dark pants and a striped shirt, his cowlick slicked mercilessly down, complained, "If I *have* to go, let me at least bring my Nerf gun." He glanced up at his father, who shook his head. "Bow and arrow? Slingshot?" Max only kept moving his head from side to side. "This is going to be so *bo*-ring."

"You'll get through it," Max said. He really was so patient with the kids.

Nick glanced back at Max again. Something in his father's eyes must have reached him, because he stopped complaining.

Max said, "Thanks, Marceline." She nodded and circled around him and the children on her way to the central hall. Max and the kids reached Lani. "You made it," he said softly. He looked so happy to see her, she forgot all about how she hated her gray skirt and she still wasn't sure she even wanted to do this.

Connie, looking a little flushed in a darling red dress and sweater over white tights with Mary Janes, was tugging on Lani's hand. "Nanny Lani, I don't feel so good," she said in a near whisper.

"Oh, honey…" Lani felt her forehead.

Max said, "What?"

"I don't know. She's not feverish."

And then Connie said, "Oh!" Her eyes went saucer wide and she put her hand on her stomach.

"What?" Max demanded again.

Alarm jangled through Lani. "Honey, are you going to be sick?"

"I…" It was the only word Connie managed. Then she vomited on Lani's gray suede shoes.

For a moment, they all four just stared down at Lani's splattered shoes in stunned disbelief.

Nicky broke the shocked silence with a howl. "Oh, gross! Connie barfed all over Nanny Lani!" He put his hands to his throat and faked a loud string of gagging noises.

Max shot him a dark look. "Nicholas." Nicky dropped his hands and had the good sense not to let out another peep. Max gave Lani a quick, apologetic glance and then knelt and laid a gentle hand on Connie's shoulder. "Sweetheart…"

Connie blinked at him—and gagged again.

Lani's inner nanny took over. She dropped her purse, scooped up the little girl and headed for the bathroom, not even pausing to see if Max followed, hoping against hope that she wouldn't end up with vomit down her back to go with what already squished in her shoes.

She did not get her wish. Connie let loose again just as she made it to the bathroom door.

Lani gulped against her own gag reflex and kept moving. Grabbing a big towel from the linen rack, she bent with Connie in her arms and spread the towel on the rug by the tub. "It's okay, okay," she soothed as she let the little girl down on the soft rug in front of the towel. Lani's mother, the pediatrician, had always offered a towel rather than the toilet in a situation like this. Kids found it less disturbing—if it was possible to be less disturbed when the contents of your stomach refused to stay down. "Right here. Just bend over this towel. That's right. That's it. Easy…" On her knees now, Connie kept gagging. Kneeling beside her, Lani rubbed her back and held her blond curls out of the way as more came up. Lani flipped the edges of the towel over to cover the mess.

Max came in quietly and stood over them. "More towels?" At Lani's nod, he went to the linen shelves and came back with three more. He dropped to the floor on Connie's other side.

Lani kept up the soft encouragements. "That's good. Just let it happen. You'll feel better, sweetie, it's okay…."

Connie moaned and more came up. Max put down a new towel over the soiled one.

Finally, Connie sighed and slumped against her dad. "I think I'm all done." The poor little thing looked wrung out.

Lani levered back on her heels and stood. "Where's her water glass?"

"The pink one," Max said.

So Lani grabbed the pink plastic glass from the counter by the sink. She splashed in a little children's mouthwash from the medicine cabinet and then filled it halfway with water. "Here." Max reached up and took it from her. "She shouldn't drink any, just rinse—and wait a minute." Lani quickly rolled up the soiled towels and pushed them out of the way, all the time acutely aware that she herself was probably the worst-smelling thing in the room now. "Can you stand up, Connie? So you can use the sink?"

"I think so."

Max rose and helped her up. She rinsed out her mouth as Lani ran cold water from the bathtub tap over a washcloth. She wrung it out and gave it to Max, who bathed Connie's face with it.

Max looked kind of sheepish. "I had no idea she was sick."

"I *wasn't* sick," Connie insisted. "But then, all of a sudden, I *was*."

"Probably just a stomach bug." Lani stayed well away from father and daughter and tried not to think about the sticky wetness down her back and the mess in her shoes. "I think I remember Gerta saying there was some stomach thing going around at school."

"I've called the family doctor," Max said. "He's on his way." He asked Connie, "How about a little rest?"

"Papa…" Connie sighed and reached up her arms to him. He scooped her up.

Gerta appeared in the doorway. "I have your bed ready, *Liebchen*."

Lani suggested, "Along with more fresh towels?"

"All taken care of." Gerta kept a cheerful expression on her face and didn't once glance down at Lani's ruined shoes.

"Nanny Lani." Wide eyes regarded her solemnly over Max's broad shoulder. "Sorry I got throw-up all over you."

"It's not your fault. It washes off and I'll be good as new." *And I hate this skirt anyway.* She had, however, loved the suede shoes. "Rest and get better."

"I'll take her," Gerta offered.

But Connie wanted her dad right then. She hugged Max tighter. "Papa will take me." And then, just a tad imperiously, "And Nanny Gerta, you come, too."

"I am right here with you," Gerta promised tenderly.

Max sent Lani a rueful glance. "I'll be back."

They all three went out, leaving her standing there in her ruined shoes, unsure of whether she ought to try and clean up a little or wait for Max to return.

She was just about to shuck off the disgusting shoes and rinse her feet in the tub, at least, when Marceline bustled in with a fluffy white robe and a laundry bag over one arm, a basket of shower accessories on the other. Lani's blue purse was hooked over her shoulder. "You poor girl." She put the purse and the robe on the chest that stood against the wall. "Get out of those clothes. I'll see what I can do about them."

Lani took off the shoes first. "I think these are hopeless—and watch where you step. It's all over the floor here, and at the door, and in the foyer, too."

Marceline was undaunted. "Not to worry. I will take care of everything while you're in the shower."

Twenty minutes later, with Connie safely tucked in bed and Gerta comfortably situated in the corner chair watching over her, Max went to find Lani.

She was sitting on the edge of the tub in the children's bathroom wearing his robe, her cheeks pink and her pulled-back hair coming loose around her face in the most charming fashion. Marceline had done her magic. The floor was clean and the air smelled faintly of citrus.

Lani regarded him solemnly, an elbow on her knee and her chin on her hand. "How is she?"

He took a moment to answer, indulging himself in the sight of her, in his apartment, wearing his robe. "She's resting. Gerta took her temperature. It's slightly elevated. The doctor should be here soon."

"Good, then." She rose as he came toward her. "I didn't know where to go. It seemed inappropriate to start wandering around your palace apartment barefoot in a robe." Down the hall, the entry buzzer rang. "I'm guessing that's the doctor."

"Marceline will answer it." He took her shoulders. Her upturned face was dewy. She smelled of soap and roses. "Anywhere you wander, I will find you." He tugged on a curl that had gotten loose from the knot at the back of her head. It coiled, damp and tempting, down her neck. "You were a champion with Connie."

A smile bloomed. "Nanny Lani to the rescue." She teased, "And what do you know? I think we're kind of late for breakfast with the princely family."

"Do you have to look so happy to get out of it?"

Now she played innocent. "Happy? Me? No way. Poor Connie is sick and I'm out a favorite pair of shoes—and do you think you could send someone to my apartment to get me some actual clothes to wear?"

"I like you in my robe."

"How many ways can I say 'inappropriate'?"

"Yes, I will send someone to get your clothes."

"Thank you."

"And you'll come to Sunday breakfast *next* week." The postponement was probably just as well. He'd told the children that she was coming, as he'd promised her he would.

However, he hadn't quite gotten around to giving his mother and father a heads-up on his plans. Now he'd have time to take care of that.

As usual, she tried to back out. "I'll think about next Sunday."

"Do we have to go through this all over again? Just say yes now."

"Don't boss me around." She faked an angry scowl.

He took the shawl collar of the robe in both hands and tenderly kissed the end of her nose. "Please."

"I know what you're doing," she grumbled.

"I just want a yes out of you."

"You *always* want a yes out of me."

He couldn't resist. He buried his nose against her neck, sucked in the wonderful scent of her shower-moist skin and growled, "So give me what I want."

She laughed and playfully pushed him away—and then stiffened, her laughter catching on a gasp. Turning, Max followed the direction of her startled gaze.

Nick was standing in the doorway, watching them.

Chapter Seven

A few choice obscenities scrolled through Max's brain.

How long had Nick been there? What exactly had he seen?

A teasing embrace. A kiss on the neck.

Nothing that traumatic, surely.

"Nicky." Max managed to keep his tone even and easy. "What is it?"

Nick just went on staring, his face flushed scarlet.

Max tried again. "Nicky?"

Nick opened his mouth and said in a rush, "Marceline said to tell you the doctor's here." And then he ducked from the doorway and vanished from sight.

Max called after him, "Nicky!"

Lani touched his shoulder. He turned back to her and she suggested softly, "You'd better go after him and make sure he's all right."

"Lani, I…" He let the words trail off, mostly because he felt like the world's biggest idiot. What was he thinking, grabbing her like that with the door wide open?

"Go on," she said. "Check on Nick. Deal with the doctor."

He dared to touch that sweet loose curl again. "I've made a complete balls up of this, haven't I?"

At least she smiled. "It's not the end of the world. Go on. I'll be fine here."

* * *

He went to the foyer first.

Dr. Montaigne, who'd been curing the ills of the princely family for decades, waited in a carved mahogany hall chair, his old-school black bag on his lap. He jumped up when Max appeared.

Max greeted him and led him back to Connie's room.

Connie knew the doctor. He always took care of her when she was sick. "Dr. Montaigne," she said gravely. "I've been very sick and it was very sudden and I threw up all over Nanny Lani."

Old Montaigne set his bag by the bed. "Well, well, young lady. Let's have a look at you, shall we?"

"Will you check me with your stethoscope?"

"Excellent idea. We'll start with that."

Max edged close to Gerta. "I'll be back. I need a moment with Nicky…" He ducked out as the old doctor started taking Connie's vital signs.

Max found his son in the first place he looked—Nick's room. The door was wide open and he was lying on his bed with his tablet computer. Max stood in the doorway for a moment, watching him, a cautious feeling of relief moving through him.

Nick hadn't run off somewhere to hide. He'd just gone to his room. And he'd even left his door open. Surely that was a good sign.

Max knocked on the door frame.

Nick glanced at him—and went right back to his game. It was hardly an invitation to talk. On the other hand, he hadn't asked Max to leave him alone.

Max dared to enter. He went to the bed and sat carefully on the edge of it. Nick went on playing his game. Lego figures drove an armored car wildly through a Lego city. Max watched a chain of vehicles careen across the screen and tried to come up with a credible opening.

All he could think of was, "Nicky…"

Nick played on, kicking his stocking feet against the coverlet as he manipulated the armored car on the screen. But then, finally, he did say, "What?"

"I…want to talk to you about…" God in heaven, how to even begin? He'd never realized before what a terrible father he was. On any number of levels. "…about Nanny Lani and me in the bathroom." He tried not to wince as the words came out of his mouth. One day he would rule Montedoro. Right now, he didn't even know how to talk to his son.

Nick tossed the tablet aside and sat up, swinging his feet over the edge of the bed. For a moment, Max was sure he would leap to the floor and run off again. But instead he kicked his heels against the side of the mattress and accused, "You said she was coming for breakfast."

"That's right. And she did."

"I thought that was kind of weird, Nanny Lani coming to breakfast in Grandmother's apartment with us."

"Because she isn't part of our family?"

"Well, she's not." He kicked the mattress for emphasis. "And nannies don't come and eat with the family."

"Sometimes they do. Sometimes Gerta eats with us in the kitchen."

"That's different than Sunday breakfast. You know that it is."

"Nick, I…I happen to like Lani. I like her very much." Was this going well? He guessed not.

"Papa." A swift, angry glare. "You were *kissing* her neck." He seemed to suppress a shudder. "And she's not even a nanny anymore, really. Trev told me so."

"It's true she's not taking care of Trevor and Ellie any-

more. She has another job now. She writes books. And I...
well, Nick, I like her very much."

Nick stared straight ahead. "You already said that once,"
he muttered. "I heard you the first time, you know."

"You're right. I said it twice because I want you to know
that Lani is important to me and that's why I kissed her."

"Is she your *girlfriend?*"

"Yes. That is exactly what she is."

Silence from Nicky. He kicked his feet some more. Max
gritted his teeth and waited for his son to speak of Sophia,
to say how he missed her and no other woman better try
to take her place.

What was Max going to say to that? He had nothing.
Zero. He was dealing with this on the fly and he knew he
wasn't up to the challenge. As a rule, he liked to plan ahead
before tackling sensitive subjects with the children. Frantically, he cast about for something brilliant and fatherly
to contribute, all about how of course, Lani wouldn't be
taking Sophia's place. Sophia was Nicky's mother and always would be.

Was that completely self-evident and painfully obvious?
He had a sinking feeling it was.

Then Nick said, "So. Since Connie got sick, I guess we
don't have to go to Sunday breakfast, after all."

Max said nothing. He was too busy trying to decide if
he should bring up the subject of Sophia.

"Papa? Did you *hear* me?"

"Erm, yes, I did. And no, we won't be going to Sunday
breakfast this week."

"But next week we will?"

"Next week, yes."

Nick grew thoughtful. Would he speak of his mother
now? Max prepared himself to provide gentle fatherly re-
assurance. Finally, Nicky said, "Sunday breakfast isn't *that*

bad. It's just that I'm the oldest. Lately, Connie is always wearing dresses and playing with her dolls. And Trev is okay, but I mean, he's only four. And the rest of them are babies." All right. Nothing about Sophia. Should he just let it go? "Papa, there's just no one to play with at Sunday breakfast."

"Sometimes you have to go places where there's no one to play with."

"Yuck."

Max couldn't bear this. He had to say *something*. "Nick, I just want you to know that your mother loved you very much and she will always be your mother. No one could ever take her place."

Nick sent him a look of great patience. "I know that."

"Well, good. Wonderful." He waited, but Nick said no more. So he prompted, "And…is there anything more you'd like me to explain to you about Lani and me?"

Nicky's brow furrowed. "You never had a girlfriend before."

"Does that bother you, that I have one now?"

He thought some more. "It's okay."

"You're sure?"

"Papa, why do I have to keep telling you things over and over again?" He spoke with more inflection now, and rolled his hand in a circle for emphasis.

Max took heart. The animated Nicky he knew and loved was back. Apparently he wasn't scarred for life, after all. "Sorry. Anything more you need to know from me?"

"Well, if she's not Nanny Lani anymore, what I am s'posed to call her?"

"What would you like to call her?" Was that a dangerous question to ask an eight-year-old boy? Too late now.

"Um. Miss Lani maybe?"

Not bad. Max hooked an arm around his son. "That sounds just fine to me."

"Yeah." Nick leaned into Max's hold and swung his feet some more. "Miss Lani. I think that's good." Max nodded. For a moment, the two of them just sat there, together, as Nick kicked his heels against the bed. Then Nick said, "Where *is* Miss Lani?"

And that reminded him that he'd left her in the bathroom and he'd better get moving. "She's still here. And right now, I need to go and see what the doctor says about how Connie's doing. Do you want to come with me?"

Nick looked up at him. He could see echoes of Sophia in the bow of his mouth, the tilt of his nose. "Do you think she's going to puke again?" His eyes gleamed with eagerness. Nick found bodily functions endlessly fascinating.

"Let's hope not." Max got up. "Are you coming?"

Nick slid off the bed, put on his shoes and went with him.

In Connie's room, Dr. Montaigne was finishing up. "She should rest for the day," he instructed. "Give her liquids, starting with a half glass of juice or a little clear broth. If that stays down, she can have more…." The old guy droned on. Max listened and nodded and promised to call if Connie took a turn for the worse.

Then Connie started in about how she felt "all better" and wanted French toast. Max left Gerta to the job of keeping her in bed for a while. He needed to send the doctor on his way and get back to Lani, who'd been sitting in the bathroom for at least half an hour since the *last* time he left her in there.

What a disaster. He'd probably never get her to come near the apartment or either of his children ever again.

They had to walk past the bathroom on the way to the door. He glanced in and there she was, perched patiently on the edge of the tub, reading a magazine Marceline must have found for her, that tempting curl of hair brushing the collar of his robe. She spotted him with the doctor and Nick, and waved him on.

And he realized he couldn't bear to leave her there another minute. It just wasn't right. He turned to Nicky. "Nicholas, will you see the doctor the rest of the way out?"

"Yes! And then I want to eat because I am *starving*."

"Once you show the doctor out, find Marceline. Ask her to order up breakfast for us."

"Yes, I will! This way, Dr. Montaigne."

"Thank you, young man." He trotted off in Nicky's wake.

Max detoured into the bathroom.

Apprehension in those big dark eyes, Lani set her magazine on the edge of the tub and stood. "How did it go with Nick?"

He wanted to touch her. But no. He'd learned his lesson on that score. Anyone might go strolling by the bathroom at any time. "Overall, I think it went well. He says he has no problem with your being my girlfriend. And he's decided to call you Miss Lani now. Trevor told him that you're not a nanny anymore."

"I'm glad he's all right. What about Connie?"

"She says she wants French toast."

Lani laughed. She really did have a fine laugh, rich and husky and full out. "She'll be back to normal in no time." She straightened the robe. "I had Marceline call for a driver to go to my place for clean clothes. He'll be here any minute to pick up my key."

"Good."

Nick materialized in the doorway and announced, "Marceline says she has enough food in the little kitchen to make us breakfast." The main kitchen was downstairs and served regular meals for palace guests and residents alike. But the apartment had its own small galley kitchen, too. "She said to ask is that all right with you?"

"Yes, that would be fine."

"Good. She can cook it fast so that I don't *die* from *hunger*." He put his arms out in front of him and made monster sounds.

Lani laughed.

Nick grew suddenly shy. "Um. Hi, Miss Lani."

"Hello, Nick."

He glanced hopefully at Max. "Marceline said she'll make toast with strawberry jam."

"Go on then," Max said, and Nick darted off, leaving him alone with Lani. Again, he reminded himself that he wasn't going to touch her, not even to tug on that sweet loose curl. "There's really no reason for you to stay in this bathroom. Come on to the kitchen, have something to eat."

She straightened the robe again. "It's only…it's strange enough, not being the nanny anymore, everything changing, coming here to your palace apartment for the first time as, um, well, not as a nanny. And to end up like this…" She looked down at the robe. "It's just awkward, you know?"

"Everyone knows why you're wearing a robe. And if it will make you feel better, Marceline or Gerta can loan you something until your clothes get here. Or I could scare up something else from my closet, I'm sure."

She aimed that soft chin high. "You know, you're right. I shouldn't make a big deal of this." She got her purse from the chest in the corner. "Get me out of here." And she held out her hand.

A perfectly acceptable excuse to touch her. Wonderful. He wrapped his fingers around hers.

It turned out to be a really lovely morning after all, Lani thought.

The driver came for her key a few minutes after they joined Nick and Marceline in the kitchen.

They ate Marceline's excellent French toast and were just finishing the food when the driver returned with the clothes she'd asked for. Marceline showed her to a spare room where she got out of Max's robe at last and into a fresh skirt and sweater, comfy tights and a clean pair of shoes.

As she was changing her cell rang. It was Sydney. "Where *are* you? I thought you were coming to breakfast with the family?"

"Long story. Connie got sick. I think it was just something she ate, because she's better already. But we ended up staying here, in Max's apartment."

"Spending your Sunday with Max and the kids. This thing with you two is just moving right along."

"I can't really talk now. Max is waiting."

"Are those wedding bells I hear?"

"Knock it off, Syd."

With Sydney's laughter echoing in her ear, Lani ended the call.

By then, it was almost noon. She returned to the kitchen to find Max there alone. She joined him at the table. They drank too much coffee and discussed the finer points of Montedoro's delicate relationship with France. Eventually, they went to Connie's room to check on her. She was sitting up against the pillows, drinking apple juice and insisting that she was well enough to be out of bed.

Max kissed her forehead and told her to rest a little longer.

"But I'm all well!" Connie cried.

Lani suggested a board game. They called Nick in and Gerta produced a game of Trouble, which Lani remembered playing when she was a kid. An hour flew by. They popped the dice in the board's central "magic dome" and raced each other around the board.

Nick won, which pleased him no end. He flexed his

skinny arms and beat his chest and crowed, "I am the *champion!*"

And then Connie yawned and admitted that maybe she was ready to take a little nap.

Nick wanted to go out to the garden and play with his Nerf gun, so Gerta took him out. Lani and Max stayed in the apartment while Connie slept. They sat in the front sitting room and talked.

It really was almost as it used to be, before New Year's. They could talk for hours on any number of subjects.

But then again, no. It was completely different than it used to be. Every time he looked at her, she knew it. They were much more than friends now.

Syd could joke about wedding bells all she wanted, but Lani really didn't know where this thing with Max was going. He was important to her, and he'd made it very clear that she mattered to him. But marriage? Neither of them was up for that.

And why was she thinking about marriage, anyway? Why was she letting a few teasing remarks from Syd tie her all in knots about the future? After that disastrous foray into first love with Thomas all those years ago, she'd been playing it way too safe. She needed to take a few chances again. And now, at last, she was. Best to enjoy every moment and let the future take care of itself.

Nick and Gerta came back inside. Connie woke up and Max allowed her to bring her dolls out and play quietly in the family sitting room next to the kitchen.

Lani said she had to go. Max walked her out to the foyer.

But when they got to the door, he took both her hands. "I don't want you to go. Stay for dinner. It will only be us, you, me and the children." *Only us.* She did like the sound of that. She liked it way too much. He kept on convincing her. "We'll stay in, right here. I'll have the meal sent up and Connie can take it easy."

It was just too tempting.

She stayed. They ate early, in the kitchen, the four of them. Connie had soup and crackers and announced that it was the best soup she'd ever had and she didn't feel one bit like throwing up.

Lani got up to go again at seven. She said goodbye to Nick and Connie and Gerta.

Marceline appeared with her gray skirt and blue blouse, good as new, pressed and on hangers, covered with plastic. "I'm so sorry about your shoes," she said. "But there was no saving them."

Lani wasn't surprised. "Thanks so much for trying."

Max followed her to the door.

They lingered there, whispering together.

"You sure you won't let me call you a car?"

"Don't be silly," she told him. "It's a quick walk."

"I want to kiss you," he said, leaning close, but not actually touching her. "But after what happened with Nick, I'm trying to control myself."

"Self-control is important."

"Self-control is overrated," he grumbled. "I'm holding on to it only by a thread."

"I admire your determination to behave."

"No, you don't. You're laughing at me."

She bit her lower lip to keep it from twitching. "Only on the inside—and you have to let me go now."

"But I don't want to let you go now."

She went on tiptoe and brushed a quick kiss across his beautiful mouth. "Good night, Max."

Reluctantly, he opened the door for her. She slipped out fast, before he could convince her to change her mind and stay even later.

There was a different guard on duty at the door she'd used that morning. He checked her ID and nodded her out into the cool evening. She took a path she knew through the gardens and she was down Cap Royale and hurrying to the old villa on her little cobbled street in no time.

A stranger in a gray coat stood under the streetlight in front of the building. As she passed him and started up the steps, he called, "Yolanda, hey!"

Startled that he knew her name, she paused in midstep and glanced back at him.

He lifted something to his face. She didn't realize it was a camera until the flash went off and the shutter started clicking. And then she just stood there, gaping at him as he took several pictures.

"Thanks a million, sweetheart," he said when he lowered the camera. And then he turned and ran off down the street.

She knew what he was. Paparazzo.

Her legs felt like rubber bands, all wobbly and boneless. But she managed to put one foot in front of the other, to let herself in the building, to climb the stairs to her apartment.

Once inside, she locked up, tossed the plastic-covered skirt and blouse on the sofa and then stood in the middle of the room trying to assess the meaning of what had just happened downstairs.

It shouldn't have shocked her so. She'd known this would happen if she went out with Max. But after Friday night, when no one bothered them, and then today, in Max's apartment with the children, everything so normal and ordinary, she'd let herself forget.

She tossed her purse on top of her skirt and blouse and booted up her laptop. It took only a simple search of her name and Max's and there she was, at his side in her little black dress getting out of the limo, sitting across from him in the restaurant, driving off in the limo again.

The articles that went with the pictures were short ones without a lot of detail, at least when it came to her. She was called a "black-haired beauty," and a "mystery date."

"Mystery date," she whispered aloud to herself. Was that like a blind date? A date who made you solve a puzzle? Someone you went out with and didn't even know their name?

There was more about Max, all the old stories, of his perfect marriage, the tragic loss of his forever-love. Of how true he was to Sophia's memory, how he'd never been linked to any woman in the four years since her death.

Until now. Until the black-haired beauty, the mystery date.

Lani shut down the laptop and told herself it wasn't a big deal, that she'd known this would happen. That she needed to get used to it.

But the stuff about Sophia kind of stuck with her.

Sometimes Lani felt so close to him.

But right now she was thinking that she really didn't understand him at all. She needed him to talk to her about Sophia. And because it seemed to her such an important, sensitive subject, she'd been waiting for him to do that in his own time. He never had.

Now she had to decide how much longer to wait, how much more time he needed before he might be ready. Not to mention, how much longer she could hold out before she just went ahead and asked him.

Monday morning Her Sovereign Highness Adrienne met with her ministers in the Chambers of State. As his mother's heir, Max sat on her right-hand side.

Adrienne often conferred with him during the meeting. Sometimes she would call him into her private office beforehand or afterward, to discuss any measures or upcoming decisions on which she needed input or more information. Max had a talent for research and she would often ask him to gather more data on a particular subject. Sometimes she simply wanted his opinion on an issue she needed to settle. So when she asked him to join her in her office after the meeting, he assumed she needed to consult with him on some matter of state.

He followed her through the gilded doors to her inner sanctum. She led him to the sitting area, where she took one of the sofas and he claimed a Louis Quinze wing chair.

Adrienne smoothed her trim Chanel skirt and folded her delicate long-fingered hands in her lap. "We missed you at Sunday breakfast. How is Connie?"

He wasn't surprised she already knew that Connie had been ill. Old Dr. Montaigne was under orders to inform her if one of the children needed his care. "She's doing well. It was some kind of stomach upset. Something she ate, we think. But she recovered quickly. Gerta's keeping her home today, just in case."

"I'll try to get by and see her."

"She would love that." He waited for her to tell him what she needed from him.

And then she did. "I understand you've been seeing Trevor and Ellie's former nanny."

The skin pulled tight on the back of his neck. He felt ambushed. But then he ordered his neck muscles to relax. He'd taken Lani out. That was major news in Montedoro. Of course, his mother would have heard about it. And he'd been planning to tell her about Lani anyway, and putting it off, waiting for the right moment. This, apparently, was it. "Her name is Yolanda Vasquez, but she goes by Lani."

"Of course I know what her name is, darling. And she's a lovely young woman."

"Yes, she is."

"A budding novelist, I hear, who just made her first big sale."

"From whom did you hear that, exactly?"

She answered easily. "More than one source. Sydney mentioned the sale quite proudly over a week ago. And Oliver, in the library, seems very impressed with her success."

He felt slightly ashamed of his own defensiveness. Of course, his mother would have heard about Lani's big sale—and remembered it. Adrienne had a photographic memory and could recall the most obscure personal details shared by people she'd met only briefly, in passing. He explained, "She has a three-book contract with a major New York publisher. The books are historical novels set in Montedoro. She's also self-published three other novels that take place in present-day Texas."

"Wonderful. You must introduce me so that I may congratulate her properly." There was a definite chiding quality to her tone.

He couldn't resist chiding her right back. "Introduce you? She worked at the palace for nearly two years. You've never spoken to her?"

"Please, Maximilian. It's one thing to ask the nanny if Trevor is eating all his vegetables. It's another to have a conversation about publishing with someone my son and heir is seeing romantically."

He confessed, "I was bringing her to breakfast yesterday."

"Without mentioning it to me or your father beforehand."

"You've always said we're welcome to bring someone special—but you're right. I probably should have said something. Lani asked me to tell you that she was coming. I didn't get around to it." His mother wore a skeptical look. He admitted, "All right. I wanted you to meet her, wanted you to see us together without my making a big thing of it beforehand…but then Connie grew ill and we stayed in." In the interest of full disclosure, he added, "Lani stayed with us until after dinner. We played a board game with the children. Lani and I talked about the situation with France. She has an excellent understanding of politics and history. The day went by much too fast."

"And on Friday night, you took her out to dinner."

"And to the villa on the Avenue d'Vancour afterward." He shifted in the chair, though he knew he shouldn't, that to move at all showed weakness.

"It *is* serious, then?"

"Yes."

A soft smile curved her lips. "I didn't really have to ask if it was serious, did I? You don't have casual relationships."

"No, Mother. I don't." Actually, there had been a few physically satisfying arrangements with discreet partners after Sophia's death. But those were more in the nature of transactions than relationships.

"There could be…issues with the French ministers," Adrienne said thoughtfully. By the terms of the treaty of 1918, two of the ruling prince's five ministers were French nationals. And while the ruling family was officially in charge of succession, the French government had to formally approve the next prince to take the throne. When his mother had married his father, the French had been outraged. As the heir apparent to the throne, they'd expected her to marry a man with money and influence, preferably a prince or a king, though a duke or a marquess would have done well enough. His father, a moderately successful Hollywood actor, had not fit the mold.

On the other hand, when Max had married Sophia, the French ministers were all smiles. They'd considered her the perfect bride for the Montedoran heir. She was not only the virgin daughter of a Spanish grandee, but she brought a large dowry, as well.

Not that any of that really mattered anyway. He and Lani were on the same page about marriage.

Max said, "The French ministers will get over themselves. They always do."

"I am a bit hurt, I must confess, that you didn't come to me and tell me about this sooner."

"I'm sorry, Mother," he said automatically.

She studied him, her head tipped to the side. "No, you're not. And wasn't there some talk about the two of you last year?"

"I'm sure there was," he said resignedly, "because I danced with her." In the four years since Sophia's death, Max had made it a point to dance only with his mother and his sisters. He intended never to marry again, and dancing only with family members was one of the ways he made his intentions—or rather, the lack of them—clear to everyone.

But in September, at the palace gala celebrating his sister Rhiannon's marriage to Commandant Marcus Desmarais, Max had danced with Lani for the first time. He'd done it again at the Harvest Ball and yet again at the Prince's Thanksgiving Ball. And then, finally, he'd claimed those five dances on New Year's Eve, when everything started to change between them at last.

His mother waited for him to say more.

He gave in and explained himself a little. "I knew what I wanted over a year ago. It's taken her longer. Whatever people whispered when I danced with her, there was nothing to say to you, nothing you needed to know, until last Thursday night when Lani and I finally came to a mutual understanding that we were more than friends."

Adrienne rested her elbow on the sofa arm and gave him a slow, thoughtful dip of her dark head. "All right, then. She's important to you and you intend to continue seeing her."

"Exactly."

"I'm glad for you," his mother said, and he knew she meant it sincerely. "Glad that you've found someone, glad that you're finally willing to try again." She extended her hand across the low table.

He took it. Her grip was strong. They shared a smile before letting go. "Until I met Lani, there didn't seem to be any reason to try again."

Adrienne regarded him steadily. "As I recall, Yolanda worked for Sydney for several years…."

"Seven in total, yes—and she prefers to be called Lani."

"Lani. Of course. I understand that Lani has been an excellent nanny."

"That's right."

"And as to her family in America…?"

"Her father's a college professor and her mother's a pediatrician. They're still married to each other, and happily so from what Lani's told me. She has a married brother who's a businessman." Max knew where this was going and he just wanted it over with. "What are you getting at, Mother?"

"Darling, it's all very well to dismiss the French ministers. But is there anything in Lani's past, anything about her that might require damage control if the tabloids get hold of it?"

There it was. The question he'd been dreading. He proceeded with care. "Lani has her secrets, yes. Her regrets. As do we all. I don't know how much an enterprising journo might dig up. And frankly, I don't really care. We will get through it, whatever happens. I have no doubts on that score."

His mother's beautiful face appeared serene. But he knew her sharp mind was working away behind the smooth facade, exploring possibilities, considering options. "She must have passed our usual background check, or Rule would never have made her part of his household. So then what, exactly, is there to dig up?"

"I can't tell you that, Mother. Lani told me in confidence."

"Will she tell me—or let *you* tell me?"

"My guess would be no."

"I could…order a discreet inquiry."

"Please don't. Leave it."

Adrienne looked tired, suddenly. She asked wistfully, "You couldn't have chosen someone sweet and uncomplicated?"

"Someone eighteen and raised in a convent?" Adrienne actually chuckled at that, though it wasn't an especially happy sound. He went on, "Lani *is* sweet."

"I only want you to be absolutely certain of your choice before you tie a knot that cannot be undone."

Bitterness moved in him. He tasted dust and ashes in his mouth. His mother knew too much. She was far too observant, and so infuriatingly wise. "There won't be any knot, so that won't be a problem."

Adrienne didn't move, but the sovereign of Montedoro vanished. She became only his mother, worried for him, wanting his happiness above all. "So you're still determined never to—?"

"Yes." There was no need to go into all this again. "Let it be. I stayed true to my vows and the throne is secure and I'm free to make other choices now."

"But how does Lani feel about that?"

"We've discussed it. She understands how it will be. In fact, she has no desire ever to marry."

"How long ago did you discuss it?"

He didn't like the direction this was going. Not in the least. "It was a while ago."

"Before you became lovers?"

"You know, this really isn't a subject I want to talk over with my mother."

An amused smile ghosted across her mouth. "Think of me as your sovereign, then. Did you discuss your feelings about marriage with Lani before you two became lovers?"

He gave in and answered her. "Yes." It had been more than a year ago, as a matter of fact. "But so what? Lani knows my position and she feels the same. And what exactly are you getting at?"

"You should tell her again. It's one thing to explain to a friend how you feel about marriage, another entirely to tell a woman who loves you that you'll never share your life with her."

"That's not the way it is. I intend to share my life with her."

"But on your own terms, with no commitment."

"That's not so. I *am* committed to her, fully. In all the ways that really matter."

Adrienne only looked at him with sadness and a hint of reproach.

And the past was there, rising up between them, reproaching him all the more. She *had* tried to warn him, to get him to slow down, to see other people, to grow up a little before he rushed into marriage. And she had been right. He should have listened to her then, but he hadn't. And he'd paid the price. "I'm a grown man now, Mother. I know the right woman for me. This isn't about contracts and promises. This is about someone I want to be with who wants to be with me. Everything is different this time."

"Is it? Oh, darling, I do hope so."

Chapter Eight

Monday, Lani's plan was to write at least eight pages by two in the afternoon, and then to put in another couple of hours researching websites and web designers.

But she woke up groggy from spending most of the night wide awake thinking about Max—about how wild she was for him, about how she felt she knew him to his soul. And, at the same time, that she didn't know him at all. She worried about next Sunday and the family breakfast. She obsessed over the incident with the paparazzo, over the pictures online of her and Max together, over when her mother or father would call her and say they'd seen the pictures and…well, she had no idea what they would say after that.

She sat down to her laptop at nine.

At eleven, when she had barely written half a page, Max called. The first thing he asked was how the work was going.

She grumbled, "I've gotten stuck on a certain sentence. I think I've rewritten it twenty times."

"Leave it. Go on to the next sentence. Sometimes you have to keep moving forward."

"Good advice. Now to try to make myself take it."

He laughed, the sound warm and deep, reaching out to her through the phone, wrapping around her heart, making her so glad he'd called. "Is that whining?" he teased. "There's no whining in writing."

"Not for you, maybe. I have to whine constantly. It's part of my process."

He laughed again. Then he said, "I'll let you get back to it, but I want to see you tonight."

"Yes," she said, without even stopping to think about it. Because she wanted to see him. Because every time she saw him, she only wanted to be with him some more. And all the other stuff, all her worries and doubts? Lately, all that stuff was starting to feel like lead weights pulling her down, trying to drag her back, to keep her from finding happiness. Maybe she only needed to let go of them, to stop giving them such unnecessary power over her. "How's Connie?"

"Dr. Montaigne says she can go to school tomorrow."

"That's what I wanted to hear—and about tonight?"

"You already said yes," he reminded her gruffly. "You can't change your mind now."

"I have no intention of changing my mind."

"Now, that's what *I* wanted to hear."

"I have a request, though."

"Name it."

"I don't feel like going out. Would you come here and we could stay in?"

"I'd like that. I'll bring dinner."

"I think you just might be the perfect man."

"Hold that thought. I'll see you at seven."

She hung up, smiling, and went back to that awful, unworkable sentence. And what do you know? There was nothing wrong with it. She kept going, pressing ahead as Max had suggested, refusing to edit or second-guess herself.

By one-thirty, she had nine good pages, which got her thinking that she had to stop staying up all night worrying.

Having an actual love life could be *good* for her writing, if she would only allow it to be.

After a quick sandwich break, she did a little website research and ended up requesting more information from two designers whose portfolios appealed to her. Then she wrote a couple of totally lame tweets, because she had to get used to the whole Twitter thing. Finally, she checked email.

She had messages in the in-box of the email account she'd linked to Facebook and Twitter, messages from people she'd never heard of. Four of them came right out and said they wanted to talk with her about her relationship with the prince of Montedoro. She trashed those.

Three of them said they'd read about her sale in Publisher's Marketplace and wanted to congratulate her and learn more about her books.

Yesterday, she would have been totally jazzed that she was already getting interest. But after last night and the man with the camera, she couldn't help wondering if those potential interviewers really only wanted what the others wanted: a hot scoop on what was going on between her and Prince Max. She didn't trash those three messages, but she didn't answer them either. She just called it a day, shut down her laptop and treated herself to a long, relaxing bath.

Max arrived with a shopping bag in one hand and a picnic basket in the other. She took the basket from him and set it on the counter of her little kitchen nook.

He dropped the shopping bag on a chair, threw his jacket on top of it and swept her into his arms. His wonderful mouth closed over hers and his tongue slipped between her parted lips, and she thought that there really was no place she would rather be than held nice and tight in Max's embrace.

"I missed you," he said, after he finished kissing her senseless.

She stared up at him. She could do that endlessly. "Do you know that you have to be the best-looking guy on the planet? I love the way your brows draw together, as though you're constantly thinking very deep thoughts. And what about the wonderful, manly shape of your nose? Oh, and the scent of you. I could stand here and smell you forever."

One side of his gorgeous mouth kicked up. "Please do—but did you miss me?"

"I did."

"Tell me all about it."

"It's been awful. Twenty-four hours without you. I don't know how I survived."

"You're right," he agreed with enthusiasm. "It's been much too long."

"Though I do feel kind of bad about taking you away from Nick and Connie."

He bent close again and whispered in her ear. "Tomorrow night come up to the palace. We'll have dinner together, the four of us."

"Yes."

His lips brushed her temple, setting off sparks. "You're saying yes a lot recently. Yes works for me in a big way."

She stood on tiptoe to whisper in his ear. "Something seems to be happening to all my fears and doubts."

"Tell me. Don't hold back."

"They could be…vanishing. I feel freer without them, but a little bit naked, too."

"You. Naked. Nothing wrong with that." He tipped up her chin and caught her mouth again, starting out with a gentle brushing of his lips across hers and then slowly deepening the caress, until her senses were swimming and desire began to pool low in her belly.

She took his face between her hands and gently broke

the scorching kiss. "If you keep doing that, we'll end up in bed before dinner."

He arched a brow at her. "Would that be such a bad thing?"

She took a moment to think about it. "Hmm. You know, now that you put it that way, I have to tell you..."

He bent, buried his face in the crook of her neck and growled, "Tell me what?"

She stroked her fingers up into his silky, unruly hair. "I don't think it would be such a bad thing at all."

That was all the encouragement he needed. She let out a happy cry of surprise as he scooped her high against his chest and carried her the short distance to her tiny bedroom. She'd drawn the blinds earlier and the room was dark. He put her down on the bed, switched on the lamp and stood back to get out of his clothes.

She gazed up at him in the pool of lamplight, dazed and admiring—and then it occurred to her she was wasting precious time. She might as well get busy getting rid of her clothes, too.

So she did. She grabbed the hem of her sweater and ripped it up and off over her head. Her bra came next. She wiggled out of it as he kicked off his shoes and hopped on one foot to tear off a sock.

It became something of a competition, both of them whipping off articles of clothing and tossing them out of the way. She started laughing. And then he started laughing.

He tossed two condoms on the nightstand and came down to the bed with her. They laughed as they kissed.

And then, somehow, neither of them was laughing anymore. He was touching her everywhere and whispering her name and she held on so tight to him, her body aching with longing, stunned with sweet delight, her mind a hot whirl of wonder and happiness.

Was this really possible? This magic, this beauty? In the long years since her eighteenth summer, she had let herself give up on ever finding this kind of joy.

She'd become careful, cautious of both her body and her wounded heart. The girl she'd once been, bold and sure, afraid of nothing, had been lost to her, stolen away by her own headstrong, youthful choices, by a thoughtless, selfish man more than twice her age.

But now...

Yes. Now.

This was hope, wasn't it? This was happiness calling her, opening to her again.

She closed her eyes and she whispered, "Max."

He answered, "Lani," rough and low and tender, too.

All thought whirled away and there was only sensation, only the two of them, locked together, only the promise in her heart, the press of skin on skin, and the sweet, endless pulse of their mutual pleasure.

Sometime later, they gathered up their scattered clothes and put them on again. In the living room, he presented her with the shopping bag he'd tossed on the chair when he came in.

"What's this?"

"Open it."

In the bag was a shoebox and in the box, a brand-new pair of gray suede pumps identical to the ones she'd worn the morning before. With a shout of pure glee, still holding a shoe in each hand, she threw her arms around his neck.

He grinned down at her and she thought how young he looked, and how totally pleased with himself. "You did say you loved those shoes."

"Thank you." She went on tiptoe and captured his mouth. They shared a long, lovely toe-curling kiss. When he lifted his head, she asked, "How did you get them in just one day?"

"You'd be surprised what a little money and a lot of determination can accomplish."

Over roast chicken and *pommes rissoles*—pan-fried, herb-crusted potatoes—she told him about the man with the camera the night before and also about the suspicious messages in her in-box.

"Welcome to my world." He sipped the wine Marceline had packed with the meal. "Where your privacy will be gleefully invaded at every turn." He set down the glass. "If you can describe the paparazzo, I might be able to see to it that he leaves Montedoro once and for all."

"It's tempting. The guy really freaked me out at first. But no."

The lines between his brows deepened. "You mean you *can* describe him, but you won't?"

"It was dark and it happened too fast for me to get a good look at him. But even if I could tell you exactly what he looked like, you're right. I don't know if I would. It was awful only because I wasn't expecting it. And even sleazy photographers have to make a living."

"Not by ambush, they don't, not in Montedoro. And they know it, too. They all know the rules here. They can take all the pictures they want, snap away to their venal little hearts' content—but they have to keep their distance while they do it. The fellow last night? Completely over the line. He deserves to be sent away and not allowed back."

She ate a bite of the delicious potatoes. "Sorry. Can't help you."

He didn't look happy, but at least he let it go. "As to the emails, can you simply ignore them?"

"I deleted the ones that were fishing for information

about you. A few of them, though, look as though they might be legit, bloggers in publishing just interested in interviewing a budding author. I thought I might write them back and ask for the interview questions. When I get those, I'll have a better idea of what I'm dealing with."

"Be careful."

She promised that she would. And then she asked him about his day.

He told her about the weekly meeting with the ministers of state and then added, almost as an afterthought, "I met with my mother alone afterward."

Something in his voice warned her. "Did you talk about me?"

He held her gaze. "We did. It was all good."

Somehow, she didn't quite believe him. "Why do I think there's more going on here than you're telling me?"

He reached across the narrow table and snared her hand. "She's glad for me, that I've found someone who makes me happy."

"Well." She felt a smile kind of tremble its way across her mouth. "That's nice to hear." He looked down at their joined hands and then back up at her, a glance that seemed just a little evasive. She asked, "You're sure that's all?"

He squeezed her hand, made a low noise that could have meant yes—or could have been a tactic to avoid answering her question.

"Max. Why do I feel that you're not telling me everything?"

"Mothers worry," he gave out grudgingly. That did it. She pulled her hand free. He glared at her. "Damn it, Lani."

She schooled her voice to gentleness. "You're not telling me everything."

"It's nothing for you to worry about, take my word for it."

"I don't believe you." For that, she got an angry shrug. "Oh, Max…"

He shot her a look from under his brows. "Let's change the subject, shall we?"

Oh, she was tempted. How simple, to let it be. To move on to some other, happier topic. But when you really cared about someone, you didn't always get to just drop it when things got difficult. "I can take it," she whispered. "I promise you I can. Won't you give me a chance?" He folded his big arms across his broad chest and sat back in the chair. She kept after him. "I know I haven't made it easy for you, up till now. I know you had to do all the work and that for a very long time, I gave you so little."

"That's not true."

"Yes it is. I created a whole new meaning for the word *reluctant.* I know you understand why now, because I finally drummed up the nerve to tell you about the hardest things. It's just, well, it's taken over a decade, for me to forgive myself for Thomas, for my poor lost baby, for…all of it. The therapy I had helped. Sydney helped, by making a place for me in her life, by being the best friend I've ever had and never, ever judging me. And you, Max. I think you've helped most of all."

"My God, Lani." He leaned in at last and reached for her hand again.

Instead of giving it, she raised it between them. "No. Wait. It's important, if we want to go on together, that we're honest with each other, that you don't sugar-coat things for me. If your mother has issues with you and me together, I need to know about it."

He picked up his wine again and saw it was empty. With a low, impatient sound, he set it back down. "You have to understand. My mother is about as egalitarian as a ruling monarch could be. She wants us—my brothers and sisters and me—to be happy above all, to build relationships based on love and respect first and foremost. But it's a little different for me."

"Because you're the heir."

"Exactly. There are other things to consider when I become serious about a woman."

Serious. It was one of those words. Enormous and yet so simple, both at the same time. "You told her that you're serious about me?"

"I did. Because I am."

Her throat clutched. "That, um, sounds really good."

He almost smiled. But his eyes remained somber. "My mother has to consider our allies and their possible reactions to any woman I become close to."

Lani knew her Montedoran history. "The French, right? Her French ministers. For them, an ordinary American girl just won't do."

"Yes, the French. She said they wouldn't be happy. I said they would get over it."

"Well, they got over your mother marrying your father."

He did smile then. "You're taking this so well and you understand perfectly."

"See? You should have just told me. What else?"

"Lani, I…" He let the words trail off. She could tell he really didn't know how to answer.

And by then, she knew. A cold shiver traveled up her spine. "Scandal, right? Your mother wanted to know if there was anything about me that might make tabloid fodder."

He gave it up. "That's right."

Her chest felt tight, and her stomach churned. "And you told her…?"

"I said you had secrets, things you regretted, as we all do. She wanted to know what those secrets were. I refused to break your confidence. She said she could make inquiries. I asked her not to."

"Will she do it anyway?"

"I don't think so."

"But did she say that she wouldn't?"

"No." He stared at her so hard, as though he could pin her in place with just that look. "I don't care."

"What do you mean, you don't care?"

"Whatever happens, we deal with it. We don't let it break us."

"Someone *could* find out though, right?" she asked in a hollow voice. "Someone could dig it all up again. The whole world could read about…all of it." She shook her head slowly, back and forth and back again, absorbing the enormous ugliness of that. "I should have thought of this. I can't believe I didn't. But then, why would I ever want to face that someday the whole world could know? I thought it was more than bad enough just making myself tell *you*."

His eyes were storm-cloud gray and his lips twisted cruelly. "Are you bailing out on me? Is that what you're doing?"

She stared at him, wide-eyed and blinking, feeling like someone startled by a bright light in a very dark room. "You shouldn't continue with me. It's not a good idea for you."

"How many ways can I say it?" Shoving back his chair, he stood.

She gasped and blinked up at him. "Um. Say what?"

He turned his back to her. She sat there, not sure what to do or say, as he paced to the living area, all the way to the sliding door, where he gazed out at the night for several seconds that seemed to stretch to an infinity.

Finally, he whirled and faced her again. "I always knew there was something that kept you from coming to me. I knew and I didn't care. I just wanted to get through it, to be the one you reached for when you were ready at last, to be the one to gain your trust and know your truth. And when you finally did tell me, you didn't shock me. It all made complete sense to me, those choices you made as an eighteen-year-old girl. I didn't—I *don't*—judge you for those choices. They caused you great pain and loss and almost killed you. But you survived. They changed you. They *are* you, a part of you anyway, a part of what brought you here, to Montedoro, to me.

"I don't really care who knows, who finds out something that happened years and years ago. To me, that's just another possible storm to weather, along with all the others we have to get through in this life. What I care about is *you.* That you know you can trust me. That *I* can count on *you,* that when the latest storm has played itself out, you're still there, where I need you, at my side."

Lani pushed her chair back and got up. Somewhere in the middle of all those beautiful things he'd just said, she'd stopped feeling stunned and broken and scared. Somewhere in there, it had become crystal clear to her what she had to do.

He watched her walk toward him, those iron eyes never leaving her face. "I'll ask you again. Are you bailing out on me?"

She went right to him, right up good and close. She laid her hands on his chest, where she could feel the power in him, feel his big heart beating under her palm. "No, Max. If you're crazy enough to stick with me, I'm not bailing."

His breath left him in a rush. "Thank God." He grabbed her close, hard arms closing around her.

She felt his lips against her hair, and for a moment she let herself cling to him. Then she pushed away enough that she could look up at him again. "I want to meet with your mother, just the princess and me. I will tell her the long, sad old story. All of it."

He looked at her so piercingly, as though he was trying to see inside her head. "You would do that?"

It was strange. Yesterday, she never could have volunteered to do such a thing. But now, somehow, she could do nothing less. "I think I have to, Max. I think it's the right thing to do."

"And then what?"

"I have no idea. But if you and I are going to continue together, it only seems right that she should know. We can start with that. And after I've told her everything, the two of you can take a meeting on the subject and decide what, if anything, you need to do."

Chapter Nine

At two the next afternoon, Lani sat on a fabulous damask-covered sofa in HSH Adrienne's private office. As always, she tried not to gape at the sovereign princess, who had to be almost sixty, but still had full lips and flawless skin. There really was something magical about Adrienne Bravo-Calabretti. She brought to mind some legendary movie star of the silver screen—Sophia Loren, maybe, with that wide mouth and those unforgettable eyes.

There was tea. With scones and delicate pots of jam and clotted cream. Adrienne poured, those slim, perfectly manicured hands dealing with the fragile china pot and the gold-trimmed, paper-thin teacups without making a single clattering sound.

Otherworldly. Definitely. Beyond the whole not-gaping thing, Lani was experiencing an absolute cringing sort of terror of this whole situation. What was she thinking to volunteer to tell this incredible woman all about how stupid and destructive she'd been once? Last night, with Max's arms around her, coming here and telling all had seemed like an excellent, brave and necessary idea.

Clearly, last night, she'd gone temporarily insane.

"What do you take?" Adrienne asked.

A Valium about now would be nice. "Just a little sugar, thanks."

Adrienne moved the sugar closer to Lani's side of the low table, next to the cup of tea she'd just poured for her. Lani put in the sugar and stirred—carefully, trying not to make those annoying clinking sounds that all the etiquette books said were so rude.

Now what? When taking tea at a table, one never picked up the saucer with the cup. But when standing, the saucer was necessary to catch any drips. Did the low table actually count as a table, or...?

The princess took pity on her and picked up both saucer and cup. Lani did the same. She sipped.

Not too clattery, thank God. And she didn't spill a drop on her carefully chosen outfit of blue skirt, white shirt and short red blazer—red, white and blue; everyday, ordinary American and proud of it. She also wore the gray suede pumps. They made her think of Max, and that gave her courage. She set down the cup and saucer and doubted she would pick it up again.

Adrienne said, "I understand congratulations are in order." Lani went blank. For what? For coming here with the intention of revealing all the ways she'd screwed up her life and broken her parents' hearts, not to mention the heart of Thomas McKneely's poor, long-suffering wife? Adrienne must have read her bewildered expression. Graciously, as with the teacup, the princess came to Lani's rescue. "Three books sold at once. We're all so excited for you."

"I... Thank you," Lani managed rather woodenly. "I've had high hopes for this series of books and I'm glad they're going to be published and published well. Very glad."

"Max says they're all three set in Montedoro."

"Yes, the stories take place in the fifteenth and sixteenth

centuries. The main characters are fictional, but I try to stay true to the period, to…history as we know it."

"And these books are called…?"

"The working titles are *The Poisoner's Apprentice, The Sword of Abdication* and *The Crucible of Truth.*"

Adrienne laughed. "I'll have you know it's never been proven that Lucinda Calabretti poisoned her husband to put their son on the throne so that she could rule through him."

"Well, it *is* fiction," Lani shamelessly backpedaled. After all, these were Adrienne's ancestors.

But Her Sovereign Highness looked delighted. "And *The Sword of Abdication* takes place in the court of Lucinda's son, Cristobal?"

"Yes, it does." Cristobal Calabretti had abdicated the throne his mother had murdered his father to get for him.

"And *The Crucible of Truth?* Let me guess. It takes place in the time of Cristobal's son, Bernardo, who certainly can't be blamed for doing what he had to do in order to regain the throne his father had turned his back on." Her huge dark eyes gleamed. "I have no idea why they called him Bernardo the Butcher."

Lani played it diplomatically. "He was a very determined man."

"We Calabrettis tend to be that way, though nowadays we are much less bloodthirsty. My husband is the same—determined, I mean. And our daughters and sons, as well. Maximilian most of all."

Max. God. For a moment there, she'd almost let herself relax. But now her throat locked up and her left leg was showing a distressing desire to bounce. She kept her foot firmly on the floor and gulped to make her throat relax. "Yes. Max is, um, very determined."

Adrienne nodded, a slow, regal dip of her dark head. "I think he will make an excellent sovereign."

"Yes."

"And whatever you've come to share with me, rest assured I would no more betray your confidence than Maximilian would." Adrienne spoke softly, with real kindness.

"I… Thank you." Lani's palms were sweating. Ridiculous, annoying tears burned at the back of her throat, forcing her to swallow again, to gulp them right down into the deepest part of her. She was not going to sit here and blubber in front of Her Sovereign Highness. "I…well, the good news is, I've never killed anyone or been arrested for bank robbery or cooked crystal meth or…" Good Lord in Heaven. Cooked crystal meth?

"It's all right, I promise you," Adrienne said in the tone people use to calm wild animals. "Take your time."

Lani wanted to cover her face, become really small, jump up and run out of there and keep on running and never look back. "I don't know where to start."

"It doesn't matter." Adrienne snared her gaze and held it so steadily. Very much the way Max often did, and suddenly the resemblance, mother to son, was so powerful, so close. "Just begin," the princess said. "I think you'll find the way. I know you will." She sounded so certain.

And really, if Adrienne Bravo-Calabretti, Sovereign Princess of Montedoro, was sure that Lani could do it, well then, she absolutely could. She said, "My father's best friend was a writer named Thomas McKneely…" And once she got going, she just kept on. On and on through all of it, her own arrogance, her pride, her complete self-righteousness, her unforgivable treatment of her own father, her certainty that what she called love justified any action; her heedless, limitless cruelty. All of which led to the loss of so much that mattered, including her baby and almost her life.

When she finished, Adrienne reached across the low

table and touched her hand. The princess spoke. She said soft, comforting things.

Lani thought that whatever happened next, it wasn't so bad, really. To simply tell the truth as it had happened, to tell it and let it stand, let it be.

Adrienne stood. Lani automatically started to rise as well. "No," said Adrienne. "Stay. Just a moment…" Lani sank back to the sofa.

Adrienne went out.

Lani heard the door close behind her. Several minutes passed. Lani sat there, wanting to go, but feeling she should wait until the princess came back and excused her.

The door opened again. She turned to look and Max was standing there.

He held out his arms to her. It was all the encouragement she needed. She got up and ran to him.

He wrapped her up tight in his warm embrace.

She clung to him, burying her head against his hard, strong shoulder. "Your mother…?"

"She said you've told her all she needed to know."

"What does that mean?"

"It means we have her blessing. The rest is up to us."

"Oh, Max." She held him tighter.

He kissed her hair. "My brave darling…"

"Brave…" The word sounded wrong to her.

"Yes. Brave."

Funny. She didn't feel all that brave. What she felt was strangely, completely free.

Chapter Ten

After that, Lani knew happiness. Weeks of it.

She got past the dreaded midpoint of *The Crucible of Truth* and forged on toward the end. Two of the bloggers who'd messaged her through Facebook turned out not to be tacky tabloid journos, after all. She gave them interviews. She worked on her web presence, hired a website designer and had two long discussions with her New York editor concerning revisions to the first and second books.

Even better than her steady progress in her career, she had time with the people who mattered to her. With Sydney, with Trev and Ellie, with Nick and Connie and Gerta. And with Max most of all.

She went to breakfast with the princely family four Sundays running. Everyone seemed to accept her, to welcome her. Adrienne treated her warmly. And Max's father, the prince consort, Evan, would smile when he saw her and ask how the book was going.

The paparazzi remained relentless. Any time she went out in public, alone or with Max, or even with the children, there was always some guy lurking nearby with a camera or a smartphone stuck to his face.

She learned to do what the Bravo-Calabrettis did: ignore them. It wasn't that hard once you got the hang of it.

And they kept their distance, which really helped. Not a one was as in-your-face as that first guy outside her building that Sunday night in late February. They all kept back, out of the way as they were required to do in order not to be packed off to France.

There were pictures on the internet, lots of them. And videos on YouTube—of her and Max out for an evening, of her shopping with Sydney, of her and Max and the children enjoying an afternoon on the family yacht.

And there were stories, in the tabloids and online. More information came out about her, specifically, about her previous job as a nanny to the children of Prince Rule, about her long friendship with Sydney, about her budding career as a novelist. The tabloids seemed to love the whole nanny angle. All the stories had headlines like The Prince's Nanny Love and Wedding Bells for the Prince and the Nanny?

Lani tried to take it all in stride. The stories about wedding bells and diamond rings kind of got to her, though. Max never talked about marriage. Neither did she. It seemed a delicate, dangerous subject in light of what they'd said to each other that long-ago night in the library.

He wasn't going to get married again. He'd said so straight out. And she'd gone and told him that marriage wasn't for her.

Only, well, something had happened to her in the course of forging her freedom from the chains of the past. She'd found a way to love again—or maybe to love for real, as a grown woman, in the way she hadn't come close to all those years ago, with Thomas.

She'd found her way to love and she loved Max. And now that she loved him, now that she was truly able to let the past go, marriage didn't seem like such an impossible proposition, after all.

In fact, marriage felt like a good thing. A *right* thing. A big step that she and Max really ought to talk about taking—not right away. There was no reason to rush it. But someday, most definitely.

She'd gone on the pill. It was nice, not to have to fiddle with condoms, and to rest a little easier that there would be no surprise pregnancy. But more and more to her, having a baby someday seemed like a good thing, the *right* thing for her.

Yes. Someday. She was sure of that now.

Her father called near the end of March. Someone had finally told him what was going on over there in Montedoro.

"Is this Prince Maximilian good to you?" her dad demanded.

"Yes, Papi. He's a wonderful man."

"You're happy." It wasn't a question. He seemed simply to know.

And that pleased her, gave her that warm and fuzzy feeling down inside. "I am happy. Very happy."

"When will you bring him home to meet your family?"

Okay, she was kind of dreading that. Just a little. She'd gone home twice since the move to Montedoro. Both times had been awkward, with her parents pushing her to move back to Texas, and her brother all over her for deserting the family, for leaving her parents without their daughter in their waning years.

Plus, well, now that she had finally found someone she was serious about, there would be the usual Vasquez Family Marriage Interrogation Squad. They all—her mom, her dad and even her overbearing big brother—wanted her to be happy. And to a Vasquez, happiness meant marriage and babies.

"Yolanda Ynez, are you still on the line?"

"Yes, Papi. I'm here. And I do plan to bring Max and

the children to meet you. As soon as we can work that out, in the next couple of months, I hope...."

He grumbled a little more, accusing her of putting him off, which was only the truth. But then he asked about her writing and she told him how much she liked her editor, about her new website and her progress on the third book of her trilogy.

And he told her he was proud of her, which got her kind of dewy-eyed. Then he said he loved her and put her mom on.

That went pretty well, at least at first. She told her mom all about how well her career was going, and her mother congratulated her enthusiastically on her success.

Then her mom came right out and asked her, "Are you going to marry this man, this prince that you're dating?"

Lani cringed—and evaded. She reminded her mother that she and Max hadn't been together that long, that it was never a good thing to rush into something as important as marriage.

And of course, her mom said, "Your father proposed to me on our second date."

"I know that, Mama, but—"

"I said yes."

"No kidding." Lani had heard the story at least a hundred times.

"You can mock me if you want to."

"Sorry..."

"All I'm trying to say is that it was the best decision I ever made."

"I know, Mama. Papi's a prize."

"Yes, he is. And a woman knows when she's found the right man."

Yeah, sure. Like I did with Thomas. "Well, Mama. *You* knew."

"What does that mean, *mi'ja?* Are you telling me you don't know your own heart? Because the heart knows. You only have to listen to it. Are you listening to your heart with this prince of yours?"

"Of course I am."

"Well, okay, then. Bring him home so that I can see if he's good enough for you."

"Oh, Mama..."

"I love you, *mi'ja.* You are always in my heart and I am so proud of you."

Out of nowhere, tears welled up. One even overflowed and dribbled down her cheek. She swiped it away. "I love you, too, Mama. Very much."

"Bring him home."

She promised that she would. Soon.

Her mother was silent. And then a few minutes later, they said goodbye.

"He's so completely gone on you," Sydney said. "Everybody sees it. But then, you're gone on him right back, so it all shakes out."

Trev and Ellie were at the villa with their new nanny that afternoon, so it was just Syd and Lani in Lani's tiny kitchen area, sharing a lunch of grilled cheese sandwiches, cream of tomato soup and tall glasses of iced tea. Lani ate a bite of her sandwich and sipped her tea and stared out the little window by the table. It provided a view of another tenant's balcony across the way, partially obscured by the crown of an olive tree.

"You're too quiet," Sydney accused. "What's wrong?"

Lani sipped more tea and watched the olive branches sway in the early-spring breeze. "I talked to my parents yesterday. They want me to come home and bring Max with me."

Sydney fiddled with her napkin, lifting it off her lap, smoothing it down again. "And this…annoys you? Depresses you? Has you feeling overcome with joy?"

"I really need to do that—go home, I mean. I haven't been back to Texas enough since we moved here."

"So give yourself an extra week when you go to New York for that business trip next month. Visit your family and take Max with you."

"It seems a little early for him to be meeting the parents."

"But you've already met *his* parents—and I don't just mean because you lived at the palace. He's brought you to Sunday breakfast several weeks in a row. That counts as meeting the parents, and you know it, too."

"Still, it's different. We live here. It's all just more natural, Max taking me to family things."

"Is this some new form of amnesia you've got now? Think back to the first time he asked you to Sunday breakfast. It didn't seem all that natural to you then. You were tied in knots over it."

"True."

"But you did it anyway. Because he's important to you and his family matters. Well, he needs to know *your* family. Take him to Texas."

There was a gray cat on the neighbor's balcony. He sat in a little splash of sun, giving himself a bath. "Okay, Syd. I'll think about it."

Sydney reached across the narrow table, took Lani's chin in her hand and guided it around so she was looking at Syd instead of the gray cat across the way. "Talk to me. Come on. You know you want to. Tell me what's on your mind, and I shall use my big brain to help you solve whatever problem is nagging at you."

"I didn't say anything was bothering me."

Syd actually shook a finger at her. "Don't be that way."

"Fine." Lani let her shoulders slump.

Sydney ate two spoonfuls of soup, taking her time about it. "Still waiting over here."

"If I take Max to Texas to meet the parents, they're going to be all over him wanting to know what his intentions are. I just cringe when I think of it. My mother is already asking me when Max and I are going to get married."

"So? I've been kind of wondering about that myself."

"Very funny. Especially since I explained to you that Max has told me he'll never get married again."

"Didn't believe it then, don't believe it now."

"I'm pretty sure he still feels that way."

"Pretty sure, huh?" Syd gave a disgusted little snort. "Has he said so?"

"We've only been—what?—together, exclusive, whatever you call it—for a little over a month."

"Not the question."

"You're getting all lawyerlike on me, you know that, right?"

"I'm going to ask you again. Since you and Max have been 'together,' has he said that he'll never get married again?"

"No. We haven't talked about it. It hasn't come up."

Syd sat back in her chair. "And what about you? How do *you* feel about marriage now that you're in love with my brother-in-law?"

"Did I say I was in love with him?"

Syd gave her that look, the one that said she was barely restraining herself from rolling her eyes.

Lani stared at her soup and her half-eaten sandwich and realized she had no appetite at all. "You're going to make me say it, aren't you?"

"No. You're going to say it because you *want* to say it.

Because it's the truth and I'm your friend and you and I, we always try to deal in the truth with each other."

"Okay. All right." She pushed her plate away. "I'm in love with Max and nowadays marriage is starting to sound like a pretty good concept to me, like a good thing to do with the person you can see yourself being with for the rest of your life. I'm even…" She let out a moan and put her head in her hands.

"Come on, sit up straight. Look at me and say the rest."

She let her hands drop to her lap again. "Dear God. I want to have babies with him. I want to help him raise Connie and Nick. I want…everything. All of it. The wedding ring and the stepkids and the baby carriage, too. I want Max and me getting old together."

"Beautiful." Syd beamed, green eyes misty. "Good for you."

"But I haven't told him any of that. I don't even know where to start. And really, as I already said, I'm thinking it's kind of soon to be bringing all that up, anyway."

"Soon?" Syd gave another snort. "You've known him since we moved here. You were friends for a year before the man even kissed you. Now you're together and it's obvious to everyone that you not only have the fireworks, you have the friendship and the mutual interests and everything else it takes to make it work. So I've gotta say that it's not in any way too soon in my book."

"That's because you're one of *those*."

"One of *whats?*"

"Oh please, Syd. You accepted Rule's marriage proposal within forty-eight hours of meeting him in Macy's. Then the two of you promptly ran off to Vegas to tie the knot. You're like my mother. Love at first sight, a marriage proposal coming at you so fast it should make your head spin— but you don't even hesitate. You just say yes."

"Tell him you love him."

"Oh, Dear Lord…"

"Trust me, Lani. It never hurts to lead with the love."

Tell him you love him.

It shouldn't be that hard, should it?

After Syd left, Lani started kind of obsessing over the idea of saying her love out loud to Max. Over how she might just tell him that very night.

I love you, Max. Four little words. Seriously. How hard could that be?

He was coming over at seven, bringing dinner. It had gotten to be a regular thing with them. Once a week at least, the two of them spent the evening at her place. Max brought the food so she wouldn't have to think about cooking after a hard day stringing words together.

How quickly the weeks had fallen into a certain rhythm. A night at her place, a couple of evenings and all day Sunday with the children. Friday or Saturday night out together, and then after the night out, the villa on the Avenue d'Vancour afterward, for slow, delicious lovemaking and maybe a little champagne.

They had it all, really, and she ought to remember that. She *did* remember that, always. She had the work that she loved. And her own place, where she could write undisturbed all day long. And a wonderful man she loved to talk to, whose kisses turned her inside out, a man who had stuck with her, refused to quit on her, during all those months she'd given him almost nothing in return.

And now?

Well, now, she simply wanted more.

She was out on the balcony when he arrived. He let himself in with the key she'd given him. She'd left the slider open behind her, so she heard him, heard that one little squeak the door always gave, heard him reengage the lock and then move to the table to put the food basket down.

He approached, his steps quiet, measured. Still, she heard them. Or maybe she only felt them all through her, in the form of a sweet shiver of pleasure and longing, as she leaned on the iron railing and stared out at the hill and the shadowed trees directly across from her.

His hands, so warm and strong on her shoulders, pulling her back against him, then easing lower, sliding over her waist, across her stomach.

She let herself lean against him with a sigh. "Max..." Already she could feel him growing hard against her back.

He kissed her temple, rubbed his cheek against her hair. She couldn't resist turning in his arms then. She wrapped herself around him and they shared a long, sweet kiss.

The balcony seemed safe enough from prying eyes. But you just never knew.

He took her hand and led her inside. She pushed the slider closed behind them and followed him, breathless, her body already humming with pleasure, to the bedroom.

I love you, Max. She stared up into his iron-blue eyes as he took off her shirt and unbuttoned her jeans.

I love you, Max, as he laid her down across the sheets. *I love you, Max,* as he kissed her and caressed her. Every touch was pure wonder, every kiss a revelation.

I love you, Max. Love you, love you, love you...

The words filled up her head as he filled up her life, her body, her yearning heart. As he blasted away her loneliness, her very *separateness*.

She felt so close to him, so right with him.

But those four little words that filled up her head?

She didn't let them out. She couldn't quite bring them to the level of sound.

Maybe it was cowardice.

Or maybe she would do it a little later, over dinner. Yes, that would be better. While they sat at the table to eat the meal he'd brought.

In time, they got up and shared a quick shower. She put on the silk robe he'd bought for her. He pulled on his trousers, and they went to the table to eat.

She opened the basket. Draped over the white napkin cradling the dinner rolls, something glittered: a diamond and onyx bracelet. "Oh, Max…"

He looked so pleased with himself, eyes shining, hair damp and curling at his temples. "Goes with the earrings." He'd given her the diamond and onyx earrings a couple of weeks before. He was always bringing her presents, usually rare research books she coveted, occasionally something pretty and far too expensive. "Here." He took it. "Give me your wrist."

She extended her arm and he put it on. The diamonds gleamed against her skin, and the onyx had a deep luster, blacker than night. "So beautiful." *I love you, Max.* "Thank you." *I love you, I do.*

He pulled her up out of her chair and she went to him for a slow, lovely kiss. "You make me happy. So very happy," he whispered against her lips.

I love you, Max. "You do the same for me."

Reluctantly, he let her go. They sat down to eat.

He waited through the meal, all the way until after they'd demolished a nice pair of caramel-glazed crème puffs, before he said, "There's something you need to see."

She peered at him more closely. Was that anxiety in his eyes?

"All right," she answered cautiously. And he got up and went over to the low table in front of the sofa. He moved a stack of books she'd left there and took a tabloid paper from underneath them. She caught a glimpse of the garish cover. It was *The International Sun*.

Her stomach did something unpleasant. She pushed her dessert plate aside.

He came and sat down again. "I was selfish. I saw you out on the balcony, looking relaxed and happy and so tempting, waiting for me. I wanted some time with you before you saw this." She only stared at him and put out her hand. He gave it to her. "Page two."

Her stomach lurched again as she stared at the cover and read the lurid headlines: "Kate's Darkest Hour," "Alien Baby Born in Perth," "Secrets of the Killer's Dungeon."

"Lani?" he prompted, sounding worried.

She tried to make light of it. "It seems there's always an alien baby being born somewhere." The effort fell flat. She made herself turn the page, where she found a color photo of her and Max by the Fountain of the Three Sirens in front of Casino d'Ambre. She wore her favorite little black dress and he looked so handsome it made her heart ache. He had his arm around her. They were smiling at each other, happy simply to be together, pretending the rest of the world didn't exist.

But it did exist. Inserted next to the picture of the two of them was a black-and-white promotional headshot of Thomas taken several years before his death. He grinned his jaunty grin straight at the camera. The headline read, Prince Max's Naughty Nanny.

"Really, really tacky," she heard herself say.

"It could be worse," he offered hopefully.

She shot him a grim glance and started reading. It was short, which was the only good thing about it, a lurid little exposé concerning the "secret love nest" she'd shared with the bestselling Texas author who, at the time of their "torrid

May-December affair," had been a married man twenty-seven years her senior.

That was pretty much the whole thing. Nothing about her lost baby, nothing about her attempt to end her life or her extended stay at Spring Valley Psychiatric Care.

Max said what she was thinking. "The rest, beyond what you see there, would be pretty hard to dig up. The medical community has confidentiality laws to abide by. Unless someone close to you who knew more started talking…"

She lifted her head from the ugly little story and looked at him across the table. "I think you're right. People did talk when I moved in with Thomas. You could say that was public knowledge. But everything else, only my doctors, my parents and my brother ever knew—and now you and your mother and Sydney and probably Rule. All people I trust who would never break a confidence."

"Then there you have it. That should be it."

"You never know, though."

"God knows that's true."

She stared down at the story again, at the picture of Thomas, who'd once torn her heart out and stomped it flat. How strange that she wasn't more upset. "I…"

"What?"

"I don't know. It was such a long time ago. I thought it would rip me apart all over again, if any of it ever came out."

"But…?"

"Well. It happened. I did what I did and I'm not proud of it. It took me years to get over it, to forgive myself. But now I *am* over it. I've moved on. Would I prefer not ever to see anything about it in the tabloids or online? Definitely. But it *is* in the tabloids. And all I can say about that is, hey. The prose may be purple, but at least what's written here is more or less the truth."

He made a low noise that was almost a laugh. "That's the spirit."

A disturbing thought occurred to her. She demanded, "Has your mother seen this?"

"Settle down. There's nothing to be upset about."

"But—"

"Lani, my mother's the one who gave it to me. Her secretary has a clerk who spends every morning scanning the scandal rags and the internet for possible stories that the family ought to be keeping in front of—for damage control. There's an art to it, I promise you. My mother's a genius at putting positive spins on negative situations."

Now she did feel a little sick to her stomach. "Oh, God. What will she do about this?"

He smiled then. "Have you *read* some of the things that have appeared in print about my family? We've been embroiled in one scandal after another since the thirteenth century. You, of all people, ought to know that. You've written three books detailing the shocking exploits of just a few of my ancestors."

She tapped the page with the story on it. "You're saying this isn't that big of a deal to her or to the family?"

"Her concern was more about how *you* were going to take it."

Now, *that* was lovely to hear. "Truly?"

He gazed at her so tenderly. "Truly."

And she got up and went over and sat on his lap. "I guess we'll get through it."

"You *guess?*" He smoothed her hair along her cheek. "I *know* that we will."

She kissed him for that, another long, slow one.

He trailed kisses over her chin and down the side of her throat. And then he stood, lifting her high in his arms, and carried her back to the bedroom. For a while she forgot everything but the glory of his touch, the wonder of his kiss and the joy she had in loving him.

It wasn't until much later, after he'd gone home to his children and she was alone in bed, that she began to see his lack of concern about the tabloid story in a different light.

"No," Syd said firmly. "I don't believe that. You're letting your doubts and fears override simple logic. Maximilian is a good man. He doesn't care about that old story because he's got his priorities right. He cares about *you*."

They sat in the living room of Syd's villa, just the two of them again. Ellie was napping. Trev and Sorcha, the new nanny, were out in the gardens.

Lani raked frustrated fingers back through her hair. "Of course he cares about me. And he *is* a good man, a good man who's been completely honest with me all along. But logic is on *my* side here. I'm Max's lover. If I have a shady past, so what? It's not like he's going to *marry* me. He doesn't care if all that old garbage about Thomas comes out because he's never getting married again. He won't have to explain me to the French ministers. I'll never be his princess, never have a baby who would end up in line for the throne. I'm his…refuge, his safe haven, the one he turns to when he needs to decompress. But my past, my… reputation doesn't really reflect on him. He can keep me completely separate from his position as heir to the Montedoran throne."

Syd was shaking her head. "What am I going to do with you? Just when I think that you've come so far, you come up with something like this."

"Something that makes perfect sense and you know it."

"Really, you ought to be ashamed of yourself."

"Syd, I'm only being realistic."

"Did you tell the man you're in love with him?" Silence echoed. "Well, I guess I have my answer on that one."

Lani knew her lip was quivering and there was a big, fat lump in her throat. "I just… I can't, okay? He's a wonderful guy. I'm insanely in love with him. But what we have, that's it. That's all there is. I need to learn to accept that. Or if I can't, I have to accept that the day will come when I need to move on."

"Or you could just get honest, just tell him you love him and you've changed your mind about certain things—and then take it from there."

"Eventually, yes. I will do that, of course. When I feel the time is right."

"Oh, honey…"

"I mean it, Syd. It's like this. He comes to my apartment, or I go to his at the palace. Every moment we have together is precious, rich, unforgettable. But then he goes home. Or I go home. Back to our separate lives—and that would be fine, that would be about all I could deal with, anyway. If he hadn't made me open up to him, made me tell him the secrets that were holding me back, helped me to see that I really can let the past go and move on from here. He… accepted me. He *wanted* me, just as I am. And now, he's done this wonderful, beautiful thing for me. And it's changed me. I want more now, more than all that we already have, more than to be his lover and his friend. I want it all. And I just don't think that he does."

Syd wouldn't give it up. She'd always made relentlessness into an art form. "You need to get with him, can't you see that? You need to tell him all these things you just told me. You need to give the guy a chance to be what you need him to be."

"But I don't even know how to begin. It's like we had a certain contract and now I want to break it and start something he never signed on for, something he's made it clear from the first he's never wanted."

"I told you—"

"I know. I remember. Lead with 'I love you.'"

"Just do it."

"Oh, Syd. Look, I'm sorry. I know I'm disappointing you. I'm disappointing *myself,* but I'm just not ready to go there yet."

Chapter Eleven

The next day, Saturday, Max had the main kitchen pack them a picnic lunch. Then he took the children and Lani to the family's private beach in the northeastern ward of Lardeaux. They parked on the point above the beach and took the steep, narrow trail down to the water's edge.

It was still chilly for swimming, but the children wore shirts and shorts over their swimsuits. They ran barefoot at the water's edge, hunted for shells and built a cockeyed sand castle with a leaky moat.

Max loved watching them with Lani. She had such a way with them. Connie liked to whisper to her. Girl things, both Connie and Lani called whatever they whispered to each other. They refused to tell Max exactly what those girl things were. But whatever they said to each other made Connie smile and put a certain confident look in her eyes. That was enough for Max. He refrained from pushing to find out the secrets the two of them shared.

Nicky was a whole other story. He could be difficult and moody. You never knew what he might say or do. Lani always managed to take whatever he tried in stride.

That day, while all four of them labored over the lopsided sand castle, Nick grew impatient with Connie's effort to construct her own separate tower.

"It's crookeder than the big tower," he whined. "And you keep making the moat leak."

"I want my own tower," Connie insisted and patiently continued patting wet sand along the base of her wobbly tower, denting the sides of the moat as she worked.

Nick jumped up. "This is dumb. I am not going to build this castle if *she* gets to just mess it all up."

Max started to say something about how they all should work together.

But Lani spoke first. "Maybe you could give her a little help repairing the moat."

"But Miss Lani, *she* broke it."

"I did not break it," argued Connie. "I only just mooshed it a little tiny bit."

"You broke it."

"Did not."

"Did so."

"Did *not*."

Nick started to lift one sandy foot, his narrowed eyes on Connie's leaning tower.

Max spoke up then. "Nicky."

Nick put down his foot, stuck out his chin and swung his gaze to Max. A stare-down ensued. Luckily, Nicky looked away first. "I don't want to build this castle anymore." He dropped his toy shovel, whirled and took off at a run.

No one else moved, except Connie, who went on patting at her tower. Max watched his son race toward the cliffs at the far end of the beach.

Lani said what he was thinking. "Good. Let him work off his frustrations with action. Nicky's an action kind of guy."

"He's also a big butthead," Connie mumbled, patting her tower.

Max almost called her on the questionable word, but

Lani caught his eye and shook her head, mouthing sound-lessly, "Leave it."

He didn't argue. She somehow always knew when to step in and when to wait it out and let the children work through a conflict on their own.

Connie sat back on her knees and stared at her handi-work. "I did kind of mess up the moat. But if I go say sorry to Nicky, he'll only be mean to me."

"Wait till he comes back," Lani suggested. "Then the two of you can fix it together."

"He'll still be mean to me."

"Are you sure about that?"

Connie admitted, "Not *completely* sure."

"So then, how about if we just wait and see what hap-pens?"

"Miss Lani, I *hate* waiting."

Lani got up and dusted off her knees. "What, you hate *wading?* Well, I was just going to go wading." She held down her hand.

Connie frowned. *"Waiting, not wading."*

"But do you want to go wading or not?"

"I do!" Connie took her hand and jumped up and the two of them ran down the sandy slope to the water's edge, laughing together.

Max watched them as they played in the foamy edges of the lazy waves, giggling and rushing backward before they got in too deep. Lani's black hair was a wild halo of curls tangled by the wind and Connie's blond mop had gone straight and stringy. The sun caught the iridescent grains of sand on their arms and legs, making nature's own glit-ter on smooth, healthy skin.

They were beautiful, his little girl and Lani. They were beautiful and he was happy as he'd never thought to be. Ev-erything made sense now. His life not only had purpose, there was real pleasure now, deep and good and satisfying. Pleasure and someone to talk to, someone who loved the same things he did.

Nicky dropped down beside him. "So when are we going to eat?" He flopped flat onto his back and squinted up at the sky. "I'm *starving*." Nick was never merely hungry. "Papa?"

"We'll eat in a few minutes."

"But how *many* minutes?"

"I don't have an exact time for you. But soon."

For about thirty seconds, Nick lay quietly, panting a little from his run along the beach. Max went back to admiring the girl and the woman playing in the waves.

But Nick could never stay silent for long. He wiggled back up to a sitting position and wrapped his arms around his knees. "Are you going to get married to Miss Lani?"

Max sat very still. Maybe if he said nothing, Nick would get the hint and let it be.

Fat chance. "Papa?"

Fair enough. He would *have* to say something. "Why do you ask?"

Nicky fisted up a handful of sand and strained it through his fingers. "You said you really like her. You said it twice, remember?"

"I do remember, yes."

"Well, when a grown-up has a girlfriend and he really, really likes her, then they get married. Philippe told me so." Philippe was one of his school chums.

"Ah." Max waited. It was a complete cop-out. He had nothing. The truth was way too complex to share with an eight-year-old boy.

"So *are* you going to marry her?"

He tried, lamely, "Sometimes people are together just because they really, really like each other. Liking each other a lot is reason enough for them.'"

"And then they *don't* get married?"

"That's right."

"That's not what Philippe said. He said people get married. That's what they *do*."

"Not all people."

"Philippe's father has gotten married five times."

"Why am I not surprised?"

"Huh? So then, you're *not* going to marry Miss Lani?"

"I'll tell you what. If I do, you and I will talk about it first."

Nick made a face. "You don't need to talk to me about it. I like Miss Lani. You can marry her if you want to."

"Well, ahem. That's good to know."

Nicky just sat there, scowling.

Max tried gingerly, "Nick, is there something bothering you?"

Nick braced back on his hands, wiggled his toes in the sand and huffed out a hard breath. "Well, I keep trying to remember my mother and sometimes I just don't, you know?"

Sophia. He probably should have known.

Max reached out an arm and hooked it around his son's neck.

Nicky complained, "Papa!" but he didn't try to squirm away when Max pulled him close. He had that sweaty-boy smell, like wet puppies and sunshine.

At the water, Lani and Connie turned and started toward them. But then Lani seemed to register that a father-son moment might be happening. She took Connie's hand and led her off down the beach a ways. Together, they squatted and started writing with their index fingers in the shining wet sand.

Max said, quietly, father to son, "When we lost your mother, you were pretty young."

"I was *really* young. Only four. I mean, *Trev* is four."

"It's natural that you don't remember very much about her."

Nicky didn't reply at first. Max cast about for something reasonably helpful to add. But then Nick whispered, "I remember she had soft hair. And she would play with me sometimes, rolling a rubber ball in the play yard of the gardens."

"See? You do remember."

"It's not a lot. It should be more."

Max felt a certain tightness in his chest. "Whatever you remember is just right."

"Did you really, really like her, Papa?"

"I did, yes." It was the truth, for the most part. Through a good part of their marriage he had liked his wife very much. And once, a lifetime ago, he had thought what the world still thought: that Lady Sophia Paloma Delario Silva was the love of his life.

"And so you got married."

"Yes."

"Hah. Just like Philippe said."

"That Philippe," Max said wryly. "He knows it all."

Max woke in Lani's bed.

It was late, he knew that. He should have been back at the apartment hours ago. But their lovemaking had been so good and she was so soft and inviting. He remembered thinking, *Just for a few minutes. I'll just close my eyes...*

Beside him, she stirred but didn't wake. The bed smelled of her. Vanilla. Flowers. Something citrusy. Everything good.

He wanted to turn into her, pull her close, wake her with kisses.

Instead, he turned his head the other way and squinted at the clock.

Four in the morning.

He needed to get back. Sunday mornings had a certain rhythm to them. Marceline brought him coffee in bed to tide him over until the big family breakfast at nine. On Sundays, Nicky and Connie were allowed to join him in the master suite. They would stretch out on the bed with him, propped up on the pillows, and drink the hot cocoa Marceline brought with the coffee. Lani would arrive later, in time to go with them for Sunday breakfast.

"What time is it?" Her voice beside him, soft and enticing as the scent of her.

"After four. I have to go…"

"Um." She moved, turning over on her side, pressing closer.

He couldn't resist. He gathered her in. "Have to go…"

"Um…"

He stroked her sleek, warm back, sifted his fingers up into the wild, fine tangle of her midnight hair. The scent of gardenias was always stronger in her hair. "You do things to me…"

Her lips, her breath, trailing over his shoulder, caressing his throat.

He groaned. "Lani…"

And then she was moving closer still, her smooth, curvy body sliding over him, until she was on top of him, her softness pressing into him, making him burn. "Sometimes I wish you would stay a whole night."

He started to say how he couldn't.

And she said, "Scratch that. I *always* wish you would stay the whole night."

"Lani, I…" And that was as far as he got. Her lips

brushed his, teasing him, and he would rather be kissing her right then than talking, anyway.

So he did—or rather, she did. She covered his mouth with her soft, warm one and there was nothing but the sweet, heady taste of her, the glide of her naughty tongue over his teeth, the rub of her body all along his.

She moved her legs, straddling him, folding them to each side of his waist.

He groaned as he slipped right into place in the cove of her thighs. She was already wet and so very ready. Just the feel of her came very near to pushing him over the top.

Somehow, he held out, held on, as her body rose and she was sliding forward, lifting him with her as she moved. The endless kiss continued, and he caught her face between his hands so he could thoroughly plunder her mouth.

Right then, without him really realizing how perfectly she'd positioned them, she lowered her body down onto his, taking him into her, all the way in.

He groaned her name against her lips. Paradise, to be buried deep in her welcoming heat. And then she manacled his wrists with her soft hands, guiding them back to the pillow on each side of his head.

"Lani…" It came out as a plea.

She lifted her sweet mouth away from him, sitting up on him. He moaned at the loss—and also at the way the shift in position had her pressing down tighter where they were joined, deepening the connection. And then she started moving, holding his wrists in place on the pillow, driving him out of his mind with pure pleasure, her cloud of dark hair falling forward over her white, smooth shoulders.

He sought her black eyes through the darkness, held them, tried to stay with her as she took him, rocking him.

But it was pointless to hold out, impossible to last. The

sensations intensified, sparks flying down every nerve, heat popping and sizzling across his skin.

He shut his eyes as he went over, and he broke the hold of her hands on his wrists, so he could touch her, grasp the perfect, full curves of her hips and press her down even harder on him as he pressed up into her.

She crumpled onto him then, her softness covering him. As his climax rolled through him, she caught his mouth again and she kissed him endlessly, crying out wordless things, her climax chasing his.

He pressed even harder into her, and with a long, low cry, she shattered around him.

"I have to go," Max whispered, his hand on her cheek, fingers weaving up into her tangled hair.

Lani pretended not to hear him, tucking her head into the curve of his shoulder and then settling against his chest. His heartbeat slowed under her ear and she felt so lovely, so loose and lazy, her body still thrumming with the echo of pleasure, her skin, like his, sticky with sweat.

For a string of too-short moments, he just went on touching her, guiding her hair behind her ear, stroking warm fingers down her arm.

But then he took her shoulders in a tender but determined grip and pushed her away from him.

She groaned in protest, grumbling, "No..."

But he was already gently guiding her to the side, sliding away from her, easing his feet over the edge of the mattress, rising before she had a chance to pull him back.

With another groan, she buried her face in the pillow.

"A quick shower," he said, bending, brushing a kiss against her hair.

She heard the hushed whisper of his bare feet as he padded across the floor.

Not five minutes later, he was back. She sat up and watched him quickly pull on his clothes.

Smelling steamy and wonderful, his hair curly, sticking up on one side the way it did when it was wet, he bent close to give her a last, sweet kiss. "I'll send the car for you. Eight-thirty?"

Her throat ached with all the things she was holding in. Her love, her longing, the future she saw for them versus the one she had finally admitted, to herself and to Syd at least, that she wanted.

But now was not the time. Not after he'd slept too late, not after she'd shamelessly kept him there longer still, using her body to get a little bit more from him, a little bit more *of* him. A little bit more of what he didn't want to give.

We have to talk.

She tried the words out in her head and didn't like them. *We have to talk.* The four little words people said when things had to change.

He arched a brow at her. "Lani? Eight-thirty?"

She forced a smile and nodded.

One more kiss. And he was gone.

She got up, pulled on the silky robe he'd given her and went out into the living area to engage the dead bolt after him. Then she brewed coffee and took it out on the balcony, into the cool predawn darkness. She sipped and stared at the tree shadows on the hill in back, planning what she would do.

She needed to wait for an evening when they wouldn't be disturbed. Tonight wouldn't do. They would be with the children all day and she would have dinner at the palace apartment, in the little kitchen, all casual and cozy, just the four of them and maybe Gerta. Later, she might stay until eight or nine, but when they were at his apartment, there was always the possibility that Connie or Nick would need him for something. She didn't want them overhearing what she had to say.

Tomorrow, they were leaving together for two days, flying to London, where he would speak at a charity fundraiser. They would return Wednesday.

She'd been looking forward to it, to the time together away from home, to the nights when he wouldn't have to get up and leave before daylight.

So then. Tuesday night maybe, after the event? If that didn't feel right, then whenever he came to her place next, she would do what Syd had said she should do. What she realized at last she *needed* to do.

She would tell him she loved him. And that she had changed. She would tell him what she wanted from him, from her life. She would do all that right away, as soon as he walked in the door, before they started talking about her day or his day or what was going on with Nick and Connie, before they made love or had dinner. She would do it and not put it off.

And then they would take it from there.

Her cup was empty. She pushed back the slider to go in and get more. And right then, on the counter, her cell started playing the theme from *Big Brother*.

Carlos? At this hour? Five-thirty in the morning in Montedoro was ten-thirty last night in Texas.

Dread coiling in her belly like a snake about to strike, she grabbed the phone. "Carlos?"

"Hey, *hermanita*." He sounded very un-Carlos-like. Hesitant. Careful. All wrong. Her big brother was always the most confident person in the room. He knew what was right and he never minded telling you. "I'm sorry if I woke you up. It's not even daylight there yet, right?"

"It's okay. I was up. I… Is there something wrong?"

And then he just came out with it. "It's Papi," he said. "You need to get home."

Chapter Twelve

Dressed in the silk pajamas he always wore when expecting a visit from the children in the morning, Max was just climbing into his bed when his cell rang. He could hear it buzzing away, over there on the chair, still in the pocket of the trousers he'd worn to Lani's.

He considered letting it go to voice mail and calling whoever it was back later. But who called at six Sunday morning? It would be a wrong number or someone who urgently needed to reach him.

Just in case it was the latter, he went over there, grabbed the trousers, fished the phone from the pocket and answered.

"Max?" Lani's voice vibrated with urgency.

Alarm jangled through him. "Lani, what is it?"

"I just got a call from my brother. My father's in surgery. Acute appendicitis. Can you believe that?" She didn't wait for him to answer, just barreled on, the words tumbling over each other in a frantic rush. "My mother's a doctor and *she* didn't figure it out. The symptoms can be a little different for older people. It doesn't seem so acute. But it *is* acute. If they'd waited any longer, it would have ruptured. He's still not okay, far from okay. They've got him in surgery—did I already say that? It's… Oh, Max, I'm sorry. I guess I'm rambling."

"It's all right. Don't apologize." He dropped to the chair and raked his fingers back through his hair. "An appendectomy then?"

"Yes. That's right."

"But it's a standard procedure, isn't?"

"I don't know. My brother made it sound pretty bad."

"Still, your father *is* going to pull through?"

A ragged sound escaped her. "I think so. I'm pretty sure. I need to fly back there, to be with them, to see Papi, to tell him how much I love him."

"Yes. Of course you do. I'll arrange for a jet." He should take her, he knew it. He should be there when she needed him. "I don't know if I can get out of that thing in London at this point…"

"Of course not. I understand." She sounded strange suddenly. A little stiff, too formal, somehow. He didn't like it. It made him feel apart from her, not family.

But then, he *wasn't* her family. He was her lover and her friend and she meant the world to him, and that was how they both wanted it.

She went on, "I mean, it's bad, but he's not *dying* or anything. At least, he'd better not. And really, Max, I only wanted you to know what was going on. As far as getting there, I can just fly commercial. You don't have to—"

He cut her off. "I will arrange for the jet."

"Oh, Max…" A tight laugh escaped her. "I don't know why I'm so freaked out. I mean, people get sick sometimes. You deal with it. It's probably mostly the guilt."

"Guilt?"

"That I haven't been back much, that I never go home. All that he did for me, all my life, especially in the hardest times. And I'm not there when he needs his whole family around him, rooting for him. Or maybe it was Carlos."

"Your brother?"

"He was the one who called me. Did I tell you that? I guess not. Carlos sounded so cautious and subdued. My brother is never subdued and…" She pulled herself up short. "There I go. Babbling away again."

"I'll arrange everything," he promised. "Two hours, tops, you'll be in the air."

"But I could so easily—"

"Don't argue. I will get you there hours ahead of any commercial flight you could find. And you want to be there fast, don't you?"

"Oh, Max. I do." A hard sob escaped her. "Yes."

"Then count on me. Pack, get ready to go, call Sydney and tell her what's happened. Do whatever you need to do. I'll be there to take you to Nice Airport at seven. Be ready."

"All right, yes. I… Thank you."

"You don't need to thank me." His voice sounded gruff to his own ears. "You never need to thank me."

"Oh, Max, I…" She seemed to catch herself. "Seven. Yes. I'll be ready when you get here."

Max arrived at her apartment ten minutes early. They were on their way to the airport at seven on the dot.

During the drive, Lani seemed distant, distracted— which was in no way surprising given the circumstances. He held her hand and gave her Gerta's good wishes. "And Connie sends a thousand kisses and orders you to take care of your papa and then be home soon."

She smiled softly at that. "Tell Connie a million billion kisses back. And of course I will do exactly as she instructed. Any message from Nicky? Wait. Let me guess.

Something along the lines of 'So can we stay home from Sunday breakfast, then?'"

"You know him too well." He wanted to be closer to her. So he unhooked his seat belt, slid over to the middle seat and hooked himself in there. "Hello." He put his arm around her. With a sigh, she leaned her head on his shoulder. Better. He breathed in the scent of her hair and tried to tamp down his apprehensions. Her father would be fine in the end, he was sure. And she would come home to Montedoro, home to him.

She glanced up at him. "Tell Nicky he gets a million billion kisses from me, too, whether he likes it or not."

"I will. Have you talked to your mother yet?"

She sighed again. "No. I'll see her soon, and she's focused on my father right now. I'm in touch with Carlos, getting everything I need to know from him. He'll tell her I'm on the way."

"The thing in London is tomorrow evening. Once it's over, I'll come to you."

Her head shot up. "You're coming to Texas?"

He eased his hand under her hair, wrapped his fingers around the warm, soft back of her neck and teased, "That's where you'll be, isn't it?"

"Yeah, but I didn't…" She seemed to catch herself.

He held her gaze. "You do that a lot lately—stop talking in the middle of sentences, as though you're editing yourself."

"I… Sorry."

"Did it again."

"I'm worried about my father."

"I know." But he doubted that was all of it.

"Max, really. You don't have to come."

"It's not a question of having to. I *want* to come." He was more and more certain that something other than her father's sudden illness was bothering her—and had been for a while now. "Unless you don't want me there…"

"No. That's not so. Of course I want you there." She was trying too hard to convince him, which only made him more certain that she really *didn't* want him in Texas with her family.

Too bad. He was taking her at her word, whether she liked it or not. "All right then. I'll be there."

Max would be joining her in Beaufort….

Lani wasn't sure how she felt about that. Glad that he wanted to be there for her, certainly.

But a little bit freaked, too. Her family wanted her to come home to Texas to stay. Failing that, they at least wanted her settled down and happy wherever she lived. To her family, settled down meant married, and she doubted they would be shy about making that painfully clear to Max.

The fact that what they wanted had finally turned out to be what she wanted didn't really help all that much. Not when she knew in her heart it wasn't what Max wanted.

Which was something the two of them were going to be talking about.

Soon.

At the airport, the driver took them right out to the plane bearing Montedoro's coat of arms. An attendant rushed forward and dealt with her luggage. Max took her on board and exchanged greetings with the flight crew.

Then he cradled her face between his hands. "They'll take good care of you. A car will be waiting in Dallas."

Now that he was leaving, she realized that she wanted him never to go. "Thank you."

"Stop saying that."

"Kiss me."

"That's better." He took her mouth gently, a tender salute of a kiss that ended way too quickly.

She trailed him to the exit.

"Call me when you arrive in Dallas," he said.

She promised she would and watched him run down the airstairs. "I love you," she whispered under her breath as he ducked into the limo. It seemed the truest thing she'd said all day. Too bad she hadn't managed to shout it out loud and proud.

Before they took off, she called Carlos. "How's Papi?"

"He's out of surgery. Groggy. Hanging in." He was still sounding strange, almost guarded, and that worried her. Was it worse than he was letting on?

"Is there something you're not telling me, Carlito?"

"Not telling you?" He spoke impatiently, with a hint of belligerence, her big brother reminding her that he was the oldest and knew best. "What do you mean?" He could be such a jerk sometimes.

She schooled her voice to a reasonable tone. "I mean, is he worse than you're telling me?"

"No, of course not."

"Thank God for that."

"Yoli Poly, you still need to come home." Yoli Poly. She'd always hated that nickname. And she didn't like his scolding tone.

"Carlos. I'm in the jet. I'm on my way. Sheesh."

"Good. You need a ride from the airport?"

"No, thanks. It's taken care of."

"She's a big girl," he teased. "She can do it herself."

"That is exactly right." She said it jokingly, but she meant every word. "And don't you forget it."

The plane took off at 8:00 a.m. Flying west, the time zone difference worked in her favor. She arrived at Love

Field at a little before noon. There was customs to deal with, but it didn't take that long.

She called Max from the limo on her way to the hospital and told him she'd arrived safely and her father was out of surgery, doing well.

"That's what I wanted to hear." His voice played through her, deep and fine, rousing way too many dangerous emotions. She promised to call him if there was any other news and he said he would be in touch tomorrow to firm up plans for joining her there. "Shall I find a hotel?" he offered.

Oh, that was tempting. Separate him from the parents and the pushy big brother. Create fewer opportunities for cringe-worthy remarks and questions about their relationship and where it might be going.

But that wouldn't be right. He mattered to her. A lot. And the people she loved had a right to know that. Plus, in her family, you didn't send out-of-town guests to hotels unless you had no room for them.

There was plenty of room at the rambling five-bedroom redbrick ranch-style house on Prairie Lane where she'd grown up. "My mother would never forgive me if I sent you to a hotel."

"There will be a bodyguard," he reminded her. "Are you sure?"

"We'll make it work."

"All right, then." Did he sound okay with the plan? He might come to her little apartment for the evening twice a week, but then he went home to a palace. He would probably be more comfortable at a decent hotel....

"Max. Just tell me. Would you rather get a hotel suite?"

"I would rather be with you."

A sweet warmth stole through her. "Well, okay, then. You'll stay at the house."

"Good."

She almost warned him that they would have separate rooms. But then again, what was so strange about that? They had yet to spend a full night in the same bed together. And never once had she shared his bed at the palace. This was pretty much the same thing, really.

He spoke again. "Lani."

"Um?"

"I miss you."

She chided, "It's been what, twelve hours since I left?"

"Maybe it's your being so far away. Whatever it is, this is the moment for you to say, 'I miss you, too.'"

She confessed it. "I do miss you." She wished he was there, in the car with her, that she could put her head on his shoulder, have the steady weight of his arm around her. Not to mention, be his wife and have his babies.

But he wasn't there. And the last time they'd talked about marriage, he'd told her he would never get married again.

She said goodbye.

When she entered her father's hospital room, Jorge Vasquez was sitting up in bed, alert and clear-eyed. At the sight of her, he grinned from ear to ear and held out his arms. "*Mi'ja,* Carlito said you were coming!"

A miracle had happened, evidently. Her father had taken a turn for the *better*.

"Papi." She went to him and he hugged her close. His grip was strong. When he let her go, she looked him over. "You seem…good. Really good."

"I'm just fine. The surgery was laparoscopic, no complications—at least so far. I've been up and walking around. They're letting me out of here today."

"Today?"

"Don't look so shocked. I'm strong as an ox and modern medicine is a wonderful thing."

"But I thought—"

The sound of her mother's voice cut her off. "Yolanda, my baby girl…" Lani turned as Iris Vasquez entered the room looking just as Lani remembered her, petite and pretty, her long dark hair threaded with silver, parted in the middle and pulled back in a low ponytail.

"Mama." Lani went into her open arms. As always, her mother smelled faintly of plain soap. Dr. Iris never wore perfume. Too many of her young patients were allergic to it. She took Lani by the shoulders and held her away enough to beam at her. "Oh, it's good to see you. Look at you. More beautiful than ever."

Lani pulled her close for another hug. "You, too, Mama."

That time, when they moved apart, her mother urged her to take a chair.

She sat down. "Carlos really had me worried about Papi."

Iris waved a hand. "Oh, I know. I told him there would be no need for you to come, but he wouldn't listen."

"No need?" Lani tried to keep her voice light, though inside she was starting to seethe.

Her mother nodded. "Right away, I knew what was going on. Textbook symptoms of appendicitis. I took your father straight to his internist and then here for surgery."

"So you're saying you caught it early?"

"Well, *mi'ja,* I am a doctor, after all. And I'm sorry to drag you all the way from the Riviera. But now, looking at you right here where I can reach out my arms and hug you, I can't help but be glad that Carlos insisted this was a good way to get you to come home."

Max was in bed when his phone rang. Lani. It was after ten in Montedoro, which meant it would be past three in the afternoon where she was.

Eager for the husky sound of her voice, he set aside

the book he'd been reading and put the phone to his ear. "How's your father?"

"Good. Really good. *Too* good."

"*Too* good? How is that possible?"

"Turns out Carlos lied to me when he said my father was practically at death's door. Apparently, he did it to get me to come home. So I get here an hour ago and my father's sitting up in bed, all smiles and so happy to see me. My mother figured out it was appendicitis from practically his first twinge of pain. The operation was laparoscopic—minimally invasive, small incisions, faster healing."

"It all sounds great—other than the part about your brother lying to you."

"I'm thinking positive. My dad isn't dying after all. The doctor's with him now and he's going home today."

"But you're angry."

"I was terrified. I want to strangle Carlos, I really do. I'll get him alone later and tell him exactly what I think of him."

"Be kind."

"Right. And you know…" Suddenly she was doing that hesitating thing again, her voice trailing off as though she wasn't sure how much she could say to him. He gritted his teeth and waited for it. "It's really not necessary for you to come here now. Everything's going to be fine and I'll be back in Montedoro in a week, two at the most."

He said nothing.

"Max? Are you still there?"

"I'm here. Are you saying that you don't want me there?"

"No, of course I'm not." The words sounded automatic and not all that sincere.

He should probably back off, leave her alone to be with her family. She'd return to him soon enough. But he wanted to go to her, to see where she'd grown up, to meet her mother and father and even the devious big brother. "All right then. I'll come directly from London, as planned."

"You scared me to death," Lani accused. "You know that, right?"

It was nine o'clock that night. Her father was resting comfortably in his own bed, her mother beside him. Carlos's bride, Martina, was in the living room on the phone with her own mother in San Antonio. Lani had dragged Carlos out to the back deck to have it out with him.

Carlos blustered, "You needed to be scared. You needed to come home." Her big brother was the same as ever. He had no shame. But why should he? He was always right, just ask him.

"You lied to me, Carlos. You manipulated me. Papi was never in any real danger."

"When there's surgery, it's always dangerous—and Mama and Papi need you. They're getting older and they need their only daughter close." Leave it to Carlos to play the guilt card early and often.

She reminded herself it was just more manipulation. "If they need me, I will be here. So far, they seem to be doing just fine."

"You are so selfish, *mi'ja*. You always have been. You do what you want and you don't care who gets hurt." Great. Two minutes alone with him and he already had the heavy equipment out excavating the pain of the past.

Deep breaths. Calm words. "What's going on here, Carlos? I mean, what's *really* going on?"

He strode out to the edge of the deck and stared off through the darkness, his broad back held stiffly, chest out. A wrestler in high school and college, Carlos never gave up until he had his opponent's shoulders pinned to the mat in a match-winning three-second hold. "Martina and I are in San Antonio most of the time now. No one's close if they need us."

She went for the positives. "Really, it's not that bad. I admit I haven't been here enough. But I will come more often, and be ready to fly back anytime it's necessary. And it's an hour flight for you."

He made a humphing sound. "You're the daughter. It's your duty to be here for your mother and father."

"Seriously?" she asked, with excruciating sweetness. "Do you even have a clue how sexist that sounds?"

He whirled on her, black eyes flashing. "You have a duty, Yoli, after all they've done for you."

She kept her head high. "Maybe I do. But that's between Mama and Papi and me. And whether or not I ought to move back to Texas has got nothing to do with why I asked you to come out here and speak with me privately. Carlos, you lied and you manipulated me to get me here. It was wrong, what you did."

He dropped into the iron chair by the railing and stared out at the backyard again. "You're getting way too damn reasonable, you know that? In the old days, you'd be crying and carrying on and calling me all kinds of names by now."

"It so happens I grew up." She waited for him to meet her eyes again. He didn't. "You need to stop thinking of me as some spoiled eighteen-year-old. I made some terrible choices and I hurt the people I love, including you. I know that. I live with that, will live with that, for the rest of my life. I hope someday you can forgive me for all the trouble I caused."

"Of course I forgive you," he grumbled. "You're my sister. I love you."

"And I love you. But, Carlos, you were in the wrong to scare me like that about Papi."

He shocked her then—by busting to it. "All right. Yeah.

It was wrong. I shouldn't have made Papi's condition sound worse than it is."

She went over and took the chair beside him. "And?"

At last, he looked at her. His eyes were softer. She saw regret in them. "I shouldn't have done it. I'm sorry. I'm sorry for…all the ways I'm being a douche. I just wanted you to come home. It doesn't seem right, you living halfway around the world."

She did long for him to understand. "I love Montedoro, Carlito. My life is there now. It's the home of my heart."

"Your home is with your family."

Here we go again. "Listen to me. You don't get to decide what works for my life. You really need to stop imagining that you do."

He looked away, then slid her a sideways glance. "This guy, this prince…"

She sat a little straighter. "His name is Max."

"There's a lot of stuff online about you and him."

"I know. And in the tabloids, too. Don't take any of it too seriously."

"There was even something about you and that SOB, McKneely."

She reached across the distance between their chairs and nudged his arm. "Don't speak ill of the dead." He made a sound low in his throat, but left it at that. She added, "It's public knowledge. What can you do?"

He held her gaze. "You're taking it well."

"Hey. I try."

"You said at dinner that the—er, Max—is coming here Tuesday."

"Well, he *was* coming to support me in my hour of need, what with my father practically dying and all…"

He scowled at her. "You made your point. Give it a rest."

"Now he's just coming to meet my wonderful family, I guess."

"Are you going to marry him?"

She'd known he would ask, and she had her answer ready. "At this point, that's none of your business."

"So then, that's a no?"

"What part of 'none of your business' was unclear to you?"

Carlos made more grumbling sounds. "I guess if you married him, you'd be a princess and live in the palace and never come home."

"Of course I would come home. I just promised I would, and more often, too. And can we worry about marriage when the time comes?" *If it ever does.*

The back door opened. Martina stuck her head out. Carlos's wife was every inch the dancer, graceful and slim, her long brown hair pulled up in a high, tight ponytail. A strong-minded, opinionated woman, Martina also had a big heart. From the first, she'd fit right into the Vasquez family. She gave Carlos a look of equal parts fire and tenderness. "Stop arguing, you two, and come inside."

The next morning, Jorge came to the table for breakfast. He winced and groaned getting down into the chair, and he only had juice and a few spoonfuls of plain yogurt. But still. It did Lani's heart good to see him sitting there, so proud of himself, so happy to have his family around him.

She had missed him—missed all of them—she thought, as she sipped her coffee and ate her mother's killer chorizo and eggs. They were dear to her and they loved her. And the emotional distance she had felt between herself and them since all the trouble eleven years ago?

Gone. Vanished. She had created that distance, she realized now. She had erected barriers against them. And now that she no longer needed to wall herself off from them, the barriers had crumbled of their own accord.

She didn't approve of the way Carlos had tricked her to get her to come home, but her brother had been right that she needed to be there. Whatever happened with Max, she would do better by her family. She would get back to Texas more often.

Whatever happened with Max...

He was still coming to be with her, to meet her family. He seemed to really *want* to come. And she wanted him there, even if it was difficult and awkward and her brother and her parents asked all kinds of leading questions, even if they came right out and demanded to know if he had marriage on his mind.

So what if they did ask? It would only prove they were braver than she was.

Carlos said, "Now that we're all here together and Papi is looking good, Martina and I have a little announcement to make."

Martina was blushing. Carlos took her hand and brought it to his lips. They shared a look of such joy and intimacy, Lani almost felt guilty watching them.

Her mother clapped and cried out, "Oh! Already? I can hardly believe it." She reached for Jorge's hand.

He took it, wrapped his other hand around it and declared, "I am a happy, happy man."

Carlos laughed. "We haven't even told you what it is yet."

Iris chuckled. "As if we don't already know."

"Could be I got a great deal on some restaurant equipment."

Iris sputtered and Martina said, "Carlos, don't tease."

And Carlos finally came out with the big news. "Martina and I are having a baby."

Iris let out another happy cry and Jorge said, "Wonderful news."

Lani added her voice to the others. "That's terrific. Congratulations."

And her mother jumped up to go hug Martina, while her father grabbed her brother's arm and gave it a hearty, man-to-man squeeze. "You have made me so happy, my son."

Lani let their gladness wash over her. She was glad *for* them, for the new life that her brother and his wife would soon bring into the world. At the same time, she was suddenly far away from all of them, remembering her lost baby, who would be older than Nicky now. There would always be a certain empty place within her, a place that echoed with longing, a place that held only regret for the life her child would never have.

But beneath the old sorrow, now there was something new. Something hopeful and scary, too. She was through with denials, through taking care of other people's babies and telling herself that it was enough. One way or another, she was ready for happiness now, ready to make a family of her own.

Max needed to know that.

And not in a week or two, when they were back in Montedoro.

Uh-uh. No more putting it off. No more making excuses for the things she didn't have the courage to say. No going along as usual with secrets in her heart, no pretending that everything was okay when it wasn't.

He was coming tomorrow. And at the earliest opportunity, she would get him alone and tell him that she loved him—was *in* love with him. And also that, for her, everything had changed.

Chapter Thirteen

The driver, Calvin, pulled the car to a stop in front of the redbrick house.

"A minute," said Max, before Calvin could get out.

"Certainly, sir." Calvin already had his door unlatched. He pulled it shut and glanced at the bodyguard, Joseph, in the seat beside him. But Joseph sat patiently, staring straight ahead.

Max gazed out the tinted side window at the graceful sweep of lawn, the long front porch and the large front door with the arched fanlight in the top. The house seemed to him so completely American, long and low, a style they called midcentury ranch. Lani had grown up here. He could almost picture her, a little girl with black braids and scraped knees, riding a pink tricycle down the natural stone front walk.

The door opened and the grown Lani came out, wearing jeans that hugged her beautiful curves and a light, lacy turquoise shirt. She closed the door behind her. And then for several seconds she just stood there on the porch, staring at the car.

He stared back at her, something dark and hot and needful churning within him. He knew she couldn't see him through the tinted glass. Still, he felt the connection anyway. Strong. Urgent. Unbreakable.

Or at least that was what he kept telling himself, even if sometimes lately she seemed to be pulling away from him.

She emerged from under the shadow of the porch roof. The spring sunshine caught deep red gleams in her black hair as she came down the walk to the car.

He pushed open the door.

She leaned in. "Change your mind about staying?" He reached out, snared her arm and dragged her inside. "Max!"

He pulled the door closed, pressed his nose to her smooth throat and breathed in the unforgettable scent of her. "I wanted a minute or two alone first."

She shot a glance at the two in the front seat. "We're not alone."

He ran up the privacy screen. "Now. Be quiet. Kiss me."

"Yes, Your Highness."

He tasted her sweetness, stroked her silky hair, considered telling Joseph and Calvin to take a long walk. But there was her family to consider. "I suppose they're waiting in there, wondering what I'm up to."

She grinned, though her eyes seemed somehow guarded. "You suppose right. How was the thing in London?"

"The usual. Long. Somewhat dull. I need to rework the speech I gave. We got several large donations, though, so I'm calling it a win. Connie sends big hugs, by the way. Nick says, and I quote, 'When Miss Lani gets back can we go to the beach again and make another sand castle and I'll be nice to Connie?'"

"Whoa. He is becoming downright sweet. You told him yes, right?"

"I said I'd check with you." He tipped up her chin. For a moment, she met his gaze, but then her glance skittered away. He demanded, "What's the matter?"

She caught his wrist, pushed it gently aside. "Later."

"So there *is* something?"

"Yes, Max. There is. And my mother just came out on the porch. We should go in."

Max liked Lani's mother. He told her to call him Max and she shook his hand and said with a smile almost as beautiful as Lani's, "I'm Iris."

Iris took the usual awkwardness with Joseph in stride. The three of them—Lani, Max and Iris—waited on the porch while the bodyguard made a quick reconnaissance of the property.

When Joseph was ready to check inside, Iris went with him in order to explain to her husband, her son and her son's wife why the large stranger with the Bluetooth device in his ear was checking in the showers and opening closet doors.

Once that was over, Calvin brought in the luggage and Iris showed Max to his room, which had a window that looked out on the front yard, a double closet and a bath just down the hall. Joseph got a much smaller room next door. Max would have to share his bathroom with the bodyguard. That was a first. He couldn't recall ever sharing a bath with another man. Luckily, Joseph was a consummate professional. He made being unobtrusive into an art form. Max foresaw no problems there.

Dinner was served at seven. There were big slabs of beef cooked on the outside grill the way Americans loved best, along with enormous baked potatoes, lots of green salad and hot dinner rolls.

Lani's dad came to the table, though he ate only a small dish of applesauce and some yogurt. Jorge Vasquez was cordial enough, but watchful, too. Same with Lani's brother, Carlos. Max could feel the men's protectiveness of Lani.

Max might be the heir to a throne, but that didn't mean he was good enough for their little girl.

During the meal, Max learned that Carlos's wife, Martina, was going to have a baby. He congratulated her. Martina thanked him and said she was very happy. Carlos took her hand for a moment and she gave him a glowing smile.

"Love, marriage, children." Jorge Vasquez looked misty-eyed. "What else is there, eh?" He aimed the question at Max, one bushy brow lifted.

"Family is everything," Max agreed with a smile. He sent a quick glance at Lani, to his left. She only nodded, her expression relaxed and neutral, but her eyes as watchful as her father's.

"I'm so glad you feel that way," said Iris, beaming. "Lani tells us you have two children already. We hope to get to meet them soon."

Already? As if he intended to have more? "Yes." He turned to Lani again. "We should plan on that."

She nodded as she had before, but didn't say anything.

And it went on through the meal, the Vasquezes taking turns dropping hints about matrimony and babies, Max knocking himself out trying to be receptive and agreeable without actually lying and vowing to get a ring on Lani's finger immediately so they could set to work providing Iris and Jorge with more grandchildren. Through it all, Lani never said a word. Max tried not to be annoyed with her, but he couldn't help thinking that it would have been so easy for her to make a joke of the whole thing, or to simply tell her parents and brother to cut it out.

After the meal, they watched a comedy on the large flat-screen television in the family room. Of course, the movie had a romance in it and when the hero proposed to the heroine, Max stared straight ahead. No way was he get-

ting caught checking to see if Lani's mother or father was
watching him, hoping he was getting the hint.

Jorge and Iris went to bed when the movie ended. Holding hands, Martina and Carlos went out the back door to
the deck.

Lani said, "There's a park a few blocks away and it's a
nice night. Get Joseph and we'll go for a walk."

The night was balmy and no one disturbed them as they
walked in and out of the wide pools of golden light provided by high streetlamps. He'd been a little worried the
paparazzi might have gotten wind of his destination when
he left Heathrow. But no. Her parents' neighborhood was
quiet except for the ordinary sounds of places like this: the
sudden bark of a protective dog, the honk of a car horn,
the whisper of the wind in the branches of the oak trees.

They walked without speaking. She seemed withdrawn,
thoughtful. And he was still a little put out with her for not
backing her family off during dinner.

When they reached the park she'd mentioned, she led
him to a bench by a deserted grouping of swings, a slide,
monkey bars and a jungle gym. They sat down and Joseph
retreated into the shadows several yards away.

And she said, "There's something I've been meaning to
tell you, Max. Something I really need to say."

And he *knew*. He was certain. The bottom dropped out
of his stomach. "You're pregnant."

Her eyes popped wide. And then she laughed. "No."

He felt relieved. And also foolish. "Oh. Well. I'm…
That's good." Did he sound like an idiot? Definitely. He
shut his mouth and waited.

She got up from the bench and held down her hand. He
took it. She led him to the swings and they each sat in one.
For a moment, she pushed herself slowly back and forth,

her head tipped up to the three-quarter moon, the swing chains making a faint squeaking sound.

Then, as the swinging slowed, she turned to him. "I've changed, Max, since I met you. Changed in so many ways I can hardly name them all. Changed way down, in the deepest, truest part of me. You've...opened me up. You've freed me. There's no other word for it. I am free now. You've accepted me, just as I am. With you, I've shared the worst of me, and still, you...wanted me, cared for me. It's meant everything, how you are, how *we* are, you and me, together." She stilled the swing and swayed there, just the slightest bit, beside him. "I know that I matter to you."

"Of course, you—"

"Shh." She reached across the space between their two swings and put her finger against his lips. At his nod of agreement not to interrupt, she withdrew her hand. "I don't know why we don't say it to each other, why I've never said it to you when I've known it for weeks now. Longer. Known it even back when I was set on denying it. For all those months when we were 'just friends.'"

He had the strangest feeling—weightless and drowning, both at once. He wanted to stop her, wanted to drag her back somehow to the safety of what they were to each other now, of all they'd had together in the past month.

But she refused to stay safe. "I don't know why we don't say it, Max. Maybe because to say it leads on to the next step and the next step is one you're not willing to take. But, well, I have to say it. Are you listening? Tell me you're listening."

"Damn it, Lani."

She stilled the swing completely. "I'll say it anyway. I love you, Max. You're everything I could ever want in a man. Are we clear on that?"

"Lani, I—"

"Max. Are we clear?"

I love you, too. You're everything to me. How hard could it be to tell her? "Yes. We're clear."

She looked at him so sadly. But he didn't need her sad look to tell him how completely he had disappointed her. "I need to…say the rest." She sounded breathless now. And not in a good way. "I know I told you once that I would never get married, never have children. I meant it, at the time. And you told me the same about yourself. You do remember that." It wasn't a question.

He answered it anyway. "Yes, of course I do."

"Well, for me, everything's different now. For me, the world is wide open again and I can be happy. I can love you and marry you, be your wife, help you take care of your beautiful children, give you more children…"

He needed to stop this. But of course, he knew he couldn't. He knew it was already too late. So he gave her what he had, which was the truth. "I will never get married again. And I don't believe in having children outside of marriage. However, if you became pregnant, I would love and accept the child."

"I told you, I'm not pregnant. I'm very careful about contraception, so you can stop worrying about that."

"I'm not worrying. I just wanted you to know."

"Ah." She stared at him for a long time, her eyes bright with unshed tears.

He couldn't bear the silence. "I told you from the first that I wasn't looking for a wife." Defensive. Gruff. God, he hated himself.

"Yes, you did. You told me you would never marry again. What you didn't tell me is why. Why won't you take a chance on a real future with me? How is it that you've opened me up, given me the ability to love again, to dream again? And you remain the same. Closed off. Unchanged."

"But I'm not unchanged. You mean everything to me."

One tear fell, shining and pure, sliding slowly down her cheek. "You never talk about Sophia."

"Lani—"

"No. Don't cut me off. Don't redirect me. I just need to know. Is it what people say? That you've had the perfect, forever love and nothing can ever come close so you're never even going to try?" She shook her head. "That doesn't make sense to me, somehow. It doesn't feel true. You never say anything about her, nothing. No fond memories. Nothing about the good times you shared, or the hard times you got through together. You are silent on the subject of Sophia. What was it with her that makes it all such a mystery, that has you swearing off ever really trying again?"

He didn't know where to start. He didn't want to start. "Just because I don't want to get married again doesn't mean I'm not trying."

She tipped her head to the side, studying him. "Okay. Maybe I was unfair. You *are* trying. Up to a point. But after that point, uh-uh. You're done. And see, that's the thing. You pried me open like a can of peaches, you know? You got inside my head and my heart and you found out all the bad stuff. I gave it to you and you took it with an open heart. I knew that it would make you despise me. But it didn't. You were wonderful, tender, so completely accepting. I want to do that for you. I wish you would let me."

"Lani." He stood from the swing so fast that she gasped. "Stop."

She gazed up at him as the swing bumped against the backs of his calves. And then she laughed. It was the saddest sound he'd ever heard. "You saw how it was with my parents and my brother. They want happiness for me, and I'm like them, as you've helped me to discover. I want what they want for me—a husband, a home, a family. And they're going to keep after you. They want you to tell them that you're ready, or at least close to ready, to give me what I want."

"Are you saying you want me to leave you here and go back to Montedoro?"

She gazed up at him, the moon shining in her tear-wet eyes. "No. I want you to stay. I want you to stick it out. But I'm warning you, it's not going to be a whole lot of fun for you if you do."

They were at an impasse. What she wanted now for her life and her future, he would never give her. What she needed to hear from him, he would never say.

He should go home. But there was a bloody fool within him who couldn't bear to lose her, who refused to surrender the field. "I'm not going anywhere, not until you're ready to come home with me."

She kept staring at him, steadily. "I want more than this, Max. I want everything, all of you. A lifetime together, to live with you and Nicky and Connie, to sleep the whole night in the same bed with you, to be in that bed with you on Sunday morning when the children come in for cocoa. The right to be there, as your wife, when you need me the most."

There was no point in telling her again that she'd never get that from him. "Let's go back to the house." He held down his hand.

She took it without the slightest hesitation and she said softly, "It's not going to be pleasant."

"What isn't?"

"None of it. You'll see."

They stayed in Texas, at her parents' house, for a week. The Vasquez family treated him with kindness and a wry sort of affection. And they never stopped working on him to declare his intentions concerning his relationship with Lani.

He could have left. He knew that. Maybe he *should* have left. But something in him held on, refusing to let go. He knew if he left her there it would be over between them.

He did not want that. He wanted things as they had been: the two of them, free to live their separate lives, connected, but freely. Committed to each other not forever, not because of some ancient words recited before a priest, but anew every single day.

She used to understand that. He was furious with her for changing. And he felt somehow bested by her at the same time.

But he was not going to leave her in Texas without him at the mercy of her family. They would be bound to convince her that he wasn't the one for her, that she needed to move home to Texas and find a nice American man, a man ready, willing and able to put a ring on her finger and baby in her belly.

After the conversation that night on the swings, she treated him as she had before—up to a point. She held hands with him and kissed him now and then, quick, chaste kisses. Alone on the back deck with him in the evening, she would laugh with him over the things that had happened that day. They might get into some debate over a minor point of Montedoran law. In front of her family, she showed him affection and tenderness.

But beyond safe discussions of her father's quick recovery and the final turning point in the last novel of her Montedoran trilogy? Nothing. He knew that was very much his fault. He wanted to speak more intimately with her, but that was too dangerous. It would only lead back to that night on the swings, to what she wanted that he didn't, to why he was holding on when she needed more and more was not something he would ever share with her.

As to physical intimacy, there was nothing beyond the

occasional fond touch, her hand in his, those infrequent chaste kisses. Even before that night in the park, he hadn't expected to make love with her there, in her father's house. But he'd hoped that maybe they might sneak away to a hotel once or twice....

So much for that idea. She had been right. It was not pleasant, being so close to her and yet feeling that she was somehow a million miles away from him. It was a lot worse than not pleasant, actually. It was a whole new way of living in hell.

And yet he stayed. He couldn't make himself give up and go.

Four days in, the paparazzi found them. So for the final three days, every time he left the house, there were photographers waiting. That first day they showed up was the worst. They came running up the walk at him, waving microphones. So he gave them an interview right then and there. It was like being interviewed by Lani's parents. Just about every question added up to: Was he there to propose and had she said yes?

He answered as vaguely as he'd answered the Vasquezes.

That appeased them enough that most of them went away. There were still the lurkers, the ones who tried to get shots of him and Lani from a distance whenever they were in open view, but it was bearable. He ignored them.

The Vasquezes seemed to take the whole thing in stride. They laughed about it over dinner and teased Max that he should just marry Lani and make all those reporters happy.

The final days in Texas went by at last. They flew home on Tuesday, leaving the house before dawn. Carlos and Martina had gone home to San Antonio two days before. But Iris and Jorge got up early to say goodbye.

Lani promised she would return in a few weeks, just for a day or two, when she flew to New York at the end of the month. There were hugs and kisses and Lani and her mother cried.

Jorge hugged Max and whispered, "You treat my daughter right."

And Iris grabbed him next. "Just be happy together," she commanded in his ear. "That's all we ask."

And then, at last, they were out of there, rushing down the stone walk to the waiting car.

He thought it would get better once they were home in Montedoro, that they would slip back into the happy, fulfilling life they'd shared before.

But it wasn't the same. She started actively avoiding him. She was too busy to have him visit her apartment in the evenings. She came to the palace to see Sydney and her family, and to be with Gerta and the children after school. But if he tried to join them, she always had some reason that she had to be going.

They were all over the tabloids. The journos made up all kinds of ridiculous stories about the trip to Texas. The headlines gave a whole new meaning to the word *absurd:* "Prince Max and the Nanny: Their Secret Engagement" and "The Prince's Cinderella Bride" and "The Naughty Nanny Snares the Prince." He wanted to talk to her about those stories, to laugh with her over them. He wanted to go with her and the children to the beach on the weekend. He longed to make love with her for hours.

None of that was happening.

Sunday, she said she couldn't make it to the family breakfast. The next week was the same. The children and Gerta saw her practically every day, but if he appeared when she was with them, she would simply get up and leave. She wouldn't spend the evening out with him and she just didn't have a free moment when he might join her at her place.

He never got a chance to talk her into making that trip to New York with him. How could he? He never got a chance to talk to her at all.

On April 20, he flew to JFK, spent the night at the Four Seasons and then spoke at Columbia University the next day. That evening, he had dinner with his brother Damien and Dami's fiancée, Lucy Cordell. Lucy and Dami lived together right there in Manhattan, where Lucy was attending fashion school. Max tried to be good company, but mostly he just wished Lani could have been there. He arrived home on the twenty-third to find that she had left that morning. Gerta told him she would spend two days in Manhattan, then go on to Texas to see her family.

She returned the following Tuesday.

And by then, he'd had enough. They needed to talk.

Wednesday, he called her. She let the call go to voice mail. He left a message for her to call him back. She did no such thing. Thursday, she came to see the children. He tried to get her alone for a moment, but she'd learned a thing or two about evasion since that February morning when he'd caught her in the garden and dragged her to the gardener's cottage.

At the sight of him, she was up and out of there. He almost took off after her. But the children were watching and he didn't want to alarm them. He still had the key to her place and he considered the pros and cons of letting himself in and refusing to leave until she talked to him.

But even desperate for her as he was becoming, he could see the wrongness of that. A woman's home, after all, was her castle. A man was not allowed to simply break in to get to her.

Next, he thought he might take up a position in front of her building and not budge until she talked to him.

Was he moving into the realm of stalkerdom? Probably. He could see the headline now: The Naughty Nanny's Stalker Prince.

It had to stop.

And he knew what to do to stop it. He'd always known, but he'd been holding out, hoping she wouldn't make him go that far. His bluff had failed. He *would* go that far if there was no other way to get near her.

When he called her Thursday evening and got her voice mail, he said, "All right. I will tell you about Sophia."

She called him back five minutes later. "I'm here. Come on over."

Chapter Fourteen

Lani sat on the worn sofa and he took the chair. He stared across the low table between them, drinking in the sight of her in old jeans and a worn white T-shirt that clung to her glorious curves, her hair a cloud of dark curls on her shoulders, just the way he liked it best.

All he wanted in the world was to get up and go over and sit next to her. Such a simple thing. But her expression warned him against such a move.

He thought of the night that she'd told him about her past. Of how furious he'd been with her, how he'd demanded she make a choice: give him her new address or never call him again.

How had they gotten here from there? How had it all turned around, their positions reversed? Now he was the one forced to make a choice while she looked at him with cool reserve behind her eyes.

When she spoke, her tone was gentle. "You don't have to tell me. You can just go."

But he couldn't go. It wasn't an option. He'd missed her too much. If telling her about his marriage would a make a difference between them, he would do it. Besides, in the past few weeks, without her, he'd had way too much time to think.

He'd kept the reality of his marriage to himself for so long. To do so had become second nature. Also, in spite of everything, he'd felt a certain allegiance to Sophia's memory, a duty to maintain the long-held fiction that she'd been an ideal wife.

He said, "I should have told you long ago. I see that now. I...*want* you to know."

She drew a slow breath. And then she nodded.

And he began, "I married Sophia convinced that we were born to love each other. That we were meant to be together forever. I was my mother and father's son in every way then. I believed in marriage, in true love between two people, love that lasts a lifetime. The problem was I didn't know the real Sophia."

Lani shifted on the sofa. "How so?"

"After we were married, I found out that Sophia had been out to catch a prince. She wanted become a princess. She wanted one of her children to rule Montedoro. She went after that goal with single-minded purpose. Later, she confessed that her family had encouraged and coached her to that end. She was to marry the heir to the Montedoran throne."

Lani's cool gaze warmed—at least a little. "Oh, Max. I'm sorry."

He shrugged. "From the first time I met her—I believe we were both nine—she hung on my every word. Already I was interested in history, in writing. She listened, rapt, as I told her stories about my ancestors. She found me fascinating, or so I thought. For a decade, as we grew to adulthood, she treated me like her king. She laughed at my slightest attempt at a joke. When I kissed her, she always seemed about to faint from sheer excitement."

"You're telling me she played you and you fell for her act?"

He tried not to wince. "You have to realize, we weren't together all that often. Never long enough or often enough for me to start seeing that maybe the Sophia I knew and the real Sophia weren't one and the same. She always claimed she loved to hear me talk, that just to be near me was enough for her. I was young and inexperienced and arrogant, too. I became absolutely certain it was true love. I believed that she adored me and we were a perfect match."

Lani shook her head slowly. But she didn't speak.

He went on with it. "I proposed to her when we were both eighteen. She instantly accepted. My mother and father tried to get me to slow down, tried to convince me to wait, to grow up a little, to see other girls. But I was a one-woman man and I wouldn't listen. I knew that Sophia was my great love."

"So you got married in a fantasy wedding of state when you were both twenty."

"That's right. And as soon as the ink was dry on our marriage license, Sophia changed. Suddenly, talking politics made her want a long nap. We no longer found the same things funny. She had no interest in the college studies I was finishing up, or in traveling with me to my speaking engagements. Reading and discussing books bored her. She preferred to sleep till at least noon, and I couldn't stand to stay in bed once the sun was up. As soon as we were married, there was essentially no way the two of us connected."

"Was she unhappy?"

"She never admitted she was. She claimed that she looked at it simply, that we were married and that was that. She *liked* me, she said. She wanted my babies, and she was proud to be the wife of the heir to the throne. When I told her how, to me, she'd changed completely, and that *I* was unhappy, she only frowned and told me to stop being silly about it. We got along well together, she said. She just didn't get what my problem was."

"You were miserable the whole time you were married to her?" Lani was incredulous. "Is that what you're telling me?"

"No, not the whole time. After a few years, it wasn't so bad."

"But what does that mean, it wasn't so bad?"

"I grew numb, you might say. And then, when Nick was born, it got a little better. Sophia and I both wanted children. Parenting was something we both valued, something, at last, that we had in common. We were a family, and that was a good thing. Then we had Connie. I was actually happy by then, fond of Sophia and grateful for my children. I learned to accept that I would never have the kind of marriage I'd planned on, never have the closeness my parents share."

Lani kicked off her shoes and drew her feet up on the sofa. "But, Max, people still talk about the two of you, about the perfect marriage you had, about how well matched you were, how blissfully happy you were together...."

"So? They had it wrong—but not completely wrong. By the end, I *was* happy with her, with our life together. And it was fine with me, that the press made up a pretty story about how much in love we were. Just as you're my *naughty nanny* and my *Cinderella bride,* Sophia and I were *soul mates.* From the beginning, the story was that we were exactly like my parents, that we shared a great love."

"But it was a lie...."

"I was the heir. Divorce wasn't an option. And even if I hadn't been the heir, I would have stayed in my marriage, because I personally believe that marriage is forever. In so many ways, Sophia was an excellent wife. After I accepted that she wasn't going to change, I wanted to make the best of the situation. So did she. For once, the press cooperated. To the world, we were the perfect couple. Beyond occasional reports about the total happiness we shared, they pretty much left us alone."

Lani seemed lost in thought. And then she asked, "Were you there when she had the accident?"

"No. I stayed in Montedoro with the children while Sophia took a long weekend at Lac d'Annecy in the French Lake District with her sister Maria and their brother Juan Felipe."

She looked at him expectantly. "But how did it happen? I know I could do a little research and get all the facts. But, Max, I would rather hear it from you."

So he told her what he knew. "Sophia was skiing and the line went lax. She just went down. They circled the boat back around to get her, but there was no sign of her. Juan Felipe and Sophia's bodyguard both jumped in to save her. Her skis bobbed on top of the water, but she was nowhere to be found."

"They never found her?"

"A fisherman spotted her body days later in a secluded inlet, floating near the shore. Her life jacket was missing. The cause of death was drowning. But she'd taken a serious blow to the forehead, from one of her skis, they said. The theory was that the head injury had disoriented her. In her confusion, she took off the life jacket and eventually she drowned."

"It's so sad and senseless."

"What can I say? Yes, it was. And after she was gone, I found that I missed her terribly. I began to see that I had been happier in my marriage than I ever realized. I began to…idealize what we'd had. I missed her so much, missed her presence, her steadiness, what I saw as her commitment to our life together. I grieved. In the end, in spite of everything, we *were* partners in life. I really believed that what we'd had, together, what we'd built together, our marriage…I believed it had meant something, that, in spite of the rocky start, the two of us had made a good, rich life. By the time she died, I'd gotten over the way she'd tricked me at the beginning. I'd fallen in love with her all over again."

Lani was watching him so closely, studying his face. "There's more, isn't there? It…wasn't what you thought, somehow."

He only looked at her.

And she whispered, "You said you *believed* that your marriage had meant something, not that it actually did."

He couldn't stand to draw it out a moment longer. He went ahead and told her. "She betrayed me."

Lani gaped. "I don't… What?"

"Six months after she died, I found out she'd been in love with another man for the whole time she was married to me."

"No…"

"Yes. Sophia had a lover—a longtime lover. In fact, she and that other man were lovers through most of our marriage, from her first trip back to visit her family in Spain a year after our wedding, until the other man died, which happened almost a year to the day before Sophia drowned at Lac d'Annecy."

Lani made a low, disbelieving sound. "But how did you find out?"

"I was cleaning out her desk and I found his letters— old-fashioned letters on plain white stationery, the kind no one writes anymore. But Sophia's lover did. Later, I went through her computer, looking for emails or instant messages from him. None. Just those letters. Over a hundred of them. They were tucked away in a hidden drawer, along with his obituary torn from a Spanish newspaper."

Lani's sweet face had gone pale. "Oh, my God, Max."

He went ahead and told the rest. "I locked the door so no one would disturb me and I read them all, every one of those letters. His name was Leandro d'Almas. He was a friend of Sophia's brother, of Juan Felipe, and Sophia had known him since she was a child. D'Almas held a minor title and he had very little money. He never married. She would go home to Spain a few times a year and they would be together in secret then."

Lani asked softly, cautiously, "Nicky and Connie, are they…?"

"Mine. D'Almas had some medical condition that eventually killed him. He was sterile and his letters were full of his frustrations that he couldn't give her children, that her children were mine. He also went on and on about his love for her, about the things they had done together in the past and what he would do to her and with her the next time she could get away from me and come to him."

"Oh, Max…"

"Those letters were tearstained, folded and refolded, tattered, read and reread. Sophia had cherished them. She should have destroyed them, but she didn't. I'm guessing she couldn't. They held her true heart. The heart I never understood, never saw, never knew…because I didn't know *her*. Even when I thought that we had come to something workable and strong and lasting together, over time—even then, it was just a lie that I told myself. I didn't know my wife at all."

She caught her lower lip between her neat white teeth. "Is that what you're afraid of with me? That I'll betray you? That if you marry me, I'll take a secret lover and lead a secret life behind your back?"

"No. Of course not."

"Are you sure?"

"Yes. Of course I'm sure."

"Then I just don't get it."

"Get what?"

"Well, Max, you wanted a real marriage more than any-thing. We could have that, together, you and me."

He longed to get up and circle around the table, to sit on the sofa with her, wrap his arms good and tight around her, to breathe in the wonderful scent of her hair. But he stayed in the chair. "I just can't, Lani. I can't do it again. I don't believe in marriage anymore, not for me, anyway. I can't…lock myself in that way. I want us both to be free to go at any time—so that every day we're together, we know, we're certain, that with each other is where we re-ally want to be."

"But you're throwing away the very thing you've always yearned for. Oh, Max. What kind of sense does that make?"

He only shook his head. "I don't know. No sense at all, I suppose. But still. I mean it. I can't do it. Not again. Not even for you. Why can't you understand?"

That soft mouth trembled. He could see the pulse beat-ing in the base of her throat. And then she unfolded her legs and stood.

He willed her to come to him.

But she only went around the low table and over to the sliding door. She stood there, staring at her own darkened reflection in the glass.

Finally, she seemed to draw herself up. She turned to him. "I'll tell you what I see." Her voice was soft suddenly. Soft and resigned. "I see that you can't get past what hap-pened with Sophia. You can't get beyond the lies that she told you, that she *lived* with you. I see that you loved her twice—when you married her and then later, after the chil-dren came."

"And both times it was a lie."

"Oh, Max, no."

"Yes. It was a lie."

"All right. I get how you would feel that way. But I see... gray areas, too."

"What do you mean 'gray'?" he demanded gruffly.

"I just... Well, I think she must have loved you, too. Not enough for you, I know that. But enough to mean that you and she knew happiness together."

"No," he insisted. "How can you say she loved me? She loved *him*. With me, it was all a lie...."

"I just don't agree with you. Yes, she lied to you. But there was also a certain truth in what you had with her. You were partners, raising a family. She gave you two beautiful children. Maybe you never knew the secrets of her heart, but I think there was goodness in her. If there wasn't, you never could have loved her."

"How can you defend her?"

"I'm not. I think what she did was totally wrong. I'm defending *you,* my darling, defending the marriage you made, the trust that you kept. As for Sophia, she's gone. You'll never be able to confront her. You need, somehow, to make peace with her memory."

"How can I make peace? I loved an illusion."

"I don't think so, Max. You didn't know everything, but that doesn't mean the love you had for her wasn't real."

"I was a blind idiot and she was a..." He let the sentence trail off unfinished. For Nicky and Connie's sake, he refused to speak the ugly word he was thinking.

Lani stared at him so tenderly, unspeaking, for an endless time. And then finally, she said, "I'm sorry for you, for her, for all of it. But what you've just told me doesn't change the fact that I want a lifetime with you. I want you for my husband. Not because you're a prince and I want to be a princess. Not because you're the heir to the Montedoran throne. There is no one else waiting in secret for me.

You're the one for me, Max. I want to marry you because I love you. Because we're good together. Because I love Nicky and Connie and I want to be there for them, while they're growing up. I want to be your wife, Max. I want to give you everything you always wanted from Sophia. But I can't do that. Because you don't trust yourself or me."

"That's not true. I trust you absolutely."

"No, you don't. If you trusted me, you would put your fear aside, take my hand and make a life with me. Deep in your heart, I think you still want what your parents have, a good marriage that can stand the test of a lifetime. But you won't let yourself have that. You're too afraid it will all go wrong all over again." Those big dark eyes pleaded with him. They begged him to swear that he *did* trust her, that he was ready to get past his fears and give a life with her a chance.

But he couldn't do that, not in the way that she wanted it. And right then, at that moment, he saw what he'd been so stubbornly refusing to see. In this, in the question of marriage, there really was no middle ground for either of them. She wanted what he couldn't give her. And it was wrong of him to keep after her, to keep pushing her to come to him on his terms. He was not the man for her. He needed to do the right thing, to let her go. There was nothing more to say about it.

He took her key from his pocket and set it on the low table. "I hope you find what you're looking for."

Her mouth was trembling again. With a soft cry, she turned her back to him. "I can't bear this. Just go now. Please."

That at least, he could give her. He strode to the door and pulled it open. "Goodbye, Lani."

She didn't answer him.

He went out, shutting the door quietly behind him.

* * *

Lani whirled when she heard the door click shut.

Her eyes blinded by hot tears, she ran over and locked it. Then she threw herself down on the sofa and let the tears have their way, let the ugly, painful sobs take her.

An hour or so later, she went online and tortured herself a little more looking at pictures of him, and pictures of the two of them together. She read the crappy tabloid stories about their relationship and groaned through her tears over the lurid headlines.

More than once that night, she picked up the phone to call him, as she'd been doing every night since they returned from Texas together more than three weeks ago. What could it hurt? she kept asking herself. To call him and tell him she was willing to do things the way that he wanted. That she couldn't bear being apart from him for another minute. If he wouldn't marry her, she wanted them to be together, at least.

But she couldn't do it. Couldn't make that call.

In loving him, she'd learned to love herself so much better than before. To respect herself and her principles. She was her mother's daughter to the core, one of those people who still believed that true love and marriage went together. It wouldn't work for her to try to be someone else. It would only make the inevitable ending more painful.

That Sunday afternoon, Max took the children to the beach. They built a crooked sand castle and ran in the waves.

When they sat down to eat the picnic Marceline had packed for them, Connie asked him why Miss Lani couldn't come with them.

He did his best to ignore the ache in his chest at the mere

mention of Lani's name and told his daughter gently that he wasn't seeing Miss Lani anymore.

Connie crunched on a carrot stick. "But I see her all the time. I saw her Friday. She came out into the garden with Aunt Sydney and Trev and Ellie. We were all together and she let me brush her hair."

Jealousy added a knot in his stomach to the ache in his heart. He was jealous of his own daughter, for getting to be with Lani, to touch Lani, when he had to make himself stay away.

Nicky said, "Papa means he dumped her. She's not his girlfriend anymore."

Connie gasped. "Papa! You dumped Miss Lani?"

He put a soothing hand on Connie's little shoulder and gave Nick a stern frown. "I did not dump Miss Lani. It didn't work out between us, that's all."

"You broke up with her," Nick accused.

"You shouldn't have done that," Connie pouted.

Was he suddenly in the doghouse with both of his children? "Ahem. It didn't work out between me and Miss Lani. Sometimes that happens. There is no one to blame." God. He sounded like a pompous ass.

Nicky peered at him, narrow-eyed. "I knew it already. I've known it for days and days."

"Erm, knew what?"

"That you and Miss Lani broke up."

"How did you know?"

"You're different, that's all." Nick sipped from a bottle of Evian. "Back like you used to be."

Connie announced, "Well, at least Miss Lani can still see *me*."

Max asked Nicky, "Like I used to be, how?"

Connie put in dreamily, "She likes me and I like her. We have our girl things."

Nick said, "You know, like this." And he made a blank sort of face. "All serious and maybe kind of sad."

Connie crunched another carrot. "She would never stop seeing *me*."

Serious and sad? Did Nick have it right?

Max told Connie, "I'm glad that you and Miss Lani are still friends."

Connie wrapped her arms around his neck and kissed him loudly on the cheek. "I'm glad, too."

He turned to Nick. "And I promise I will try not to be so serious and sad."

Nick shrugged. "It's all right, Papa. That's just how you are, I guess. You were always that way. Except, you know, with Miss Lani."

A week went by. And then another. He saw Lani now and then. In the garden. In the library. They would nod and smile politely at each other and leave it at that.

It hurt every time he saw her. A deep, fevered kind of ache. But at least then he felt something.

Because his son was right. He'd gone back to his old ways, to living his life at a distance, as though there was an invisible barrier between him and the rest of the world. The familiar numbness he'd known for so long had claimed him again.

Most of the time, he simply went through the motions. He felt alive only in snips and snatches: when he held Connie on his lap and read her a story. When he helped Nick with his studies. Or when he caught sight of Lani and gave her a false smile and his love for her welled up, hot and hungry and alive.

Other than those brief flashes of intense feeling, he was his old self in the worst kind of way.

His mother got him alone after a Monday meeting with her ministers and asked him what had happened with Lani.

She knew, of course. She always did.

He told her it was over and he didn't wish to speak of it.

"May I make a suggestion?"

"No."

She suggested anyway, "Consider putting your pride aside. Stop punishing yourself for making the wrong choice once. Think of your children, of all you gained by that wrong choice. And move on. Ask Lani to marry you. Let yourself be happy."

"This has nothing to do with pride, Mother. And Lani and I are finished."

She didn't argue further. But he saw in those legendary dark eyes that she thought he had it all wrong.

On the last weekend in May, his sister Alice married real estate golden boy turned international investor Noah Cordell in Carpinteria, California. Most of the family attended.

Max went and took the children and Gerta. The wedding was held in the big Spanish-style house at Noah's estate. Alice came down the curving staircase, arms full of Casablanca lilies, wearing a daring white wedding gown that fit her like a second skin and dipped to the base of her spine in back. The spectacular dress had been designed by Noah's talented younger sister, Lucy, the one who was engaged to Damien.

Max felt a jolt of aliveness when Alice stood with her groom and said her vows. They were happy, Alice and Noah. Happy and willing to take the biggest risk of all, to bind their lives together.

Most of his siblings had taken that risk. Only his two youngest sisters, Genevra and Aurora, remained single—

and Damien, too. Dami and Lucy planned to wait a while to marry, until Lucy had gotten through at least a couple of years at fashion school. But then Max overheard Lucy laughing and saying she didn't know how long she could wait to be Dami's bride.

So there you go. Before you knew it, they would all be happily married. Except for him.

Because he was both prideful and cowardly, and completely unwilling to take a chance like that again. He was willing to trust neither himself nor the woman he loved, just as Lani had said.

Noah's sprawling estate not only had one of the finest horse stables in America and extensive equestrian trails and fields, it also had artfully landscaped gardens rivaling the ones at home in Montedoro. To escape the crowd in the house for a while, Max left Nick and Connie in Gerta's excellent care and wandered outside, where the weather was California perfect and trees shaded the curving garden paths. Lost in his thoughts, enclosed in the usual bubble of numbness, hardly noticing the beauty around him, he walked past the infinity pool and down one path and then another.

Until he rounded a curve and there she was: Lani. Sitting on a small stone bench beneath a willow tree, her back to him, her long black hair dappled in sunlight and leaf shadow.

Max stopped stock-still on the path as the world instantly flashed into vivid three-dimensional life. Everything glowed with color and light. He smelled dust and eucalyptus and the haunting sweetness of some unknown flower. He heard birdsong. Something rustled in a patch of greenery to his left. And from back the way he'd come, the sound of voices and laughter drifted to him.

And then she turned her head. He saw her face in profile.

It wasn't Lani.

The vivid world subsided into dull reality once more.

The woman saw him, gave him a nod.

He returned her nod and walked on by.

It happened again that night. He caught a glimpse of black hair and the sweet curve of a woman's shoulder. The world exploded into life.

Until he moved closer and saw his mistake. Only another stranger. The bubble of numbness descended as before.

He didn't start wondering if he might be going insane until after he was back at home and it happened three more times: a woman in the marketplace buying oranges; another at a formal dinner in the palace's state dining room; a third in the library.

Each time everything flashed bright. The world pulsed with vibrant intensity—and then flattened away to grayness once again.

He was an intelligent man. He got the message. Not only did his mother and his children think he was crazy to let Lani go, even his subconscious was out to teach him a lesson now.

Max was just stubborn enough that he might have soldiered on in his gray bubble, telling himself it didn't matter if he'd lost his mind, he'd messed up on forever once and he couldn't afford to risk it again.

But then he started dreaming of Sophia.

In the dream, she wore her favorite white tank bathing suit and she stood on a narrow ribbon of pebbled beach at the lake where she'd drowned. She shaded her eyes with the flat of her hand, her mouth twisted in exasperation, glaring at him. "For such a smart man, you have always been so stupid. Go. Have the love you've dreamed of at last. Live. Live until you die." And then she dropped her hand and dived into the water.

He ran in after her, shouting her name. But no matter how he splashed about and called for her, there was no sign of her. She was gone.

Until the next night, when he would dream the dream again.

After the fourth night he had the dream, even he knew he could hold out no longer. Love and life were calling him.

And they were never going to shut up until he finally gave in and answered.

Chapter Fifteen

On the third Friday in June, just as night was falling, Lani finished the final book in her Montedoran trilogy. Satisfied with the ending at last, she saved her work. She was just closing her laptop when the intercom buzzer sounded from downstairs.

She got up and went to see who was there. "Yes?"

He said only her name. "Lani."

Her hands went numb and her heart stopped dead—before recommencing beating so fast and hard she felt certain it would batter its way right out of her chest. "Max?"

The old intercom crackled. "May I please come up?"

Had someone died? If Connie or Nick… No. She'd seen them both just yesterday. They were fine. She wouldn't accept any possibility but that they remained so.

"Lani. Please?"

Numb hands shaking, she buzzed him in. And then she undid the locks and opened the door and stood there on the landing, her heart going a mile a minute, listening to his swift footfalls growing louder as he came up the stairs.

She leaned over the railing and watched him run up the second flight to her floor, his chestnut hair as unruly as ever, a little too long, curling against the collar of his blue shirt. She knew how soft those curls would be, the way they wrapped so sweetly around her index finger.

He looked up and saw her. "Lani." His eyes in the light from the stairwell were more blue than gray. And did he have to be so handsome it hurt her just to look at him?

She retreated, backing across the landing and through the open door of her apartment. He reached the landing and came for her, matching her backward steps with his forward ones, until they were both over the threshold.

"Lani." He reached out, grabbed the door and pushed it shut behind him, closing them in together.

She was breathing too hard, her poor overworked heart going faster than ever. "I don't... Is everyone all right?"

He just stood there and stared at her. He seemed to be breathing as hard as she was. "God. Lani."

"Tell me. Nick and Connie...?"

"Fine," he said. "Everyone's fine."

She put her hand to her chest in a vain attempt to calm all the pounding in there. "Then what's happened?"

And he reached out and took her by the arms. His touch sent shivers dancing across her skin. She gasped. And he said, "Yes." And then again, "Yes." His voice wrapped around her, deep and rich and so well-remembered. It made her throat clutch just to hear it. "Alive," he whispered. "With you I am alive." He pulled her closer, bent nearer and breathed in deeply through his nose.

"Max." She made herself say his name louder, more firmly. "Max, what in the world is going on?"

"Tell me I'm not too late."

"Too late? It's a little after nine, I think."

"I don't mean the time." He gripped her arms tighter. "Is there anyone else?"

"Anyone...?" She gaped at him. "You mean another man?"

"Yes." His straight brows drew together. He looked angry. Or maybe terrified. "Is there another man?"

"Uh, no." She shook her head.

He mirrored the movement, his head going back and forth in time with hers. "No." He glared. "You said no."

"I did, yes. I said no. There is no one."

"Lani." Desperate. Pleading. "Lani…"

And then he pulled her even closer and he kissed her.

Oh, dear sweet Lord, his kiss.

How had she kept going without his kiss?

Her thoughts were a jumble. Her body was on fire. Her heart ricocheted against her ribs.

And she couldn't stop herself. She slid her hungry arms up over his hard, warm chest and wrapped them around his neck, pulling him closer, sighing in surrender against his parted lips.

When he lifted his head, he said, "It's no good without you. I keep seeing you everywhere. But then it's not really you, just some stranger with black hair. And then I started dreaming of Sophia."

"Sophia? You're not serious."

"Yes, I am. She kept saying, 'Go. Have the love you've dreamed of. Live until you die.'"

She blinked up at him. "Sophia. In a dream…"

He nodded. "I know. Madness. I've been wondering if maybe I've gone round the bend. But I've come to the conclusion that I'm still reasonably sane. I'm just stubborn and full of pride. And scared. Yes, I am. Scared, most of all. But I do love you, Lani. I trust you completely." He touched her hair, guided a dark curl behind her ear. It felt so good. Heaven on earth. His hands on her skin again, caressing her. At last.

And he wasn't finished. "I love you so much. I love you and my life is one big, gray cave of numbness without you.

I love you and my children love you. My mother thinks I've been an idiot. She told me to stop being stubborn, to put my pride aside and ask you to marry me."

She hitched in a sharp breath. "Your mother said you should marry me?" She stared at him, stunned. "But the French ministers—"

"Don't worry about them. They'll come around, they always do." He reached into the breast pocket of his blue shirt. "I want only you, Lani. I love only you. You're the one I saw in my heart, always, even before I knew you. You're the one I should have waited for. But I didn't wait. And still, there was good in that, just as you said all those endless weeks ago. There was Nick and Connie. And I was true to my wife even if she wasn't true to me. I kept my vows. And life went on."

"Oh, I'm so glad you see that now."

"I do. It's what you said. What else is there but to let the bitterness go? I swear it to you. I'm done with letting my pride and my anger rule my life. I trust you, Lani. And I trust my own judgment in choosing you."

"Oh, Max…"

"You are my hope for the future, Lani. You are everything bright and true and vivid and alive. I want to be with you. *Truly* with you. I want to be your husband, if you'll only have me." His legs gave out.

Or so she thought at first as he was slowly sinking to the floor. She put her hands over her mouth and let out a soft cry.

And then he was there on one knee right in front of her, reaching up to take her left hand. "Marry me, Lani." He slipped a ring on her finger—an impossibly beautiful ring, with three giant sapphires surrounded in diamonds on a platinum band.

Her eyes blurred with tears. "Oh, Max…"

"I know it's taken me way too long to come to this, to come to you," he whispered, his voice gruff with emotion. "I know I've hurt you."

She touched his upturned face. "You've only ever been honest, I know that. I never faulted you. I just wanted more."

He pressed a kiss in the heart of her palm. "And now, if you'll have me, if it's not too late, I want to *give* you more. I want to give you everything, all I have. My life, my love. Forever."

"Oh, my darling…"

"Be my bride, Lani. Marry me."

"You mean this?" she demanded breathlessly. "You *want* this?"

He didn't waver. "More than anything. Marry me, Lani."

There was only one answer by then. She gave it. "Yes."

He swept to his feet and wrapped her in his arms. "Say it again."

She laughed. "Yes, Max. I will marry you. I will be your wife."

And he grabbed her closer, claiming her lips in a kiss that promised all the joy she'd never thought to share with him. "Together," he whispered.

She nodded. "You, me, the children…"

"Through the good times and all the rest," he vowed. "From today onward. No matter what happens, we will get through it. As long as I have your hand in mine."

* * * * *

Welcome to your new-look

Cherish™
series!

TAMING HER
ITALIAN BOSS

Fiona Harper

THE BABY TRUTH

Stella Bagwell

A BRE
BEGINN!

Michelle M

EXPERIENCE THE ULTIMATE RUSH
OF FALLING IN LOVE

The same great stories you've come to know
and love, but in a sparkly new package!

See the new covers now at:
www.millsandboon.co.uk/cherish

A sneaky peek at next month…

Cherish™

ROMANCE TO MELT THE HEART EVERY TIME

My wish list for next month's titles…

In stores from 16th May 2014:

☐ Becoming the Prince's Wife – Rebecca Winters

& A Brevia Beginning – Michelle Major

☐ Taming Her Italian Boss – Fiona Harper

& Fortune's Prince – Allison Leigh

In stores from 6th June 2014:

☐ Nine Months to Change His Life – Marion Lennox

& The Single Dad's Second Chance – Brenda Harlen

☐ Summer with the Millionaire – Jessica Gilmore

& The SEAL's Baby – Laura Marie Altom

Available at WHSmith, Tesco, Asda, Eason, Amazon and Apple

Just can't wait?

Special Offers

Every month we put together collections and longer reads written by your favourite authors.

Here are some of next month's highlights— and don't miss our fabulous discount online!

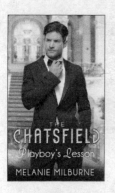

On sale 6th June

On sale 6th June

On sale 6th June

Join our *EXCLUSIVE* eBook club

FROM JUST £1.99 A MONTH!

Never miss a book again with our hassle-free eBook subscription.

★ Pick how many titles you want from each series with our flexible subscription

★ Your titles are delivered to your device on the first of every month

★ Zero risk, zero obligation!

There really is nothing standing in the way of you and your favourite books!

Start your eBook subscription today at www.millsandboon.co.uk/subscribe

Join the Mills & Boon Book Club

Subscribe to **Cherish**™ today for 3, 6 or 12 months and you could **save over £40!**

We'll also treat you to these fabulous extras:

- 🌹 **FREE L'Occitane gift set worth £10**
- 🌹 **FREE home delivery**
- 🌹 **Rewards scheme, exclusive offers…and much more!**

Subscribe now and save over £40
www.millsandboon.co.uk/subscribeme